M000310566

SWORD PUNK

SAVING SEOUL

STEVEN KELLIHER

MONOLITH
BOOKS

CONTENTS

To all of the people who have been a part of my martial arts journey over the decades, from the parents who signed me up for my first Tae Kwon Do class at age 14, to the coaches, sparring partners and cornermen who built me up over the years in various gyms and dojos across the northeast, and the doctors who tried to put me back together again after a dozen fights too many.

Most of all, this book is dedicated to Shihan Mario Mastro, who supported me win or lose, and taught me to take more from the latter than the former, and whose wise words could only have come out of a Boston fighter's mouth.

"I may be old, but I'm still hell for a minute."

All in all, it's not a bad mantra to grow into.

1

THE FREE CITY OF SEOUL

I didn't know who I was kidding skulking around like a hooded ghost in the neon night. Certainly not Joon. He always knew when I came around, even if I didn't always have the good humor or patience for a visit.

It wasn't really raining, but it was misty. On the forested mountain paths, the vapor probably would have cast an ethereal beauty over the landscape, glittering like starlit dew on bark and leaves. That wasn't to say that the mist couldn't be pretty here, in the Free City of Seoul, it was just that it only stayed pretty if you kept your eyes up, drinking in the microscopic jewels of water that passed like a film through the blues, yellows and blazing reds of the cityscape.

But my eyes were usually down at street level, as they were tonight. Down here, the mist coated everything, mixing with the gasoline oil in the street to form the worst sort of rainbows, and clinging to window panes and brown bricks and tipped-over traffic cones. It drew the hoods up over the ears of passersby, making it easier for them to fall into the sort of danger that lurked in this part of town, and easier still to ignore others falling into it around them, in the alleys like the one where Kenta had found me.

Danger had never been shy about this part of town, but it had always been sensible, keeping to the shadows. Skulking in the alleys and slithering in the sewers. Now, it was a beast grown brazen as the old fool had been in life, before the same pride that had kept the whole neighborhood—hell, half the city, it felt like —safe had ultimately seen him pay out the rest of his debt in blood.

I often found myself pacing on the sidewalk outside of Ken's Place the evening before a fight. I always thought it was going to bring me comfort, and remind me of more pleasant times. But when I was there, listening to the cars and cycles whiz past and cats and drunkards retching beneath nearby eaves, I always ended up thinking about Kenta's death instead of his life.

I suppose that's why Min visited Joon even more seldom than I did. She'd always been the smart one.

"Go in or leave, you ass," I whispered, rebuking myself for hesitating more over the decision to speak to a friend close enough to be my brother than I did before engaging with some of the most violent men and women in the East in semi-lethal combat on a weekly basis.

Ken's Place was a better name for a bar or a restaurant, but you couldn't mistake it for anything other than a dojo if you had a glance inside the fogged windows and glass door. A bar would have done better business. Of that there could be no doubt, but no other place could make better men.

I was getting old enough not to realize when a saying belonged to me or to the man who'd taught me.

In truth, I don't know why I was so hesitant to speak to Joon. Our last few conversations had been contentious, but that wasn't uncommon for the two of us. Brothers never seemed to mince words at the best of times. Those raised in combat could hardly be expected to buck the trend.

"Just say hi," I told myself, frozen in the mist just out of sight from the main door. I could hear the muffled sounds of children's Kiai leaking through the window panes of the dojo, their little war cries acting as the chorus to Joon's clipped verses as he ordered them through katas far more advanced than you were supposed to teach kids who could barely ride a bike in a straight line.

Are you going to tell him?

The question came up unbidden. It reminded me of all the choices I'd made, especially in recent nights. It reminded me of deals struck. Bargains made. Joon had wanted me out of the League since I'd joined it, but I doubted if even he would want me to leave it on these terms.

I sighed and decided to walk toward the front door of the dojo, ignoring the gnawing guilt at the choice I made along the way. Surely it was the moral choice, to spare Joon the burden of the truth. He didn't have to know about my bargain with the League, and through them, with the organization that had been directly or indirectly responsible for the death of our master. Let him bask in the bliss of ignorance.

I did tell you Min had always been the smart one.

Just before I reached for the slick aluminum handle of the fogged-up glass door, I heard the sound of something hard meeting something soft, followed by a grunt. It wasn't a low sound. Not low enough to belong to an adult, and before I turned from the door, I could already feel the blood rushing up into my temples, making my ears warm enough to feel like they could start steaming in the drizzle.

There weren't many things that got me angry enough to rage, but hitting a kid was at the very top of a short list.

I glided past the windows, aware that Joon saw everything that passed by his inherited dojo. There was no choice but to go in and speak to him now. But first, I had to take out the trash.

The alley between Ken's Place and Shark's Convenience was wide. Black iron stairwells that doubled as fire escapes climbed the brownstone walls, passing over cracked windows and flapping plastic sheets. It looked like a scene out of a 1980s comic book. If you had told me I was in classic grunge New York City, I'd have believed you. It was strange. The more neon-lit the cities of the world seemed to get, the more dark places seemed to crop up, like mold.

Two men in leather jackets and studded jeans loomed over a black-haired kid who crouched defiantly against the rain-soaked wall. The kid was propped up on one foot. He rubbed at his cheek with one hand and clutched the strap of his pack tightly with the other. A black-and-silver handle stuck out of the pack, and I recognized it as the end of a sai that should have been hung up on the wooden pegs on the dojo wall. His face was mixed Korean, and his hair was spiked in the wet. He looked a lot like me, which didn't help my mood, and certainly wasn't going to help his accosters.

The kid noticed me first. He drew in a sharp breath at first, likely afraid that another thug had arrived to cut off his escape. However, his look morphed from fear to confusion when I pulled my hood down to reveal my own mixed features and my personal brand of spiky black hair. When recognition dawned, he broke into a smile, and the thugs turned toward me.

These two were harder to place. They could have been Japanese, but there was something about them that recalled soviets. Either way, their lack of recognition showed that they weren't from around here.

As did the fact that they had chosen to assault one of Kenta's … one of Joon's students mere inches from the dojo.

"Akio!" the boy shouted, causing one of the thugs to step threateningly closer to him. He shrank back.

"You two aren't from around here, are you," I said.

They exchanged a glance. I could tell by the way their hands twitched toward their pockets that the only thing they were packing was switchblades. Either they were too low level to carry guns, or they were smarter than they looked. I was critical of the SPDF in many respects, but Min's department had managed to get a lot of Tokyo's guns off of our streets in the last two years.

"Okay," I sighed. "Listen. I'm on a bit of a time crunch tonight, so here's how this is going to go—"

"Move along," the thug on the right said. He was a little smaller than the other one, but the command came with a forward step which exposed him as the alpha. The thing about alphas, however, was that they were only as strong as their pack. And a pack was only as strong as its selection of prey.

"You really aren't from around here, huh?" I said.

"This is Akio," the boy said. "He's a League champion!"

One of them spit onto the wall, causing the kid to squirm backward grimacing. Funny, the things kids focused on.

"That true?" the spitter asked.

I shrugged. It wasn't really the point I'd been trying to make.

"Latex and glow sticks," the other said. "The real thing happens out here." He spread his arms out like a messianic figure, and revealed a short, black-handled knife with a deft flick of the wrist.

I was through talking, and my conscience had already been cleared on account of the warning I'd given them. It wasn't a warning on the back of what I'd accomplished on the professional martial arts scene. It was one on the back of these streets and alleys, where I'd grown up, and where I'd received as many lessons as I'd been forced to dole out. This was still Seoul, no matter what the Hachinin had to say about it, and Seoul still belonged to us.

Still, I always felt better when the other guy threw the first punch, so I simply walked forward. Not fast. Not slow. Just steady, like I was on an evening stroll.

It had the desired effect. The knife-holding thug screamed in at me with bad intentions. By the movement—a crescent-shaped downward slash—he was clearly used to killing, but certainly was not anyone who knew what he was doing around a blade. I flashed forward, deflected the swinging hand up by striking his forearm with the back of my wrist, and turned into him, sliding my heel in between his too-wide stance while I guided the knife hand over my opposite shoulder, snapping my fingers over his wrist like a vise grip. I didn't hesitate in bringing his arm down over my shoulder. I didn't pay much attention to the positioning of his elbow. The point of the move was to throw him. The ensuing snap was just graham cracker crumble on top of the cake.

The knife clattered to the pavement with a ting while the thug's body followed after, trailing a different sort of scream and a much nastier-sounding crash.

Chances are, the other thug was simply staring slack-jawed, unable to react quick enough to make a decision on either side of the fight-or-flight debate, which is why Kenta always added the third 'F' into the equation.

"Freezing's the worst of the lot, friend," I said as I dug an elbow into his boney midsection, folding him over and only just escaping the half-digested street sausage he wolfed up into the alley as he toppled.

I reached down and pulled the kid up, tousling his hair and giving him a light slap on the cheek to jar him out of his shock. His lip was bleeding from where he'd been struck.

The lead thug had struggled onto his knees while the other one continued to heave. "Now, now," I said, holding up a hand. The thug clutched his broken arm, his eyes shaking as he looked from the knife to me, weighing his odds.

"You two have any employers I need to be made aware of?"

The knife thug frowned while the retching thug looked askance at him.

Not Hachinin, then. That certainly made things more simple.

"You're going to walk out of this alley and turn left, and keep walking until you're well past Sister Red's, and then you're going to keep on walking," I said. "You're going to do it before I start counting. Trust me when I tell you that, despite my reputation as the more emotional of the two of us, if Joon catches you sniffing around here, he'll kill you and feed you to whatever street dogs are going to be at that sausage soup as soon as this party's over."

The thugs didn't waste time arguing. They scrambled to their feet, one clutching his arm to his side and wincing all the while as the other stumbled with both arms clutched over his stomach. When they had gone, I looked back at the kid, who continued to stare after the thugs, his eyes glazed.

"Hey," I said, snapping him back into the present. He blinked up at me. In the rain, he looked even younger than I had thought. At heart, if he was anything like I had been at his age, he was a lot older. He was brave like all Seoul youths were brave, but he could still be given a scare. Given the way he looked at me—with a mix of admiration and something else—it could have been me he was afraid of, now that he'd seen me go to work without a glowing League suit and thousands of cheering fans for window dressing.

"Let's get you inside. And don't worry about Sensei Joon. He'll forgive the tardiness."

The kid nodded, all earnestness. Still had some innocence, then. That was good. More than I could have said at his age.

"Thanks, Akio," he said, seeming to flush with embarrassment. "I'll take the long way next time."

I didn't know what to say to that. Joon would have encouraged him, but my instinct was to tell him that he shouldn't have to plan out a route least likely to put him in the clutches of street thugs or the things far worse than them. Things that wore nicer clothes and scanned the city streets through tinted windows in cars as expensive as tanks.

"Now you can see why Sensei doesn't want me around the dojo," I joked, leading him out of the alley and checking to make sure he wasn't sporting a limp or exhibiting any signs of concussion.

"Why's that?" he asked, confused.

"I'm always breaking things."

He only shook his head. "Sensei Joon is always talking about you," he said.

"That so?"

I opened the fogged-up door of the dojo and scanned the street as I ushered the boy inside. No sign of retribution. I breathed a sigh of relief as I stepped inside, and I felt Joon's eyes on me before the door closed behind me.

"Ah," he said, his voice ringing out clearly from the front of the dojo as the children and teens on the red and black mats paused in their katas. "Uncle Akio has decided to grace us with his prese—"

I shot him a cutting look and nodded toward the kid. Joon's eyes were as sharp as his black bangs. He took in every detail of his student, likely noting cuts and bruises from the front that I hadn't even catalogued, and nodded almost imperceptibly.

"Bow onto the mats, Jace," he said. "And tell Akio to do the same."

Jace smirked at me and did as he was told, and I found myself kicking my shoes and socks off and sliding them onto the rug to the side of the dojo floor along with all the grimy, torn pairs from the feet of Seoul's treasured youth.

Joon wore a blue training gi and had his hair tied back in a tail. His hands were clenched into fists and rested in front of his belt as he readied to start class. Most of the kids were already drenched in sweat from their kata-laden warm-up. Joon might have had a better bedside manner than Kenta, but he was an even more demanding teacher.

I hung my hoodie on a brass hook on the wall and stepped forward, bowing onto the mats as Jace raced past me, having pulled the twin sais out of his training pack. As I walked toward the front of the dojo, Jace hurriedly hung the sais back on their wooden pegs to Joon's right. Above the forked metal weapons, two dark wood sabers with more scars than those Kenta had sported hung crisscrossed: my old training swords, which had never broken, no matter how many times I'd tried.

I could feel the children's eyes on me as I walked between them and took my place next to Joon. I turned and adopted my own ready stance, feet shoulder-width apart, fists down in front of my belt, which was leather instead of cloth. In the place of a gi, I wore jeans and a black tank top. The kids were no different. Joon had managed to scrape together old gi pants for some of them, but most wore sweats or shorts, and none sported colored belts. That was a practice we'd never taken to.

Jace took his position at the back of the dojo, bumping into a German-looking girl with sandy hair and green eyes, who shouldered him away.

"Uncle Akio will be teaching class tonight," Joon said, stepping aside. "He's going to show us what he's been teaching those fancy League fighters all season long."

Joon had a funny way of punishing people.

I scanned the three rows of street roughs, picking out the ones who held themselves with surety and which ones had dipped shoulders and twitchy eyes. There were eleven altogether. They were young. Very young, in places, but tough. I nodded.

"Feet together!" I intoned. They complied. "Bow!" They did, and the earlier worries of the night melted away as we set to work.

Two hours later, as the last of the kids—Jace, his hair plastered with sweat instead of misted rain this time—spilled out onto the Seoul streets, Joon and I sat on the wooden shelf before the bay windows. I had to move a few old trophies aside, and before we could settle into anything approaching small talk, all the worry Joon had kept suppressed throughout the class came bubbling out.

"How many were there?" he asked, his eyes boring into my temple. "Were they armed? Did they bear the ma—"

"No infinity marks," I said, holding up both hands. "No horizontal '8' on their wrists or necks. They weren't Hachinin." Joon relaxed visibly. "Just a couple of thugs. Junkies, most likely."

Joon almost spat. It was a bad habit it had taken him years to quit.

"They're either getting braver or dumber," he said, his tone sounding murderous.

"They won't be coming back," I said.

"Not those ones."

It was true, and I didn't argue with the implications. The streets were getting worse by the month. The local businesses and the local families knew that Kenta's death was going to shake the aura of security in the area, but I don't think anyone could have guessed how quickly the drug routes would be redirected in his absence. It had been a tragic event for Joon, Min and me, but for the neighborhood, it was more like a pin being pulled on the world's slowest-ticking grenade.

"It's getting worse," Joon said. "They might not have borne the mark, but they probably run drugs for the ones who do."

I shrugged, then stood up and crossed the dojo floor, climbed the short stairway toward the back office and went to fill a soggy paper cup from the fountain set into the back wall. I took a drink, reminding myself not to say anything stupid.

"They're like vultures," Joon said. He was looking down at his feet, then craned to look out the window, where cars and cycles hissed through the puddles, sending up fins of reflected neon spray from the emblazoned buildings that cloistered around our childhood clutch of blocks.

"And Kenta was the lion," I said, walking back down the stairs. I made my way over to my hoodie and checked the damp, grimacing as I thought of the unpleasant walk back to my apartment.

"Three years ago to the day," Joon said, still looking out the window, his voice drifting like the ghosts he was thinking about. "Tomorrow."

"Long time that feels short," I said. "Short time that feels long."

Joon nodded and then seemed to shake himself back into the present.

"What's going on, Akio?"

"What?" I said as I slipped my socks back on and donned my sweatshirt. "With the city? Same thing that's happening to every city in the world."

"With you," Joon said. "Much as I enjoy your company, you haven't exactly made yourself common around the dojo these days. Ever since—"

"Ever since I joined the League," I said. "I know, Joon. And you do remember why I joined in the first place, right?"

Joon pursed his lips. At turns, he could look like a samurai or a disapproving librarian. Sometimes both.

"It was never your debt to pay off," Joon said. "It never should have been his to pay off. Protection money in the year—"

"Then it would have been yours," I countered, stopping the tired old argument. "Or theirs," I added before Joon could raise a complaint. I nodded out the door, and Joon swallowed and frowned.

He knew I was right, and he hated it.

"Guilt is a poison, Akio," Joon said. "You couldn't have stopped it. If you'd been there, you'd have been gunned down right alongside him."

"I like to think of it as a fire," I said, not really believing it. "We've all got debts to pay. Just a matter of choosing which ones."

Joon chuffed.

"What?" I asked.

"Min said something similar before she joined the force."

I ignored what felt like a barb, even though I knew Joon didn't mean it that way.

"The debt is almost paid, Joon," I said, coming closer than I thought I would of telling him the truth. "Almost. And then. Then we'll see about the rest of it."

We didn't meet each other's eyes.

"I'll come by the arena tomorrow night," Joon said. I nodded and pushed the door open, smelling in the mix of pavement, ozone and city wet.

"Akio."

"Yeah?"

"We always thought Kenta was invincible."

"Yeah."

"He wasn't."

"No."

I knew what he meant, but we left it at that, and I tried to guide my mind away from decisions of the recent past and toward the immediate future. I had a fight to prepare for, and for at least one more night, I was allowed to win it.

2

YELLOW AND BLUE

I could tell you I hated it.

The lights—all red, blue and neon purple. Shades and strobes that would put your grandmother in the hospital.

The sounds—the pounding of the ceremonial drum. The roar of the rabid crowd. The crackle of electricity as the announcer slammed the porous surface of the microphone with a voice that had gone from silver to hoarse over the course of the night.

I could tell you I hated the smells—the tang of sweat as it mixed with the sweet smell of sulfur and smoke from the fireworks and flares. The faint rot of the sticky audience floors, where the cement had long ago given way to a paste that infected the place and filled it with a pregnant musk.

I could tell you I hated all of that, but I've never been very good at lying.

Another roar to make my heart swell as the announcer made the introductions. Another boom and slap as a half-naked man struck a white canvas drum that was somehow louder than it was comically large.

A bow as a woman with long black hair dressed in blue armor with gold accents faced a man dressed in gold armor with blue. His hair was short-cropped and silver-white, and his eyes were a startling blue. Lit lenses for effect. And as I watched from the shadowed entryway, holding one of my blunted blades at my side, twirling it absently as the other rested in the sheath across my back, the first grimace crossed my face.

This, I did hate. The way a contest of honor was made a mockery on a public stage. The way martial artists turned from fighters into showmen. The way technique gave way to bluster, glory to adulation.

But then the fight started, and my martial mind took over.

Sang Hee was a sight less benevolent than her name would suggest, but she was damn fun to watch. She was also a former Olympic gymnast, which, given the elasticity of the stage on which they fought, put most opponents at a sound disadvantage at the outset. What made her truly interesting, however, was the fact that she was rich beyond belief. An heiress from the north whose money was difficult to trace, but impossible to miss.

It went without saying that competing in the most high-impact sport in the world was a … strange choice for someone like her. But there was always more to the story.

She leapt into a front roll and drew her quarterstaff, which ignited during the roll, glowing blue-white. Instead of coming up in her usual bounce, she stayed low and spun, carving the canvas with the lit weapon and whipping it back toward the golden boots of Dae, who wasn't half as great as his name suggested.

He did manage a dodge. What's more, he managed a good one, hopping just over the lit staff and moving forward instead of back, as Sang Hee had no doubt intended. He brought his own weapons out from across his back—twin double-bladed hand axes that glowed golden-yellow—and carved the place where Sang Hee's head had been. Now she rolled back, landed the flats of her palms on the canvas and somersaulted up and over. She stood motionless, her staff thrumming and pulsing like a lantern as she held it stiffly behind her back.

"Close one," she said, her voice amplified by the mic in her collar.

The crowd roared. She was an entertainer, through and through, and even I got caught up in it, bringing my hands up for a clap before I noticed a particular shadow staring from the President's box slightly above and to the left of the fighting stage, looming like an emperor's coliseum perch. Instead, I leaned from my place beside the red corner doorway at the edge of the arena and spat, the glob spinning down into a chasm that seemed bottomless. There was a distant glimmer of iron netting, small consolation should any fighter be tossed from the platform. It wasn't unheard of. I'd sent a few there myself in the last three seasons.

They'd all survived, far as I knew, but sometimes their echoing screams woke me in the night, cursing me for their humiliation. I might not have killed them, but I'd effectively ended their careers. Being thrown from the ring marked the height of dominance. True fighters kept themselves in until they were weaponless or unconscious.

The two before me were true fighters. Of course, I didn't think either one could stand up to me for long. I'd beaten Dae the season before. I'd never had the pleasure or misfortune (depending on whom you asked) of facing Sang Hee, a fact that had allowed us to be more cordial to each other than most were on the circuit.

I figured it was a given I'd see her in the Finals. But Dae had been training. We all had, no doubt. But Dae had really been training.

The golden-armored fighter never attacked Sang Hee straight on. If he stepped into the arc of that whipping staff, it might crack his skull along with his purse. Instead, he approached at angles, darting in with one blade—the golden blades standing out starkly atop black handles—before following it up with the other. Sang Hee was on the defensive. Dae attacked so often that she couldn't afford to attempt any circular attacks. Instead, she turned her staff into an approximation of a blunted spear, jabbing it forward like a striking snake. She landed two solid hits, the resin weapon making dull thuds as it connected with the mix of rubber and plastic of Dae's battle armor.

Seeing him reel back coughing reminded me to adjust my own padding. I placed my rubber blade back in its X sheath and gripped the suit just inside the collar, pulling. It was always too tight across my front and too loose across my back. I could almost hear the skintight material stretching as my blood warmed to the task.

It was a good fight. A damn good fight.

Dae had already lasted longer than Sang Hee's last three opponents combined, and it looked as if he had no plans to quit.

Sang Hee, for her part, was the picture of calm. Right up until she wasn't.

Apart from the one cheer when she'd made her voice heard, the crowd had been holding their collective breath. Now, a smattering of voices began to carry a chant. Soon enough, the rest took it up.

"Dae … Dae … Dae … DAE … DAE!"

Sang Hee had been forced to the edge of the platform so that her back heel was suspended above the black depths. Now Dae did come on straight, spinning so fast the yellow glow of his axes turned him into a lit top with a sunny corona.

Even from a distance, I could see Sang Hee's smile, and my heart froze as she waited until the last possible moment before bringing her staff around her back and spinning with it. She did what should have been impossible. If she had stepped forward, Dae's lead axe would have broken her orbital. If she had jabbed straight ahead with the butt end of her weapon, he'd have turned it aside and smashed it with one weapon and her nose with the next.

But she didn't step forward and she didn't plant. Instead, she stepped back, or seemed to.

As Dae reached her—rather, as he reached the place she'd been, Sang Hee swept her front foot back behind her, spinning so that just the ball of her rear foot remained balanced on the edge of the platform. The momentum of the spin kept her from tumbling over into the abyss, and the momentum of her staff, held at its very end, brought her back around. She came in at an angle as Dae stopped his spin and attempted to plant to keep himself from going over. He looked shocked, standing where Sang Hee had only just been. She might only have moved a foot to the right, but it was enough.

To his credit, he managed to get one axe up to block, though he held it too close to his head for my liking. Sang Hee didn't care. Her staff met the haft between the two blades with an echoing crash and sparks flew as pieces of lit resin—blue and blinding yellow—broke off from the embattled blades. Dae let out a cry as he tumbled, the force of the blow passing through his block and cracking him in the temple. He landed in a drunken tumble and came up unsteadily.

And then Sang Hee was on him. He did well. Very well, all things considered, but when Sang Hee had you hurt, there wasn't much point in fighting it. Best you could hope to do was last long enough to make an impression on the fans.

I swept my gaze over the crowds—all sixty horizontal rows of them—and even now, I could see their screens lighting up as the promoter terminal asked them to rate the performance of both fighters. Sang Hee would get a 10, as she always did. But then, performance scores only mattered if you lost. Now, Dae needed to dig in his heels and launch a counterattack if he hoped to earn anything above an 8—anything that would keep him in the League through to the next season.

The commentary booth was just ahead, suspended above the ring and lit by that sickly white glow that could only mark streaming cameras. The white-haired blowhards gesticulated wildly, red-faced and spitting, either praising Sang Hee's performance or lamenting Dae's latest big-stage failure, and both seemingly using more energy than the fighters in the ring.

Dae was quite popular with sponsors, or so I'd been told. Quite popular with the League, in other words.

As it turned out, he also wasn't ready to lose, at least not quite yet.

Sang Hee had launched into a furious assault, her feet never set and her staff always spinning, until it slowed long enough to mete out its battering, blunt-force trauma on Dae's forearms and shoulders and the center of his chest. Still, he'd managed to keep the thing from cracking him full in the head, and when Sang Hee set her feet long enough to send a jab forward that might've taken an eye out, Dae launched into a spin of his own.

I don't know if he'd been playing possum or not, but it sure looked like it. One minute, he'd been reeling under that blue-white buzzing onslaught, and the next, he'd executed a perfect counter spin. Sang Hee saw it coming, but she'd already committed to her forward strike. In a moment the highlight shows would be going over for days, Sang Hee lifted the butt of the staff up to block. She managed to divert the angle of the first axe, and might have caught the other if it had followed the same path.

But Dae was more clever than he looked. At least, more clever than he had been last season. Instead of following the same horizontal path as the first blade, Dae's second axe came up and over his head. Sang Hee's eyes widened as she sat back and leaned her head out of harm's way.

"What a dodge," I said, knowing it didn't really matter.

Dae hadn't been aiming for Sang Hee's head, and in her panic, she'd left her staff too far out in front of her. Dae couldn't help but grin as the axe chopped down and hooked back, the curved bottom of one glowing edge catching Sang Hee's weapon and ripping it toward him. Instead of catching it, he flung it back, where it struck the canvas and then careened off into the blackness, buzzing the whole way down. I watched it until it faded from view, far, far below, where the building met the damp streets of Seoul.

There was a pregnant pause, and even the chants of "Dae" stopped for a breath as Sang Hee rolled and executed another perfect somersault. She landed on her feet and wiped the sweat from her brow.

An explosion from the crowd, and now the white-haired men in the booth looked as if they might go right over, falling into the ring below or joining Sang Hee's staff in the netting that might kill them in their silken suits.

Dae was the winner, so long as Sang Hee knelt before him. He stood there, axes hanging by his sides. He even loosened his grip on the hilts, dimming the yellow glow of the blades. He smiled a smile of victory and waited for the inevitable.

But Sang Hee did not kneel, and despite myself, I leaned forward so far I nearly fell into the pit myself, forgetting that the bridge from the red corner had been retracted until the fight was through.

Judging by the collective intake of breath, the crowd was as surprised as me. Judging by the way the glass in the President's booth grew darker, the executives must have pressed themselves up against it, watching in macabre fascination as Sang Hee strode calmly toward her doom.

Killing was illegal in the Korean League. Looked bad for sponsors. Looked bad for the sport, if you could call it that. But it had happened before, and it would happen again, as long as fighters like Sang Hee let their pride get in the way of their livelihood.

Now, Dae had nothing holding him back. Sang Hee had chosen not to kneel, which meant he had no choice but to make her. He actually grimaced. Dae might have been a sponsored fighter, but I'd heard he was a decent man from a hard-working family. He had no desire to kill one of the League's most popular fighters, but it seemed Sang Hee had a death wish. That, or she knew something the rest of us did not.

As it turned out, the latter turned out to be the case.

Dae reignited his yellow blades and held his axes up across his chest as if in prayer. He actually closed his eyes for a spell, and when Sang Hee was nearly on him, he exploded into motion. Dae cut and slashed, spun and charged without a thought to mercy or poise.

Sang Hee ducked and darted, leaned her head back and raised her hands to parry the very air the axes trailed behind them, but though her feet were never still—twisting and pivoting as she adjusted—they never took a backward step.

Dae was getting angry, and anger made him sloppy. He was armed, but that shouldn't have made him careless, especially against a foe as experienced as Sang Hee. But then, we all need to learn somehow, and nothing learns you quite like pain.

Sang Hee stepped forward in the midst of Dae's latest torrent. He actually looked surprised for a second, as if he couldn't believe she would actually step into what could be a lethal range even for blunted resin blades. She stepped in even closer—too close now for the next swing to threaten her, and wrapped her arm around his right arm, locking up his elbow and twisting. He grimaced in pain and started to bring his left blade forward, but Sang Hee had him. There was an audible snap that echoed in the silence and Dae grunted rather than screamed.

Sang Hee slammed her hip into his and sent him up and over her back, keeping his broken arm locked the whole way down. He lost his grip on that blade as his arm went slack, and when his back crashed into the canvas—however unyielding it might normally be—the force jarred a shout from him and a gasp from the crowd.

To his credit, Dae managed to force a scramble, bringing his remaining blade in and striking out with the short hilt rather than the business end. The rubber slammed into Sang Hee's nose and started a fountain of spurting red that had her rolling backward. Dae stood on wobbling legs as Sang Hee eyed him like a cat, crouched, teeth bared in a snarl. He looked pale, the pain from his arm warring with the shock of how quickly the bout had changed.

Dae should have cut his losses and knelt. He didn't. I couldn't help the smile that broke my face as Sang Hee channeled her pain into a furious assault that was nearly as potent as anything she could do with a weapon. In the place of a staff, she sent her legs into momentous spins, taking me back to my tae kwon do days. In the place of roundhouses and spinning back kicks, Sang Hee's all took on a strange, circular flair that could only be explained by her time spent as a gymnast. The kicks came at such odd angles and moved with such velocity that Dae could do little more than dodge. When he struck out with his lone axe at a passing heel, the other came in on the end of a traditional wheel kick and cracked his jaw with a sharp echo.

Dae fell as Sang Hee rose, bringing her head back to the center line. His axe went spinning down to join her blue staff in the depths of the Soul Dome—a winking yellow firefly that heralded his imagined death.

Sang Hee stood motionless but for the rise and fall of her chest beneath her blue and golden padding. She was slick with sweat, her black bangs plastered across her face. The blood ran freely over her mouth, staining the canvas at her feet, where the hot lights would bake it into a syrup I'd have to be careful not to slip in when I was up.

Dae wasn't getting up, and for a moment, I feared him dead. And then I heard him groan. We all did. It was comical and heartbreaking all at once, and Sang Hee dipped a bow to him that seemed a sight more genuine to me than the crowd took it.

"And your winner and first finalist of Season 6!" The announcer was lit once more in a flood of pulsing colored lights while Sang Hee looked beyond him, staring up past the rafters and out into the rain-soaked skies she could not see through the steel and aluminum roof. "Sang Hee!"

The roar was deafening. It easily supplanted anything I'd got last season. I wasn't jealous. Quite the opposite. I was excited.

Sang Hee turned her bow from the vanquished Dae and turned more flourishing versions to the adoring fans, careful to make sure she twirled for the cameras that hung on their wiry webs and swung from gyroscopic motors that whirred like buzzing insects. She paused when she faced the President's box and did not bow, but rather stared, her crimson face making her look anything but friendly—anything but subservient. I didn't think the box was low enough or close enough for her to leap to it, but she looked like she wanted to.

The crowd loved her for it. They hated the League. Hated what it stood for. Hated the black suits from the Land of the Rising Sun as much as they hated the men who funded them and almost as much as they hated the thought of missing a single match in the League's short and storied history in Korea.

Of course, it was all a part of Sang Hee's act. Hero of the people. Fan favorite. Korea's own. Unsponsored. On that point, at least, her act held weight. Of course, being a former Olympian and the daughter of a billionaire afforded a person certain advantages in that department. Still, she didn't have to fight. I could respect her for that.

The rumble of the crowd was supplanted by the vibrations below my sock-thin boots as the gears turned. The walking bridge slid out with an oily hiss, stretching toward the ring, all black planks and oval white lights along the borders.

Sang Hee timed her walk perfectly, stepping onto the walkway without breaking stride just as it connected with the square platform. She hid her limp well as she walked toward me. Dae couldn't say the same, unfortunately, as a pair of medics rushed in from the blue corner walkway and peeled him up off the canvas, depositing him unceremoniously onto a stretcher.

The crowd had already forgotten Sang Hee by the time she passed me by. She showed me a red smile, and I was surprised to see a plastic glaze to her eyes that suggested Dae had struck her harder than she had let on. She swayed a bit at the end and I leaned toward her. She caught my shoulder to steady herself and played it off as a playful greeting to the crowd, patting me on the rear as she trundled past.

"Thanks," she whispered as she stole into the dimly lit hall and cut a path toward the locker room.

"Great show!" I called behind her. She just waved without turning back. "See you in the Finals," I said to myself. I didn't know if my heart was beating more furiously for that or for the fact that I was due up next.

I had already gone through my stretching routine in the locker room and I'd been standing here for seemingly an hour as the last few bouts had gone off. My muscles were warm and my mind was keyed to the task. All that remained was to see the thing done.

I looked up at the display that hung in the air above the ring. It was a black sphere of plasma during the bouts that turned to a glowing repository of highlights, advertisements and pulsing annoyance between fights. I chewed my lip in anticipation of the performance scores.

Sang Hee came up first. "W," as was the case with all winners. It was a wonder they showed it at all. No surprise there. It was greeted by a loud and throaty cheer as her key demographics swooned.

"Come on … come on," I whispered to myself, as if Dae's incoming score had anything to do with me.

A louder cheer went up when the second number came up next to the sable-haired, blue-eyed image of the South Korean male.

"10," I said, satisfied. "Not bad, Dae. Not bad at all."

Performances, after all, weren't all about winning. I dare say, if they let the audience give me one, I'd be lucky to break a 7, given how one-sided many of my fights tended to be. What was the word the Seoul sports media used to describe me this season? Workmanlike.

Nothing workmanlike about winning. After all, I'd had enough of bloody wars. Season 4—my first—had been full of them. Season 5 less so, and this season, I couldn't recall a single fighter having landed anything that did more than smart. Of course, Sang Hee had faced the tougher competition. I wouldn't argue with that.

Maybe King Kwan would have something to say about it. I'd heard he packed quite the punch.

The black screen faded for a spell and the lights went down. Now my heart was hammering in my chest.

"Next up!" the announcer screamed, his voice going from hoarse to reedy. "Your second Quarter Final match! Openweight division. Nine victories each to their names this season. Zero defeats."

Of course there were zero defeats, or else we wouldn't be here. The Korean League had taken all but the most controversial rules from its mother League in Japan. 64 fighters. Single elimination. Rinse and repeat.

I ached to step out onto the bridge, but the suits had been clear that I wasn't to mess with the presentation any more than I had in the past. My fights were getting stale enough, they said. In paying my debt, it seemed I was affecting someone else's bottom line. I spat into the airy depths again, and the spotlight tech chose that moment to focus on me.

It was blinding bright and I squinted. The crowd cheered, though not as loudly as they had for Sang Hee. Reduced to Dae-level applause. I nearly shook my head. Maybe I'd make this one more exciting for them. Maybe I'd keep him in it.

That was what I thought, but my heart beat even faster, if it were possible, and my palms had begun to sweat. The truth was, I'd never fought Kwan before. I only knew him through observation. We hadn't met during Season 5. Lucky for him, each of us thought. Lucky for him.

Thing was, it really was a stroke of luck that had prompted Kwan's exit from the previous tournament. Kwan wasn't much of a dodger. He was huge and massive all around. Close to seven feet and weighing in at close to 300 pounds. But he had near impregnable defense, by all accounts. He used a shield with a glowing red blade surrounding it, like a disco Frisbee. It had been a prototype he'd been testing out last season. Resin must not have been cast right. It shattered under the weight of Mal Chin's Euro-style sword, and then there'd been nothing to defend himself with. He'd taken a beating, and a bad one. It was a wonder they had let him compete at all this year, and a wonder he'd made it this far.

Mal Chin certainly hadn't. The nasty Korean might have lost in the Semis, but he'd acquitted himself reasonably well. He'd been in an accident soon after. A fatal one, if you could believe it, and the media hadn't done a whole lot of digging into circumstances that had seemed less than legitimate from where myself and a whole lot of others had been sitting. But then, few tears had been shed on the circuit. Mal Chin had kept to himself. He hadn't done much media and his run during Season 5 was seen as something of a Cinderella story. He had few fans to speak of. Didn't look like that was going to change anytime soon.

I'd grown so used to blocking out that reedy announcer's voice that I had to blink to notice that Kwan was already standing in the ring. Every considerable pound of him. He wore a mask—a black one that covered the bottom half of his nose and all of his mouth. His armor was a deep and inky green, and he looked to have a new version of that black bladeshield he'd used last time. He didn't pace, just stood there like a titanic statue of muscle and supplements, not that I could accuse him without being sued.

"And now … fighting out of the red corner … a man who needs no introduction …"

But a man who's going to get one anyway.

"A man who followed up a first-round exit from his Season 4 debut with an undefeated stretch that earned him the Season 5 Championship and shows no signs of slowing down …"

My feet were itchy and my palms had gone from damp to dry. My heart had slowed and my vision had cleared and focused. My thoughts narrowed along with my attention.

"Introducing … PRINCE AKIO!"

A louder cheer than I'd been expecting. I didn't even remember to spit at the intentional misread of my name. Akio Prince. Didn't have to get very creative to turn that one around and use it as a moniker. But then, it hadn't been my choice. It seemed fewer and fewer things in my life had come on the end of choice, lately. But then, choices were more akin to choosing which mountain to attempt to climb rather than which path.

Damn bastard always popped into my mind in the seconds before a fight. And he never seemed to offer advice regarding the contest at hand. Everything had been big picture to him, which is why he'd missed so many moments. But that wasn't the story at hand.

I sighed and breathed it all in. I might as well enjoy it. After all, if the suits got their way—those cigar-toting fatsos in the President's box—I'd be taking a dive tomorrow night. At least the debt would be paid.

Thoughts best left for tomorrow. Maybe Kwan would do me a favor and beat me tonight, fair and square. I didn't think it entirely likely, but stranger things had happened.

"Right, then," I said to myself, and stepped onto the walkway. "Time to play."

3
KING KWAN

The fans would never take to me.

That was what they'd said. I had a foreign name. Two foreign names, and neither from a place the great people of the Democratic Republic of Korea held a whole lot of love for these days.

Prince. Prince could be an Englishman. My father had been American, far as I knew. Maybe that had just been the moniker he'd used on whatever business trip he'd met her on—a Tokyo gal working a Tokyo bar, no doubt. But Akio. Akio was given by my mother, right before she gave me away, shipped me off to a land of freedom and opportunity. I'm sure she meant well. Sure.

I didn't learn the meaning of the name until much later. My friends used it ironically. My opponents derisively. At least, they had.

"Hero," they'd say, referring to the traditional translation. "Whatever will we do?"

"You could always run," I'd tell them. "Much good it'll do you."

Of course, all of this was quite beside the point. And the point, right now, was King Kwan himself, standing like a mountain of a man, all green resin armor and black bladeshield. They were playing my highlight package on the black sphere above. I could see the glow of the viewscreens reflecting those pale ghost faces in the crowd, playing some version of the same old, complete with my latest statistics. There would be an algorithm running in the back, computers spitting out odds and chances based on our respective weights, records, strength of opposition and—it goes without saying—propensity to cash out on big bets.

The bookies had been losing money on me every week. You'd think they'd have learned when the streak stretched to 12 in a row, spanning two consecutive seasons and play-in bouts. You'd think they'd really learn when it had reached 14. And then, when it hit 18 just three days ago, you'd think there could be no sane man in all of Seoul or watching on his monitor at home, bag of chips and flat soda by his bed, who would bet against Akio Prince.

But then, every run had to end, and when it did, a whole lot of common folk would lose a tiny smidge of money, and a whole lot of bookies would go a long way toward earning back their losses.

I sighed for comedic effect. Not so the crowd could see. Just a little touch for Kwan and me. As it turned out, the rumors were true: Kwan was not the joking type. In fact, the longer I stared at him and his dark eyes—no colored lenses for this one—the more I wondered if a man like Kwan had a type at all.

I studied him. Studied his armor; it was thick, but no doubt legal, in keeping with the regulations. It didn't look overly flexible to me. There were plastic plates over his gargantuan pecs connected over his sternum, and his belt fed to a thick row of rubber ribs that curled around his torso and likely fed up to the base of his neck. Not one for dodging, Kwan. Not one for moving much at all. Not that he had to.

I studied his weapon next. It was big. Much bigger than it looked on the few highlight videos I'd seen in passing. I wasn't one to study tape. That was more Joon's prerogative. But then, I had never been one to listen to Joon all too closely in any case, and so, I really had little idea what the thing could do other than light up like any of our other weapons and more than likely crack my skull without much effort.

Helmets had gone out of fashion in the midst of Season 2. They had never been mandatory—a loophole the Seoul Athletic

Commission had never seen fit to fill—but the promoters assumed fighters would want to afford themselves as much protection as they could when die-cast resin staffs and dull blades were whipping around, spinning with devastating force. Exactly why they'd gone out of fashion was a matter up for some debate. Some thought they actually limited a fighter's vision, and thus made things even less safe than they already were. I subscribed to that camp. Others simply chalked it up to another vain excuse for sponsored fighters to flaunt their pretty faces, colored lenses and new hair dyes for the cameras, risks be damned.

I also subscribed to that group.

Speaking of pretty faces, there was mine, looking out over the stands from the screens above as the highlight package started to wind down. I'd grown bored enough with inspecting Kwan's—it wasn't all that much to look at, truth be told—and wanted to see how much longer the highlight package would run. A face that verged closer to the isle of Japan than whatever Eurocentric suburb my father had crawled out of. Black hair cut short and spiked, and eyes that were a dark blue. Dark enough to look black to some. I had long lashes and thick eyebrows, one of which bore a nifty scar down the center—a mark from my kick-boxing days. My nose was slightly crooked if you looked at it from below, but I could pass for handsome and often chose to.

"Trick?"

The gruff voice pulled me from my private contemplation. I looked at Kwan, standing there like a silent gargoyle. I couldn't see his mouth behind the ninja mask he wore. It made him look like a cross between an old-school fighting game legend and a hulked-out super villain.

"Pardon?"

Kwan tilted his head to the side as he considered me. The movement admitted a beam of bright-white light from the commentary box that had me wincing before he straightened and bathed me once more in his black shadow.

"Everyone in this League has a trick, Prince Akio," Kwan said. "Tricks from the cage. Tricks from the ring. Tricks from the street. Some even bring tricks from wars they fought in, tours in the Middle East and North Africa. Americans aren't fond of tricks. They're straightforward. That's why I like them. But you're not American."

"The Chaos Countries." I nodded, but Kwan only watched me. His voice was low, but not as low as I had expected. It was sonorous and oddly soothing. Somehow, it made him more frightening. He seemed entirely in control, and entirely uninterested in the lights and the crowd, the glitz and glamor. That made him dangerous in my estimation.

"So, then," Kwan said, leaning forward so that I could see his eyes. No color to them. They made mine look like bright oceans of azure. "What's your trick?"

"Well," I said, becoming aware of the dimming lights in the crowd as the display screens winked out and the almost silence of a full arena took over, "I've always been rather quick. Speedy, some might even say."

"Quick," Kwan nodded. "Speedy." He didn't seem impressed, which was all well and good to me.

In truth, I had no trick. At least, not in quite the way Kwan thought. I was fast. That was no lie. No use in being modest about it. I was also strong. Stronger than my average frame might suggest. I was agile enough, though I'd block more often than Sang Hee and less often than Dae, dodging where I could. I hit with power when I wanted to, and I was precise.

All of those were attributes. All of those made up the fighter that I was. The fighter I'd become through countless hours spent in the dojo with Joon, endless bouts in Thailand where my knuckles were covered with ropes and my body with oil. Long, grueling exchanges in the cages of North America, where the stars of MMA met to play and make their great fortunes before their traditions, too, began to die off.

But no, Kwan. None of those could be counted as my trick. Even together, they didn't make up anything more than a clever riddle.

My blood began to rise as Kwan's bladeshield lit. Red pulsing light ringed the lightblade along its edges. In that, it seemed we were the same. The crowd's silence had begun to grow restless, and my heart began to hammer in my chest, admitting a flood of that sweet, horrid chemical into my veins. The one that made my eyes glaze and my sweat dry up. The one that made my muscles twitch before I called them to action. The precursor to my trick.

Adrenaline is one hell of a drug. Don't let anyone tell you otherwise.

"My trick, Kwan," I said, reaching up with each hand and pulling my swords from their sheaths, "is fear."

He actually laughed. Just once, but enough to show me what he thought of it.

"Not yours," I said, earning a confused stare.

Kwan took a step forward and I took two back, whipping my black resin blades to the sides. The crowd let out a collective gasp as the weapons elongated, growing from three feet to five from hilt to angled edge, though they'd seen it a dozen times before. I pressed the padded hilts and the straight inward edges of the blades began to emit a darker version of the red light Kwan's bladeshield emitted. Mine didn't pulse and flicker. Only glowed like devil's teeth, and that was what I called them.

"Your own." Kwan offered it as a question. "Your trick is your own fear." He didn't dismiss it out of hand like others might have. If anything, his eyes went a little wider and the circular path he paced around me grew a little wider. I could feel his power as he moved. It was like watching a big cat pace on the other side of a chain-link fence. It wasn't something you could get a feel for on a digital screen.

"You know, Kwan," I said, turning and beginning my own circular path to match him, "you might just be smarter than you look."

He didn't like that. He didn't like that one bit.

For once, the crowd reacted before I did, screaming in unison as Kwan burst into motion. He was far quicker than he looked. It was a good thing I'd kept some space between us or else I'd have been flattened on the spot.

I leapt back far enough to avoid the behemoth's lowered shoulder but not nearly far enough to escape the range of that sweeping black shield. It sped toward my princely crown trailing red light. I rolled beneath it, forward instead of back, retracting my blades back to their shortened forms as I came up just before his bulk.

I stabbed forward, landing a solid hit with the right blade that sparked on contact, alerting the crowd to a concussive blow, but Kwan only let out the barest hint of a sigh and I expelled a heavier one as the right hand he'd hidden behind the sweeping shield caught me in the gut and sent me rolling back out into the center of the ring.

Apparently, Kwan was intent on pulling my trick out of me.

He was on me like a hound on a hare, and so I was forced to put that aforementioned quickness to the test. I rolled and came up slashing, my blades sprouting back to their full length. I fought in an orthodox stance, keeping Kwan's right hand at bay with my left blade and holding the right aloft and above my head, waiting for the right time to strike.

Kwan was more clever than he looked. He didn't charge again. Not right away. If he had, I'd have brought that right blade crashing down on his head hard enough to sleep a bull, which meant it might've had a good chance to give him a mild headache.

No. If I wanted to have a chance at beating him, I'd have to get that pesky shield away from him.

I darted forward, keeping on the balls of my feet, moving like a fencer. I jabbed with the glowing red tip of a resin blade. It didn't connect, of course, but it had the desired effect, forcing Kwan to lean away from the bright light. I kept on him, waving my lead sword like a torch before the cave of a hungry bear, bewildering … annoying. Stinging.

Finally, Kwan had enough of retreating. It was unbecoming, and so he put that bladeshield to use, knocking my lead sword aside, which, of course, was just what I wanted him to do. I chopped down with the right sword as my left was pushed away, and in the place of an armored elbow, the broad center of the shield was there to greet the red sparking edge of my strike.

"Clever," I said, marveling at how quickly Kwan had managed

to halt the momentum of his swing. Instead of passing the bladeshield right by us both, he'd stopped it in time to take the full might of my strongest hit. I didn't consider that he wasn't done with his attack, and the next thing I knew the shield screamed forward with 300 pounds of force behind it. The strike gave me a spurting nose that must have put Sang Hee's to shame.

Now when I spun away from the exchange, there was nothing of show or strategy in it. Sheer momentum. I wiped the blood from my upper lip. My head was clear, meaning I'd had the wherewithal to lean back quick enough to take some force from the blow. I widened my stance and readied for another charge, but Kwan, it seemed, was now content to take his time.

You could learn a lot about a fighter from just a few brief exchanges. After all, fights were nothing if not exchanges. Questions and answers. Sometimes a bout took one or two. Sometimes it took a short novel.

Kwan was aggressive and defensive. Fast and slow. He seemed to be more a master of breaking rhythm than following it. Still, every fighter set patterns, and I was good at reading them.

For now, Kwan let me examine him from nonlethal range. He was confident. More so, he was controlled. That didn't mean he was going to let me stand unchallenged for long. It just meant that if I wanted to find a way to win, I'd have to do it with offense and not some clever trip.

I was getting nervous, and my nervousness began to morph into fear as Kwan skipped in again, his flashing shield keeping me on the edges of the ring as I dodged. I wasn't nearly as nimble as Sang Hee, but my blades were strong as the hands that held them, and I managed to divert the heavy thing enough to keep it from connecting solid. One glancing knock to the ribs and I'd hear a crack. What's more, I'd more than likely find myself screaming out into the abyss as I careened down toward that iron netting far below, where I'd join Sang Hee's staff and Dae's yellow axe.

I decided I'd had enough of retreating, and also that I'd like to take back some of Kwan's respect. I attacked. Trouble was, my head was a little fuzzy from his first—and to this point, only—hit, and so the cross strike I landed to Kwan's mountain of a jaw was rewarded by a full-on gut punch with that damn bladeshield. That one nearly laid me low, but I managed a roll and hooked my other sword behind the crook of Kwan's knee, hilt planted firmly in the canvas. I heaved as I rolled.

And stopped dead. Kwan had tensed, seeing the move before I'd made it. It took all of my considerable poise to keep from crying out as I left the sword on the spot and scrambled out of the way as that shield crashed down onto the section of canvas where I'd just been. The sound put the half-naked man and his ceremonial drum to shame, and I swallowed as I rose, single glowing blade in hand, and squared my stance.

Kwan picked his bladeshield up with a sucking sound, and I thought I heard a faint tearing that echoed in the airy confines. Had his blow actually ripped the canvas? Can't say I'd seen that before. Judging by the collective gasp the crowd let out, it was new to them as well.

The hulk turned toward me. His dark eyes darted down to the single blade I held out toward him like a ward and he seemed to remember the one I'd left behind like an afterthought. He stooped to pick it up and I thought about taking the opportunity to attack. I'd like to say I refrained out of some shred of the respect Kenta had instilled in me, but the truth was, I was concerned about falling into another one of Kwan's clever traps.

As it turned out, he surprised me, just not in the way I was expecting. He snatched my discarded blade from the canvas and twisted it in his huge, green-gloved hand, admiring the resin and the lighting effects. It was a nice sword, if I did say so myself, and I sighed at the thought of Kwan tossing it into the abyss, where it would fall to the lowest levels of this cursed arena, to be dismantled or stolen by a janitor or street punk. Surely he would.

Instead, Kwan tossed it toward me like Joon might have in the dojo after having knocked me down. Tossed it like a kid tosses a ball to a friend.

I caught it, never taking my eyes from Kwan. He gave a nod, and the crowd, holding its breath during the silent exchange, exploded into applause for the rare show of honor.

I inclined my head and crossed my red and black blades in front of me before dipping into a bow in the old style. I did take my eyes from Kwan, and he did me the honor of not seizing the moment by kicking me right off the edge of the platform.

"An honorable man," Kwan said as I raised my eyes and then my head and began to circle. The blood had dried into a raisin paste below my nose and on my upper lip, and my head had ceased its swimming, allowing the pain to settle in and the fresh fear with it. "Few enough of those left."

"True."

I dare say that over the course of the next three or so minutes we treated that sold-out arena to one of the best fights the League had seen in its short gestation.

You see, when I got hit hard enough to draw blood, and when I truly felt the balance of a contest swing against me, I got this … mask that came over me. Sort of a film that slid over my eyes, slowed my breath even as it quickened my heart and my hands. It was a lucky thing my blades weren't sharp. A lucky thing for Kwan.

I gave the mountainous brute everything he could handle, feinting high and cutting low. I rapped him on either temple with the hard flats of my blades and took his counter on the end of its swing, spinning away only to come back in right after. I made him swing that bladeshield often, and more of the time, he caught nothing but air. When he did land a partial blow, I let him see that it didn't hurt enough to stop me, that it might even be spurring me on.

Of course, if he had landed it fully, I'd be waking up in a hospital bed with different sorts of lights shining down on me. Kwan had to know it, too. That's why the big bastard didn't give up. Not even close.

When his weapon got a bit heavier and his slashing swipes a bit more labored, he changed tack, hiding that clever right hand behind the black and red disc. He blinded me momentarily with a squeeze on the handle that flared the red blade to life and left trails on the backs of my eyes. He followed it up with a right cross that split the white scar on my eyebrow, and I gave him a matching one across the nose with a cross-angled, overhand chop with my left blade as I charged in rather than falling back.

Hit the skin hard enough—blunt weapons or not—and it'll split, especially when you've got the scar tissue folk like us tended to sport.

The League said the crowds weren't into blood. They were wrong. The popularity of the brutal Kyoto League proved that much, no matter what the buttoned-up suits in Seoul said. They loved it. Craved it, even as they hid from it behind splayed fingers.

I knew Kwan was just about done when he stopped circling. We had been making something of a funnel that had grown tighter as the fight had grown fiercer, exchanging blocks and blows at medium and close range as the spiral tightened. Now, I kept my circuitous route going, swords tipped down below my knees, but Kwan only turned to face me. I reversed directions, never taking my eyes from his, and he twisted to match me. I smiled to let him know I had him, and he showed the first hint of emotion since the fight had started.

It was a mix between a wheeze and a growl, and it warmed my heart to hear it.

I darted in straight then changed course, picking my blades up, spreading them to either side and launching into a spin. Kwan leaned back to avoid the twin stab and raised his bladeshield to ward off my three-strike spin, but he'd missed the setup.

You see, I liked my blades. I really did. They increased my reach and—against a less cagey opponent, or one grown tired enough from the fight—they were more than capable of ringing a skull hard enough to knock the toughest fighter out cold. But my swords were little more than window dressing for my true art. The art of all fighters, should they learn to embrace it.

The art of kicking ass. And I do mean that quite literally.

I planted on the back of that whirling tornado of red light and black resin, dug my rubber heel into the rip Kwan had made in the canvas, and lanced my right foot back as my head came around my shoulder. It was a long moment of agony for Kwan to see the kick rocketing toward his midsection and a longer one when it connected, as I chose that moment to put the pop into it, as Joon would say, extending my hip that extra centimeter that made Kwan's gut the perfect resting place for my foot and his floating rib the perfect sacrifice for our violent collision.

He stumbled as I chambered my kick, pulling it back toward my body. His eyes widened at the force I'd generated, as much from surprise as from pain. I always focused on the body. The League might have closed down most of those hand-to-hand organizations, dropped knuckles and elbows in favor of bright lights, cast resin and body armor, but fighters who came out of those circuits knew that, no matter how tough you were and no matter how bad you wanted to, there was no walking off a clean body shot.

Kwan, however, was up to the task. But pain made even the most experienced veterans sloppy, and King Kwan was becoming rather predictable. You see, in addition to my dashing good looks and better kicks, I was good at reading patterns. Very good. I know I mentioned that before, but it really can't be overstated. I was a visual learner, and Kwan had given me a lot to look at in our short time together.

Kwan managed to keep his feet long enough to let the worst of the impact pass him by. He choked out a shaking breath and a bit of pink drool leaked out to stain the canvas, steaming in the heat the spotlights gave off. His eyes weren't so dark now, with the whites showing all around the edges, and a vein the size of a nightcrawler had started from one military-cut sideburn and burrowed its way right up to the crown of his too-large head. I could hear his breath wheezing from behind his ventilated mask.

Instead of swiping with a bladeshield that had grown heavy indeed, Kwan feinted a charge straight in. He knew my response would be a right-hand chop, so I showed it to him. At least, I showed him the start of it, raising my sword above my head and starting it downward. He smiled a smile of victory and halted himself, jutting his shield arm forward rather than across his body. It was a broken pattern, and it would have caught most fighters off guard.

But Kwan. Oh, great and mighty, simple Kwan. I'd already done that move tonight, and so had you.

Instead of striking down toward the crook of Kwan's elbow, I stopped my strike and instead leapt, my right boot landing on the ridged surface of the black shield. I swept my swords out to either side for balance, like the wings of a falcon, and saw the first glimpse of fear in the monster's eyes. His bladeshield flashed and flickered as it bore my full weight for a brief moment.

Kwan couldn't pull his shouldered charge entirely, so I rode the momentum of the lift and pulled my shoulder blades back, carving crescents in the hot, musty air with my arms and extending my hips forward, right knee leading the charge.

Directly into Kwan's cheek.

The snap had me grimacing even as I felt the sharp rush of imminent victory. Of a foe vanquished.

It was true what they said about the big ones. Kwan fell hard, and he fell loud, while I landed on my feet, glowing blades out to either side. I looked back at Kwan over my shoulder. He wasn't moving, and for a long half minute, the crowd was mostly silent. Even the static chatter coming from the commentary box cut out, where before it had been a buzzing gnat at the periphery of the contest.

There was a generous helping of red beneath Kwan's left eye where my knee had struck that had begun to pool, and as the adrenaline began to ebb away, I had the sickening feeling that I had just blinded the man. My knee had already begun to throb through the plate, and I could feel something loose behind my kneecap that I hoped wouldn't stop me from competing in the Semi Finals.

The crowd roared only when they saw Kwan roll over and catch himself with his right hand, his bladeshield flickering as he struggled to one knee. The blood that had buried his eye spilled onto the ruined canvas like fresh black tea, and I heard someone lose their soda and corn in the bottom row behind me.

For a moment, I thought Kwan would regain his feet and make me deprive him of consciousness, which would likely be akin to killing him in his current condition. But then he brought his hands up under his face and left his shield behind, where the red light dimmed and then went out completely, leaving the mighty weapon looking like a discarded sewer cap. The brute's shoulders shook, and I thought he was crying before I recognized the sound as laughter.

"Kwan ...?" I asked, turning to face him directly. Decorum said that I should sheathe my blades, but I didn't feel comfortable doing that quite yet.

Kwan remembered himself and unclipped his mask, pulling the polymer off of his nose, mouth and jaw. He seemed to remember me. He looked up and I winced at the sight of his face, which had already gone purple where I'd struck him. Of course, the slashed nose and cheek made him look worse than he was, but the orbital on his left side was no doubt cracked.

And yet he smiled. It wasn't as manic as I'd thought now that he'd calmed some.

"Some trick," Kwan said. "Some trick you have, Prince Akio."

4

LAST NIGHT OF FREEDOM

As it turned out, Kwan wasn't the only one who appreciated my tricks. As soon as Kwan's bladeshield lost its glow and the crowd became aware that the behemoth—tough as he was—seemed unlikely to rise to the challenge, a roar went up that took me pleasantly by surprise.

I turned in slow circles as the bright, white competition lights winked out and the personal viewscreens began to light the myriad faces surrounding me and looking down on me. I wanted to hate them, the many faces of the Free City of Seoul, but I just couldn't bring myself to do it. Hating was a hard thing, Kenta had always said. Damn it if the old man wasn't right.

I would have said Kenta never met some of the folk I had, and that was true, but there was no doubting he'd met plenty worse. He'd fought in the American Wars, after all. Lost plenty more than his thumb and half an ear down in hot, humid Central.

The sound of cheering began to fade as I slowed my spin. I'd timed it right. About thirty seconds. Thirty seconds of fanfare, and then they waited to see what was next.

"Maybe I do hate you, after all," I whispered.

I heard a groan in the fluorescent semidarkness. I had all but forgotten poor Kwan, who was just now struggling into a seated position. He started to sway and I knelt down to help steady him. No cheers for that. I doubt anyone noticed. The League had plenty of fans—a growing subset of the Democratic Republics of Asia Major—but few fans of the older, more pure martial sports had made the migration.

Joon thought it was the pageantry, but he was speaking with a serious recency bias. Pageantry had always been present in prizefighting, if not in martial arts. Forms might have had a warlike purpose to the ancients, but they were pretty dances meant to earn children gold-colored plastic trophies these days. No. It wasn't the lights, nor the screaming fans or squawking commentators. It wasn't the television deals or the gambling or even the money that turned off the purists. It was the weapons. More so, it was the armor. Separate a man from his enemy with a bullet, and you're talking war. Separate him from his enemy with a length of sharpened steel, and you're talking classic war.

Separate a man from his enemy with hard resin and LED lighting, and you're talking something that looks like one and acts like the other, and so ends up caught in a sad, worrisome middle ground.

There my mind went, wandering its usual ways. Kwan didn't seem to notice. Another strip of pink drool leaked from under his upper lip and gave me the urge to dab it with my gloved thumb and forefinger. I refrained.

The hiss of gears announced the approach of the twin walk-ways, and the sound of booted footfalls from the blue corner tunnel signaled the arrival of the medical staff. I laughed as I saw how many of them they'd brought.

"A royal retinue, here for the King himself," I said, clapping Kwan on the back. He grunted something unintelligible, his head no doubt swimming with whatever my knee had put into it. Speaking of which ... the thing was beginning to throb so badly I could barely limp.

"Step aside, please."

"You got it, Doc," I said and I did. The team of six—I counted them—helped Kwan into a sort of lurching, stumbling half crouch and deposited him onto the flat bed of a tractor thingy with as many wheels as there were medics. Kwan waved weakly at the crowd as he passed and got a halfhearted sympathy cheer for his efforts.

I stood in the center of the ring, waiting just long enough to ensure there would be no post-fight interview. No sign of that greasy-haired weasel they'd used in Season 5. More cost-cutting, I guess. I shrugged and sheathed my shortened blades in the catches on the back of my suit and made my way back onto the red corner bridge, sparing a disinterested glance back at the black sphere monitor as it lit up in that void the rafters made. It all looked a bit like some sort of cyber beehive, with the lit backscreens of cell phones and server menus acting as the buzzing workers around the spherical monitor's weighty presence.

"Bow to your queen," I whispered, and to no one in particular.

Just before I turned away, Kwan's face came up on the screen. Some statistics flew by the margins—figures I doubted if anyone in the crowd bothered to double-check—that attempted to reduce whatever it was Kwan and I had just done into a series of numbers on a digital canvas. I didn't think Kwan had landed sixteen hits on me, but then, I could still smell copper within the ruin of my nose and my ribs were beginning to swell enough to cause my suit to start to feel like a boa constrictor.

Performance Score for Losing Fighter, "King" Kwan: 8.6.

"Not bad, Kwan, though I'd have bumped you up for that first trick. Clever thing, that."

Now that I was caught there on the center of the bridge like some vain fool, I might as well wait around to see what the fans had given me.

Performance Score for Winning Fighter, "Prince" Akio: 9.8.

"Well how about that. Can't blame those ratings on me this week."

I turned back to the painted tunnel, or started to, when my eyes froze of their own accord on the tinted glass of the President's box. There was only one figure standing there now, his shadow positioned off-kilter and his head facing my way.

The ever-present shadows. Always watching. Always scheming.

I really shouldn't have, but I worked up enough saliva—the blood helped—to send a gob of spit off into the echoing chasm where dead weapons rested until their lights winked out. To my chagrin, the shadow did not so much as twitch from its place, but I gave him the full ire of my stare, knowing it wouldn't do anything to help me sleep through the night.

The white lights turned on from either side of the arena as the coliseum readied for the final bout of the night, and the one that would decide my opponent in the Semis. I hadn't a clue who was fighting, but it was clear that the arena was waiting for me to make my exit. I obliged them, that damn shadow leering in my periphery as I took my awkward leave.

Seoul was a free city. The most free, according to the state media. Which is to say, the more of it you say you've got, the less you'll really know.

But who was I to judge?

It wasn't all the Hachinin's doing. The corruption, I mean. I shouldn't have lingered on it and trust me, I tried to shake the thought as I left the bout behind, but the tunnel was painted red, after all, and it put me in a similar mood.

There was a man with a purple suit standing to the right, where Locker Room A was situated. I paused at the intersection, curious as to who would be coming out next—I never paid attention to the rankings—but purple suit shooed me away like I was a fly.

Fine.

The hallway was darker on the lonely road to Locker Room B, and I passed a plasma screen on the way that I hadn't noticed before. I paused before it. It was a tournament chart, with animated likenesses of all the participants from Week 1 to tonight. Kwan's big mug still glowed on the screen, which hadn't yet updated to log the latest results. Handy thing to know about, seeing that I was in the tournament, but I found that I got more nervous not knowing whom I'd be fighting until it was too late to prepare in any sort of meaningful way. Strange way to operate as a fighter, but then, being nervous led to being scared, and as old big King Kwan had learned not so long ago, being scared made me the opposite of soft.

Footsteps to my left, and I turned to see Sang Hee gliding with too-perfect steps in my direction. She wore a suit—pants and all—but she wore it well. When she saw me, she smiled in a devilish way. Her nose was a little swollen, but if you hadn't seen it happen, you might only think her a little chilled. The blood had only seeped a tad into the hollows beneath her eyes.

"Just a little tired," she said as she came to stand in front of me. "But thank you for the concerned look."

"Concerned?" I laughed. "If you're banged up, it only increases my chances of taking this one all the way."

"Not banged," Sang Hee said, winking when she caught my look of confusion. "Not yet. Does help me relax after a fight like that, though. Thanks for the offer."

"I wasn't ... I mean ..." I floundered about. I wasn't keen on sleeping with opponents, former or potential ... though I had made exceptions before. Sang Hee seemed to delight in my discomfort, and I wondered if she was pulling a fast one on me, but then her eyes began to rove not at all modestly, and she stepped a little closer.

"Let me buy you a beer or three, Prince Akio," she purred. It was strange hearing her put on a sultry voice, seeing as I'd just witnessed her beat the tar out of one of the best fighters in the world as if it were nothing. Maybe it had gotten her temperature up.

"Drinking alone, tonight," I said. "The way it should be for all us brooding types."

She shrugged and took a half step back, and I let out the breath I hadn't realized I'd been holding.

"Not alone," she said, and I turned my embarrassed look into a questioning one. She jabbed a thumb over her shoulder. "Friend's been waiting in there. Was in there when I got out of the shower, which would have been more fine with me had he been willing to humor me for a bit of ... ah, never mind." She gripped me on the shoulder. "See you in the Finals next week."

"I don't even know who—" I started, turning back to the chart. Kwan's name was now faded, as if he'd died and been erased from the surface of the Earth and not simply from one in soon to be hundreds of seasons in a meaningless exercise in corporate greed and consumer escapism.

"Janix will win," she said, answering my unspoken question, "and I've no doubt you can manage a win over a rookie, fiery as he might be."

"I'm scarcely more than a rookie myself," I put in. Janix. Janix. The name, I was sorry to think, did not so much as flirt with ringing a bell. That would have been fine, except that I couldn't quite work myself up to being afraid of him if I didn't know who he was or how he fought. More importantly, how he won.

Ah, well. I'd just have to fire up YouTube later on and troll for his most vicious highlights of the season, get myself all worked up. YouTube. Weird name for an entertainment conglomerate, I'd always thought, but then, it was one of the oldest companies that still kept its original name.

"Guess it was a weak year, with me making it to the Finals," Sang Hee said, the model of false modesty.

Sang Hee was the most talented fighter in the League, with me being the only argument to the contrary. She'd debuted in Season 3, got knocked around a bit in the Round of 32, and then taken the next two seasons off. She'd come back better. Much better. In fact, I can't say I've ever seen someone improve so much in such a short amount of time. She'd come into the League as a glorified gymnast. Now, she was a queen of war.

"You haven't made it, yet," I said easily, but she ignored the comment.

"I will. I'm fighting Kaya Brent." She pointed at the animated leaderboard and my eyes found a dark-skinned face tilting from side to side. She had braided hair with as many bows as there were colors in the rainbow, and then some.

"She's no good, I take it?"

"Good as the rest." Sang Hee shrugged. "She's American,

though." She looked at me quickly, her cheeks reddening some. "No offense."

I held up my hands and smiled. "None taken. Never spent much time there, myself."

"Right." Sang Hee was already looking back at the screen. "Nothing inherently wrong with being American. Not even when it comes to martial arts. It's just ..." she shook her head, "they're still caught up in that old stuff."

"Ratings are down across the board," I put in.

"Boxing or MMA?"

"The board meaning everything, but they don't seem to be taking the hint that the rest of the world's been moving on for the last fifteen years."

Sang Hee sighed, but I couldn't tell what she meant by it. Was it condescension toward our wayward Western brothers and sisters, or sorrow for the departure of the old forms of televised violence?

"She's brave," she said. "I'll give her that much. Doesn't even have a professional team behind her."

Neither did I, and as far as anyone could tell, Sang Hee's Team Azure was comprised of herself and whatever trainers she kept on the payroll. Probably all signed NDAs and the works.

"She emigrated?" I asked. It seemed strange to be talking about someone so much while having little more than an exaggerated cartoon graphic to stare at. I tried to keep from looking at my own, which verged on my Japanese side much more heavily than my American.

"I guess. Not a sponsor to her name."

"Sounds like we'd get along."

Sang Hee turned a doubtful look my way. "What? You're not exactly the most sociable of the League's fighters."

"I didn't realize there was a reading group," I said. She rolled her eyes. "What are we here for, Sang Hee? Certainly not to make friends." I was getting a little more irritable than I should be. Maybe it was the post-fight exhaustion taking over. Adrenaline dumps always did a number on me.

She simply stared at me … maybe for a solid twenty seconds. "Duly noted."

I shrugged the way a child might when he doesn't get his way, unsure if I'd been led. Could Sang Hee add 'master emotional manipulator' to her impressive list of credentials?

"Anyway," I said, "I think you're underestimating the two of us." She raised her eyebrows. "Who would have been the favorite, if not us?"

"Korain didn't enter this season," she said. "Nor," she emphasized the word, "did he enter the last one."

It was a good point, and not well taken. Korain had won the first-ever League tournament. He'd done it with flying colors, and most expected him to return the following cycle. He hadn't. In fact, he hadn't even been seen until he swaggered right back into the hall—glided, more like; Korain wasn't as much of a show-off as his fans were—at the start of Season 4. Would have been just my luck. I wasn't ready to fight him. Turned out, I wouldn't get the chance. I lost in the first round, and to a relative nobody. Some Russian sambo champion older than my dead grandfather. Lapse in attention. Sometimes that's all it took. There was plenty of luck involved in the fight game. Trick was in learning how to see it as more a matter of attention than chance or divinity.

"Sure I can't interest you and your friend in a round …" Sang Hee started.

"No, thanks," I said, washing thoughts of mighty, brilliant Korain away. "I'd rather not get familiar before I'm forced to be less than chivalrous, should we meet—"

"See you then," she interrupted, squeezing my shoulder hard enough that I felt it beneath the padding. "Now," she released me, "I'm off to see about getting my staff back. I don't plan on fighting every bout bare."

"Might do monster ratings," I called over my shoulder as she waved without turning and walked away.

"Ha ha," she said without humor. "Just remember, Prince Akio, I got a nice, long look at you against Kwan."

"Likewise."

I heard the whirring that preceded the stretching of the red corner bridge and felt an urge to creep back along the corridor to see what this Janix was all about. But then, it didn't really matter, did it? Not the way things were supposed to go tomorrow.

The way they were going to go, I reminded myself as I continued down the hallway.

The locker room was lit in a hypnotic fluorescent blue that stung the backs of my eyes and made my temples throb almost instantly. It was at once too bright and not nearly bright enough. I barely noticed Joon. Almost knocked right into him, leaning with his back to the white metal coffins that housed musty rubber suits and soda-stuck boots from the other fighters. He was dozing, and I simply leaned against the lockers facing him, crossing my arms and waiting for him to notice me.

It smelled like any other gym—old sweat and the mildew flavor of whatever grew in it. Which reminded me, I needed a shower. No matter how new the world got and no matter how many chemicals they stuck in the soaps and lathers they sold at the premium training stores, beauty salons or hotel bathroom tray tables, they still hadn't cracked a better way to stop those damn gym spores from sinking their hooks in you if you didn't get dry as quickly as possible after a match or spar.

He really was tired, back of his head resting against that cold metal as if it were a lounge chair, glasses threatening to drop from the tip of his nose. Joon had hair the color of black ink where mine verged closer to brown. His was also longer. Where mine stood up in chaotic spikes like some chi-riddled anime hero, his hung more in the tradition of a samurai—some vague rebellion against an oppressive father who had emigrated from the war-torn north—though he seldom tied it.

BOOM!

I rammed the side of my fist into the tin lockers, rattling the whole standing row like a mechanical viper. That got him up. It got me up as well, or at least straight, as Joon, wild eyes still obscured with the coagulated gel of sleep came at me with a balled fist of his own.

He caught himself before he broke an already broken nose, and I thanked him for sparing us both the carnage of a practical joke turning into one of our famous, property-destroying brawls. They always seemed to spring up out of nowhere. Come to think of it, we were overdue.

"Akio." Joon breathed out a sigh that was part relief, more exasperation. He bent over and put his hands on his knees.

"Why don't you ever just wear jeans?" I asked, frowning at the black gi pants. "We're not in the dojo, are we?"

"Whole—"

"World's a dojo." I waved my hand at him as I turned toward the locker I'd been leaning against. "Can't get the old fool's voice out of your head either, eh?" I pressed my palm to the black plate of glass. A thread of yellow lights blinked across the top of the display before the whole line came up red. I tried again. Same thing.

"Gloves, Akio."

"Right."

I peeled my rubber gauntlets off and tossed them toward the bench, not caring much where they landed. Now when I tried the latch sprung and the door swung open, admitting a view of my pitiful belongings. Jeans like those Joon should be wearing, only full of holes, and not at all in an attempt to be fashionable. White shirts, few of which looked clean. Socks. Those would require the ole smell test. A half-melted white and green-speckled bar of one of those fancy bars of chemical soap I was telling you about. And a jacket. Red leather like the legendary Akira, whose name was close enough to mine to draw joking comparisons I'd decided to run with. That had cost a pretty penny, but Joon had insisted that not all of my Season 5 winnings—the ones that didn't go toward Kenta's debt—go to the electricity bill at Ken's Place.

"Sang Hee tells me you won," Joon said.

"Me standing here, alive and mostly well apart from the smashed-up nose and raccoon eyes didn't tell you that already?"

Joon didn't answer.

I reached past the hanging shirts and pushed my fingerless,

padded training gloves out of the way until my fingers brushed the mercifully cool latch on the front of a mini fridge I'd rigged into the outlet along the back wall. I'd had to remove the back of the locker to hook it up. Lot of work to go through just to have a cold beer at the end of a match, but when I pulled a pair of frosted green bottles out and heard the hiss and fizz after popping those aluminum caps, I sighed a thank-you to my past self for the effort and plopped down onto the bench where Joon had been sitting, letting him take my leaning place against the lockers.

I took a long, freezing pull on the bottle. German lager is the best lager. Don't think so? Fight me. Fight me if you don't think German lager is the best lager.

All the while, I tried to ignore Joon's steady, silent, domineering presence. I could guess the look well enough: a cross between a jaded, jacked librarian and a disapproving dad. He wore them both well, which might have been the scariest part.

When I set the half-drained bottle down with a hollow ring on the lacquered wood, Joon took his own pull, which was more a sip. All dainty. I was annoyed before he opened his mouth.

"How was the fight?"

"I won," I snapped. "Not that you were there to see it." I swallowed, knowing it was uncalled for. Not yet, at least.

"I'd say I was sorry to miss it, but I'm not, Akio. I suppose I inherited our master's disdain for," he looked around, "all this." He held his hands out to his sides, and already I could feel my skin itching under my skintight suit. "Besides, I knew you'd beat that oaf."

"He was better than I thought."

Joon shrugged, unconcerned.

I couldn't shout Joon down on the first account—the 'all this' account—because I agreed with him and he knew it. After all, Seoul was only a free city when the Hachinin weren't looking.

"The Yakuza went legit," Joon said, reading my mind. Of course, they didn't go by that name anymore. That was the name that had gotten them and all their previous bare-knuckle brands banned from the networks. I just stared at him, knowing what was coming. "Maybe you should too."

I took a steadying breath.

"'Legit,' in this case, meaning sponsored?"

"Would that really be so bad?" Joon took another pull and slid one locker door closer. "If you had a sponsor, Akio, you wouldn't have them chomping at the bit to get rid of you. An unsponsored fighter winning the League one year is a fun distraction. An 'anything can happen!' type of thing they can spin in the promos. Doing the same thing again, training out of a dojo/dustbin called Ken's Place while the sponsored fighters are flying in trainers from all over the world? Not so much. Makes the sponsors wonder why they're footing such heavy bills. Makes them wonder if the whole thing isn't a work. Makes the bosses want to make it one, and not in your favor, Kenta's debt be damned."

He was right. He was stone-faced, logic-hardened, level-headed correct. Which was precisely why I was so seething mad.

"'Times change, kid,'" I said. "'Times change fast, and you're going to change with them.'" I leveled a hard stare at Joon. "That's what he said to me."

His brow furrowed in thought. "Kenta?"

"Not Kenta," I said. "Goro." I speared a finger toward the empty doorway and into the dim, flickering hall. The echoes of the arena drifted in. Janix and whoever he was fighting were having a lengthy row. "The boss. God, if you will."

"Goro pulled you into his office last week?" Joon said, seeming shocked. "The order came direct from Goro of the Hachinin?"

"There's that word again!" I slapped my knee. Joon didn't seem impressed. "Hachinin. Hachinin. What does it mean, again?"

Joon sighed. "You really should brush up on your Japanese."

"Who needs it, these days? Audio translators on every watch."

"You don't wear a—"

"Communicator, then," I cut in. "Display screen. Computer. All of it."

"It means eight."

That didn't sound right to me. My look must have showed it.

"Eight people."

That made more sense. Matched the tattoos we'd grown accustomed to searching thugs and ne'er-do-wells for.

"Not the most original name for a crime syndicate," I said, finishing the bottle with my next drag. I reached my hand out toward Joon, wiggling it when he didn't act immediately. He reached in and grabbed another green bottle, passed it over.

"I'd hardly call the Yakuza a crime syndicate," he said.

"Of course they're a crime syndicate. Don't let the glitz and glamor fool you, Joon. None of their money is clean."

"I'm not saying they're not a crime syndicate—"

"You literally just said they're not a crime syndicate."

"I mean they're not *just* a crime syndicate," Joon said, imploring. "Calling them that is like," he waved his hand around in a meaningless gesture, "it's like calling a wolf a dog."

"A wolf is a dog."

Joon just shook his head and I drained another half of my bottle.

"Think that's going to make it easier tomorrow?" Joon asked, eyeing me. Eyeing the bottle, more specifically.

"This?" I turned it over in my hand, pretending to read the label. "Not nearly strong enough. I've got some other stuff for that. Who knows? Maybe this Janix fellow will be up to the task without me having to help him along."

Joon was angry. I knew he was angry because he didn't look angry. I'd known him a long time. Long, long time. At least he wasn't angry with me.

"Maybe it's for the best," he breathed out in a sigh and I closed my eyes, setting the bottle down. It clanged against the empty one and made a hollow ringing sound that made my blood want to boil even more than it already was. "Sorry."

"Yeah," I said. "Yeah. Me too."

Joon actually laughed. It was a small, innocent sound, and it sounded genuine. It should have made me even more angry. Instead, it just had me staring at him expectantly, wondering what in the world he could find funny at a time like this.

"It's just..." Joon shook his head, and that's when I noticed the tears in his eyes. Not from laughter. That had already blown out. He seemed at a loss. "Just when it looked like you were starting to take to this new stuff, to earn something from it in your own name, they come and take it away from you."

I watched him for a few moments, thought about gesturing for him to snatch me another bottle and then thought better of it.

It was sad, when you thought of it that way. I'd come to the League late, relatively speaking. No early adopter here. There was less of Kenta in me than there was in Joon, who had largely foregone a competitive career, but there was still enough of that old bag of muscle and bones to make me cringe at the colored suits and swords, tight-fitting leather and sponsorship dollars.

I had taken to tae kwon do early, winning all the regionals before placing fifth in the Olympics at age 14—yeah, those were still a thing, though hardly as prestigious as they had once been, since half the original countries had either ceased to exist or had recused themselves over the course of the last few decades. I was fast, lean, agile. All the things that still made me a tough out for virtually any opponent, except I had managed to pack on some muscle in the years since. I was twenty-eight now. My time spent in the rings and cages of the Japanese and American MMA organizations had molded my body to be more resistant to damage and more capable of doling it out, even if my movement still largely recalled my fleeter, faster days of youth.

No, I hadn't loved the idea of the League and all its bright baubles and glow sticks at first, thinking it little more than a glorified forms competition with weapons that looked more like retro future toys rather than the real thing. But then I'd lost that first match, and I was hooked. The feeling of striking and being struck with those bright resin blades was intoxicating. It changed the whole game up, the various makes, weights and models of the blades used, and the relatively lax regulations—for now—on what could and could not be used in the arena added much more than a new wrinkle onto the combat sports archetypes.

Styles make fights. That's what they'd been saying ever since the archaic boxing days in the West, when fighters had laughably only been allowed to use their fists in an effort to discover who was the best fighter in the world. When MMA came around, it got much closer to the point of it all. The real point. Now. Now, with blades in hand—resin or otherwise—I felt like I was truly in combat. Truly in peril.

"They aren't taking it away from me," I said, breaking the silence that was no longer tense but more mournful. Joon blinked at me as if he had forgotten the original point. "I lose tomorrow, make a lot of money doing it. Finish paying off the debt, and they'll put me back in for Season 7."

"They told you all that, huh?"

Of course I'd feared it to be little more than some dim mollification when it had come from Goro's greasy, cigar-stained lips. Now that Joon said it, I knew what a fool I'd been to dare hope.

"Well," I said, reaching out for another bottle in spite of my former absolution. Joon obliged. "At least there's the extra money."

"Screw the money," Joon said, his disgust evident. He had always been that way. I had been too, but money paid bills, and we had a lot of them. Joon had a lot of them if he wanted to keep Ken's Place open. He told himself it was about teaching them, and maybe a good part of it was, but a growing part was skewing toward giving them a place to sleep. The dojo had become something of a nursery in recent years, and the great Free City of Seoul wasn't having it.

Joon shook his head and straightened, stepping away from the lockers and slapping his palm on them to make a brassy rattle as he did.

"You don't have to take a dive to make money, Akio," he said, speaking quickly so as to preempt my inevitable eyeroll. I spared him it, this time. "How much are the sponsored fighters making these days?"

"Haven't checked," I said, taking a sip. Also, I had checked, and I'd rather not think about it just then. My chest had begun to itch as the salt and sweat congealed beneath my suit. I really needed to get myself cleaned up. "Besides, you take one check, you take them all."

Joon wouldn't argue with that, so he let me have it. I knew he hadn't yet reached the point he was itching to get to, but Joon liked to take his time with these things.

"Seen Min recently?" he asked.

"Nope."

"She's a detective, now."

"Good for her." He looked like he wanted more. "Fighting the good fight, and all that."

"You could be, too, Akio," Joon said. "Put those talents of yours to good use. Put these clowns down for good, if that's what you're after, and do it legit."

"Bah!" I slammed the bottle down a little harder than I had intended. Seemed the bench was a little lower than I'd thought. "No way to put these boys down without getting your hands dirty. And I already promised Kenta—and you, for that matter—that I wouldn't do that."

"Fighting in rings and cages is one thing, Akio," Joon warned. "Fighting in the streets and on the rooftops, and against armed Yakuza thugs, is something else. Min has more than resin blades at her disposal. She's got a task force. She's got allies. She had years of precedent in the Seoul legal system—"

"And where has that gotten the Seoul Police Force?" I asked, bored with the topic. "More importantly, where has it hit the Yakuza?"

"There's a reason Seoul isn't in nearly the same state as Tokyo," Joon argued. "There's law and order on our streets. It may not be perfect, but at least the cops here aren't tattooed assholes you pay simply to keep them from robbing you. It's all territories, there."

"Same here," I said, even if I only half believed it myself. "Cops control one corner, Goro's thugs another. Don't let anyone fool you into believing otherwise. It's better than Tokyo. I'll grant you that, but Min's power rests in that holster I'm sure she keeps tucked out of sight, not in her computer system or anonymous tip line."

Joon looked as if he were about to argue, but something caught his attention and had him scanning the dim red hallway.

"What is it?"

"Fight's over," he said, tilting his head like a dog might.

"Janix?"

Joon shrugged, then perked up. I could hear them now, boots scuffling and squeaking over the laminate.

A man in a gaudy purple suit the color of poison filled the doorway. I had already forgotten him from earlier. He was medium height but pumped full of the same supplements I guessed Kwan to be on. He wore shades, though I could see a black strap against his temple that suggested the presence of a hidden eye patch. Something about him was oddly familiar, but I couldn't place him under all the pomp and circumstance. He looked like he was waiting for Joon or me to ask what he was doing standing in the doorway, as if we didn't know already.

I let him sweat it out and took another pull on my beer, smacking my lips and breathing out in a relaxed sigh.

Poor guy actually cleared his throat. Joon just looked away from him and went back to leaning against the lockers.

"Akio Prince."

I gave him a wave.

"You are planning to compete in the Semis tomorrow, right?"

"I made them, didn't I?"

He didn't immediately answer, but tossed a suspicious look at Joon, who ignored it with aplomb. Who was this guy to toss suspicious looks, when he was little more than a Yakuza—a Hachinin—henchman?

"Just checking," he said, unsure how to proceed.

"I know the deal," I said, feeling the words as acid that dripped, burning all the way down. I did my best to ignore Joon's gaze. "Who am I fighting tomorrow, anyway?"

"Janix." He smiled. "He looked good tonight, which is why

you're not seeing his opponent limping his way into the locker room. Hospital trip for him. Might not have needed to pay—"

"You haven't paid me," I said. "Not yet."

"That's right."

I looked at him. Looked right through those shades. He did well not to flinch, and I frowned at him. "Now I remember. Hey, weren't you the guy Korain beat in Season 4?"

He swallowed. "Korain beat a lot of people in Season—"

"The guy he beat badly," I amended. I touched the spot under my right eye and Purple Suit Man went beet red, refusing to answer.

"You know what you have to do tomorrow," he spat, and I do mean that literally. He glared a challenge at Joon. "Shame your friend here can't pay the electric bill. Food stamps not keeping the lights on at ole Ken's—"

"That's enough of that," I said. I said it flat, without inflection. He stared daggers at me and I just looked straight ahead, counting the dents in the tin door in front of me so as to keep from snapping his neck. He hadn't done well against Korain. He wasn't cut out for the League, not even when he'd had two eyes. With the mood I was skating toward, he'd do a lot worse against me.

He was smarter than he looked. He kept his mouth shut, turned and walked away, though he made a lot of noise doing it.

"What's that about not taking checks?" Joon asked.

"Hasn't paid me—"

"Yet."

I raised my eyebrows as I met his accusing stare. "What have we been talking about this whole time, when you're not droning on about Min? You knew I was taking a fall tomorrow."

"Akio," Joon said, but I just kept on keeping on.

"Whole League's already tanking as it is," I said. "Ratings aren't down because a Japanese-American-Korean … whatever the hell I am, started winning and didn't endorse the latest brand of shelled pistachios. There's something better. Always something better, and we ain't it. Kyoto is all the rage. Might as well cash out while the getting's good. That, or maybe they'll make Season 7 interesting and adopt Kyoto rules."

"Akio …"

"This Janix fellow might be great, for all I know. Maybe he'll beat me clean, take the entire question off the table. Allow me to pay off Kenta's debt and keep my dignity. And with the extra—"

"I won't take the money."

There it was, like a cold stone tossed down a deep, deep well.

"Like hell you won't take—"

"I won't take it." He took a step toward me, met my eyes and leaned in. "Not me, Akio. You're not doing this for me."

"Think of the children," I started, but Joon was having none of it.

"Not for me."

With that, he, too, turned and walked out, leaving me with the fly-like buzzing of blue fluorescence and some sick-green bottles for company.

I sat there for a while, doing my best not to think of anything in particular. Then I stood, stripped down to my skin, which was already purpling where Kwan's bones had struck mine, and made my way to the showers.

Maybe I would join Sang Hee for a drink after all.

5

WATCHING TAPE

To say my head hurt the next morning would make a mockery of understatement.

I rolled over, feeling like I was drowning in satin and fluff. I wasn't used to such a soft bed. The fall to the hardwood floor was only two and a half feet, but it sure felt like more. I let out a groan as my knees and elbows struck the unyielding surface and then I laid there, allowing the pain to help orient me to my surroundings.

"I've never seen you look that bad in the Soul Dome," a light voice said. I answered it with a groan. "You'd think you would take it easy, given that you're fighting tonight. Just a few hours."

It was quickly becoming apparent that Sang Hee wasn't planning on leaving me to soak in my own misery on the floor of what I guessed to be her bedroom. I let out another exaggerated groan of protest and pushed myself up onto my feet, wavering a bit.

"No way this is Germany's fault," I said, pressing a palm to my eye.

"What?"

"Beer," I said, waving at her distractedly.

She laughed. "Started with beer. Turned into a hell of a lot more."

"That how you got me all the way up here? Drugged me and decided to take advantage?"

The ensuing silence told me she didn't like that. I looked at her. She was leaning against a white painted door frame wearing a blue satin robe that did little to obscure the lean, muscled and shapely form beneath. Her hair was wet and she held a steaming mug of the most glorious-smelling coffee. Colombian.

After a few moments, I reacted to her raised eyebrows and roving eyes and discovered that I was still quite nude. Casting about, I didn't see a way to remedy the situation immediately.

She jabbed a thumb over her shoulder. "Clothes are in the front hall. Pot of coffee on the burner. I suppose I don't need to ask if you're so inclined."

"We didn't waste time, did we?"

"I'd say it was all you," she started and then winked, "but I must admit I played a part in getting you up here. You should still have what it takes to beat Janix later on, though I saw the highlights."

"And?" I asked, brushing past her. I felt the cool satin touch my thigh and couldn't really do much about the thrill it rekindled, along with the physical evidence therein.

"He's good," Sang Hee said, turning to watch me as I stumbled through a kitchen that, while small, probably cost more than the entirety of Ken's Place, attempting to reacquaint myself with gravity and basic motor functions. "He's better than I thought, that's for sure."

"Always going to be new kids."

"He's pretty old. Experienced."

"A veteran?" I asked, not really caring. I'd decided to forego a search around the studio penthouse for my clothes for the moment. The coffee was much closer. I grabbed the stainless steel pot and poured myself a cup into a clear glass mug. I noticed a blue symbol set into the side as I lifted it.

"I know how you feel about sponsorships," Sang Hee said.

I shrugged and took a drink. It was too hot and I winced and gritted my teeth as the black substance burned its way down my throat.

"I'm not sponsored anymore," she said, as if she needed me to believe it. Not sure why my opinion mattered to her either way.

I should have refrained, but I couldn't help but slide my doubtful eyes over the penthouse and all its gadgets, not to mention a back or front wall made of full-length windows that spanned the space from floor to ceiling. It was a cloudy day, the sort that made it impossible to tell the time, and the blue, red, green and many-colored lights of Sorry Seoul bled in through the panes.

"I mean," Sang Hee said, her annoyance evident, "that I'm not sponsored by anyone else." She strode past me and opened one of the lacquered cabinets, pulling out another mug, along with a stein, what looked to be a sippy cup and a martini mixer. All were engraved with the same image of a crackling blue staff.

"Ah," I said, pretending to be impressed. "Can't-beat-'em sort of thing."

"There's no shame in making money at this," Sang Hee said. "Better I make it selling my own stuff. Make myself into a brand. At least that way I can control it. No scantily clad women-empowerment bullshit. Just a staff and the one who wields it."

"Poetic," I said, taking another sip.

"Whatever." She nudged me in the side, right in one of the deeper streaks of purple Kwan had given me. "Much as I'd love to have another roll, I've got to get to my father's place in the suburbs, and I don't trust you or particularly like you enough to let you lounge around in the nude all afternoon."

"Right." I set the half-drained mug down and moved to the living room, conscious of Sang Hee's eyes on me as I attempted to bend over to pick up the jeans that had somehow ended up draped over the corner of a dark wood display table. Soon enough, I gave up trying to bend and executed something of a controlled fall onto my rear, which succeeded in getting the pants into my hands. I fumbled with them like a child might, pulling them on and grunting in pain as my core contracted with the effort.

Sang Hee shook her head and strode past me, picking up the

rest of my articles and dropping them unceremoniously at my feet. Probably would have taken me a lot longer.

"What are you going to do, Akio?"

"Me?" I pulled a white cotton shirt over my head and didn't bother hiding my wincing. The next day was always worse. "Probably just head to the arena, wait it out."

"I know what you're going to do," she said, watching me carefully. "I meant, what are you going to do, Akio. About tonight?"

I met her eyes. They were pretty, almost light enough to appear yellow, like sunflowers. They were also piercing, and I couldn't quite know what she meant. Was she aware of my verbal agreement with Goro, if caving to unspoken threats and cashing out despite that meaning an exit before the Finals could be considered an agreement? Or did she simply mean, how was I going to fight Janix when I struggled with a pair of Levi's?

"Adrenaline's a hell of a drug," I said, looping on a brown belt. "I imagine I'll settle right in once I get a solid warm-up … or when Janix starts hitting me."

Judging by her continued staring—and studious sipping on her mug—I'd guess she didn't quite buy it.

"Do you at least want to know what sort of weapon he uses?"

"A glowy one?" I joked. She pointed at the small stainless steel table in the kitchen, tucked into a little alcove beside the divider into the living room. There was a view pad propped up at an angle. From the white and red coloring, I could see that it was open on YouTube.

I turned a wide smile on Sang Hee and actually meant it. "You've been up watching tape for me? You really do care."

She rolled her eyes and walked past me, sitting down in front of the screen with her legs off the side of the chair. She pulled it toward me, tapped it with her thumb, and the highlight reel she'd been watching started again. I decided to humor her and leaned in, then backed up a bit when she squirmed with me hovering over her shoulder.

Turned out Janix was blond. More impressive, it looked natural. It was also long, and judging by the bouncing signs in the first row, which were all pink and red and loaded with glossy stickers, he had his demographic locked in.

"German?"

"International man of mystery," she said.

"I love those movies."

"What?"

"Old classics from Britain. Or, maybe from America, but starring a bunch of Brits."

"Anyway," she said, ignoring me, "nobody really knows where he's from. Germany's a common guess, but his accent doesn't really say sauerkraut."

"Accents are fading away all over." I shrugged. "Doesn't mean much, these days. Australian?"

"Too clean-cut."

"Good point, and culturally insensitive to boot," I ribbed.

"What's culturally insensitive about pointing out that I find Australian men to be testosterone factories?"

"Culturally insensitive to Janix, I meant."

"We don't even know where he's from."

"Exactly," I said. "And we shouldn't make assumptions."

That got her to turn around and fix a stare that wasn't so much withering as genuinely shocked at the depths of my cleverness. Or maybe my idiocy. Who could tell?

I nodded at the screen. "He looks pretty smooth. Very flashy, though. What are those?" I squinted and leaned in again, ignoring her squirming this time. "Kali sticks?"

"Something like it."

Janix was tall and lean. He wore a suit made of the same rubber composite as the rest of us, though his was somehow even tighter. There weren't many visible spots of padding. Small half-plates over the pecs, but nothing on the shoulders and surprisingly little on the legs. That said he valued his mobility.

As for his weapons, they were short sticks that couldn't have been more than a foot long each. They glowed a bright amber, like sunset, and I had to blink to make sure I was seeing properly.

"No black?" I asked.

"What?"

"On the sticks." I pointed. "Pure glow. You'd think you'd want a bit of black there."

"True."

The reason you wanted a bit of black on your weapons was because black signified the presence of resin. Well, even that wasn't really saying it properly, since we used the term 'resin' to refer to the hard bits of weapons and armor. Whatever chemical composites of plastic, rubber and metal your smiths put together for you. The League allowed pretty much everything, given that it glowed. Had to please the fans and the cameras with the pretty light show, even though the organizers tried to convince us every year that it was more a matter of letting the judges see who was landing what, in the event that a bout went the full thirty minutes to a decision.

Spoiler: they never did. Way too much force flying around in there for someone to take more than a few solid blows without collapsing, giving up or both.

Anyway, the reason Janix's orange sticks stood out to me was the fact that they didn't appear to have a shred of resin to them. They seemed almost totally luminous. Sang Hee's staff was similar, but it didn't glow half as bright as these, leading many to believe she'd found a smith who'd somehow managed to make a highly durable resin that also emitted light. Good branding, indeed.

"Does he use the same smith—"

"Nobody uses my smith," Sang Hee clipped.

"You kill him? To keep your secret, I mean."

"I pay him. A lot."

"Exclusivity." I nodded. "Good stuff."

"Was he in Season 5?"

"No," she said.

"And nobody knows where he got his experience?" I must have sounded dubious.

"France, some have been saying."

"On the streets?"

Sang Hee shrugged. "Could be. He certainly moves like one of them."

"He does," I agreed. "Can't say I've ever fought a savate specialist."

"And he is a specialist," Sang Hee said, pointing at the screen. I didn't know Janix's opponent and didn't really care. The guy was a bulldog of muscle. He used a double-sided axe and swung it about like a character in a fantasy novel rather than a martial artist. It certainly looked like it packed a punch, but I didn't see much else to his game that impressed me.

We were about three minutes into the match, and I couldn't recall Janix having lashed out once with his weapons, though he had bent his lead leg on numerous occasions as if he were about to. When he circled, he kept his opponent on his left side, then his right, never squaring to him directly. He had a bounce, but not an exaggerated one. His stance might've pegged him as a karate specialist, or even a tae kwon do fighter, but something about the way he held his hands reminded me of the old American Philly Shell boxers. It was a weird combo.

As was the first one he landed.

"No way," I breathed, watching it develop in slow motion.

You see, Janix was something of a peacock, and I say that with all the love in my heart for him. He'd lulled ole Bulldog into a false sense of security about his safety while giving him the impression that he was under no immediate threat. Not only were Janix's sticks too short to give him much range, he hadn't attempted to close the distance between them much at all. At least, not obviously, but Janix was tricky, and I'd seen enough kickers to know how they set their traps.

Janix had been dancing along the borders of the ring, bouncing and high-stepping, never coming closer. All the while Bulldog chased him, and with each strike he lunged a little farther, swung a little more off-balance, pursued a little more recklessly. Janix retreated, retreated, retreated. But his retreats shortened each time, first by degrees, and then by inches, until, on Bulldog's most wild swing, Janix slid just out of range, and I do mean just. If he'd had even a smidge of the hair on his chin that Sang Hee seemed to prefer, he'd have lost it.

I expected the kali sticks to greet the brute's overenthusiastic temples, one after the other. Instead, Janix slid his back foot up to meet his front and then chambered the front, lancing it up and out before slapping a stinging hook kick back across Bulldog's bearded face. The blow wasn't a hard one, but his next one was. Instead of retracting the kick, Janix rechambered, standing on the ball of his back foot and bending his left at the knee before lancing it out once more. Now, he twisted hard into the canvas, rocketing a roundhouse that snapped into the other cheek of his adversary with a sound like a wood clapper.

"I haven't seen that pulled off in a fight in a long, long time," I said, marveling as Bulldog fell back onto his butt, the double kick leaving his body unsure exactly which direction to spin in. He recovered well enough. Seemed he'd fallen more out of shock than impact.

But boy was he embarrassed. And boy was he angry, neither of which was very good—in my esteemed opinion—when you had someone who clearly thrived off of both switching his stances like some sort of bird-like mating dance in front of you.

The lights could get to anyone. In my younger years, the lights had gotten to me, but that was an old axiom on the fighting scene the world over that was an attempt to sum up the intense, seemingly insurmountable feeling of pressure that greeted fighters when they stepped onto the big stage. In this case, it turned out to be quite literal.

Instead of launching right into a new kick as soon as Mr. Bulldog—his real name was on the bottom of the display, but I'd grown into thinking of him this way—regained his footing, Janix exploded into a forward boxing combo.

Or at least, he seemed to, but once more, it looked as if nothing Janix did was quite as simple as it at first seemed.

Mr. Bulldog reeled backward, blocking the first few blows of those glowing sticks with surprisingly deft turns of his great axe, green lights flashing along its edges at each impact. But something was off about the whole exchange.

"You see it already?" Sang Hee was watching me watch the footage she'd already seen. "You don't miss much, eh?"

"Nothing, if I can help it."

I leaned in farther, so much so that Sang Hee stood and moved out of my way. I didn't offer an apology as I sank into her seat without taking my eyes from the screen.

Janix kept his combos going, stringing one after the other, keeping all of his opponent's attention up. I could see the other man's eyes begin to squint as the bright sticks flashed before him, could see him begin to blink and flinch like no fighter should. Blinking in range of your opponent got you hit. Flinching set patterns for him to exploit.

I knew it was coming because I was a kicker myself. I also recognized pretty early into the seeming assault that Janix was pulling his strikes. Those orange rods of daylight weren't meant to end the fight. He probably knew that actually connecting with them would put him in lethal range of that swinging axe, which still had plenty of mustard on it.

Instead, Janix used his weapons the same way he used all of his bouncing, shuffling and shifting movements: they were distractions. He might sting you with them, rap you on the nose or clip an eyebrow, but his finishing set was all about the feet.

Bulldog eventually had enough of retreating—that and he had reached the edge of the ring. I didn't think him likely to pull off an advanced, impossible pirouette like the one Sang Hee had managed earlier that night, but he probably thought he'd get Janix off him by setting his feet and putting his all into a counterassault with that weighty weapon.

He was half right. Janix did retreat, sliding back in that side stance to avoid the last desperate swing of a cornered bear, but while the attack had spared the axe-wielder from a renewed assault of those glowing sticks, he was still in range of Janix's punishing kicks, and now he had nowhere left to run.

There was nothing fancy about the finishing kick. Janix simply leveled him with a swift and no-nonsense side kick to the gut. Mr. Bulldog shot off the platform and sank into that lonely abyss to greet that unforgiving iron netting, green-bladed axe following him down along with a scream that was decidedly less manly than the man it trailed.

"Still think you'll just sleepwalk your way through him?" Sang Hee asked. She was leaning against her stove. She'd put a leather jacket on and her keys were dangling from a finger. I got the point and pushed myself away from the table.

"Probably not," I said. "He's good." Not good enough to beat me given a true contest, but good nonetheless.

At least her question showed that she was unaware that I had no intention of winning in the first place, and, I guessed, unaware of my forced meeting with Goro, or the Purple Suit Man.

"Thanks for the joe," I said as I moved to the door. "And the bed." She smiled in a mischievous way.

"You earned it."

I didn't know what that meant, but took it as a compliment. I really didn't remember much from the night before, but I was starting to hope it would come back to me in due time. I'd need something to get me through the long months of shame that would dog me heading into a seventh season I had no idea if I'd grace with my presence or not. Maybe I'd just take the money and run. And by take the money, I meant give it to Joon, help him pay off the old place and all the collectors, or maybe even build another one entirely. Lot of zeroes in the check to come. Sponsored sort of zeroes, assuming my balance—Kenta's, that is —was what they'd told me.

"Where you living?" she asked as we stepped out into the hall. Apparently I didn't have a jacket with me. The walk to the Soul Dome was going to be miserable.

"Crummy apartment on the edge of the river. Sometimes at Ken's Place."

She looked up at me as she waved her condo card over the pad on the front of the door, which beeped and turned red. "That old dojo near the center?"

"That's the one," I said, smiling like a proud father ... or son. "Home sweet home."

She shrugged and we began walking toward the stairwell. I

didn't see any other doors in the hall. When I looked over my shoulder, I saw that the hall beyond Sang Hee's condo turned around a corner and continued on.

"Mats and some heavy bags," she said in answer to my unspoken question.

"They've got a gym up here? Just your condo and a gym?" It seemed like a weird use of space, not to mention the oddity of having stuffy urban professionals passing by your door at all hours of the night to catch a sweat.

"I've got a gym up here," she clarified, stopping me in my tracks as we reached the end of the hall.

"This is your building? You own it?" I must have looked dumbfounded. She laughed as if it were ridiculous.

"Just the floor," she said, opening the door to expose the cement stairwell beyond. "The buildings I own are too far from the Soul Dome to see the damn thing."

Like that made it less impressive.

"Good luck tonight, Akio," she said as we reached the bottom and passed onto the wet street, neon lights making the river and all its bridges look magical, so long as you disregarded the cold corporateness of it all. "I know it could be taken as a threat, but I do hope I see you in the Finals next week."

I smiled at her but didn't know what to say. I felt sick, and I didn't think it had anything to do with last night. For the first time, I was allowing the utter shame of my future actions to haunt me in the present. More specifically, my future inactions.

I'd made peace with taking the loss. I'd lost before and I'd lost badly. No matter how good my current run was, I knew it would end sometime. Just wanted it to end on my terms, or at least on someone else's. Someone good enough to make it end on the back of their triumph.

Someone like Sang Hee.

We shuffled a little awkwardly at first and then she said goodbye and started off in the opposite direction, and I turned my thoughts to the road ahead, and the night that lay at the end of it.

I tried to shake off those thoughts as I walked through rain-soaked Seoul, the place I'd resided but never really thought of as home. The thoughts that told me I was a coward to take the fall, and the words my other side shouted back that said I'd be as much of one for letting my pride take me through to another win just so I could watch Goro make good on all the threats he hadn't said.

Maybe Janix would beat me legit and make the whole point moot. I'd get the money I'd been promised, and I'd keep my own pride even if the small public support I'd started to generate would peter out on the back of the loss.

Maybe Janix could do it. I even had myself convinced of it by the time I reached those silver and black doors at the back of the behemoth of cement and metal that was the Soul Dome.

Deep down, however, I knew he wouldn't. I'd never felt so horrid about the prospect of winning.

6

THE FALL

I thought I'd been knocked out.

Would have been a first, if so. I'd lost, before. I'd even been stopped, which is the polite way of saying I'd had my ass kicked six ways from Sunday in various places and by various people using various styles throughout my many years on the full-contact martial arts circuit.

I'd even lost in the League the one time, back in my debut. But through it all, I'd never been knocked out.

Sitting here now, or kneeling ... well, sort of wavering on all fours like a drunk, beaten dog, red-tinted drool leaking from my swollen lips, I thought perhaps I had just been knocked out.

Then Janix kicked me again.

This one was a heavy blow that made me remember all the rest of them. It sank into my rib cage and sent me rolling on my side until I stopped and managed to spare enough breath for a single cough, right hand hanging out into the abyss. Amber light stung my eyes and had me craning over to see Janix pacing back and forth. He looked wild, wide-eyed, like a demon of chaos. He was bleeding from his nose and one of his eyes was a purple mass of ... purpleness.

I groaned. The sound jogged a memory from that morning: me hitting the hardwood floor in Sang Hee's condo. And with that came all the rest of the memories, especially those much more recent. Those that had led me to my current predicament.

You see, when I'd dressed for the night's contest, I'd done so while still turning over the prospect of doing the wrong thing for the right reasons or the right thing for the wrong reasons. Either I threw the match and made a mockery of a combat sport I only pretended not to love and earned myself—and by extension, Joon and Ken's Place—a lot of cash, or I beat Janix down en route to a Finals showdown with Sang Hee that would never come, since I'd have directly spat in the face of Goro of the Hachinin.

Never mind the fact that I believed my Finals match with Sang Hee would do incredible ratings, especially since the tabloids had caught me leaving her place this morning. Of course, I didn't know that until I entered the arena and saw it playing as a part of the highlights package pre-fight. Still, I knew Goro wouldn't suffer me to win, not after I'd already shaken that fat, greasy hand. Not after I'd given my word.

It was funny, in a sick sort of way, how these gangsters tried to affect the appearance of honor the higher up that slimy, blood-soaked ladder they climbed. But promises between snakes meant nothing. There was a reason their tongues were forked. They'd tell you the truth on one side and a pretty lie on the other.

The data showed that Janix was the star on the rise, and that a Finals match between him and Sang Hee would crush the number I did against … whomever it was I fought in Season 5.

I was to lose the match with Janix, the League had decided. Kenta's debt would be forgiven and I'd earn myself a nice check to go along with a slap on the ass on my way out the door.

The decision should have been simple. It was simple. Trouble was, I couldn't quite decide which side of simple it should be. So I'd made it complicated. Instead of winning the fight outright or losing in style, I'd decided to try for a happy medium. I'd dressed for my Semi-Final showdown with Janix of … wherever it was Janix was from, but I'd done so without my blades. Left those in the locker, chilling right alongside my green-bottled German beer.

After all, Janix never seemed to use those orange sticks of his to do any real damage, the part of my mind that wanted to win thought. After all, I can't possibly defeat an armed man, no matter his weapon, using my fists and feet alone, the part of me that wanted desperately to lose, but knew I couldn't make a convincing show of it, thought.

And so, here we were. Here I was, drooling bloody spittle into the same abyss I might as well throw myself down, the way things were going. As it turned out, Janix was a good fighter. As it also turned out, those fancy orange sticks hurt like hell, and as soon as Janix had discovered that trading kicks with me wasn't a winning proposition, he'd done the only logical thing and started beating my face in with them.

I hadn't really considered that, by not bringing weapons into the arena, I'd actually dialed up the drama to eleven and the stakes with it. If I won, it would probably make me into a star. It would also undermine everything the League was built on: chiefly, that old-school, hand-to-hand combat leagues were irrelevant in the face of glowy swords and shining shields.

I also hadn't really considered the fact that, by not bringing weapons into the arena, I'd basically begged Janix to beat me to within an inch of my life for insulting him so brazenly. I had to admit, even from this lowly vantage, that my stunt looked to be the height of arrogance.

Who was I kidding? It *was* the height of arrogance.

Ah, well. All that remained was to take my lumps—if there was any space left on my body for them—and to get the damned thing over with.

Janix had certainly given me a lot of time to recover. Either he had enough sympathy or chivalry not to kick me again before I'd gained my feet, or his anger hadn't yet run its course and he much preferred the thought of kicking me while I was standing. Of course, I could have surrendered. It was the expected thing to do for an unarmed fighter. Many had booed when I'd made the walk across that lonely red bridge without my black and glowing red blades in their X sheath, thinking I meant to forfeit then and there.

The thought had crossed my mind. I figured it would honor my verbal contract with Goro and piss him off all at once. But then, the Yakuza had never played fair. Why would the Hachinin, who were supposed to be eight of the biggest, baddest bosses in the whole syndicate?

"Up!"

There it was. That weird accent. Janix was a silent fighter, usually. They'd played his pre-fight package on the black sphere during the introductions. You know, where they ask you why you like punching and kicking other humans for a living ... beating them with sticks, etcetera. He'd kept his answers short enough to remain mysterious. It was playing well with the young female demographic and probably many more besides. I hadn't been able to place it then and I still couldn't.

"Up!" he shouted again, loud enough to create a murmur in the crowd that had grown ghostly silent as the match had verged closer and closer to an execution. I hadn't noticed the silence until now.

Perhaps that had something to do with Janix's desire to see me stand and fight. Appearances, and all that. Lots of folks watching, both in the arena and at home, and Janix was the new golden boy dressed in white, the new Korain, as it were. Of course, I didn't see him dropping his weapons in favor of a good old-fashioned rumble. Lot of people I'd met in the past few days were smarter than they looked. Or maybe I was dumber.

When I stood on wavering legs and wiped the crusted blood from my chin, my smirk must have shown through.

Now the crowd woke up. It was a mix of cheering and jeering, and it took my still-clouded mind a bit of time to figure out who was getting what. Janix recognized it before I did, and, his complexion being a hell of a lot lighter than mine, his face confirmed it. He turned almost as red as the blades I'd left in the locker room and the luminous stripes that separated the joints in my armor. I had worn that, at least.

The chants were muddled and chaotic, loud enough to be called raucous. Janix still had his share of fans, but many of them were silent, either cowed by those who had suddenly turned to the side of Prince Akio, or unwilling to endorse the wholesale slaughter of an unarmed man in the League. I even saw some parents leading children who probably shouldn't have been in the Soul Dome in the first place up the steep flights toward the white brightness of the concourse hallways.

"Ah-Kee---Ohhh! Ah-Kee---OHHHH!"

"Looks like they've seen enough of you, Janix, my boy," I said, acutely aware of the fact that the mic in my collar would project my voice from every armrest and viewscreen in the place. I wasn't much of a trash talker, normally. Hell, I couldn't remember the last time I'd employed my incredible real-world snark to the fight game. Maybe never.

I hadn't suddenly turned into a massive dickhead. There was a method to my madness, and it revolved, quite simply, around making Janix really, really mad. It might have seemed like a strange strategy, given the fact that Janix himself had used it against the axe-wielding bulldog from Belarus in the Round of 16. Maybe the League was therapy for the long-haired lad. Hell, it seemed to be for the rest of us.

Fighters have many strengths, Kenta used to say, *but don't bother yourself with learning about those. A man has a nice jab? He'll eat you with it and you'll have to fight through it. Woman has a mean ground game? Deal with it. Guy blinked before he feints? Now that's a fatal flaw, and one worth exploiting.*

A man has many strengths, Akio, but he only needs one weakness to lose the damn thing.

Kenta should have listened to himself as much as we had.

Judging by the beet-red coloring of Janix's face—apart from the blood I'd managed to wring from it already—and the wide set of his stance, I'd landed squarely on his weakness, which meant a lot of bookies were about to lose a lot of money.

I moved back into the center of the platform, just a few paces from Janix, and took my stance. Right foot back and turned out, front foot pointed forward. Soft bend in the knees. Lead hand up and open palm, rear balled into a loose, snapping fist. Chin, as always, tucked. No bouncing. Not now. Not with my head swimming and my ears ringing.

"I'm going to beat you, Prince Akio," Janix said. He meant it for me and me alone. His tone said it and his whole demeanor shook with the private nature of it. "I'm going to beat you bad."

"It is France, isn't it?" I asked it like I'd had an epiphany. Even lifted my chin for effect.

The crowd drank it in and spit it back. They were calling for me to be raised on a feathered couch and paraded through the streets of Seoul, right on to the once-golden roads of China and south, to the sea. They were calling for my coronation.

They were also calling for Janix's head. And who was I to deprive them?

I'd grown tired of being led, so I decided to do the leading.

I launched into a blitz jab I'd picked up in my younger years on the mats and foam floors of karate dojos on the south coast. A singular attack in the spirit of the samurai. One hit, one kill.

Of course, I'd led with my front hand, which wasn't going to do anything more than make Janix's eye a little more purple. Of course, that wasn't my intention to begin with.

Janix dodged the leaping strike. He dodged it with ease, actually. That was fine. That was the point. When he came in for the counter right cross with that glowing orange rod, I'd duck it, hook him under the armpit and neck and lock him in such a squeeze that he'd wake up three stories down, ass as sore as the rest of him as he slept on iron netting.

Only Janix didn't counter as any sane, gullible man would. Instead, he spun, twisting to the right and away from my lead left. His feet executed a pirouette that was only slightly less perfect than Sang Hee's and I winced before the blow had even landed. It didn't help. Janix's right hand swung around on the back of his turn and cracked into the back of my skull. It stung like all hell, but lucky for me, we were so close that the nape of my neck and the meat of my brain stem ate much more knuckle than resin.

It didn't stop me from careening, uncontrolled toward the very same abyss I meant to send Janix flying down into in the deepest, softest slumber. I managed to stop myself, tottering on my tiptoes, legs splayed, arms waving like one of those old coyote cartoons. My vision was partially obscured by the blinding floodlights that illuminated the open-air commentary box, which hung suspended a stone's throw above me.

All I could do in my current predicament was guess. There was a lot of guessing in fighting. Don't let anyone tell you different. Sure, better fighters made more educated guesses, but it was guessing all the same. You could get faster and stronger. You could improve your reflexes and your visual recognition skills and increase your proprioception, which was the end-all, be-all at all the high-tech gyms in Asia. But guesses often won fights, and guesses often lost them.

I guessed right, and I guessed right because Janix did exactly what I would have done.

Instead of shouldering into my back or even risking a straight-line kick that I might have twisted and managed to lock between my arm and side, Janix sank down into a low squat and spun, one knee brushing the canvas and the other leg striking out behind him, ankle turned down and soft-booted foot in a blade. The closer sounds of the fight were always louder for me than the farther ones of the crowd. I heard the nylon and polyester of his boot racing across the canvas like a viper over a sand dune, and timed my jump accordingly.

I didn't bend backward, plant my hands on the mat and execute a somersault as Sang Hee would have. As I might have under different circumstances. Instead, I merely hopped like a rabbit, up and back, clearing Janix's sweeping leg with ease and placing myself off to the side of his rotating torso.

I landed with knees bent and figured I had Janix dead to rights as he completed his spin, his eyes wide with recognition but turning away from me. A well-placed knee to the side of the head or jawline—depending on how quick Janix turned—would do it from here. I might need a bit of a leap to get it done, so I started into it, pushing hard off my rear leg and thrusting my right hip forward.

The crowd could sense it. The moment. There were many moments throughout a good fight, but there was ever and always only one that mattered. It was the beauty of combat sports.

Janix had different plans, and they verged heavily on hanging around and continuing to pester me for a while longer. Instead of raising his forearms over his head in a vain attempt to block the full force of the same knee that had finished King Kwan the titan, he decided to part with his precious baton. One of them at least. As he came around, he launched one of them at my head. It looked like a disc of sunset as it spun toward me.

It couldn't halt my momentum completely, but it could certainly make me execute something of a controlled flail as I tried to divert the missile off course. The glowing orange resin polymer cracked off of my forearm and went spinning off into the crowd, drawing gasps of excitement and a scream that promised the League would soon have another lawsuit on its hands and another settlement to pay. I felt my knee connect with Janix, but his grunt and the awkward angle at which I'd struck meant I'd caught him mostly in the shoulder of his throwing arm.

We went down in a tangle, and I hit hard, since my arms were up in that flailing motion I mentioned. The air rushed from my lungs as the canvas did nothing to cushion a fall Janix assisted, wrapping his arms around the back of my knees and spearing me down with the point of the shoulder I'd just struck. At least he got it too. Got it bad, from the sounds of things. I didn't hear the crack, but judging by the force with which I'd struck, Janix's collarbone had snapped on the takedown.

Still, he was a tough one. Far tougher than he looked. I had to give him that. I still might have to give him a hell of a lot more, the way things were going, but I didn't think so. Bad as things looked for me, we were closer to my world now than his, what with one of his bright batons removed from the field of play.

I tried to force a scramble up but Janix snatched me by the throat with one of the rough biker's gloves the League called gauntlets. I panicked for a short spell, but the squeeze wasn't so hard, Janix having lost a good bit of strength in the limb on account of his shoulder. His eyes were even more wild than before, his sweat and blood-soaked bangs hanging over my face.

As I struggled to roll onto my hip and then to buck Janix off, I wondered almost absently why he wasn't trying to choke the life from me with two hands instead of the one. And then I remembered the second baton. Remembered because it was pretty hard to miss, hanging there just a wingspan away from my brow, clenched white-knuckled in white gloves.

In the movies, everything slows down in moments like this. Your surroundings fade while what's in front of you sharpens, brought to life in vivid detail. That's because it's true. Adrenaline is a hell of a drug. The colors of Janix's silver and red-striped ivory armor, the pores and blemishes on his lumped-up face, the sweat dripping from it all, mixing with the blood and taking on its vital sheen. All of it was so clear in that moment that I could have made a painting.

Janix might be a good guy or a bad one. More than likely, he was—like the rest of us—some horrible, unenviable combination of the two, an amalgamation of all the rights and wrongs he'd committed in his thirty-odd years of life. Some men were born into fighting, but most of us found it and used it to cover up that ugliness at our cores, or to hide from it.

All this is to say, I didn't really care what sort of man Janix was in that moment. I didn't care what his past was and I didn't care what his future would be. All I cared about is that he was about to dash my brains in with a glowing polymer rod in front of 20,000 people who alternated between being deathly silent and murderously loud.

Remember that trick I told you about? More specifically, the one I'd told Kwan about? Janix was now the second opponent in a row to force me to pull it from my bag, even if I helped him along by showing up absent my blades and all manner of sense.

Never back a wolf into a corner. Never make a tiger fear for his life, unless you plan to snuff it out.

Janix's moment of hesitation—of mercy—cost him.

I considered myself an honorable fighter, but I left all that aside in the moment.

Janix's head was too far above me for me to snatch him by the back of it, so I reached for the next best thing: those white-blond locks of his that were hanging over my face. I let go of his choking wrist and grabbed a whole fistful of hair in my left hand, yanking him forward and shooting my head up, chin tucked so that my brow ate the worst of it.

I was lucky not to catch a row of teeth on my forehead. We both were, I suppose. I did manage to crack Janix right below the eye—the one I'd already purpled with an elbow on one of our close-range exchanges earlier in the fight. I heard a crack now and spared a hope that I didn't send a shard of orbital lancing back to sever the man's retina. Nobody deserved that just for trying to bash a man's face in in the call of duty.

Janix was full of surprises, and a part of me thought he'd simply brush this blow off like he had the rest of them and find a way to turn it around. He didn't.

As he fell back, I rose up, reaching desperately for his opposite hand, which still clung stubbornly to the glowing orange baton. I managed to free one of my pinned legs and swung it back behind me, pushing at the low angle to continue my bridge, and we soon found ourselves in close to the opposite position we had just been in. Janix didn't land on his back particularly hard—it was a short fall from his knees—but I landed a lot harder, sinking my knees into his torso, one in the gut, the other in the crook of his arm, right below the shoulder I'd done some damage to.

Janix cried out. He thrashed like a mad dog and bucked his hips, trying to dislodge me, but I wasn't going anywhere. I had his left arm in a vise grip with my right hand, and I put a squeeze on that.

"Drop it," I said evenly. The crowd must have been on pins and needles watching the reversal of fortunes and the tense state we found ourselves in now. Well, tense for one of us. I was starting to feel more relaxed. More in control, in any event.

"Janix ..."

He stilled and looked at me with one pale blue eye. The other one was already swollen shut and looked to be in a nasty way.

"You need medical assistance," I said. "Let them give it to you without adding anything more to the sheet."

He snarled at me, but there was less pepper in it than there had been before. Janix was trying to save as much face as he could. After all, he'd somehow allowed a weaponless fighter to take him down. We needn't bring up the fact that he'd had me dead to rights on more than one occasion. Or maybe we should. Maybe that made it all the worse for him. Maybe that was why I heard the fibers of his glove straining around the dim buzzing of his amber baton, as if it had a mind of its own. As if there was no way he could let it go now.

Not unless I made him.

I sighed and took some of the weight off of Janix's chest, which brought a whole lungful of air rushing back in. He gulped it eagerly, which was exactly what I had in mind. I pressed back down in the hollow between his rib cage and Janix stamped his feet like a child throwing a tantrum, or a man suffocating to death. I used the momentary lapse in attention to switch my grip from his wrist up to his weapon and grabbed it near the tip, folding it back against his fingers until I heard a few pops and felt it give.

You see, close-range fighting, and I do mean close range, was all about bending the body in the direction it didn't want to go. Follow the pain. I wasn't as studious as Joon. I'd always been more of a savant, but even I could get the basics.

I stood and allowed Janix to roll over onto his side and spill his bloody guts onto the canvas. The crowd probably would have laughed under less strange conditions. Instead, I heard an audible sigh, as if they, too, were relieved to have the brutal contest over with.

Amber weapon in hand, I stepped away from my prone adversary and spun in a slow circle. The stands were dark. Our fight had even managed to tear the majority from their phones and watches for a few brief, bloody, glorious minutes. The contest was over, but it seemed that even the production crew was so at a loss, they had yet to push the master switch that would project the holographic voting display up before each seat.

What sort of a number did you get for something like this?

I twirled like a ballerina beneath the sea, slow as a dream, until I faced the section of the arena where no stands stood, where the ugly, jutting subway car of glass made up the President's box. It was raised up above the combat platform just enough to appear out of reach, and just close enough to be a constant reminder of the would-be emperor's presence. There was only one shadow pressed up against the glass, bulky and misshapen, the rest of the executives having withdrawn as soon as I'd decided to make a real show of it.

"For you, President Tokyo," I said, brandishing Janix's still-glowing weapon. I held it out and dipped my head in the most shallow bow I could manage, and then I flipped it, end over end, into the bitter dark.

The crowd roared, swooned and beat their feet. They knew that President Blue, an American businessman-type who introduced every highlight package, was merely the face of the League. They likely knew that the shadow against the glass was Goro of the Hachinin. The former name meant nothing to them. The latter everything, here in the Free City of Seoul. The free city that wasn't free. Not really.

The people of Seoul liked to hate the Hachinin, but they didn't know the truth of it. They didn't know that the stories and the rumors were the barest silken sheets covering something much worse. They didn't know that the Hachinin owned the Japanese suits, and that the Japanese suits owned more of Seoul every year.

They couldn't have known that Goro was a devil, nor that I had crossed him.

I had always resented the fans for their ignorance. In this, and for the first time, I envied them.

Things were about to get much worse for me, and despite my occasional arguments to the contrary, I wasn't sure they would ever get much better.

7

THE PURPLE MAN

I dressed quickly.

Rather, I stripped down, falling twice as I struggled to rip the mix of rubber, resin and military-grade plastic from my body and stuffed my suit into the locker, hearing the ting of those green German bottles in the ice box. I didn't have time.

I knew it like a shadow on the heart.

I didn't have time to shower. I didn't have time to clean the cuts and bruises that were nothing if not ripe, fertile grounds for all the rot a place like this carried. I didn't have time to phone Joon or even Sang Hee—not that I had her number—for help. Nothing had happened that even told me I needed help. That I was in danger.

I knew it because I had just crossed Goro of the Hachinin in front of 20,000 screaming, adoring fans. It didn't matter that I'd done it on national and international network cameras. It didn't matter that the headlines would look suspicious. I had just crossed Goro of the Hachinin, and I needed to run.

My bag was lightly packed. My outfit—faded blue jeans and a white beater—inauspicious. Most of my meager belongings that weren't martial in nature were tucked away in the attic I counted as a refuge at Ken's Place. I couldn't go there now. Not with things being how they were. I had to get out, and my thoughts spun as I tried to figure out where. Certainly not my apartment.

I paused before I stole out into the hall. Pipes dripped in the silence, echoing. How quickly an arena could empty, spilling its cheering, jeering guts out onto the brightly lit streets and alley-ways. The thought occurred to me, ever so briefly, of marching right up to Goro's office, then and there, throwing myself at his feet and apologizing. Or perhaps I'd play it off like some trick meant to garner ratings.

The crowd couldn't have known it was you I mocked, I'd say. *What does it matter what sort of show I put on, as long as it's a good one?*

That was the extent of my foolish, wishful thinking. Goro was not a forgiving man, nor a modest one.

Maybe I should just kill him and be done with it.

Strangely enough, that thought lasted longer than the previous ones, though not by much.

I moved back to my locker, fished inside and fumbled with the red and black suit I'd pressed in haphazardly, finding the clip that fastened my crossed scabbards to the back. The black straps looked a little strange crossed over my shoulders and clipped into my belt like suspenders. Looked even stranger when I filled them with my resin short blades. Just a guy in his jeans, walking down the streets at night … with his professional League blades jutting out above a red leather jacket, like an anime street runt.

Still, the jacket did rather complete the package, and helped to protect me from my own smell. I caught a glimpse of my battered face in the changing-room mirror, took a deep breath and passed into the hall.

My nerves were on edge, stretched tight as razor wire. I felt fear, which made me dangerous. Exceptionally so. Still, while I could probably take a single thug with a gun, so long as I saw him coming, there was nothing I could do against a squad of them. Guns were difficult to conceal in Seoul, but not impossi-ble, and I was betting that if anyone knew how, it was Goro and his outfit.

No security in the hall. No ambush waiting in the damp cement stairwell. I craned my head over the painted blue rail and saw nothing below but the stone floor lit by a flickering wall-mounted lamp.

It was the longest descent of my life. I sprinted down each flight and crept past each red painted door, hands twitching toward my scabbards. My blades wouldn't likely kill on command, but they'd make anyone think twice.

No attack came. No bullet spray. No hurled grenade.

I reached the bottom of the cement stairwell without incident, with my heart hammering against my chest and my body expelling another round of sweat that brought all the arena smells bubbling back out. A part of me wanted Goro to get it over with, to challenge me here, in close confines. Send his best men and see how they fared.

I knew he was more clever than that and cursed him for it as I took another steadying breath and opened the door to the street beyond.

Of course it was raining. I swore under my breath and moved past the door guard, making sure I met his eyes as I went. He was clean, bare hands clasped in front of him. No gloves. A hint of discomfort with my attention, which meant he wasn't pretending everything was fine. He hated his job and he hated the weather: two things mercenaries and hired guns reveled in.

Seoul was okay in the daytime. The buildings were alternately tall and squat, pressed together like modules. At night, it was brilliant—a kaleidoscope of colored lights that recalled Tokyo's skyline without going full bore into the garish, dizzying displays down every alley.

The city was known for its mountains. The rolling peaks bordered and bisected the glittering city, from Bugaksan to the Philosopher's Path on Mangusan to the steep and treacherous Bongsan that looked out over the Han River, you couldn't find a pebble in the streets that hadn't originated along those forested paths. Many of those paths remained today, but the Achasan Mountain had been taken over by the sociopolitical elites. Everyone who was anyone in Seoul lived in glass houses along the tar and concrete roads that now marred the once-majestic mountain that had offered the best views of the surrounding city. That was the place that popped into my mind, and I didn't have much time to deliberate.

I didn't have a car. Instead, I crossed a busy intersection on yellow, listening for signs of pursuit more than looking, and made my way to a city bike rack that was bathed in the warm yellow light and drifting smell of salted pork from an open soup restaurant. It was 30 credits for a standard rental. 130 to unlock the one I wanted.

The premium models forewent the tiny wheel motor that made the standards little more than glorified bicycles, taking large motors which turned them into something more like the cycles the Texans used in their arena races. One swipe of plastic —some things never change—and the front wheel unlocked. I gripped the leather handles and eased the red mass of plastic and engineering out over the bar, checking the gauges to ensure I had enough power to get where I wanted.

There it was. The tingle at the nape of my neck that I'd been waiting to feel. The one that had never been wrong before, and wasn't about to start now. I might not have fought in any wars, but a fighter had stronger instincts for self-preservation than most. One trained by Kenta doubly so, as the old man had always been more about defense than sport.

Of course, it could have been the other instinct fighters had, whether they wanted to admit it or not: the instinct of a predator. Every jungle needed them. Even the neon-glowing, steel-and-cement ones. Especially those.

I was being hunted, and I wasn't about to tip off my pursuers by turning to look at them, though my slight pause as I fussed over the control panel likely did enough damage on its own.

I took my seat and left the helmet sitting on its holster. The safety alarm from the rack blared, instructing me to put on the helmet, and now the cook from the soup restaurant added his voice to the mix. I turned his way, meeting his eyes over the steam of his grill, forgetting that my face was a bloody horror. He stumbled back in fear at first, and then his expression changed, and he looked from me up to the small LED screen the patrons at his short bar were glued to. I squinted in the wet. The details were impossible to make out, but the blue ticker at the bottom which signaled the city news channel and the white ring displayed in the center of the screen were impossible to mistake.

Highlights. Highlights from my fight.

"Shit."

League match highlights were always played on the sports stations. But that blue ticker meant I'd done a hell of a lot more than I'd even feared. And I could guess which part of my display had the anchors riled and thrilled as if they'd just hit the jackpot. I was betting it had nothing to do with the fight itself.

One rev and I sped off, nearly taking out a stray cat and a late-night gaggle of women shoppers, all of whom darted out of the way. Their complaints made it impossible to separate feline from female, but I didn't have time to apologize.

I stayed on the sidewalk as long as I could, which, cursedly, wasn't very long at all, since the lane was choked with bar-goers. The back tire of the cycle slipped a bit as I plunged into the street. Fresh pavement was great for the buses. Not so much for a bike in the rain. At least, not for what I had planned.

There were a few expected horn blasts at my unexpected arrival in the center lane, but another sound rumbled below it. It was the engine of something sleek. Something expensive and expected.

So be it.

Instinctively, I twisted the handles, frowning as nothing happened.

"Right." City bikes.

I pressed the pedal all the way down. Instead of the scream of the engine, I heard a series of pops and sparks coming from under the thin red hood. High acceleration, but not fast enough. No sustain. That's electric for you.

There was another stop light ahead, and another crowd emptying the sweaty confines of some seedy establishment. I slowed down as green turned to yellow. The rumble drew closer and louder, and I knew it wasn't going to work. I gunned it, speeding through as the red changed, and the car following produced another pop to draw a few dramatic screams from the crowded crosswalks.

At the next street I swerved and turned left, leaning hard and pressing my left foot down on the peg. I felt the rear wheel slide on the slick surface of the road just as I felt the sting of head-lights as my pursuers approached. I managed to chance a look before making off, and felt more anger than fear as I glimpsed a pair of black suits and two pairs of black shades behind the windshield of the following car, their looks expressionless, even serene.

Professionals in every dripping, ironic sense of the word.

The road I was on was largely empty. I was at the southern-most point of the city, and the road continued on for a short time before shooting me over one of the many bridges across the Han. Then the road climbed sharply up and to the left before a sheer wall of concrete. This wall marked all that was wrong with the world. A place built out of more unnatural than natural. An artificial expanse meant to provide premium housing to those who could afford it. All the doctors and actors and military industrial-complex privateers who resided here at least part of the year.

They had torn the trees of Achasan down and drawn the monolithic concrete mountain up. The result was a sparsely populated mountain estate for those with means who wished to get away from the wiles and noisy ways of the city below, sacri-ficing the transit lines and easy-reach grocers for glass condos and gaudy fountains.

Not to mention precarious roads meant to evoke the sensa-tion of driving the still-famous Pacific Coast Highway in California.

It might have been a dumb idea, but in my experience, safe was never the way to go when you were being chased.

The road twisted sharply to the right as the bike and I started our climb. The black muscle car was only just beginning its own climb as I rounded the third bend. We continued on like that for what felt like an hour, with me rounding each bend and climbing each rung of the cliffside ladder just as my pursuers cleared the one below, engine roaring and tailpipe popping all the way.

On the final bend, I couldn't help but look down at the city and all its lights. It was beautiful, doing its best to imitate the light it stole from the stars far above. In the far distance, the forests to the north and west stretched out, and the true mountains beyond them.

At the top, the first of the mountain condos leered. The lights were off in this one but on in the next, each one looking like a glass nest. Looking far more fragile than they were, with their modern security settings, and a few with more old-fashioned forms—wrought iron gates, or big dogs sleeping in the foyers which looked like bears.

The road leveled out, and I breathed a sigh of almost-relief as the final pop of the black car's final turn sounded. They'd burned too much on the climb. The engine must be heaving now, the wheels burned to shit, if not stripped away to the rims. You couldn't race up this hill without a bike or something designed to do it.

You sure as hell couldn't race down.

I came to a stop at a line of stones set into the road that marked the highest point on the Achasan.

The black car had ceased its roaring. Its breath was ragged now, but I heard it rumbling along. Just as I heard the soft squeal the brakes made as it eased itself to a slow, grinding stop. I twisted on my seat and gave them a full view of me, cuts, bruises and all, and kept my eyes wide despite the blinding glare of the headlights.

The car was close, now. No more than a stone's throw from my back tire. But the doors remained closed and the windows as well. The rain started up again, pattering on the black hood and throwing up ominous steam, sizzling like so many eggs in the fryer.

I showed the black shades a confident smile I only wanted to mean and turned back, catching sight of the family gathered in the blue-lit living room that was visible down the hall of the glass structure at the zenith of Seoul. That was probably the reason the tail didn't rise to my insult. Too public. Even here, at the top of the world.

Maybe they only wanted to take me in. Bring me to Goro.

Make me answer. Maybe I had become too big a name to whack. After all, it would be obvious to all the right people and plenty of the wrong ones. After the stunt I'd pulled, there would be no mystery as to the disappearance of Akio Prince.

It would be a tragedy the fans would talk about for weeks, the rest of Seoul for the length of time it took them to finish their morning coffee.

No. There was no mercy for the Hachinin. I knew less than little about them, but every kid growing up in the mainland knew about the Hachinin. They were taboo. They were everything that was wrong with the world today, the worst sorts of business high lives and corporate low lives. Men who oozed confidence and dripped corruption. Smart men. Strong men.

Men who could gun you down in the rain and have someone else pick up the debt you were too dead to pay.

I almost laughed at the absurdity of it. How much of a fool was I? I couldn't go to Joon. I couldn't go to anyone they knew I knew.

Then the engine revved behind me. Let me know they were still there, that they weren't going to stop. A face painted itself on the backs of my eyelids. A stern face with chestnut eyes light enough to appear amber, like dripping honey. A face I hadn't seen in a long time, seemingly in another life. A face that belonged to a name Joon had dropped the night before.

Surely she could help. Get me out of the country, if nothing else. She was a bigwig now, after all. An untouchable, even for the Hachinin.

I leaned the bike back onto the center and leaned over the handles. No showmanship this time. I just went, leaving nothing behind but the trail of a red taillight and the screeching tires of my hunters, who'd been caught by surprise.

I went fast. Faster than I should have gone. Faster still because the road helped me along as it poured me down the west-facing side of the mountain and toward the edge marked by a thin silver rail. I started my slide for the first turn earlier than I thought I needed to. It was a good thing, as the road was more a thin black river now, and I had nothing for grips.

Whatever the thugs were driving, it had to be custom. The wheels didn't lock on the slide, but followed me well enough, and now the engine was sounding closer. I thought I heard the slight squeaking of glass against rubber as the passenger side window slid down and my heart began to hammer in my chest as I tensed for what must come next.

The spray and pop of bullets striking the pavement prompted me to lean too hard into my next slide. I rounded the bend in a panic, my left elbow tearing open, along with the leather covering it, as my bangs kissed the slick ground. Somehow, I kept the bike up, wheels turning, as we passed each other on opposite sides of the rail. The driver only looked ahead, teeth gritted as he tried to control his own machine on the precarious path I'd led them down. I couldn't see the passenger, but I imagined him loading another clip into the silenced automatic he clutched. Silent as death and far scarier than any bang could have been.

No more games.

As I rocketed toward the bottom of the mountain road, I killed the lights, hoping that would make a tough target even tougher to hit. I thought of weaving, but I had far less momentum than the luxury tank screaming down the road behind me, and any wrong move might send me into a deathly spiral.

I prayed for a civilian car to peel into sight, cross the bridge down at the bottom and start its slow, meandering climb up the hillside we'd been disrespecting with our deadly haste. Anything to stop the bullets, grant me a respite and a chance to merge back into the chaos of the city.

For once, I got an answer, and for a few adrenaline-fueled moments, I thought it was a good one.

As I leaned right and began my final slide toward the bottom of the road, a pair of headlights flashed on the other side of the narrow span. I heard another series of pops and even felt a splash as one bullet struck the deeper water at the bottom of the hill.

For a second, I thought I might spin out, but I managed to

keep control and start forward again. Something tore across the leather on my back, and I cursed myself a fool for not having kept my arena armor on a bit longer. It might not stop a direct shot, but it sure would slow it down.

I raced toward the bridge, eyeing the black water that churned past. The light from the city beyond didn't reach over here. There were nothing but dark office buildings framing the other side of the span.

Another bullet tinged as it struck the plastic of the bike, and I felt the fear grip me so tightly it lost some of its effect. It would have been bad for them had we been in the arena, fighting with glow sticks and waxing poetic in our own minds about the virtues of a sport that did nothing but churn out injured, some-times braindead veterans and make bookies rich. But we weren't in the arena. There were no spotlights, just headlights. No air horns and clappers, just the roar of a maxed-out engine and the horrible patter of rain and the silver missiles that sliced through the droplets, each one seeking my heart. There were no yellow and white streamers or confetti. Just the dark of the night, the mud of the riverbank, the black of the pavement … and the purple of the ugliest suit I'd seen.

I squeezed the triggers and put the brakes on, locking the front wheel and bringing the bike to a horrible sudden stop. I let out a startled yelp as I kept going, flying right over the handles of the bike and slamming down onto the iron of the bridge. I rolled without intent, end over end, and covered my face as the bike hurled itself over me and passed me by, skidding to a sparking halt in front of the Purple Suit Man and his black beast of a car, which matched the one that had chased me down the mountain.

It took so long to release a breath that I thought for certain I would suffocate. When I did, I coughed, my ribs feeling like shards of brittle glass all along the length of my right side where I'd struck the bridge. I pushed myself up onto my hands and knees and watched the red drool paint a smaller river within the inch-deep one flowing by me on the iron span.

Any second now, the black car would roll right over me. But then, I didn't hear the engine any longer.

The old-fashioned way, then. The way they did it in old westerns and modern gangster films alike. The worst way, and the quickest.

Of course they had orders to bring me in, so that Goro could administer whatever passed for judgment in his demented black eyes. Of course the men chasing me would try to do that, if they could. Shoot out my tires. Maybe one to the shoulder and two to the knees. Enough to keep me from fussing.

But Purple Suit Man knew better. He'd fought in the arena and he'd seen me do it. I felt the weight of my resin blades pressed against my back. If I lived through the night—it seemed more doubtful by the minute—I'd likely be sporting bruises down the length of my back in the shape of them.

"Goro want to speak with me?" I croaked out, wavering onto my knees and flailing toward the too-far rail as I struggled to orient myself in the accusing light of the cars on either side of the bridge.

"Something like that," he said. I couldn't see him until he moved to block the light from one of the headlights. He was illuminated by the one behind me, as were his gaudy purple suit, slick black hair and oily black patch over one eye.

"You really need to ditch that suit," I said. He smiled, taking the jibe in his stride. He reached into the fold of said suit and brought out a pistol with a barrel twice the length it should have been.

"Silencers for the guns," I said, "not for the engines. You bozos aren't half as smart as you think you are." I pressed my palms into the meat of my thighs and made my way to my feet, swaying unsteadily. My vision was swimming.

"What difference does it make?" the genius asked. I laughed and didn't have to feign the humor.

He must have heard the sirens before I did. He straightened from against the black hood of his vehicle and turned his one eye up at the cliffs we'd raced down from.

"Blue lights?"

I heard the men behind grumbling in a panic. I turned to show them a smile.

"You boys just raced a ten-cylinder engine through the quietest neighborhood in the city, paused at the top long enough for any one of six glass condos to get your plates and fired an automatic weapon that, while silent, certainly gives off flashes. What did you think was going to happen?"

The purple man looked panicked for a few moments longer, but he recovered well enough. "Clever move," he acknowledged.

"I thought so."

"It won't save you."

"I didn't think so."

I glanced behind him, half expecting and fully hoping to see blue lights coming from that direction as well. But then, we were on the edges of the city proper, and the eastern entrance to the concrete mountain was more easily accessed, especially on a Friday night, when the main throughways were choked with the pedestrians I'd managed to avoid killing earlier.

"So, then," he said, taking a half step forward. "How does Akio Prince want to die? From the front?" He waved his gun and then nodded over my shoulder. "Or the back." He was still smart enough to keep his distance. Judging by the watchful silence behind me, the dull boys were too.

"Well ..." I reached up slowly. "If you'd permit me, the direction doesn't matter to me so much as the situation." I gripped the hilt of one resin blade and drew it, surprised he let me. He had no reason to fear it. I wasn't anywhere near close enough to strike, and drawing a weapon at all suggested I had no desire to run. Not that there were many places to go in the present circumstance.

"Fine by me," he said with a shrug. I drew the other blade, whipped them out to either side and let them slide out to their full lengths. I gripped the handles and saw the red light bleeding up from the polished fiber that ran along the center of each blade, standing out starkly against the black borders.

The purple man glanced once more at the cliffs. The lights

must have been getting closer, judging by the widening of his remaining eye.

"Front it is."

Before he could squeeze the trigger fully, I launched my right-hand blade toward him. It spun end over end in the driving rain, a red scythe that had him diving to the side as it crashed into the windshield of his car and shattered it. He hit the road hard and then I felt a force like a punch on the back of my throwing shoulder blade.

The momentum of the bullet and the throw combined to spin me around and sent me slipping to one knee, my already numb right hand reaching out to grab the rusted railing of the bridge, my left hand dragging my remaining blade along the rain-soaked metal. The passenger leveled the automatic on me, ignoring the shouts of the driver, who had already scrambled to get back in his car, panicked much more by the approaching sirens than by my futile attempt.

The passenger was a hero in his own mind. Probably earn a nice promotion for killing me, assuming the purple man didn't take all the credit. Might even get to smoke a cigar with Goro himself.

"Screw it," I said as he smiled. As he went for his own trigger squeeze, I put everything I had left into my legs and what little I had in my right arm, giving a roar that rivaled any engine as I hurled myself over the rail as the bullet storm struck the place I'd been. I spun as I went over, managed to hang by my ruined, pulsing arm long enough to find a seam between the panels in the bridge, and stabbed my remaining blade into it.

The bullets clanged off the rail, and either a piece of shrapnel or another of the silver devils buried itself in my left collarbone, assisting my fall into the Han.

The water was deeper than I'd thought, and faster moving. I gasped and tried to make for the north bank, but there was nothing to grab but slick clay, and nothing to grab with but rapidly numbing arms.

I gave up the fight and rolled onto my back, doing my best to float above the rain-infused rapids and to keep my eyes open.

Through the curtain of rain and the blur of pain and blood loss, I saw the two pairs of headlights race away, back toward the city streets, where they'd no doubt ditch them in one of a thousand of Goro's hiding places. I then saw the blue lights coming down the last ramp on my side of the mountain.

Last, before the darkness took me, I saw my red blade, stuck up in the center of the storm above the river like a silent sentinel.

That should be enough.

8

BETTER OFF DEAD

I remember bits and pieces of that night, and the few that followed.

I remember fighting to keep my head above water for a while. And then I remember losing.

The water was rough, I told myself. Far rougher than it had any right to be. Of course, the truth was that the bullet had just given me more than I could handle. Taken too much blood. At least the river was cold enough that I didn't feel the pain, much.

I remember scraping along the edges of the bank. When I finally caught hold of something—some trash or maybe some scrub grass and sludge growing along the bottom—I clung to it like I'd found paradise. Like I'd found a reason to live. Or just a more comfortable place to die.

"Remember how Kenta died?"

The voice sounded like a dream. I would have played it off like one, but then the pain rushed in.

It shouldn't have hurt this bad. Of course, I'd never been shot before—let alone twice—but the dim part of my brain that was currently lighting up like a circuit board knew it shouldn't have hurt this bad.

I woke up flailing, reached for my back and felt the wrapping she'd just been digging her thumb into.

"Some bedside manner," I said groggily enough that it came out more as a malformed series of mumbles.

"What's that?"

Min had that flat look she used to wear before her fights. Before she'd do anything that was about to turn out very badly for someone else. I looked at the floor in front of the couch, my expression sheepish.

"Water," I said, pressing a hand to my pounding forehead.

"Excuse—"

"Min," I said, drawing it out like a younger brother. "Please."

She sighed and stood up. I felt the leather cushions expand. By the time she was back, I'd already started to nod off. She sat next to me and laid her palm across the wrapping again, making me flinch. When I looked at her, she smiled this time, softly and with genuine care.

She handed me a tall, cool glass of water, and I touched it to my lips. My throat, dry and cracked, was soothed, and I drank deeply, wondering absently how long I'd been out. Min stared at me over the lip of the glass. She had large brown eyes that were complemented by brown hair she tied back in a tail. Her face was soft and rounded. She wore black gi pants— seemed old habits die hard—and a loose-fitting gray night shirt, and sat cross-legged against the opposite arm of the couch.

Overall, she looked like a gentle thing, but I knew her strength and her toughness. If she'd had half a mind to, she would have been ranked in the League without issue.

As it turned out, she'd always been a hell of a lot smarter than me, and a hell of a lot more driven than Joon.

I lowered the glass, cradling it between my hands in my lap. I still had my jeans on from the night before … the week before. Whatever it had been. The blood had stained brown. I picked at the spots absently, ran my fingers over the wrapping around my bare chest.

My forearms and ribs had purpled, scrapes having turned a

violent, beet red—the markers of Janix's assault. It hurt to breathe, but I'd never been one for painkillers.

Beer, on the other hand.

Min read my mind and handed me another cold glass, this one green and bottle-shaped. I took a long pull and she matched me with her own, a blue bottle with white writing.

"Still drinking that American crap?"

She gave me a withering stare and then smiled, but the smile dropped soon enough, as if she just couldn't keep it glued to her face, seeing the state of me. It was hard to look at her, so I didn't. I looked down at my hands instead.

"Thank you," I said without looking up.

Min made a sound that was difficult to gather the meaning of. It could have been motherly concern. It could have been disappointment. Probably an odd mix of the two. Mostly, it just sounded tired, and I felt a pang in my chest that had nothing to do with my recent ordeal.

I sighed and looked around the room. We were underground, in a basement, by the looks of things. There was a stairwell with a stapled-down gray rug heading up onto the landing of a house I didn't recognize. The shag carpet seemed like something out of a 1970s catalogue. It was steel-colored. The walls were dark slate panels. There was a TV set into the wall directly in front of us, overlooking a black glass fireplace and a squat coffee table. In the corner, I saw a large white desk—more a wall of desks and tables, all pushed up together and each overflowing with manila files and hot-burning lamps. There was an open laptop, the luminescent screen buzzing softly.

"Working?"

"Always," she answered.

"It's no Tokyo, at least."

"Not in the open," Min said derisively. "But, seems like it's a pretty near thing for you."

There it was. No avoiding it, now. I took another sip. Made it a long one.

"Hell of a way to get my attention."

"Which part?" I asked, turning one of my clever looks on her.

It didn't work. None of them ever had. "My low-speed chase up that concrete monstrosity we call a mountain, or my epic last stand on the Bridge on the River Kw—"

"Sticking that glow stick of yours into the side of the bridge," she said. "Must have been tricky, planting it as you went over."

"Do you—"

"It's locked up in evidence," she said. "I wasn't the only one to notice it. Had to wait a solid hour before I could pull myself away from the scene long enough to search for what I assumed was going to be a dead body, all bloated and blue—"

"Okay," I said, waving a hand. "So, this is public?"

She nodded. "How could it not be?"

"Damn."

"Yup. As if the city news wasn't already enamored with your bold … whatever the hell it was you were trying to prove against Janix—against Goro, for that matter—now the conspiracy theorists are running wild in the streets with news of your demise."

"They don't know—"

"They don't know you're alive, no," Min said. She looked at me as if I should thank her, again. "If they did, I assume you'd be dead already. Or we both would. Or all three of us."

"Joon wasn't involved," I said, again without meeting her eyes.

"No?" she prodded. "Seems like just the sort of thing you two might cook up. Fight for the downtrodden. Stand up against organized crime. Make a stand on a rain-soaked bridge at the edge of town, for nothing and no one but yourselves."

"Oh yeah," I said. "This is the Min I remember. How's that fight going on your side of the aisle? How many of Goro's thugs have you locked up? Did you even catch the ones I led you right to? How's Purple Suit Man?"

"Who?"

"Exactly."

She shook her head. Looked as if she'd been slapped. I felt bad, but I also felt angry, not as much at Min as at the situation I'd created. More so, the one this city—this country, this world—had let fester beneath their noses all along.

"What the hell, Akio. What the hell got into you?"

I leaned forward and pinched my nose, squeezing my eyes shut tightly. A grizzled, scarred face with soft blue eyes flashed on the backs of my eyelids.

"We learned from the best," I said.

Min didn't say anything. When I looked up, she was red and fuming, with water gathering around the rims of her eyes.

"What?"

"Shame on you," she said, nearly breathless. "Shame on you, for putting this on him."

"You're the one who brought him up," I said, ire rising. The conversation was starting to become familiar, retreading familiar ground. We all become what our fathers made us. It's just a matter of interpretation.

"You've been living a dream, Akio," Min said. She had already regained control, which made me want to do the same. "When you're in there fighting for fans and adoration, I'm doing real work—"

That was rich. "Kenta didn't only leave that dusty old dojo behind, not that you cared enough to know."

She winced. "What?"

"Debt, Min," I said. "You know Kenta had a debt, and you know debts to the Hachinin aren't just forgiven, even if you're dead."

She swallowed.

"It's not enough," I said. "Your work at the precinct."

"Then what do we do?" she yelled, nearly spilling her drink. She set it down with a hollow thud on the table. "What do you propose? That we embarrass Goro of the Hachinin in front of the world? That we all get ourselves on the same red list you're on now? One I don't know how on earth I'm going to get you off of? Seoul has its problems, Akio. I know it just the same as the next beat cop. But it's a damn sight better than what's going on elsewhere."

"Not good enough," I said. "Where's our next generation, Min? How many young recruits do you have banging down the door who aren't strung out on Goro's shit? How many orphans are plying their trade in the sweat-soaked, mildew-infested dungeons, fighting and dying so that those lucky few can claw their way up the regional ranks and populate the League with its next generation of fodder? What happens when they buy out the schools like they did the networks? What happens—"

"Listen to yourself, Akio," Min said. "You sound like you're putting together a list of your own."

"Maybe it's time someone did."

She just looked at me. It wasn't anger I saw in those eyes I'd known since I was old enough to scrub the mats at Ken's Place. It was heartbreak, like she was seeing me throw it all away. It made me feel like I'd already lost.

I looked at the black screen above the fireplace. "Anything good on?"

"Mostly you," she said, not reaching for the remote. "Biggest story on both sides of the week, one for your heroic moment of defiance, the next for your absence. Akio," she sighed, sounding like she didn't want to start a new argument, but unable to help it, "you got your wish. You called Goro out. Him and the whole League. It worked. It worked just as you hoped it would. The Hachinin got egg on their face, there may as well have been singing and dancing in the clubs, in the bars, in the streets. Hell, even the boys at the station were singing your praises: that's Prince Akio for you. Heart and Seoul, is what he's about. Show those old Yakuza bones we're not afraid of them, that they don't own us."

She was silent for a spell.

"But then you go ahead and get yourself killed in the next breath, far as they know," she said. "You haven't been made a martyr, Akio. You need to accomplish something to do that, not just throw a silent tantrum on a public stage. You need to do something." She sounded like she was on the verge of tears, and looked back toward that buzzing screen on its white desk. "I don't know. I've been in contact with Jacinto—"

"Your old partner?"

"He's stationed in Cameroon."

"Thought they had a handle on that whole thing."

"Kenta's not there anymore, remember?" Min said, only half joking. "The African continent was doomed the moment his squad left. It's just gone on too long to be sexy on the news these days. I think the West is still getting a kick out of it."

"Nice change from the Middle East for them."

"True." She shook her head, knowing she was being led off the present track. "Akio, I think I can get you papers. But ... God. I don't know if it's going to be enough. Not if you join some regional or—heaven forbid it—work your way up to a national standing. They'll find you. You're marked by the Hachinin, now. There's no fighting that, only hiding from it."

"Never really been my strong suit."

"I know."

More silence, and this one stretching. Min knew this wasn't a fight she was likely to win. She thought she was looking at a dead man, and was just wondering how long it was going to take him to realize it, to see sense.

"You're right, Min." She sighed, her relief almost palpable. "About me being a fool. About my tantrum, as you called it." She winced. "My little show on the bridge, which earned me nothing but a bullet—"

"Two," she added and I nodded appreciatively. It was starting to come back to me.

"But you're wrong about the solution."

"Oh?" She didn't sound like she agreed, but for once, she seemed willing to hear me out.

"You said so yourself," I said, speaking as nonchalantly as I could. "I haven't really done anything worthwhile. Nothing that would earn me more than a passing mention over some half-drained bottles at last call, maybe for another month or two. Nothing that would get people motivated, get them to start asking tough questions, especially of the people asking the questions these days."

Min started to shake her head, but I wasn't going to be stopped.

"Goro prides himself on the show," I said, nodding along to myself, as if I were in a fever dream. "I'll give him one. I'll give him a good one. One that'll get him seen. One that'll get all of them seen. Their whole Seoul outfit—the same one you and yours haven't been able to crack—"

"We've cracked it fine, Akio," she said, frustration mounting. "It's just, the world doesn't work the way you think it does. The way we all thought it did, when Kenta taught us to solve all of our problems with our fists and feet. You took it to heart, Akio, but you took it literally. At least Joon is using the martial arts to get kids off the streets—"

"Why are they on the streets in the first place, Min? Shadows run the world. You've got all the information on the Hachinin. You've got all the info on Goro's enterprises—whatever you want to call them—operating on Capitalist Democratic soil. Why haven't you been able to make anyone talk? Why haven't you been able to link him to the networks? Why haven't you been able to tie the League money back to Tokyo? It's all right there, right in front of everyone's noses."

"Nobody's going to talk, Akio! Because if they do, they'll end up—"

"Like me," I said, staring at her as if I'd just won. She blinked, not sure how to respond.

"That's it," I said, leaning forward as she leaned back, regarding me like I'd simply lost my mind along with my head under that bridge. "Can't you see it, Min? I've got nothing to lose, now. I can do what you can't. I can rattle them, hit them where it hurts. Who better?"

"Even if you could," she said, slowly, hating herself for humoring me, "none of it would be valid. I can't take testimony under threat."

"We're not trying Goro of the Hachinin in a court of law," I said. I was even beginning to frighten myself. "We're trying him—"

"On the end of one of your red blades?" Min asked, her eyes widening. When I didn't respond, she looked at me with fresh horror. This was the Akio she remembered. This was the one she'd lost touch with—rather, that she had cut herself off from. The one who was less disillusioned with the world and more angry with it. Angry enough to lash out. Angry enough to kill.

"Would it be wrong?"

"This isn't a game, Akio." Min laid her forehead against her open palm. "You're talking about something different than fighting in a League match. You're talking about war, and war without rules."

"Even war has rules," I said. "Kenta taught me that."

"He also taught you how to die, it would seem."

It was meant to rattle me. All it did was harden me, turn me more into the stone I'd been getting closer to for years.

"For honor?" I asked, mocking. "For something he believed in?"

"For old debts," Min said. "Alone. And in the rain."

I swallowed. She had been the one who had found him, after all. The brave, mighty Kenta. Hero of Sixth Street. Difference-maker in the lives of small, fatherless children.

A single tear tore itself loose from Min's eye, falling like a grudge.

"It was raining when I found you, you know," she said, her voice nearly breaking. "I sank up to my ankles in that stinking muck. Walked for an hour. I found you in a shit-stained pool on the edges of an aluminum tunnel. I thought you were dead, anyway. And Akio," she sniffed, "I almost left you there. It wasn't heartache I felt. It wasn't sadness. It was anger. And not at the ones who'd put you there."

I wanted to look away. I wanted to look at anything in that moment that didn't make me feel the way she did. The way that only she could.

"I was angry at you, Akio. For making me do it. For making me turn you over, hoping against hope I'd see those pretty eyes open, see that stupid grin, hear one of those famous apologies you don't really mean."

I almost said I was sorry right then and there.

"I know," she said. She wiped her eyes and drained the rest of her glass, stood a little shakily and moved over to the steel mini fridge she had sitting in easy reach under the desk with all that ugly manila. She grabbed a couple more bottles, foregoing the glasses this time, and brought them over, snapping the lids off on the edges of the table—which chipped, making me cringe— but Min didn't care. She'd never been materialistic.

"So," she said, handing one over and half draining her own in a swig, "you're going to kill Goro of the Hachinin—"

"Eventually," I said, inflecting my tone with just the timbre of bravado I knew she hated. She smiled through it. "Right after I'm done with Purple Suit Man."

"Who?" she asked, frowning. "The one who shot you?"

"The one who gave the order," I said with a shrug. "One of the door guys at the Soul Dome. Ex-fighter. Middling." I looked at her. She stared at the blank screen. "Know him?"

"Thinking." She did, for a while. Long enough that I thought she'd forgotten the point.

I pictured myself as a red ghost, terrorizing the Hachinin en route to a public execution of Goro. It was a nasty, passionate vision, and one that I knew was unbecoming. Still, I'd always been more honest with myself than Joon was. No matter who my father was, and no matter what Kenta had preached, I had always been closer to him in practice. The real him. He and I had known it, even if we never said it. I could see it in the way he had looked at me, not with pride—as he looked at Min and Joon —but with consternation. With the weight of destiny, and not that of the grand variety.

There are no heroes worth talking about anymore, Akio, he said to me once, when I'd got myself knifed for the first time trying to stop some local gangsters from roughing up a drunk who prob- ably deserved it. *Heroes end up dead. People remember their names, but they don't live by them. They don't live for them. They live for themselves. The trick is in making them see what they are. What they could be.*

That was Joon. Building people up rather than breaking them down. But I'd been Kenta to his core. He said those things because he wanted desperately to believe them. But there was a fire in him that was also in me. An anger at seeing injustice, and being powerless to do anything to stop it.

"Sang Hee win?" I asked, jarring Min into wakefulness. I felt a pang of guilt, wondering how long she'd been looking after me. She probably hadn't slept in days.

"Obviously," she said, giving me a stare most men know well. The sort of stare your girl gives you when another comes up. She shrugged. "The American chick did alright, all things considered."

"Brent?" I nodded. "Heard good things about her."

"Oh, don't worry," Min said, sitting up. "She didn't mark up that pretty face too badly. You're looking a damn sight worse."

I cringed on the inside, but tried to play it off. I had forgotten that my little tryst with Sang Hee had done more for my public image—for better or worse—in the hours leading up to my Semi Final, than any of my in-ring performances had in the previous seasons. Of course, I hadn't really stopped to consider that the thought of two lovers—if you could call us that—meeting in the Finals would be too good a story to pass up. I also hadn't considered that everyone I'd ever known, in the Biblical sense, would know of it as well.

Min had never been one for jealousy, though.

"I didn't end it," I said, raising my eyebrows.

"Ah, Akio, Akio!" Min drained the rest of her bottle and then set it down with a wobble. "Just because I broke up with you doesn't mean I don't have a right to give you shit about every woman you spend a night with for the rest of your meager existence."

"How does that work?"

"I don't make the rules."

What was I going to say to that?

"Sang Hee looked good," she said, nodding, her martial mind taking over. I could tell she was replaying the fight in her mind's eye. She had that glassy look. "Brent got her licks in." She shrugged again. "But, if you ask me, our girl was looking a little worn out."

"Pining for her lost love?" I purred.

"More in the physical sense, I meant," Min said absently, either not seeing or ignoring my deep blush. "News of your … disappearance, hasn't really played on the major networks. Takes three days for them to file a missing person's report now. Plenty of time for them to cook up some PR scheme about how you fell in with the wrong crowd at your afterparty. Ran afoul of the true bad eggs of Seoul … as if they aren't all directly tied to Goro and his ilk." She went to take another swig, but set the empty bottle down with a look of profound disappointment and then reached for mine.

I handed it over.

"What have they done with the season, then?"

"They've taken a very short recess," Min said. "Of course, everyone knows what happened. Knows you're missing. There's been some outrage, but without any real coverage, and no questions being lobbed at the League outside of the superficial variety. I'm sure they'll simply match Sang Hee up with Janix, once he's got a chance to heal up. More likely …" she paused and swallowed, but then said it anyway. "They're seeing if they can confirm your death before risking you dropping in and causing a spectacle on the grand stage, or having the department do it for you."

"You already said you couldn't do anything—"

"I said it wasn't that simple, Akio," Min said. "But if you've got information that leads to an arrest, a real arrest, and not some fall guy—"

"They're all fall guys," I said, exasperated.

She opened her mouth to speak but then let it drop. I did too. I'd put her through enough as it was.

"Did you tell him?" I asked.

"Who? Joon? No. Didn't want anyone connecting dots best left separate, for now." I nodded. "Of course, they already know everything about you, but shadows don't like stepping into the light unless they're forced to. As for Joon, I couldn't well tell him you were alive, Akio. That's not on me."

Min was starting to sound as if she'd already had a few before she'd roused me.

"Better this way than the alternative," I said.

"What's that?"

"You've always been the scariest one of the three of us," I said.

Min smiled. "I noticed you didn't say I was the best."

"You're not," I said evenly. "But you are the scariest."

She smiled again. She knew it was true.

"You need to tell him, Akio," she said, her eyes losing focus.

"I know."

I wrinkled my nose, catching a whiff of something that I assumed was me.

"Yes," she said, nodding. "Imagine working next to it."

Speaking of which, I had the sudden, unholy urge to piss like a racehorse. Now that it hit me, I was shocked I hadn't soaked Min's leather couch. Of course, I had no way of knowing whether I had.

I stood and tried to stretch. My body made me think better of it.

"You've seen better days, Akio Prince."

"Speak for yourself."

"What's that?"

"You could go far in the League," I said, making my way toward the stair, "if you got in shape again."

That earned me a glare that was only partially in jest. She rocked herself back up into a rigid, straight-backed position.

"Who's to say I'm not?"

"Gun range is hardly the same."

Min looked to be grinding her teeth. She looked like she wanted to leap across the room and throttle me right there. She could give me a fit in her prime. That hadn't been so very long ago, but a lot had happened in the interim. I'd stayed in the gym, on the mats, in the fire. She'd thrown herself behind a desk, or behind a wheel, listening to a scanner call out the city's sins, only a few of which she could even do anything about. Only a few of which didn't have to do with Goro.

"You've got a look about you, Akio," she said, shaking her head and settling back, sinking deeply into the cushions. She looked beyond exhausted. She closed her eyes, and before I made my way up to find the bathroom, I saw a tired smirk spread across her face.

"I did like the look on his face."

"Whose?"

"Goro's," she said without lifting her head. "They showed him on the way to his car behind the Dome. Camera operator probably got fired—if not outright killed—for lingering with the shot. He was red-faced. Red like a tomato. Red like blood."

She was snoring before I hit the landing. I replayed her words all night. They didn't feel as wrong as they ought to.

9

OLD HABITS

It took Seoul Media—the real media, which is to say, the one that got the most eyeballs and told the least truths—three days to run a story that had Goro's greasy mitts all over it.

Min and I watched on the main floor.

League contender Akio Prince, who defeated Janix in Friday night's Semi-Final bout, has officially been declared missing by the Seoul Policing and Defense Force.

I glanced sidelong at Min over the name of her police force, which I'd always found to have an oddly fascist lilt to it. She rolled her eyes.

"Contender *and* champ," I corrected, with a wag of my finger. Min ignored me.

Prince was last seen by eyewitnesses renting a speed bike outside of Yoon Bar on Sixth and Twenty-First. Witnesses described Prince as looking tired, bloody and—

I held up a finger as if I were directing an orchestra, waiting for the inevitable drop after the rising crescendo.

… and, well, more than a little inebriated.

I even mouthed the word, knowing it was how they'd spin it. Min might be giving me the cold shoulder, but it had more to do with the same annoyance I felt, not to mention the fact that I still hadn't informed Joon that I was, well, alive.

"I told them this was a missing person's case and that foul

play was suspected," Min said. She had started the morning with black tea, but had already graduated to a silver can.

Prince's rental bike was found on the southwest side of the city, on the banks of a drainage vein. Searchers have been looking for him for the last seventy-two hours, with divers having been dispatched to the reservoir…

"Already giving me up for dead, I see," I said with a shake of my head.

"May as well be."

"What's that?"

She only crossed her arms and kept on staring at the screen, muttering to herself on occasion when whatever falsehoods the anchors had been fed by Goro's sources came tumbling out of plush, robotic lips.

"Going to look pretty stupid when the city—the world, for that matter—finds out I'm well and good. Goro, that is."

"And when," Min said, not trying to hide her annoyance in the least, "might that be?"

I shrugged. "Haven't quite decided yet."

"Did it ever occur to you, Akio, that Goro's people fed the station this shit because they plan on making it so? That they plan on finding your body in that reservoir you were so close to actually slipping into before I found you?"

"Of course it has. Like I said … they're going to look pretty—"

"You're a dead man as soon as you make yourself known!" Min shouted. "Likely before, and with me along with you."

I turned a more serious look on her and she bit back whatever was on the tip of her tongue. "You know I won't let that happen, Min. I'd never let that happen."

"Yeah," she said, getting up in a huff—not that I could blame her. "Sometimes, it isn't up to you, Akio. The sooner you learn that, the better off you'll be. The better off everyone who's ever known you will be."

She went into the other room. I heard her flip the coffee maker on. She couldn't decide between depressants and stimulants, it seemed. I wondered if it was a part of her usual routine, or if it was on account of dealing with me in close proximity for the first time in a long time.

I looked around the place, still marveling that Min had got herself set up so well. Her current residence was a far cry from the cramped apartment she had had the last time … well, the last time I'd been around. This place shared some similarities with the glass villas atop the mountain where I'd taken my midnight ride, though it came off as being less pretentious. Bay-view windows looked out over a yard that was as big as you were going to get while still being within the city limits. Wood paneling ran throughout the house, sort of reminiscent of a mountain-view cottage, like those you'd find in the mountain forests that surrounded the city. There was a screened-in back porch that I hadn't been permitted to check out on account of me being some combination of missing, hunted and presumed dead, and there was a single bedroom tucked just behind the TV that hung from the wall opposite me, above another coffee table —this one glass rather than wood.

The day was dreary, the same storm that I'd nearly died in having left behind a wet haze, like a low-hanging cloud that coated everything in the city in its slick, muggy malaise.

Today was the first day I'd been able to get away without having to have my bandages changed by foregoing them completely, much to Min's chagrin. I kept reaching up under my shirt to itch at the taped patches that likely wouldn't be coming off for another few days. Wasn't going to win that argument.

"Do you plan on changing your clothes?" Min called in. "Or are you just going to wear those stained jeans and that ripped shirt for the rest of your life, however long it lasts?"

I gave my armpits a sniff. "I washed them."

"I washed them," she corrected. "And I told you I had extra clothes."

"No thanks," I said. "Just because we're no longer dating doesn't mean I have any desire to wear your ex's cast-offs."

"Suit yourself."

"Speaking of," I started, "any luck on getting any info on said suit?"

"You said it was at the Dome," Min said. "No way I'm going near that place without good reason."

"That suit is as good a reason as any," I complained. "Most of last year's winnings went into it."

She came into the room holding a steaming white mug and stood with her hips tilted and one shoulder down, letting a string from her black tank top fall with it. I didn't pretend not to notice. She stared at me expectantly.

"Joon already told me."

"Told you … what?" I said with my most innocent expression.

"Really? We're going to play it like this?"

"Like … what?"

"Like … I know Ken's Place had quarter-inch blue mats a year ago, and now they have inch-thick red ones. Like … I know there used to be two sets of kali sticks, likely from the 1980s, and now there are, what, two dozen sets of all manner of resin blades, staffs, sais—"

"Alright, alright," I said, waving the rest away. "You're making me blush."

"How much did you keep for yourself, Akio?" she asked, plopping back down onto the couch.

I shrugged and she sighed in exasperation. I'd been making her do that a lot over the past few days.

"You were going to need something to get you by after you were done fighting. Once Kenta's debt was paid," she said, her voice softer, less accusatory than it had been. "You could afford to live anywhere you wanted, if you got an investor. Sat down with an advisor. Don't know why you sleep in that dump on the west side."

"I sleep in Ken's attic, too," I said, earning another of those withering stares. I'd almost forgotten how much I missed them. Almost.

"What does it matter, at this point?" I asked. "You said it yourself, I'm a dead man walking."

I expected her to go the other way, to shout me down or to tell me it wasn't so, that they could find a way around it. That we could ship me off to North America, or put me in witness protection. Min knew me better than that. She knew I wasn't joking when I said the things I'd said the other night. She also didn't want to fight. At least, not verbally.

"Department doesn't miss you?" I asked.

She shrugged. "I'm working a case. I'm not on the beat anymore. That ... and they know better than to give me a hard time."

"I can believe that. Graduated to paper pusher pretty quick, eh? I always thought—"

"That I hated the idea? Yeah, well," she took another sip and blew out a long and weary sigh, "I do. But, I've already learned I can effect more change behind a desk by keeping an eye on the rest of the department than I can waving a baton around on one corner or the next."

"Department still needs an eye on it, then ..." I left it hanging. Min didn't disagree with me quick enough, which said all it needed to.

"Bad eggs in every walk," she said. "Less than there used to be, I'd guess."

"Fair enough."

I stood and stretched. I almost caught myself, froze, waiting for the inevitable shock of pain to hit. It didn't.

"Feeling sprightly and spry, then?"

"Close to it," I said. "Looking pretty?"

"Back to your usual ugly self."

"What's that say about you?"

"I was younger then."

"Not by much."

I moved toward the back of the room, running my fingers along the wood paneling on the way to the Japanese-style canvas slider that led to the porch I wasn't supposed to wander onto.

"Akio—"

"What does it matter?" I asked, my own sense of exasperation beginning to grow. "You've got a row of trees between your place and the neighbors."

I wrinkled my nose, picking up a scent I hadn't before. It was a familiar one, and it was coming from under the thin, wood-framed slats that separated the living room from the porch.

"The hell?"

"Akio, don't—"

I slid the door open before she could finish. I expected there to be sunlight streaming in from the three-quarter windows. I expected a wicker chair, maybe a little couch or a loveseat.

Instead, my eyes had to work to adjust to the gloom. I stepped down half a foot onto the mats and walked into the center of the makeshift dojo, Min silent behind me.

The space was only a little larger than the basement I'd awoken in a few nights earlier. The walls were wood paneling, though they weren't the same as the modern dark wood found throughout the rest of the house. These were old, dried pine, with splinters still jutting out from the corners. The ceiling was covered with old spray-board panels. A few were missing, and the white insulation could be seen; one panel had a bird's nest tucked up inside.

I turned in a slow circle, saw the old wardrobe at the back of the room, or the front, depending on your perspective. The sight brought back memories I didn't know I still had. Brought them in a rush, and one that nearly brought me to my knees with the blast of intoxicating, heart-wrenching nostalgia.

There were two brass poles standing on either side of the wardrobe with candles set into the tops. They weren't lit now, but as I moved up to them, I could tell they had been lit not so long ago. No dust marred the wax. No dust marred any of it. The mats were smooth in places due to the passage of thousands of feet, or dozens of feet thousands of times. To the right of the wardrobe and behind one of the brass holders, two flags were pinned to the back wall, beside one another rather than above or below. The Korean flag we all grew up seeing on every street corner, and the red sun of the Japanese we weren't supposed to covet.

It wasn't a political statement, but rather an homage to the arts. The true arts. The martial arts. Arts that had no borders aside from those of the mind. Arts that could take a rich man and make him as noble as a poor one, or take a street urchin and make him a man.

I saw Min step into the doorway out of the corner of my eye, and paused. I hadn't realized I had been reaching for the handle to the wardrobe.

I expected her to look angry, or hurt. Instead, she looked proud. Her eyes shone in the dim light. She flicked a switch I hadn't bothered to search for, and a single bare bulb that hung from a wire wedged between two of the panels overhead flickered to life with a soft and pleasant buzzing.

"This is it," I said. "This is it, isn't it?" I spun around, taking it all in again, eyes wide.

Min had taken her socks off and stepped down onto the mats with a bow I'd forgotten in my excitement. I felt my face color in shame. She walked toward me and then turned to the wardrobe, brushing the handles with reverence. She didn't open it.

"I thought they sold the place," I said. "Before …"

"Before he went," she said, quiet as a breeze. "Yeah. Mom sold it. After he was too sick to come home. After it was … too much for her to keep."

I shook my head. "I …" I started and then stopped. "I was only here a few times, back when Kenta kicked me out—"

"He never kicked you out, Akio," she said, shaking her head. She was examining the flags on the wall. "You two were too similar to solve your problems through conversation." I could see her ears pull back on either side of her ponytail as she smiled.

"It isn't how I remember it," I said. "Well," I nodded toward the living room as she turned to regard me, "this is, but none of that."

"New owners made plenty of improvements," she said, bending her fingers at the knuckles to show what she thought of those improvements. "I haven't had the time to unmake them. Not all bad, I suppose."

"At least they left your father's dojo."

She shrugged. "Didn't so much leave it as ran out of time— more likely money—to demolish it. They hid it behind that dark wood paneling. I just knocked the wall down and put in the slider."

I put my hands on my hips and smiled, almost at a loss.

"What?"

I laughed. "You just bought it back? How did you afford it?"

"We aren't paid as poorly as some would have you believe," she said with an eye roll. "Besides, it's not like I own the place outright."

"Bank owns everything." I shrugged. "I'd say you own it as much as the next."

She nodded at that and then she stepped into the center of the room, spread her feet out to shoulder width and let her arms hang by her sides.

"That old suit still in there?" I asked, staring at the wardrobe hard enough that my sight might pierce it.

"It is."

"I remember it," I said, speaking in an awed tone.

"I could tell," Min said without turning.

I whirled. "How so?"

"Seen that League getup you wear," she said, not moving from the spot, just staring straight ahead, or else standing with her eyes closed, shoulders down, the picture of calm. "You might have covered the dye with flashing lights, and you don't wear a mask, but the red and black, the twin blades. I remember the impression that old thing made on you. You woke my father up in the middle of the night when you stayed here, nearly spitted yourself on the end of one of those blades."

"Thought he was going to kill me," I said, turning back to examine the wardrobe. I could almost see it, the red-scale armor, the shoulder pauldrons with their razor tips, like tongues of flame. The mouth mask, blood red, and the black cloak that went with it all. I could almost see the outline of the twin blades crossed in front on their wooden pegs, see the insteps and forearm guards, all of it red and black and polished to a dull sheen, like it was wet.

It had been a family heirloom, traced back to the ninja clans of the isles. I'd never known if it was true, but I'd believed it enough. Believed it because I wanted to.

I heard Min behind me. She breathed in, filling her lungs up fully as she brought her arms up from her hips out to either side, fingers straight. She raised them slowly, bringing them together high overhead, and then reversed the movement, until her arms were once more at her sides.

"The rising sun," I breathed. It was the start of a kata I hadn't done since I was a kid. One of Kenta's favorites, and, as it turned out, the one that had bonded him to Min's father so long ago.

Min turned around to face me. She slid her right foot back, turned her left foot inward. She tucked her right hand up to the underside of her chin and held the left farther out in front.

I smiled. "What happened to your concern over my well-being?"

"You don't want to wear the bandages," she said, "don't see why I have to take it easy on you."

"Fair enough."

I turned my head and stretched my neck to either side, exulting in the pleasant cracks and snaps that accompanied the movement. I slid my own foot back into a stance that was wider than Min's.

"Playing with those glow sticks in the arena's changed your stance," she commented, raising her eyebrows.

"You saying that's a bad thing?"

"You're flat-footed."

"Might look that way," I said, though I had to admit, I was feeling a little heavy. I lightened up my stance and took some of the weight off of my heels. "You're welcome to try m—"

Min had brought her right foot up to the back of her lead heel without me seeing. It was one of her oldest tricks, and still —apparently—her best. She lanced a side kick at my midsection with the lead leg, covering an extra foot and a half of distance by disguising her forward creep.

I managed to flex my core and slide back enough to take some force and effect away from the blow, but Min was always quick to go for the kill. She dropped her lead leg to the mats, twisted on the ball of her foot—the bottoms stained red and callused from her practice on this very floor—and brought her rear leg around for a second—and far more powerful—kick, one that unleashed the full power in those loaded, twisting hips.

Lucky for me, I'd seen Min fight before. I'd fought her before, and while this was the move that had nearly cost me gold in the TKD Worlds all those years ago, recognizing it then had saved me, and recognizing it now likely did the same.

Rather than sliding back, as most would be compelled to do in the situation, I darted forward, jamming Min's movement and making the heel of her second kick glance off of my side as I closed the distance between us. I led with a backfist, landing it on the right side of her face. She was leaning back, putting as much force into her kick as she could, so the blow didn't land hard enough to do more than make her blink.

That was all I needed.

I followed it up with a right cross, confident that I'd catch her more flush this time, maybe even drop her onto her butt and force her to give it up. If I stayed on the outside with Min, she'd eventually pick me apart. In close, fighting in a veritable phone booth, there wasn't a whole lot she could do to stop me. Size and strength would always matter in a fight, just as speed and cunning would, but only if you could enforce them.

As it turned out, Min remembered my tricks just as well as I remembered hers.

She did drop, only it wasn't the result of my cross that sent her down. She sank into a crouch just as her kicking foot bounced off of my hip and touched the mat, and then she planted her fingers and twisted to the other side, bringing her left foot around, low, sweeping the blade of her foot across the mats. I saw it out of the corner of my eye, recognized the movement, but I'd committed to the punch.

I felt her Achilles slam into the meat of my calf hard enough to let me know I'd have another nasty bruise in the morning, and also hard enough to take me right off of my feet. I landed on my ass and turned the fall into a haphazard back roll. When I came up Min had already gained her feet and I saw a blur of flesh lancing toward my face.

I couldn't dodge the roundhouse, so I blocked it. Stung like hell. And this time, I managed to hook the foot under my armpit as she retracted. I stepped in, accepted a jab to the nose that felt a little harder than Min had likely intended, and hooked my stepping leg behind her own foot, tripping her down.

As soon as Min's back touched the mat, she hipped up and rolled, managing to bridge me halfway over before I'd recovered my balance. When I tried to slide into a mounted position, she gave me another punch, this one a thrust to the jaw that sent a flash of hot anger through me and had me working to cool it. It also allowed her to escape into a roll herself.

She came up in a crouch, fists clenched, feet sliding, as I wiped a trickle of blood from under my nose.

"I see our argument's not quite through," I said, looking at the red smear on the back of my hand.

She blew a stray bang that had come loose away from her eye and gave a quick little shrug.

"Just remembered how stupid you're being," she said.

"Stupid?"

"Selfish, then."

"Whatever."

I accepted the next jab and landed a hook to the ribs. Judging by the sound she made, it connected solid, but even that indrawn breath turned to a growl, and Min locked both of her hands behind my head and launched a hard knee up into my gut, nearly taking the wind from me.

"The ... hell ..." I said through gritted teeth as we spun in a locked embrace, Min alternating knees as I crossed my arms down in front of me to stop them landing in my midsection, or below it.

When her attacks slowed some, I seized the chance and weaved my arms up between her own and mimicked her hold, grabbing her behind the head and pulling her forward. With both of us holding each other the same way, we had no space to throw anything meaningful. It was a waiting game, seeing whose arms would give out first, and even if I hadn't been bigger and stronger, I had the inner grip, and Min knew that as soon as she let me go, she'd give me the opportunity to land something nasty.

She gave another growl that morphed into a sound of anguish as she released her hold on the back of my neck and tried to duck forward and out of my own hold. Rather than send a knee screaming up to smash her nose apart, I let go of her neck and dropped my hands to her shoulders, shoving her. She hit the mat and scrambled to get back to her feet.

"Enough!"

Min rose and looked like she might come at me again, but she stopped, seeing my look. We both stood there, chests heaving, red-faced and angry more than excited now, Min in a looser, more chaotic version of her stance and me straight, tall and relatively defenseless. If she'd have wanted it, she could have kicked me from there before I could do anything about it, sent me into another sleep it might take an hour or a week to wake from.

Finally, she straightened as well and brought her hands up to retie her hair.

"Sorry."

"No you're not," I said, shaking my head. My heart slowed down quickly, though my blood was slower in cooling.

Min eyed me, then glanced toward the wardrobe. She closed her eyes and tilted her chin down toward her chest, breathing out a heavy-sounding sigh.

"I'm sorry, Akio."

She meant it, now. I knew she did. I didn't say anything back.

"It's just …"

"Might as well say it. Have it out."

"You're really going to do it," she said more than asked, though her eyes looked like a doe's when they opened and met mine. It was hard to see her look at me that way. "You're going to go after him."

"Him," I said with a shrug, wiping a spot of blood from a cut on my lip I hadn't noticed until now. "Them. What's the difference?"

"Akio." Min held her hands out, palms turned up. "You can't take on the Hachinin of Seoul—"

"For starters."

She looked as if I'd just slapped her. "What's that supposed to mean?"

"You know exactly what it means," I said. "Goro is the face—the jowls, more like—of the Hachinin in Seoul, but we all know where they're based."

"So, what? So you're going to take down Goro, the most powerful man in Seoul, which would make him just about the least powerful man in Tokyo, and then you're going to hop on a boat and take your private war to the island, clean up the neon streets?"

"You're going to clean up the streets, Min," I said, realizing how ridiculous it sounded but too emboldened to give it up, "I'm going to make it possible. Get it started. Trim the fat. Literally."

Min opened her mouth to speak, but nothing came out. She tried a few times, long enough that I began to wonder if I'd actually gone far enough as to put her into a state approaching shock.

"You said it yourself, Min," I said. "I'm a dead man walking. I know you think you can help me, or that you did think it. You might have even thought it as recently as this morning. But I can see it, now. I can see it in your eyes, and in the way you stare at the phone before it rings. You know there's nothing to be done for me, nothing your people could do to get me across any sovereign border that would have me, even if I did agree to go, which I won't. You can't because you don't have any people. Not any that you can trust."

"Plenty of good cops left in Seoul," she said.

"Plenty that share coffee with the bad ones, and likely without even knowing it." I didn't believe the last part. I had a natural, long-standing mistrust of most all authority figures, even trainers. It had taken me years to warm up to Kenta, a man who had opened his dojo to me as the first and only true home I'd ever had.

"Look around you," I said, sweeping a hand out to encompass the whole of her father's musty old dojo, and all that lay outside its walls. "The streets might not be running with red, but the gutters certainly are. More of it every year. Goro's bullied his way into some legit cash in the form of the League, but it's nothing but a vanity project, a means of covering the gold in all those Tokyo coffers with pyrite. His real product is in the streets that are the veins in this city and in the next one. His real cash is in the veins and rotted teeth of the kids who weren't lucky enough to get rescued by a dojo master like I was, like Joon was. Kids who weren't lucky—"

"To have parents," Min said for me. I winced. "I've never made any bones about that, Akio. I never denied it. You were the one who used to accuse me of playing orphan because I dared to be your friend before you'd be mine."

I wasn't going to say sorry for that again, and Min wasn't asking me to.

"This city is bleeding, Min," I said. "It may be lit up more brightly than most. And it could be a hell of a lot worse, but I'm telling you, it will be, as long as Goro's sitting there on his leather throne, basking in cigar smoke and adulation from League crowds that silently curse his name but never within earshot of anyone they don't know. Anyone wearing a suit, a mic, even a pen. He's like a ghost, seeping into everything like a rot. He's in the media. He's in city hall. He's in the department, Min, and you know it. It's right there for everyone to see. Right in front of their tablet-lit noses. And we've let it happen. Seoul isn't being invaded, Min. It's already been taken. I think it's time we take it back. Goro isn't the end, but he's a hell of a start."

"And you really think this … crusade, or whatever the hell you're going to call it, is going to change the way things are?"

"Not right away," I said. "Maybe not even in a year or three. Not my actions alone."

"What? You going to start recruiting?"

I bit my lip, kept the fresh cut from scabbing over. "Not for what I'm going to do. I'm not going to hand out pamphlets or cut promos. Those mouth pieces," I pointed back into the living room, "will be doing it for me. They'll play my misdeeds on the evening news. They'll squawk about it until they're red in the face. They might even show some emotion doing it, and if that happens, when that happens, we'll know we're getting to them."

"Them," Min said, shaking her head slowly. "They. Goro. The Hachinin. The devil himself. It hasn't even started, Akio, and you already sound like it has no end. Is this really for the children, or is it for you, Akio? Your own personal brand of vengeance."

"What?" I scoffed. "Because he tried to get me to throw a match?"

Min only eyed me, steady and unflinching. "Goro didn't make you, Akio. This city did. This world did. It's not a perfect place. It's flawed and in some places it's even rotten. Your life hasn't been as fair as most. Neither was Joon's. Neither was mine, no matter what you think. But, Akio, this is madness you're talking about, here. And if you're going to be mad, at least do it for the right reasons, not some half-cooked mission to cleanse the Far East of all its sins."

She waited for a response that didn't come.

"If Goro dies," she said, swallowing, "there'll be another like him."

"Seven, to be exact."

"I'm not talking about the damn Hachinin, Akio," she said, squeezing her fists once again. "I'm talking about judges and street thugs and … and yes, even cops. It's not going to stop. They're like weeds."

"Pull the right one up," I said, "and the rest come closer. Their roots are tied, but they're buried deep. They just need the right sort of tug."

I turned and looked at her father's wardrobe. I could sense her fear and her sense of expectance as I did.

"And if I fail, I'll do it in such a way that it'll serve as a warning. A warning to the Hachinin and to those like them. And a signal to those who oppose them."

"Some already do, Akio," Min said. "Some have been."

"Then help me. Help me for a little while. Help me do it my

way, and then you'll have what you need to do the rest of it the right way."

I couldn't tell by her silence if she was considering it or just too stunned to speak. I didn't look her way or meet her eyes because I was afraid of what I'd see there. The silence stretched.

Min walked behind me, headed for the living room. She passed like a silent wraith and then paused at the doorway.

"This is for you, Akio," she said, head down. "Nobody else. At least make your peace with that before you …"

She left the rest unsaid and stepped up onto the carpet, leaving me beneath the lone buzzing bulb.

I heard the front door open, and the car start up a minute later. It was getting to be evening, and Min had put off going into the station too long on my behalf already. The questions would come more frequent and more probing if she didn't make her presence felt.

I stood there for a while, staring at that wardrobe without opening it.

10

RED PATH

Min had left my League armor hanging in the spare bedroom. I watched it spin lazily on its hanger for a while as I leaned in the doorway, sipping on my fourth cup of coffee that hour.

I had to squint to make them out, but the bullet holes were there. I'd sport the scars of them for the rest of my life. So much for League armor.

Again, that closed cupboard loomed in the shadow of my mind like a ghost. I could almost see the red-scale armor in my mind's eye, the worn, crisscrossed threads along the hilt of the masterwork blade. Those scales were designed to slow the sharpest swords in the East. To put up an argument—however futile—against the almighty katana.

How would they fare against lead and powder?

I often joked Min had joined the force because she was smarter than me. The truth was, she was just less selfish. She told me in those first few years that my ignorance was bliss. I had the luxury of seeing the world in shades of black and white while she had to navigate the gray. She said it not like she was lecturing me, but rather like she envied me. Min had the same bug I did. The same drive. The need to act and not simply to react. But the devil, as they say, is in the details.

I was a dead man, or as good as one. That would make it at

once exceedingly difficult and somewhat easy to move about in the open.

But in death, I was free.

It was why Min envied me even as she feared for me, and even as—much as it pained me to recognize—some part of her couldn't look at me the same way after tonight.

The sky outside was clouded, and morning gave way to after-noon without a change in the light. All in all, it seemed Seoul was in a perfect mood to reflect my own.

Tough luck for those who were soon to be in my way.

I started to turn from the doorway, but something caught my eye that I hadn't noticed before. I set my lukewarm mug down on the black rosewood dresser and crossed the carpet to the night stand. There was a manila envelope sitting there, slightly askew, as if it'd been tossed there in haste—likely just before Min had left for work.

I frowned and hesitated as I reached for it, a knot of guilt welling up in my gut. This was Min's work. She'd likely left it here by mistake, and I wasn't about to go digging.

That is, until I saw something—someone—familiar.

A white page had slipped free of the cover. Something about the black and white photograph gave me pause. I pinched the corner between my finger and thumb and pulled it out just enough to see, and felt a dizzying, throbbing pulse in my temples.

It was a mug shot, just like you'd see in all the old serials. It was a Japanese man with a square face and jet black hair, spiked much straighter than my own. He had a thin goatee, and though he wasn't wearing the shades that would have allowed me to place him even quicker, there was no getting around the poison glint in his right eye ... the one Korain had carved out in the bloodiest League match to date sometime after this photo had been taken.

I flipped the cover open and frowned at an old brass key that slid across the page as I did. I brushed it away without sparing it a second thought and lifted the small packet, my eyes running over the black letters and skimming past the gray smudges the industrial copier had left behind.

"Hello there, Kuzu Tokoro," I said to myself, not feeling the least bit insane. "Known as 'Zoo' to friends and associates."

There was all the strangely familiar police jargon, none of which I understood and all of which I recognized. Various charges were listed, including aggravated battery, felony assault and over thirty counts of intimidation of witnesses.

I shook my head and snorted as I flipped through. Given his charges, and given the evidence against him, our friend Zoo should have been rotting in a Seoul prison for the next twenty to forty. (And by rotting, I mean enjoying free MREs and basic cable from a box room that was probably larger than your average studio high-rise these days.) The figures on the last page took on a numeric bent, and went a long way toward explaining Zoo's absence from the system in the classic definition of the term.

"Pockets," I said, whispering it in disgust. "What deep pockets you have, Mr. Tokoro. If I knew being a glorified doorman paid so well, I'd have given up on the League ages ago."

Zoo's bail numbers started out modestly enough. A few grand here and there, nothing a drug runner or even a streaky gambler couldn't cobble together in a pinch. With each successive charge, however, the price grew, going so far as to hit six figures in his last two trips to Min's place of business.

As if I didn't know it by the way he'd tried to kill me on the bridge, there was now no doubting that Zoo was Goro's man. But that wasn't what got my blood pumping all over again, just as it did before my matches. What raised my pulse and had me sweating despite the damp and cool confines was the fact that the Seoul police knew it, and there wasn't a damn thing they could do about it.

This was Min's white flag, planted firmly and without comment. It wasn't a blessing. She'd never give that. Not openly. But it was just about as close to one as I was going to get.

The next section that drew my eye was one entitled 'Haunts.'

Took me a bit to get what that referred to, until I started piecing together the various names and associating them with local strip joints and sports bars—the kind with more bookies than patrons. These were Zoo's usual hangouts, and I was guessing they hadn't changed all that much in the intervening years.

The one at the top of the list was no surprise to anyone who grew up in the poorer neighborhoods of Seoul. The ones the bright neon lights did well to hide and the law chose to ignore, for better and worse.

Sister Red's was just a well-placed stone's throw from Ken's Place. It was something the old bag had grumbled about so often when I was a kid, sitting on the stone step out front and watching the bleeding drunks stumble past on a Wednesday night. Took a few years to realize Sister Red's—and a host of other even more seedy and less kempt establishments in the vicinity—was more a blessing for Kenta, Joon, me and the rest of the runts than a curse. For being close to the heart of downtown, the eight blocks or so surrounding Ken's Place had done a remarkable job of stubbornly rebuffing all but the most recent and aggressive attempts at gentrification, which kept the rent cheap.

Lucky us.

"Sister Red's, then," I said, almost licking my lips. It was Friday, and since there had been a delay to the League Finals on account of poor Akio Prince's disappearance, my friend Zoo wouldn't likely have anything on his busy purple schedule other than absorbing the sights and sounds of the Seoul nightlife … and whatever vengeance it might bring.

That, and I might get a few names out of the equation.

I told myself that all I wanted to do was rattle the cage—maybe rattle a few cages. I couldn't well traipse out into the streets in my League armor, all bright and glowy, and without my blades to accompany me. Much good they'd do me in a real, lead-filled scrap like the one I'd only just survived a few nights prior.

The gears were already turning, and the guilt rebuilding, when I closed the folder and went to turn toward the door. The back of my hand brushed against the brass key I'd swept aside earlier, and now I stared hard at it, caught between breaths. It looked familiar. The color and the rust, if not the shape.

A ghostly image of the wardrobe in Min's father's backroom dojo pushed its way to the front of my mind.

I smiled.

"Knew you'd come around," I said, flipping the key and its silver ring up and snatching it out of the air with a wince as my stitches pulled.

I dressed as quickly as I could, which wasn't all that quickly, considering. Once I had my League suit on, I took a gander in the full-length mirror on the opposite wall, next to the bay-view windows. I squeezed my fists and tested a few lazy jabs with my lead hand, catching the glow out of the corner of my eye as the red lines that bisected the resin plates on my shoulders and continued in twin lines down my arms and the sides of my legs responded to the motion, and lit with that bloody red glow.

I pushed less convenient thoughts aside as I passed through the living room, ignoring them as easily as I ignored the mindless prattle of the platinum blonde on the TV, with her salt-and-pepper co-host nodding sagely against a blue backdrop and over a blue and white ticker. I knew Min was using me—rather, that she was allowing me to be of use—like a hunter uses a pack of hounds and a bundle of smoking thatch above a fox den.

Min knew I was going to do something stupid. Might as well make it useful, and give the Seoul police—Min, at least—a fire to put out that might lead to a meaningful arrest that would precede another meaningless trial. It wasn't that there weren't any good legal suits in Seoul. It was that the best ones were from Tokyo.

I stepped down onto the mats of the dojo floor, feeling a little icky as the rubber soles of my boots scuffed the canvas, leaving black streaks behind. I flicked the switch on the wood paneling, listening to the ting and crackle as the lone hanging bulb flickered weakly to life.

The cherrywood shone like something frequently polished, at

least on the outside, and I focused on the brass lock separating the twin doors.

I sank the key in with a grinding sound and exhaled with a mix of reverence and regret as I twisted it to the right. There was a click, and I stepped back and pulled the handles, spreading my arms out to my sides as I opened the wardrobe.

It was difficult to see in the half light, so I stepped aside and let the bulb illuminate the shrine to Min's father, the only other thing approaching a father other than Kenta in my own life, however briefly it was for. I thought I glimpsed him for a moment, but then his face was gone, soft, strong eyes fading away to be replaced by the armored suit that should have been in a museum somewhere, or on a true shrine in the Okinawan islands, surrounded by diligent students and polished daily.

There was a red-scaled suit made up of a chest plate, shoulder and forearm greaves, and insteps that didn't so much glow as smolder. They hung from tightly wound threads on wooden pegs, and above the chest plate was a red mask in the style of a Shinto demon, with that wide mouth that was something between a sneer and a lion's roar. The nose was harsh and the eyes dark, and the mask seemed brighter than the rest of it. Brighter and bloodier all at once.

Just in front of the suit and below it, laid horizontally on gold-plated catches with obsidian poles beneath, was a sword that stretched from one cherrywood panel to the other. It was as wide as my wingspan with arms outstretched and fingers pointed, and as I reached for it, tentative, like a child expecting at any moment to be caught and reprimanded, I knew that I wasn't worthy of it.

It was heavier than I'd been expecting. I switched it to my left hand and went to unsheathe it, pulling harder than I needed to. As it turned out, Min had oiled it—must have done so recently— as it slipped free with a snake's hiss followed by a faint ring, like a Tibetan bowl.

I stood there, admiring the way the blade drank in the amber light of the flickering bulb and turned it to a sunset ribbon, like a river below the far horizon. As I turned the weapon over, I thought of my resin blades. I suppose I'd been playing at sword fighting long enough to think I knew what to expect when I put it into motion.

I laid the black scabbard down on its gold-dipped catches and did just that, angling slowly into a form I remembered from my younger days, when I'd been forced to practice them after angering Kenta. This is one I'd learned with a mop or a broom, if memory served, and each time I missed a step, delayed a pivot too long, or turned my body before my eyes, I'd have to put it to use cleaning the spotless dojo floors until I was convinced I'd actually rubbed all the dye from the canvas and made more of a mess than I'd cleaned.

Forms were always more Joon's speed than mine, which told you a lot about each of us.

When I put the katana into motion, it parted the still, damp air with the faintest whisper in the place of the whoosh and whistle I'd expected. It felt strange and unwieldy in my hands, but not for long. Soon enough, that sword and I made music together. Silent, humming music, fainter than the beating of a sparrow's wings. I left my plans to the side, and felt my anger ebbing away as I stepped and turned, guiding the bronze-colored length of steel until I felt as if I were being guided by it.

Minutes turned into an hour, and by the time I was done, I thought I understood the smallest piece of how the elders had claimed each blade had held a soul of its own. I thought this one was good, and a hell of a lot more pure than mine.

A part of me expected some sort of rejection. Maybe I'd angle wrong and slice the bare wire that held the buzzing bulb. Maybe I'd lose my grip and send the majestic thing tumbling to the mats with a hollow, bouncing thud. I didn't, and when I stopped and straightened, I gave the inanimate object a nod whose meaning I'd be hard-pressed to explain, even to myself.

I blinked myself back into the present and felt a trickle of thicker stuff beneath my armpits, mixing with the sweat. I'd pulled at my stitches and was starting to feel the sting as my suit rubbed against the irritated wound beneath. Not totally done, then.

I felt calm as I stepped up into the living room once more. It was getting dark, and a part of me felt foolish—what would Min think if she walked in right now and saw me standing in her living room, sweating bullets, dressed in my League suit and holding her dead father's naked blade? However, the greater part of me felt a growing sense of purpose, and one that turned me back down onto the mats and back in front of the open wardrobe.

League plate might not stop a bullet completely, and I don't know if this scale would either, but a combination of the two couldn't hurt. I left the katana leaning against the wall, observing me with its silent regard, and strapped the red-scaled pauldrons over my shoulders, the greaves to my forearms, pulled the chest plate over my black suit, and strapped the insteps to my shins.

I tested a few boxing combinations, feeling light and lean now that my muscles were warm. I saw the red glow of my League suit beneath the samurai armor, and came away thinking the marriage that should have been gaudy seemed somehow to fit. I told myself I strapped the red goblin mask on over my sweat-soaked hair because I feared recognition, but the truth was, I was in a theatrical mood.

I stood in the kitchen, trying not to catch my own ridiculous —admittedly quite badass—reflection in the now-darkened windows, waiting for night to fall in full. When it did, I snatched a tablet off the counter and pulled up a digital map of the city, trying to find the most nondescript route to Sister Red's.

I was feeling more clever than a spy when I managed to climb the wood fence—and then the six beyond it—without alerting any of Min's neighbors or their neighbors behind them. By the time I hit the more brightly lit areas as the quiet residential district ran up against the first bits of mechanized industry, I felt more like an alley cat.

In the comic books, the dark hero had no problem traversing the rooftops by night. It was as if the whole of any modern, twisted city had a city above the city, a vast network of interconnected walkways and alleys above blinding neon lights and flashing car lamps. Maybe that was true in Tokyo, or in the oldest of the new cities of America, but Seoul's skyline was too irregular for me to make a serious go of it. Instead, I stuck to the ground, basking—rather, slinking—through the shadows, largely ignored by the sorry lot who made them their homes.

Maybe it was too dark for them to catch me in full view—to wonder why some crazy was slinking around in samurai armor with a sword at his belt—or maybe they simply didn't care, confident that they were too far below the regard of even crazed criminals to fear any direct attention from one.

More than likely, some of them gave me up as a ghost of their subconscious—a passing wraith with a blood-red face and black eyes—and a reminder of their sins, and those of the new world.

Next time, maybe I'd forego the samurai getup and simply put on a hoodie and take the night bus.

I had grown so used to the odor of trash and refuse as I skulked in the brick-bordered alleys in the old part of town that I wasn't entirely sure I wasn't the source of it by the time I reached my destination.

The alleys weren't places for kids, not even street kids. I'd never hung around these parts, even though they were merely a stone's throw from the busy, bright and bustling intersections I'd spent most of my youth around. The alley I was in ended just ahead. It angled sharply to the right, forming an L that was only broken by a chain-link fence that bulged with the week's garbage.

I heard the blaring of horns and the beating of street drums, the pop and shake of car motors and the sharp whine of street bikes. Closer, I heard rusted, congealed hinges squeak as a back door opened, and I crouched low.

The door was a long time in closing. I listened past the malformed argument as some lowlife or other was sent packing —unceremoniously, by the sounds of things—by the undoubtedly lower lives that minded the door. They laughed as their latest discharge cursed them to the depths, and before the door closed, I heard the steady bass and odd tune of electronic dream music wafting out from the backrooms. It was the sort of music that was only hypnotic to those who were already held in the sway of booze, pills and whatever flesh happened to be on display on a Friday night in Central Seoul.

Sister Red's. No doubt about it.

I smiled beneath my mask as the door closed with a slick screech, and waited impatiently as the drunk who'd been wronged like no other patron before him made his slow, stumbling way out of the neighboring alley in search of the next most reputable establishment that would take him.

He'd be lucky to live out the night.

I closed my eyes, snaked my right hand across my waist and touched the hilt of the blade I'd borrowed. I took a steadying breath, trying to push down the creeping doubts.

What if Kuzu wasn't at home? What if he was in any number of his other local haunts, tending to his other seedy matters?

What was I doing?

"No choice," I said, knowing it wasn't true. I said it in a whisper, at first, and then repeated it, a little louder. "No choice. No choice. They have left me no choice."

It sounded like the rambling of a madman, like some personal mantra that had long since lost its meaning.

Trouble was, it worked.

By the time I opened my eyes, I had gone right past a slow simmer and was in the midst of a steady boil. My muscles tensed alongside my fingers, so much so that the slick pavement below me and the cement wall beside me began to take on the reflected glow of the red rivers in my suit as the resin came alive. The glow was one of an untold number of silent tells to my martial mind that my body would soon be called upon to act, and when the first adrenaline dump hit me—the hardest one to take—I breathed in and let it infuse my blood with that liquid fire.

Liquid courage, some liked to call it. And a hell of a lot more effective than anything you'd get over a beer-stained counter.

Liquid fear, Kenta had said. It had taken me a long time to understand what he meant by it. Adrenaline increased the senses not by degrees, but by orders of magnitude. Sights got sharper. Sounds got louder. Smells grew so intense you could taste them, but all of it was in service of preparing the body to fight … more probably, to flee in the face of morbid danger.

Kenta had always operated on the notion that there were two sorts of people in the world: predators and prey. The only thing that separated the one from the other was in how they dealt with that liquid fear when it first struck.

Most would let it flood their veins, constrict their heart and clench their throat, make their teeth chatter and their eyes blink more rapidly than a strobe. Most would want to run, and most would be so caught in the grips of their own body's chemical infusion that even that craven, intelligent act would prove beyond them.

But some would stand for a different reason. Some would clench their fists and their jaws. Some would crouch not in fear, but in preparation. These were predators, and despite the name, there was nothing inherently evil in considering oneself among them.

The world needed predators, just as it needed prey. What was I out here for, basking in the damp shadows of the city that had raised me even as it had abandoned me, if not to hunt?

When the rusted hinges started their irritating squeal anew, I tensed, feeling the muscles of my thighs bunch and the rubber stretch. The lines in my suit flashed as if responding to the beating of my heart, so much so that the door guards stopped their throaty exchange, caught between breaths.

"What's that glo—"

I pressed down hard with my back foot, the light resin boot of my League suit allowing me to feel the bumps and grooves in the pavement as I did, and tore into the neighboring alley like I'd been fired out of a cannon.

I moved my eyes before my head as I streaked toward the open door, taking in the pair of black suits who stood just outside—one leaning with his back to the green door, the other with his head turned toward me, body away, one foot propped up on the cement stair.

"The fu—"

I shouldered into that one hard enough that I felt a crunch as the ball sank too quickly into its socket, crushing all the soft, sinuous stuff between it and the smooth joint that stopped it. The man's collarbone snapped, unable to stop the momentum, and he went down in an agonized tangle, rolling violently and reaching for his belt as he did.

His partner detached himself from the open door and started down after me.

A fellow predator, then. I almost smiled, but let the mask do it for me. These two weren't wearing shades, so I could see the white edges take their eyes as they responded to a sudden threat they likely hadn't had time to fully process before it was on them. As I raised my right foot up and slammed it down on the leg of the first thug, grimacing as the shin bone snapped underfoot, I wondered absently if these two had been the ones that had accompanied dear old Zoo on his midnight ride.

I glanced at the one I'd struck, my eyes darting to his hands, which had dropped the black implement he'd pulled from his waist and were now clutched around his shin, cradling it like a babe. The gun I'd expected revealed itself as a baton. Nasty thing in the right hands—or the wrong—but not nasty enough to land you in prison for carrying.

A shadow passed over my face and I raised my left arm at an angle, accepting the blow of the hard black resin, preparing for the dull pain to ring through my forearm as it connected. The extra armor, as it turned out, wasn't just for show, and I barely felt the blow as I turned it aside, wrapped the swinging arm with my blocking one and used the bottom step as a launching pad, ramming my left shoulder into the goon's chin.

He fell back just before the door completed its swing. Lucky for me and unlucky for him, his head was big enough and wide enough to act as a doorstop. He squirmed and reached up, bracing against the frame, and I pressed my knee down into the center of his chest, feeling the air wheeze out as I did. I hooked my right hand into the door and took just enough pressure off of his temples to bring his attention down to the more immediate concern—namely, the glowing red demon crouched atop his chest.

A part of me experienced a thrill I hadn't expected at the fear
—the true fear, now—I saw in those eyes.

"Who the ... hell—"

A little more pressure stopped that quick enough, and this
one's fellow goon wasn't coming to his aid anytime soon. He
was still writhing and whining at the bottom of the steps, close
enough for the bustling street to see and hear him, and far
enough for any with half a brain to ignore him.

"Consequence," I said, hissing it out with even more venom
than I'd intended.

He tried to say something else, but his eyes were enraptured
by the red glow along the suit veins of my right arm. They
widened in a mix of pain and horror as I moved it slowly across
his field of view, wrapping my black leather fingers around the
red-roped hilt of the katana. He frowned a bit, as if he didn't
quite believe it, so I eased the top inch of the hilt free with my
thumb, allowing the ruby glow to catch the steel.

"What ..."

I eased up ever so slightly, conscious of the chaotic wash of
sound coming from the deeper darkness of the club. There was a
purple haze to it, and smells that mixed sweat with cigar smoke
from the backrooms. Still, I heard no signs of pursuit. Seemed
these two thugs were the only means of defense that Sister Red's
had these days.

"What do you want?" he wheezed out when he had enough
space in his lungs to do so. I pressed back down as soon as the
question was out, delighting in the way he squirmed beneath
me. Maybe this was one of Goro's men or maybe he was an inde-
pendent lowlife. Either way, he was the worst sort of predator. I
could see it in his eyes, and it went a long way toward erasing
any guilt or cousin doubt that might try to worm its way into the
back recesses of my mind.

"The right question," I said, putting a bit of gravel into my
voice. It was doubtful anyone would recognize me by sound
alone, but, there weren't too many vigilantes running around
with red glowing League suits these days. Shinto mask and
armor notwithstanding, a discerning eye would likely make me

immediately. Perhaps they'd think me Akio Prince's killer and thief rather than the true thing.

"Kuzu Tokoro," I said, drawing it out. I showed him my teeth in that wide mask's grin. His brow crinkled in thought when I eased up again, allowing the pain to recede enough for him to think without forgetting it entirely.

"Zoo …"

Now his eyes widened.

"Ah," I said. "He's at home, then."

A quick nod.

"Not the most loyal hound."

Despite his current predicament, this one wasn't quite as cowardly as he appeared. He spit, but made sure to turn his head and aim it at the cement rather than his accoster.

"Zoo doesn't own me," he said, even going so far as to raise his chin, as if it made him proud to say it. As if some other local mob boss or underling didn't own him. "He's in there." He nodded toward the purple darkness beyond the door. "Room 6. Same as always." He went to say more, then hesitated.

I pressed down, conscious that the whimpering of the thug behind me had died down some. He'd be getting up as soon as I was out of sight, was likely judging his chances of making a run for it on a broken leg even now. Would he make it to the street before the Red Demon of Seoul was on him, blade flashing, mouth grinning?

"Spit it out," I said. "What were you going to say just then?"

"He …" he coughed, but I didn't let up this time. "He ain't alone, ghosty."

I made a show of looking up into the hallway, taking in the flickering lights and the faint sounds of womanly laughter. Might have even been some moaning beneath it.

"I figured as much."

"No," he said, oddly persistent. "Not girls. Zoo's … always got company. You'll see."

My heart beat faster of its own accord, before I'd even worked over the implications. I stood, ignoring the sounds of coughing and retching as the thug rolled onto his side and curled up, greedily forcing air into his bruised chest and aching ribs. I stared into the gloom, my eyes adjusting on an agonizing delay.

Goro? Could he be talking about Goro, or one of his underlings? What luck, to find Zoo entrenched in such a seedy establishment, and with just the sort of company I'd hoped to find him in.

I smiled to myself as I pulled the door open a bit wider, letting the rusted hinges squeal as the metal slab clicked shut behind me.

11

THE DEMON IN ROOM 6

I didn't have long. Soon enough, the thug on the stairs would be up and around the corner, squawking into his mobile to anyone but the police.

Now that my eyes had adjusted some to the gloom, I saw that purple glow emanating from a bend in the hallway. I took a step forward, but instinct made me pause.

"Bursa!"

I flinched at the volume and closeness of the shout. As it receded, I heard footsteps coming toward me.

"Coen! You two lock yourselves out again? We've got one of the locals making a—"

I flattened myself against the wall as the woman—more a girl, by the looks of her—came into view. She blinked at the sudden change in lighting, and I cursed myself as I forgot the red light on my League suit.

As her eyes moved from the closed door at the back of the hall over to me, I sprang into motion, slamming her against the opposite wall harder than I had intended and closing my hand over her mouth, stifling the ensuing scream.

Her eyes widened as she took in the leering mask and the dark eyes behind it. I could feel her heart beating, even through my armor.

"Shhh."

I let it out slowly, and withdrew half an inch, enough to let her breathe. I kept my hand firmly pressed until I was sure she was focused on me and saw me as a real thing, and not some strange, horrifying fever dream.

"I'm not here for you," I said. "Not you."

I let the implication stand, that I was here for someone, and that they weren't going to be happy to see me. Keep the threat there, lest she get any ideas.

"I'm going to remove my hand, and when I do, you're going to be quiet."

She nodded a little too hurriedly for my liking. I looked her in the eyes. They were a pretty hazel. She looked to be a mix of Korean and something else. Maybe Swedish, and she was older than I'd first thought her to be. Certainly old enough to be working in a place like this, but dressed much more conservatively than most females in the establishment would be.

"What's your name?"

I withdrew and she released a quivering sigh, clutching one hand in the other. Her eyes roved over the rest of my gaudy, ridiculous getup. They lingered on the hilt at my waist, and I gave a slight nod, showing her that, while I was undoubtedly crazy, I certainly wasn't in a harmless way.

Still, she did well to hide her fear, or to gain control of it.

"I'd rather not say."

"Smart."

"Thank you."

I heard a door open from the hall and sank into a crouch, watching her eyes as she leaned to look. My hand began to stray unconsciously toward my belt. When she looked back at me and gave a nod, my hand was back by my side.

"How many in the front room?"

"Are you going to hurt them?" she asked.

"That depends on them. I'm here for someone in particular."

She frowned, gauging the truth of my words. Her eyes twitched toward the hallway. There was a slight buzzing in the air, the work of the neon signs that hung above the door frames of the private rooms.

"Room 6," I said, remembering.

Her look was confirmation, and it showed me just what I wanted it to. Zoo might count Sister Red's as one of his regular haunts. Maybe even considered it a second home to him. But, if the doorman and this gal were anything to go by, he had yet to make many friends here.

"He ..." she started and then stopped. I took a step toward her, looming. It did the trick. "He's not alone."

"So I hear."

She watched me, swallowing as my eyes fixed on hers, unblinking.

She nodded toward the hallway. "Last one."

I lingered on her a moment longer and then started away.

"You didn't kill them."

The way she said it had me frowning back at her. She was looking toward the metal door to the alley. When she looked back at me, I had a frightening impression that she saw right through the mask.

"I'm sure someone else will, given enough time," I said.

"Same could be said for a lot of us," she answered, evenly.

I didn't know what to say to that, and I had no way of knowing she wouldn't immediately fetch help, but I left her standing there in the purple darkness as I stalked the buzzing, flickering hallway toward door number six, and the purple man inside.

Soon enough, I found myself standing before the door, bathed in the sick glow of the flickering bulbs overhead. They were hot and had me sweating in my suit and mask. I looked up, and saw that the source of the purple glow was the paneling above, translucent sheets of melted plastic with tangled wires in the crawlspaces. No escaping through the vents in this place, not like you saw in the movies.

Then again, I hadn't exactly come dressed for subtlety.

I listened for a short while, unable to suss anything out beyond the rhythmic thumping bass. There were five other doors, some slightly ajar and empty, others playing host to their own private parties. There was a red glow not far removed from the colors of my suit and armor coming from the far end, and a louder, more insistent thumping coming from the direction of the main room.

I don't know why I stood there as long as I did. Maybe I wanted to be seen by more of the help, like the girl I could still feel watching my back, eyes an expectant smolder, almost hungry to see what I'd do.

I looked down at the doorknob—painted in gaudy drips, like everything else in the place—and was surprised to see my hand shaking as my covered fingers brushed against the brass.

Oh, Akio. What are you getting yourself into now?

I sighed and closed my eyes, steadied myself. When I opened them, my hand was closed around the knob. I twisted and pushed, and when I moved into the stuffy room on the other side, the cloud of cigar and weed smoke must have obscured me enough to make me grow into an approximation of the demon whose skin I had donned.

"Jeon!"

A violent fit of coughing came from one of the seated shadows on the couch across the way.

"Jeon! That you?" He waved in front of his face, trying to clear a path through the smoke as I let the door close softly behind me. "We need a new girl in here. Thought you went to fetch one. Other one's used up. She quit on it, hit the showers. April, or whatever her name—"

"June," the other shadow put in. My throat tightened and I felt my fists clench absent of conscious command. I knew the voice. It was steady as a snake with just a bit of gravel on the bottom. "Her name is June."

"June, right," the other said. The smoke had cleared enough so that I could clearly mark the positions of their hands and legs. The speaker, chest still shaking with a silent fit of coughing he was struggling to get control of, held something out to the other, who sat still. He ignored the chatty one and leaned forward, trying to peer through the murk.

"Put that damn shit out," he said. "Can't see a thing in here."

"Jeon—"

"It's not Jeon, you idiot! Look at the size of him."

"Ah," the first one said. "Bursa or Coen? Jeon send you in here to clear us out? Well, we'll pay for another hour. Just tell her that. We'll even tip. Hey, what's—"

My eyes found the movement as Zoo squeezed his friend's knee, willing him to silence. As the mist cleared enough to admit a bit more than hints and shadows, I took in the layout of the room, and everything happening in it.

There was a long, short table just before me and just a foot or so in front of the damp, stained couch the shadows sat on. There was a rack to my left, and I could see a heavy coat with a blue marking leering at the corners. Some distant part of my mind recognized the symbol, but I was too focused on the two before me to pay it much mind.

Zoo's hand shifted from his friend's knee and flashed into his waistband. I guessed it wasn't the first time he'd done it tonight, but I knew the intent here wasn't quite the same as it might've been when June was dancing.

"That's not June, you twit!"

His hand flashed out just a hair slower than mine, and the blue and purple of the LED lights strung across the ceiling admitted flashes of two distinct sorts of metal. Zoo brandished his gray stock, while I opted for something cleaner. Something that would have drunk in and sent back the reflected light of the moon and stars overhead had we been in the open fields of an ancient valley.

Kuzu Tokoro hadn't been fast enough for the League. Even if he hadn't been matched up with Korain in the first round, he'd have run into Dae, or Kwan, or Sang Hee, or Kaya Brent.

He certainly wasn't fast enough now. Not for me.

There was a spark as my cross-body swipe met the gray barrel and sent the gun spinning away. It hit the edge of the table and tumbled to the floor, lost in the steam and smoke that was now settling to waist level. Zoo did well not to cry out, but I'd caught one of his fingers with the slash. He gripped his bloody hand to his chest, leaning over double and rocking like someone in a ward.

His friend blinked dumbly at him before he turned his slow, dumb, still-blinking eyes over to me.

"Wh …" he started. "What …"

I stood before them in all my strange, nightmarish glory, right hand held out, sword tip nearly brushing the wall. The red veins of my suit pulsated with the ruby glow that washed the room and took it over, poured into the grooves of my mask and lit the ridges of the scales and greaves on my shoulders, chest and legs.

"This man," I started, leveling the tip of the katana just under Zoo's chin, close enough to graze the stubble, "is Kuzu Tokoro." I tried to keep any inflection from my voice, but I sounded hungry. I was, in a manner of speaking. I remembered the overpass, and being under it. "He is guilty."

To his credit, Zoo didn't quake in his overpriced white sneakers, just stared at me with that one good eye. The patch on the other had been knocked askew, showing a hint of the pink and red horror beneath it.

I turned my head slightly to look at the other man. This one did quake. I didn't have to ask if he was guilty. His face showed it. I almost didn't have to ask who he was, as his eyes kept switching from me to the black table just in front of him. I followed the direction of his rabbit's gaze, feeling like a hawk, and settled on a black leather wallet stuffed to the brim with the colored paper that made an establishment like this tick without the need of pesky trails in banking systems.

There was something next to it. A small cut of metal, like a pin … or a badge.

"Well, well well," I said, eyes fixing on the emblem. Now I recognized the insignia on the jacket hanging by the door. "Bit of a seedy establishment for one of Seoul's finest to find himself in, isn't it?"

He swallowed, and, if it were possible, began sweating even more profusely than he had been. He'd let the joint in his right hand burn all the way to the tip, and yelped like a startled cat as the embers burned the tips of his fingers. He shook it out and sucked on it like a pig.

"Lost, officer?"

I felt Zoo shifting on his sodden cushion and pressed the razor tip of the katana up past his bristles so it touched the skin, delighting in the slight whimper he made. He held his hands out to his sides.

The officer cleared his throat. I tried to place him, but my association with Min had only given me a passing acquaintance with a small number of the untold thousands of officers within the city limits. This one was middle-aged and stupid.

"What do you want?" Zoo growled. He was made of stronger stuff than I'd imagined. Even now, his eye kept glancing back at the door, as if he expected a royal retinue to barge in at any moment to free him from the demon's grasp.

"A great many things," I said. "But tonight, I'll settle for names."

He made a strange sound. I didn't quite recognize it until I realized it was laughter. Careful laughter, enough to keep his throat from being split on the end of the blade that pressed up against it, but laughter nonetheless. It made me angry, and it made me come close to losing control, which made me angrier still.

"Something funny?"

Even officer so-and-so seemed to share my shock. He stared wide-eyed at the criminal seated next to him as if he were crazier than the sword-brandishing demon standing over them.

"Names," Zoo said. I could tell he wanted to shake his head in the most condescending way possible. I remembered that about him from the Soul Dome, when a few weeks prior he'd first fetched me to be invited among Goro's esteemed, august company, and again when he'd come upon Joon and me after my win over Kwan, a not-so-subtle reminder of the debt I owed on the back of a loan I'd never asked for or been granted. "They always want names, and I always tell them the same thing."

"What's that, Mr. Tokoro?" I asked, gritting my teeth and pressing the edge of the blade just a little farther, enough to draw a bright-red droplet of blood that sparkled like a twisting ruby in the light.

"There's only one that matters," Zoo said, all pretense of humor dropped. He looked at me dead on, unflinching.

We stayed like that for a time, staring. To break it, I pulled the tip of the blade away. Zoo relaxed visibly, and now I saw the sweat standing out on his brow. Instead of sheathing the sword, I continued to pull it away, until the dull back was hovering just above my left shoulder. Zoo frowned.

"I suppose you're right," I said, my tone flat, and—judging by the panicked expression on the face of Zoo's associate—just the way I intended. "Guess I won't be needing anything more out of you, after all."

I twitched my right hand forward, red suit veins flashing, but the officer's loud, mewling plea stopped me.

"Wait!"

I stopped, and Zoo held still as he looked from the razor's edge of the katana over to the other man without so much as twisting his neck.

"Surely there's something we can work out here."

Strange. I hadn't even threatened this one. But then, I suppose it stood to reason he assumed I'd kill him just as soon as Zoo was dead.

Whatever works.

"Bold of you, to wear that coat in here, bring that badge in here, where anyone could see. Unless ..." I drew it out for dramatic effect, mildly concerned at how easily I had begun to put a character together to match my getup, "...you're here to arrest Kuzu Tokoro for another of his heinous misdeeds." My two eyes swiveled to Zoo's one and held his gaze long enough to call up something I wanted to be recognition, but likely wasn't. "Including his very recent ones."

Now his eye twitched down, looking past the red-scale armor and the blade I held. Now, he saw the black resin and the red-ruby veins. His eyebrows raised, and when next he looked up into my eyes beneath the demon's mask, he seemed afraid. I hadn't realized how much I'd needed to see it.

Ironically, the look saved Zoo's life, brought me off the killing edge. At least, it would have, if he'd have been less brave and more craven, like the city's protector that sat next to him.

As it turned out, the aforementioned Bursa or Coen—whichever one whose leg I hadn't shattered—had managed to rustle up something approaching a local militia. This was more than likely made up of whatever criminals or ne'er-do-wells from the main room who were drunk or sober enough to make a try for a madman with a sword.

The door was unlocked, but even if they'd known it, I doubt they would have spared us the dramatic entrance. I heard the girl I'd come upon squeak as she heard them approach. She sounded as if she'd had her ear to the door, listening to the macabre scene inside and likely imagining me inflicting all manner of horrors on Zoo and Officer So-and-so.

I grimaced, my eyes holding Zoo's one in the moments before the latch shattered and the half-dozen sacks of beef poured themselves into the squat, smoky room, brandishing everything from broom handles to switchblades.

I thought of carving Zoo's throat right there, but the longer I spent in that room with an unsheathed katana, the more bodies I'd make, and the greater the chance some of them wouldn't quite have deserved it.

I whirled toward the door and took a bearded, vaguely Russian-looking fellow in the temple with a backhand swing of the sword's hilt. He went over with a dramatic crash, breaking all manner of cheap ceramic crap made to evoke the sort of Eastern erotic mysticism westerners ate up when they were in town.

Not killing the rest of them proved difficult. A left punch to the gut folded the next in line, but the two behind him managed to tangle me in a grapple that only an easy slash across their twin midsections freed me from. These were the drunkest, showing less valor and more liquid courage as they swung their lazy hammer fists and jabbed their sharp edges at me, oblivious to the mortal danger they were in.

One knife did find a place between the red scales of my chest plate, but the resin beneath it did the trick. I stepped back as far as I could, turning at an angle so quickly the blade snapped—

cheap make—and the wrist behind followed soon enough, as I brought the hilt down on top of it with a crunch.

One of my tall, dark and ugly victims from the alley watched it all wide-eyed from the doorway. He held the night stick I'd already seen once tonight, but didn't seem overly thrilled at the prospect of using it, nor at the now-dwindling chances his hastily assembled team had of taking me down.

A hard knee to the gut finished the job of folding the knife-wielder all the way down, and the next in line released me and actually surprised me by making an intelligent choice in the midst of the chaos.

He went down, diving to the side with a look of such unbridled fear, I could have blushed. Bursa/Coen followed after, shielding his eyes and falling back in a strange, lurching panic that saw him drop his weapon, and it was beginning to dawn on me that I wasn't the only scary thing in the room, even if I was the craziest.

I heard the click as the hammer stretched back past its first catch. I didn't have time to spin before the next click, which could undoubtedly discharge the bullet from Zoo's regathered gun right into my spine, making the immortal Demon of Seoul anything but.

Lucky for me—and unlucky for the pair of men—sport fighting had been the least of Kenta's concerns when it came to training Joon, Min and me to face the dangers of a world that had gone through chaos and come out trailing its vapors.

I felt the corner of the knee-high table against the back of my thigh and lanced a kick back, catching the leg and driving the surprisingly heavy thing back across the dingy carpet with speed. Zoo cried out as the corner slammed into his knee and spun him round.

The gun discharged, and I only knew it went wide of the mark because I didn't collapse in a twitching heap before I got to him.

I brought my right hand around, the hilt of the katana gripped tightly in my palm, its edge singing its faint, keening song as it parted the murk and whipped across. I felt the faintest

impression of resistance, but my hips were twisted wrong, so I
spun back the other way, leveling the blade in front of me as I
prepared to take Zoo's hand with the next chop.

He stood there facing me, his one eye wide, both hands down
at his sides, shaking. The gray metal gun was still held loosely in
his right hand. It clattered to the ground like an ended statement. I saw his mouth open first, his jaw going slack, and then a
thin red line appeared across the exposed flesh of his throat. It
opened a bit wider as he leaned, the droplets turning to a trickle
that became a syrupy pour as he fell forward, breaking the table
and landing face first on the floor just in front of me.

Quite dead.

As it turned out, he wasn't the only one. Officer So-and-so
should have let out a scream like the coward I knew him to be.
Instead, he, too, had slumped over, and when I pulled my eyes
from Zoo's prone form and traced them up to the couch, I saw
the resting place of the bullet he'd discharged, his aim off on
account of my maneuver.

The effect on the next gallant heroes who'd charged in to
save the day was pronounced. One let out a roar and made for
me. I only turned toward him, giving him the full view of my
blood-red mask—more so, of the eyes beneath. I knew how I
looked in that moment because I knew how I felt.

Numb.

He froze there in mid-stride, hand cocked back. He allowed
himself to be led from the room, and I heard shuffled footsteps
and squealing as they dragged one of the fallen drunks across the
laminate floors of some back kitchen.

I heard muffled shouts and knew the police—the real ones,
likely with Min in tow—would be along in short order.

I turned in a daze, flinching as I noticed a figure standing just
outside the doorway.

The girl from earlier. She stood there, staring, not looking
nearly as frightened as she should have, given the circumstances.

I didn't know what look to show her and I didn't know what
to say, so I simply sheathed the blade that wasn't mine, and

made for the hall. She stepped aside to let me pass. I turned back and forced myself to look upon the scene I'd caused.

I'd been wrong. It wasn't numbness I'd felt. It was something else. Something close to shock but not nearly so crippling.

The truth was, I'd seen Zoo. It had happened quickly, and I'm not sure I could have halted the momentum of the swing even if I'd tried, but I had seen him, because Kenta had always taught us to strike with our eyes before our bodies. I had seen him, and I'd seen the path the katana was about to make, and the pitiful resistance it was about to meet.

I hadn't tried to pull it back.

Rattle the cages. That's what I'd told Min I wanted to do tonight. That's what I'd told myself, right up until the moment I found myself inside one. As I cast one last look at Kuzu Tokoro and his bloody sins, I didn't feel guilt.

I won't say it felt right. I won't couch it in justice or gild it with false claims of honor. But I'll tell you, here and now, it felt more than a little far away from wrong.

It wasn't the killing that would scare me later. It wasn't the way I'd gone from glowing toy blades to a real one as easily as a kid playing a VR game. It wasn't the fact that Goro and his Seoul-based ilk would be after me in force, just as I'd wanted them to.

It was the fact that it had been so easy.

"Who are you?" the girl asked as I moved toward the back door, wondering almost absently if I'd meet a hail of bullets on the other side.

I paused and kept staring straight ahead.

"Just a ghost," I said.

It didn't feel like a lie.

12

CONSEQUENCE

I should have felt some relief at the fact that I'd just survived a chaotic situation I had no business coming through unscathed. But the silence had stretched for half an hour already, and any silence with Min at its heart was one wont to make a grown man quake in his boots.

Especially if he knew her.

You know how a tsunami is always preceded by a slow ebbing away of the tide? Like the coast—the whole world, for that matter—is taking a long, considered breath, expelling its sins before accepting the wave of death and destruction? That was the silence Min wore as she moved about the kitchen of the home she'd grown up in and that I had invaded, doing everything she could to keep from glancing at me as I worked through a bowl of oatmeal and thumbed through every amateur blog and social media page I could, searching for mentions of what had happened last night.

Nothing. Not a peep.

On the one hand, it was a good thing. Searches for Akio Prince came up with two-day-old stories about the latest tragedy to befall an enemy of Goro of the Hachinin. Of course, they never mentioned his name.

Kuzu Tokoro was more of a ghost than I was, apparently. Not

even an offhand mention. It seemed Goro kept those close to him out of the media.

I'd become so absorbed in my fruitless and increasingly frustrating search that I'd failed to notice Min's absence from my field of view. Always a dangerous thing.

This time, I hadn't just done something stupid. I'd done it while wearing the armor and wielding the sword her father had kept as an heirloom—perhaps an unanswered prayer—to ancient murderers time had changed to the approximation of heroes.

I saw a blur of gray and white come at me from my periphery, and nearly tipped over in my chair as I leaned back to avoid what would surely be a killing blow. Not that I didn't deserve it, but still, being bludgeoned to death by a former lover turned friend wasn't my ideal going-out party.

Min slammed the thick pile of paper onto the oak table so hard I swore one of the cracks sprouted legs that made spiders out of the amber whorls. I blinked, trying to suss out what it was, as Min's palm pressed it down, veins standing out on the top of her hand. I could feel her eyes on me, but didn't dare meet them.

"Is that a newspaper?"

She made a sound at the question that was an odd mix of annoyance and amusement. Less of the latter.

"Didn't know they still printed any."

"Not many," Min said, dragging her palm and fingers away from the black and white pile, seemingly with effort. "But there are still a few hangers-on." I looked up at her, my eyebrows raised questioningly. She sighed and put her hands on her hips. She was still dressed in her work clothes. Well, the clinging, disheveled clothes she wore under her work clothes. "I never canceled mom's subscription to the Seoul Sentinel."

I nodded in a way I only recognized as condescending by the look Min returned. I hadn't actually bothered to look at the headline, still sodden and slick with the sheen of fresh ink.

I dragged the pile toward me and turned it. I frowned, blinked and wiped away sleep that hadn't threatened me on the slow passage of night to morning, knowing what images would await me in my dreams.

'Sword PUNK' Makes Mince of Local Thug

I read it once, then twice.

"Punk," I said absently. "PUNK," with more force. I looked up at Min, who regarded me with hands still firmly planted on hips. Now she looked less like one considering homicide and more like a mother considering how not to go through with it. "Why did they capitalize it?"

"That's what you took from the article?"

"I didn't read the article, yet."

Min gestured impatiently. I sighed and dove in.

The feature was written in a style that struck me as old-timey, inverse-pyramid, albeit poorly taught. I suppressed the urge to roll my eyes as I searched out the pertinent bits. He talked about the death of said 'thug,' albeit without mentioning his name or that of his less than august employer. He went into gory, colorful detail on the state of the backroom, and the manner of poor Zoo's end. He didn't exactly exult in it, but he certainly didn't condemn the act.

When pressed for the identity of the attackers—likely a rival gang or an international outfit (possibly Scandinavian) who would move with such open hostility toward the powers that be in bloodless Seoul— witnesses offered little in the way of detail, albeit to claim—and to a person—that the bloody deed was accomplished by a single attacker, from the incapacitation of the doormen (highly trained mercenaries, according to local law enforcement) to the near-decapitation of their lord underling.

I skimmed the repeated account of the assault, near as the writer's 'witnesses' described it. They got enough right to let me know they'd been to the scene, and enough wrong to let me know my lonely corridor girl hadn't opened her mouth. Toward the middle, he looped in the bar manager, and thus, I learned the origin of my now-dubious title.

Mickie Sinz (this writer was unable to ascertain the authenticity of the proprietor's name), noticeably agitated about the night's events due to the unwanted attention it might bring from all sides, referred to the perpe-trator as 'some sword-strapped punk,' pausing in his tirade long enough to

acknowledge that he had to have serious training, or a serious lack of
sense, to do what he'd done as quickly as he'd done it. After all, our
sources inform us that firearms were recovered from the scene, which
matched black market records for the deceased. The casings recovered on-
site were fired from the same barrel, meaning our so-called 'punk' appar-
ently did bring a knife to a gun-fight.

What followed was a series of twice-baked theories layered atop nonsense about who this mysterious, obviously well-funded and highly trained attacker might be. The writer seemed hell-bent on discovering who was pulling my strings, despite the fact that all of his interview subjects seemed to be under the impression that I was simply crazy, or hopped up on any manner of chemical cocktails, and would never be seen or heard from again, either because you-know-who would be dealing with me, or because I wasn't likely to get so lucky with a blade against suits and gunpowder a second time.

Min had been following my progress, or guessing at it. She pulled her chair out with a slow grinding sound that she knew I felt like nails on a chalkboard. She sat with a heavy thud. It was enough to make me forget the trouble I was in and start a bit of my own annoyance to simmer.

I pushed the brick of paper away, wondering how they still managed to stuff enough op-eds and coupons into the package to derail a train day after day.

"Happy now?" she asked. She had her arms crossed and was tapping her index finger on her forearm. She looked tired, and I felt another pang of guilt because of it.

"Not particularly," I allowed. I flicked my chin toward the paper. "Still don't understand why they felt the need to jam the caps lock on—"

"Akio!"

"What?"

"You killed a man last night!"

That brought a fresh swallow. I noticed that she didn't say I'd killed two men last night.

"You killed a man wearing my father's armor, and wielding my father's sword." She shook her head and blew out a shuddering sigh that seemed to bring her close to the breaking point, but she closed her eyes and steadied herself. It looked like it took effort. "We can deal with all that … mess," she waved her hand around in a meaningless gesture, "later. The point is, your cage-rattling, if you want to call it that, didn't go the way you thought."

"How would you know?" I couldn't help the edge in my voice, and knew it sounded defensive. I may as well write Min's argument for her, but I was done having it. A man was dead on the end of my wrath.

"Akio …" She sounded defeated more than exasperated.

"That was Kuzu Tokoro I … ended, Min," I said, "no saint. Not some small-time thug. Not the door muscle I bruised up to get to him. Not the dirty cop—another one—I decided to scare the shit out of rather than end alongside him. Zoo botched it." She winced at that. I didn't know if that meant the department had told them or kept a lid on it. Maybe the investigators had managed to move his body to another scene. More damage control. Everyone had a PR department now, even the police.

"That's not my point, Akio—"

"Then what is your point, Min? What exactly did you think I was going to do? These sorts of people don't threaten. And they only speak one language. It just so happens to be the one we've been trained in most of our lives."

"They're not calling you a hero, Akio," Min said, surprisingly calm. "They're calling you a punk, and the way you've been acting, I'm not entirely inclined to disagree." I ground my teeth. She must have seen my jaw working. "You haven't made a state-ment. You've made a scene. You can't fight the Hachinin on your own, Akio. Taking down Zoo is like flicking a flea off a lion's back."

I reached for the paper and scooped it back up, waving it like a victory flag. "This is a start," I said, and before Min could argue, I plopped it back down and snatched the tablet back up.

"You're not in the news, Akio," she said. "You're not trending …"

She frowned, likely at my smirk.

"No," I said, turning the screen toward her. "But it looks like more folks in this lonely city are carrying their mothers' ancient subscriptions than either of us thought."

She let out a clipped laugh, but still came away with a shake. "A few mentions of 'Sword PUNK' on the—"

"Scroll," I said. Now it was her working her jaw. She tore her eyes from mine and set to it. I waited.

"Akio, it's hardly flattering. Your accidental alter ego is more meme than—"

"It's a start," I said, leaning back. I must have looked like the picture of victory.

"A start to what?" she asked, dubious. "Your glorious insurrection? You think the people are going to rise up and follow you in that fucking armor as you prance right up to Goro's palace and wring his neck to the adulation of the masses, the weeping of babes and the swooning of—"

"That," I interrupted, "or, more likely, the increased attention will flush out the rats I'm hunting."

"The wolves, you mean."

"This is the Far East, Min. Wolves don't rule these lands. Tigers do."

She raised her eyebrows at that. She'd had a lot of practice, dealing with Joon and me. Even Kenta, to a lesser degree.

"And you fancy yourself a tiger, do you?" Min's tone showed that she saw me as being closer to an alley cat.

"It doesn't matter what I see myself as, Min," I said. "It matters what the people see me as, and what Goro and his ilk fear me as. It matters what I can do in a room with a sword or two. It matters who I can do it to."

She pursed her lips, forming a star, and apparently thought better of furthering yesterday's argument. I was already a dead man and Min knew it. What was doom to a dead man?

"I'm not a dragon slayer yet, Min," I allowed. "But Zoo was a beast all the same. It's a start, even if we can't see the end."

"What if it's a quick end, Akio?"

"Then I'll do my best to make it a bright one. One the talking heads won't be able to ignore."

I jabbed my thumb over my shoulder toward the flickering light coming from the living room, where the day's news—absent tales of punks, swords and recently deceased lowlifes—tumbled loose from red lips and polished porcelain teeth.

Min looked right through me, just as she had when I'd first revealed my idiotic, Pyrrhic, utterly selfish plan to her the first time.

A symbol to the people? A ray of hope in a sea of neon lights most were too enamored with to see the teeth they concealed?

Who was I kidding?

"Convince yourself before you try to convince me, Akio," she said, standing up. She filled a mug with coffee that had already gone cold.

I let her cool a bit.

"What was the word at the precinct?"

"What do you think?" she asked sarcastically, after taking a swallow and grimacing, either at the taste or the question. "Discounting whoever it was you saw in Zoo's company—reports haven't come in yet, and there are a lot of cops in Seoul—and whoever he was friendly with in the department, the mood was one of … say, jubilation?" She half turned toward me. I wasn't smiling.

"They're not looking for me … er, the killer, then?"

"Looking is a strong word for whatever it is we're meant to be doing to track down Kuzu Tokoro's killer, Akio. He wasn't exactly a shining beacon."

I stared dumbly for a little too long, and Min's brow crinkled as she considered the look.

"You really think we're that bad, huh?" She set her mug down with a clang on the marble that threatened to chip it. "You think we're so overgrown with bad weeds that we'd be hunting down Zoo's killer on one of Goro's errands."

I settled for a shrug. "I mean, there was a cop—"

"A dead one, now. There have always been dirty cops, Akio," Min said, pressing a palm to her forehead. "Dare I say, there always will be, so long as they're human. But no, Akio, the department isn't after you, even if they are officially." She looked earnest. "There are a lot of good people behind the blue, if you'd only give them the chance."

"See, Min," I said, "I fear we don't need any more good people in uniform. Near as I can tell, the world could use a little bad to cancel out the worst."

I thought she might shout me down on that one. Instead, she smiled. "That what you think you are, Akio? A bad man?"

"Doesn't much matter what I think."

"You only think it matters what you do," she said. "How could it?"

"How could it not?"

Min opened her mouth to speak, looked toward the door as if she expected someone to walk through it, and then looked back at me.

"I was never the conscience of the group, even if I did enforce the rules," Min said.

I nearly smiled as I took her meaning, but the thought of who it was about gave me pause.

"Akio," she started, "you need to talk to him—"

I stood up and made a show of stretching. Min gave me a sad stare that turned into a withering one. She went to speak again, but I cut in.

"He knows I'm alright."

"How can you say that?"

"Because you told him so," I said. Min's white face colored some. She swallowed and blinked. When I didn't say anything, I saw a bit of that familiar defiance in her eyes.

"I thought about it," she said. "But it isn't on me, Akio. We're connected. The three of us. If he knows you're alive, it's because he feels it. Nothing else."

I glanced toward the paper I'd slid to the other side of the table.

"Joon's never been one to read the local gossip," Min said, following my gaze, and with it, my concern.

"He's got his own personal spy network in that dojo," I said. I let out a sardonic laugh, my mind going back to when I was chief among my own grubby, largely merry band of Seoul urchins. "Besides, Joon may ignore everything from the League to the latest North African incursion, but nothing within a stone's throw of Ken's Place escapes his notice. Zoo died just a few doors down."

"If he has put it together," Min offered, "he'll be glad to know it was you, and not someone he has to guard the children from."

We both knew it wasn't true.

"So, you're going to talk—"

"You know I can't do that, Min," I said, hating how it sounded before the words left my lips. "I can't risk it—"

"Your association with Kenta's dojo isn't a secret to Goro," Min said. "That's how you got mixed up with him in the first place."

"He isn't in Tokyo," I said. "Bad as Seoul has gotten, even the Hachinin have to tread carefully here."

Min adopted a victory grin, taking partial credit for that. Then she frowned.

"But you can risk involving me."

"Not for Joon," I said. "I won't involve the dojo. I won't involve—"

"Ah, yes." Min rolled her eyes. Could be that it was meant to be playful, but it still stung some. "Think of the children."

"I'm a dead man walking—"

"You can say that again."

She swallowed whatever she was going to say next.

"Sun's up," she said, changing the subject. "I assume you'll be retiring, resting for your next … mission, should we call it? This Zoo situation was meant to be a beginning, after all, wasn't it?"

"Damn right."

Maybe some part of her thought I was going to give it all up, after all, take her up on her witness protection offer. Retire into the West at the ripe old age of twenty-eight. Maybe I could saddle up with the Canadians, shore up the North American border. Word was slow coming from the West these days, but when it did come, it came bloody.

"Who's next on the punk's list?"

So much for the Red Demon of Seoul.

"One dispatched underling isn't going to get Goro sweating any more than a trip in the elevator does now, strenuous as that may be for him."

I moved toward the spare bedroom, eyeing the flat screen as I went. I knew Min's expression by the silence that stretched.

"You do have a list, then …"

I turned toward her, running my fingers through hair that had gone from sweat-soaked to greasy to brittle in the long night hours. "Didn't write anything down, no."

Before she could say anything else, I glanced toward the closed wood slider to the dojo garage.

"Who owns SMC?" I asked. "Who really owns it, I mean."

Min snatched the remote off the glass and steel-gray coffee table and flicked the screen on with a shake. As the familiar crackle filled the room and the black plasma tickled the hair on the nape of my neck, I saw that persistent blue and white ticker at my periphery.

"You want to know who owns Seoul Media Corps …"

She tilted her hips like she might have while standing over me on the red mats of Ken's Place. "Well, there's Blu Soda, Gyro Motors, Snax De—"

"Not corporate sponsors, Min," I warned, turning toward the predictable platinum blonde plastered across the screen. She was mixed Korean, and far from natural. She had those bleached white teeth that made cream look brown, and those dead eyes that saw nothing but the flickering white scroll ghosting across a buzzing black monitor—the soulless gateway to the hearts and minds of the city.

"Akio …"

"I'm not going to kill him, Min," I said. "Or her."

The look in her eyes told me it was the latter.

"You seriously don't know?"

"Know … what?" I asked, hesitant.

"Gabriella Burtahn is one of the premier heiresses in the East. Dare I say, in the world."

I frowned, and Min shot it right back.

"This isn't some reality TV bullshit, Akio. She's a seriously big deal. Pops left her the whole thing."

"Recently?" I asked, staring in wonder at the broadcast.

"No," she led me like I was a child. "You've seen her face a thousand times. She's on every street corner, hanging from every other market display. She's made herself a brand apart from SMC. I think she fancies herself a humanitarian or some bullshit like that. Vegan by day, money launderer and political stooge by night. Of course, she's hardly the one typing the transcripts."

I was stroking my chin as Min went on about Princess Gabriella.

"And who owns Gabriella?"

"I think you know that," Min replied. "It's a dangerous world out there, now. Especially for an heiress. Protection is cheap, but protection from Goro can only be purchased in favors."

Seoul Media Corps had been pumping the League for the last two seasons when no other mainstream Korean outlet would touch the neon barbarism. They'd also been dishing the dirt on all of Goro's political and business rivals between weather reports and traffic updates, and even ran a nice two-minute tragedy piece on poor Akio Prince after he went missing so recently. Already forgotten, but certainly not forgetful.

"The Hachinin want to own Seoul, Min. Own the news, own the entertainment, and soon enough, own the people."

"Akio ..." Min let out that warning again, but lighter. She knew I was beyond helping at this stage. "What could you possibly—"

"You wanted me to do things your way, right Min?" I interjected. "On the level."

"This hardly sounds—"

"I need everything you have on Goro of the Hachinin."

"If you're looking for the stuff that sticks, it's going to be a short list."

"Doesn't have to stick in a court, Min. Well ... not a real court, in any event."

Min actually laughed. She seemed to sway a little as she did. I hadn't seen her spike her coffee with anything. She had quick fingers, but maybe she was just tired. I'd brought a lot down on her in the last week, after all.

"I need whatever you've got. Any scandal he's been tied to, or that his underlings have been tied to. I need a floor plan of Triton Tower—"

"How do you know she even stays there?"

"It's the highest place in the city," I said, as if it were obvious. "Every queen has her perch. Every hawk her brooding nest."

Min took a step toward me, frowning over the sudden uptick in the broadcast's volume. "Why not go straight to Goro's offices at the Dome, if you've got such a death wish?"

"My wish isn't for me," I said. "Besides, Min," I smiled my most confident smile, "think back on Kenta's teachings. Things get stupid when they're afraid."

"You carving up Kuzu Tokoro hardly scared the street vendors outside the club," Min sighed.

"I'm only one man," I said. "But Seoul is comprised of the many. Let's let Goro hear them, see them, feel them, and with more than just a two-hour social trend."

Min thought better of saying anything else. That, or she was finally ready to give me up for dead and retreat to the warm comfort of her bed.

"Fine," she said, and somehow I knew she'd have it all waiting for me on the kitchen table before she left for the precinct that night. She was exhausted, and she was angry with me. Still, I saw the ghost of a smile lurking, that mischievous spring lighting her step as she traipsed away toward the basement door.

Min didn't believe I could bring Goro—never mind the Hachinin—tumbling down any more than she believed she could. But she knew I could cause a scene better than anyone. I might not have the personality for League interviews or highlight intros, but when the lights dimmed, my own shined brightest—all ruby red and smoldering. As much as she feared for me, she was looking forward to the show.

As a matter of fact, so was I.

"And Min," I said, watching her fingers blanch as they caught the frame and slowed her path around the corner of the living room, "Goro is afraid of me. He just doesn't know it yet."

They said dying absolved one of the fear of it.

Thing is, I'd never taken a castle before. This one had a princess at the top. I only hoped it didn't have a dragon in the depths.

13

THE TOWER

Unlike the Soul Dome, Triton Tower was planted firmly on the north side of the city, tucked just under the beginnings of the woodlands the previous government had managed to plant and rewild in the time before I was born, and before the current iteration of neo-capitalism had taken things over.

The silver and black tower dwarfed the greatest of the gnarled trunks behind me, and they had the advantage of being set up on a great slab of rock and soil. I hadn't done much in the way of sneaking. There were hiking trails scattered throughout the hills. I'd simply kept the light off in the veins of my League suit and made sure I left at the witching hour.

Now, here I sat, perched like some brooding hero—more likely, a self-righteous villain—letting the damp wind blow the shame from the bright, glittering jewel of the city over the tower gates. There was a strange tang to the air when the wind swept it from the inside of the gated compound. It was like sulfur and metal mixed. Perhaps a hint of money.

Or maybe that was my imagination.

I surveyed the grounds, trying to channel some of Joon's legendary patience.

Upward, where the tower gave up its luminous bulbs and plunged into the backlit darkness of the night sky, the spire was all shadow for what seemed like a mile. But there, higher and higher, the black narrowed some, and red took its place, not unlike the lights in my artificial suit.

That was the nest, then, already bathed in my colors. That was the roost of the Princess of Seoul—one of the great heiresses of the New East—and one who would soon be answering to me. How mythic, that such a vast media empire could be wielded by one so small.

But then, Gabriella only owned what the demons of the isle suffered her to in their domain. The ghosts of Japan, a land that was said to be as beautiful today as it had ever been, and as deadly. A land whose current masters had cast out the old—the titans of industry and commerce replaced by the deadly calm and assurance of ones without conscience and with no end to ambition. These were men who wore painted skin beneath their suits.

These were the Hachinin.

And here, in this tower, nestled among lights and furs and all manner of vain indulgence, was one of their stooges. One of their willing slaves.

In the frozen wastes of Russia, it was said that trained wolves guarded the wealthy and feasted upon those bold, daring and desperate enough to try for their winter stores. In the amber-lit Germanic and French regions, automated turrets whirled on oiled motors—spinning cogs of industry and death meant to protect those who made the rules mainland Europe thrived and writhed beneath. In the Americas, they still had men guarding walls. Men with black metal that shot it back.

I had always hated guns. Found them distasteful and the worst combination of personal and cold. A man with a blade or baton had to meet you on the field. A machine was just following the programming that made up the entirety of its universe—its god and its purpose. But a gun. That took squeezing, and aiming, and it could be done from far away, free of consequence and full of luck, if men on the other side of the field had them too.

I watched for over an hour, and saw no guards, no guns, no dogs. No sign of organic or artificial motion at all.

The lack of guards bothered me. The lack of movement. The

seeming lack of life within or beneath the towering structure that loomed like an unwanted lord over his scuttling subjects. But the allure of what lay inside that red-tinted nest won out, as I knew it would and as Min feared.

She'd stayed up through the previous night and had regaled me with tales of Goro's many trespasses. I was beyond anger and heat. Instead, I felt a coldness come over me that felt a lot like the way I was before my fights.

Strangely, what was missing in all that cold and dark was the customary fear, and that was another cause for concern. How careful could I be if I didn't have fear to rule at least some skeletal part of my choices? How deadly?

I suppose that was for us both to find out—the princess and me. I suppose, that night, I was going to find out who I really was. The incident with Zoo—the folly—was rash, the actions of a man recently thought dead—recently halfway there. Tonight was different. Tonight, I made a conscious choice, one I'd slept on.

An owl glided past on silent wings, nothing marking its passage but for the quick shadow it cast on my ruby mask, dying it the color of poisoned blood and blotting out the sight of a moon whose demeanor I couldn't suss out on either side of judging or encouraging.

I took it as the sign I'd wanted, ignoring the warning of Min's conscience, which had buried itself, hooks and all, deeply within the hollow confines where mine had nested once before, and slid down the slope.

Once I reached the bottom, I adjusted my belt, checking to make sure my sword was still firmly sheathed at my waist, and checked that my mask was secure. I touched the gray, springy fence gingerly with my gloved hand, then climbed the gate like a spider, doing a handstand at the top so as to avoid any barbed or razor wire that might have been too fine for me to see in the shallow lighting at the edge of the concrete yard. I landed in a crouch, right hand straying toward the worn hilt at my hip, and surveyed the scene.

I was only a few feet closer to the base of the tower than I had been moments earlier, but now I felt the swell and pulse of danger beating at my temples. I felt hot and stifled with the mask. I nearly squeezed my palms, which would prompt my suit to glow for the crowd's delight, until I realized I wasn't in the arena and that any crowd I attracted in the present circumstance would be one I'd do better to avoid.

There were shipping containers scattered about the yard, placed almost haphazardly. I snuck around one and looked toward the front gate, which faced a single, winding road that curled around from west to south, leading back toward the city below.

I settled to the task, replaying Goro's many trespasses as I crept through the yard. It made me angry, and, as Kenta had always been fond of reminding me, and as I had always been fond of reminding my students who were really Joon's, anger made things stupid, and stupid got things killed.

Before I knew it, I was standing before the glass and steel-framed doors to the tower, the cement entryway lit with a soft blue glow. I tensed, waiting for an alarm to sound, or for a speaker to crackle to life.

There was nothing.

As I reached for the handle, thinking to try my luck before I resorted to shattering the whole thing with a League armor-enforced kick, I heard that chittering sound again. It still sounded like birds, or bats, only now it was more persistent. It was a sound of many things and not one, and it had a steady whirring beneath it, like a belt running on an oiled loop fast enough to raise steam.

I looked up with a feeling of dread, and the red eyes that looked back at me had no fear of the demon's mask I wore, nor of the sword girding my hip. These eyes were lifeless, and intent.

These eyes were many.

As if on command, the chittering stopped and the dozen or more lights dimmed before flashing brightly, and when next they spoke, they did so in a series of sharp clicks and screeching wheels and cogs that sounded like banshees on the wind.

The first of the beasts dropped from directly above me,

forcing me to dive and roll toward the door. I came up hard against it with my back, drawing my sword as I framed my body against the base of the tower.

The rest of them had dropped onto the platform as I'd made the move. They were machines—bots reminiscent of crabs or spiders. They had thin legs, and red eyes blinked atop flat black discs in their centers. In the place of arms, they had long, cane-shaped pincers that rose up higher than I was tall, and hooked down. They recalled mantises.

I didn't see any automatic weapons attached to harnesses or girding buckles and latches. I didn't see holes that might hide explosives and other hidden horrors. I only saw a small army of metal mantises, red-eyed and flat, chittering and chirping as they considered how many pieces to slice me into.

"What the hell happened to the days of flashlights and batons?" I asked them, gritting my teeth as I awaited their reply.

It came much faster than I anticipated, in the form of a razor pincer spearing toward me like a hurled javelin. It came fast enough to let me know the things weren't playing around, and that SMC didn't take trespassing lightly. There wouldn't be any questioning or subduing with these scorpions. There were no cameras on the fences and no razor wire because they wanted to make sure that whoever was foolish or determined enough to break in never got another chance to make trouble for the big leagues.

As I dodged, things slowed down. I saw the shards of glass spinning around me, falling down to tumble on the cement, where they reflected the red bugs' eyes and turned them up like bloody rubies. I felt the pressure on my back give way, and tucked the fall into a roll that brought me end over end into the main lobby and its cold black marble.

Before I came up, I thought of the last thing Min had said to me before I'd set out for my second suicide attempt in as many days.

You're not a spy, Akio. You weren't trained to engage in corporate espionage or to skulk in shadows and bring down empires. You're a fighter, through and through.

She wasn't wrong, that one. Although, as I came up in a crouch, fists clenched and red suit veins pulsing their own macabre glow that the black floor drank in, I felt myself smiling.

I was a fighter. That much was true. Far as I knew, there had never been an empire taken down without an army of those, and with a few great ones at their head.

Well, I certainly wasn't an army. But I sure as hell was good enough that modesty came naturally. A tiger is modest while a jackal boasts.

"Why do you think that is?" I asked the chittering creatures as they spilled into the semidarkness that was my domain.

They didn't answer, but that didn't put me off all that much. I figured it was nothing personal.

The tower lobby was more a grand entryway. This didn't seem a place of business, but rather one where business people got away, held meetings in smoke-filled rooms, and got up to all the things they were rumored to on the isle of Japan. There were pillars that could have been slate gray or white, for all I could tell. They framed the sides of the vaulted chamber. There was a grand staircase behind me, and I could see the balustrade curl around in front, two stories up, forming a gallery. I only had to hope there weren't more of the things waiting up there.

It seemed almost absurd that my only visitors were of the artificial variety, given the stir I'd already caused. But then, maybe this wasn't an office building. Maybe it truly was the grand, opulent nest of Gabriella Burtahn.

I nearly spit at the wastefulness, and thought that maybe I'd give her a true fright on top of the demands I'd be making. Someone with all this couldn't be an innocent bystander. Gabriella was in a tower too high to be too far below Goro and the Hachinin.

I raised my borrowed sword and held it across my body, just beneath my eyes, blade up. It drank in the red light, turning into a ribbon to match the lifeless glow of the unblinking beads staring back at me from the starlit doorway.

"Time to see what you can do against throats not made of the usual stuff," I whispered.

The sword was polite enough to answer.

As the first of the surprisingly cautious hunks of metal and alloy flashed toward me from the darkness among the pillars, I flashed the red ribbon across and felt only the faintest tug of resistance. The red light on the front of the body disc blinked furiously and two pincers clattered to the marble floor, twitching spasmodically.

I brought the blade overhead and slashed down harder than I needed to, shattering the glass on the crawler's head and parting a chunk of the shell behind it. And the first of the red lights went out with less than a hiss and fizzle.

"More plastic to you than I thought," I said, raising my voice so the others could hear as they chittered to one another in the gloom, their crab legs taking them around me in the darkness, swirling like a pool of death.

I circled, holding the sword out before me. The little beasts might be little more than resin and high-quality plastic, but those pincers were razor-sharp, and a kick—even in League armor—wouldn't do much more than put me in a blender.

"Come on, then," I sneered, feeling a little silly for the venom I injected into my tone, given that I was surrounded by a bunch of robots rather than men or dogs.

They did.

I slashed again, bringing the sword up and across my left side as if it were an axe kick, and took another of the red beads out, feeling the sword bite and pull a bit more sharply this time. I ducked mostly on instinct and rolled to my right, coming down a little harder than I'd intended. As I did, I felt the first stabbings of fear as a forest of lashing talons rained down around me.

I managed to squirm, roll and execute something of a controlled fall that worked well enough. Still, one razor arm tore through the leather on my leg, scraping a gash on the right side of my shin. Another embedded itself in the marble with a crack, shattering it like an eggshell and taking some of the spikes of my black hair along with it, mercifully sparing my scalp.

The beast above me was having a hard time extricating itself from what would have been a fatal blow, and hesitating had never been a good move against me. I tensed my core and brought my knees up to my chest, avoiding two other crawlers, and spun on my back like a top. I brought my sword hand around and sliced through the thin part of the pincer, then planted my feet.

Before the crawler could turn the other on me, I lunged forward and buried the blinking disc with my bulk, spilling us both across the black frozen surface of the lobby like drunken, demonic dancers. The crawler tried to free itself, and then turned its calculating mind to offense, bringing its legs up to find whatever holds they could in the veins and seams in my armor. One snaked its way under my mask, drawing blood as it scraped along my chin and lips, smacking against my teeth as it sought out something soft to puncture.

I let out a snarl that was a marked separation from the synthetic noises the crawlers made, and balanced myself atop the disc. I plunged my blade in, tip down, and felt the crawler shudder and gasp in its mechanical death throes.

The machine's dying was chaotic enough to keep the remaining crawlers at bay, at least for the time being.

I stood atop the tangled ruin of metallic legs and wiped the dribbled blood from my chin, watching as the dwindling swarm —I counted nine—began to arrange themselves in smaller clusters in front of me.

"What's the matter?" I jeered. "Scared? Come now, friends. You still hold the numbers."

I had no idea how the AI worked in creations like this. The most advanced machine I knew how to operate was a coffee maker, and that not well. But I figured they had some sort of shifting hierarchy, the algorithms and calculations running on which of them would make the best sacrifice.

At least, that's what I told myself. The reality was, there were still nine of them, and one of me. And while Min's father's sword had given a more than fine accounting of itself to this point, I had doubts about how long it could stand up against steel and alloys.

One crawler near the center raised its disc body higher than the others, as if it were trying to see over the thicket of metallic limbs, and sent out a series of sharper chirps that had the others bowing out of its way. As one, they parted, and the crawler stepped forward, bent pincers hovering in front of it hungrily.

"Not a jackal, this one." I nodded my respect, then stepped off of the broken form of the crawler beneath me and moved back toward the broken glass of the entryway, shifting into the shaft of moonlight. The crawler watched me, its fellows beginning to spread out along the bottom of a stairway I now saw in its ornate moon-painted detail.

This wasn't an office, nor a place to conduct business. It was a penthouse. A penthouse built for one, and guarded by soulless things.

I wasn't tired yet, nor was I wounded apart from the shallow gash on my leg that had already begun to run dry, creating a crusted paste over the seam between my skin and League rubber. The first rivulets of sweat ran down my brow, sticking my bangs to it, and I'd had enough close calls in the scrum to make me nervous.

That was good.

The lead crawler paused just a stride or two before me, and while the others fanned out on either side of it I saw them clearer this time, my eyes having adjusted to the gloom. I saw their gray, shadowed legs and their wavering pincers even as their red lights went dim in the wash of moonlight from the courtyard.

The lead crawler tensed to spring, and I tensed to intercept it, but then that plasti-metal disc in the center of the joints quivered, the red light blinking as if it had just been presented with new data, new information. Ignoring me at its own peril, the lead crawler straightened, switching the direction of its recorder toward the ornate staircase. The others paused as well, leaning over their own bent legs and shifting side to side to get a clearer view.

I resisted the urge to follow their line of sight, thinking it must be some advanced tactic to divide my attention. I gripped my sword hilt tighter, and even considered making a break for the bottom of the stair rather than rushing them head-on, as they no doubt expected and wanted me to do.

The lead crawler sent out another series of chirps and beeps, these ones sounding somehow more frantic and less controlled and commanding. I expected those at its back to respond, or to explode into motion. Instead, there was a deeper, rougher and more grating sound that answered from on high. It was like gears grinding over chains caked with sludge.

Again, I resisted the urge to look in the direction of the crawlers' collective red gaze. And then I saw those red orbs blink more rapidly than before, and those metal legs scrape and scramble, the body discs bumping into one another as the calculating pack turned into a chaotic jumble. It was as if they were trying to flee, and while I cut an imposing enough figure, I doubted it was because of me.

The sound started just as I took the bait, beginning to swing my head toward the staircase. It was a soft sound at first, almost like a fan blowing, or something spinning.

Midway up the stair, I saw the beginnings of a great shadow. I swallowed as my eyes took me to the top, where the lord of all crawlers crouched on bunched, metallic legs. It looked to be painted—either black or green in the tradition of military equipment—and in the place of a small disc, it was built more like a tarantula, with a meaty body, thick, bent legs and a row of blinking red lights instead of just the one.

I was so taken with the sight of the massive crawler-tank hybrid that I'd forgotten to check for the source of the strange, windy sound that echoed in the airy gloom of the gallery. There was a gunmetal-gray blur hovering like a giant moth just above the creature's eyes, propped atop its back like the shell of a hermit crab.

I squinted, my heart picking up the dread before my conscious mind did.

I recognized the primordial shape of the spinning turret before it started spitting its yellow flashing fury into the black marble.

There was no time to think or consider, and I decided on

instinct that the pillars supporting the upper gallery were too far for me to make for. Instead, I dove amidst the gnashing limbs of the crawlers as the turret tore apart the tile on which I'd been standing.

The great legs bent, the concrete on the uppermost stair cracking and yawning with its bulk, and it swung the screaming turret with terrible, halting precision.

The chirps and beeps raised, and while some of the crawlers managed to disentangle themselves from the mass, making for the edges of the lobby or scraping toward the broken door, those that remained were parted from whatever programming they called a place to ghost. I was nearly through the pack, having picked up a number of scrapes, gashes and shallow pierced holes as I swam through the thicket of sharps, when I heard the horrifying sound of metal tearing the air apart as the bullets moved through the atmosphere directly behind my head.

I'd been shot before—just a few days prior, actually—but the sound a pistol makes is more a pop, like a quiet joke with a weighty punchline. The tarantula's turret was a storm unto itself, a roaring of a beast loud enough to wake sleeping dragons. Still, it was that sharper, closer sound of torn and dying air that filled me with dread.

And had me charging the titan head-on in my sudden need— my mortal drive—to make an end of the thing that was set on my own.

I couldn't see the bullets passing me, but I could hear them tearing through the invisible currents their forebears left behind like airy rivers. The barrel spun on at the top, the yellow flashes lighting the gallery and all its rich paintings and adornments, and the neck looked to be changing from slate gray to a smoldering orange, like coals first coming to life.

The red row of lights took in my approach, and as I reached the midway point of the staircase, the spider's forelegs bent lower, the spinning geyser of doom tipping downward. I dove and rolled to the left, just before the metal river dug a trench into the crest of the section of stair I'd just come up. My left shoulder slammed into the wooden balustrade and snapped the timbers clean, sending a pair of polished rails spinning toward the lobby floor and trapping me for a second that would have cost me my life, had some mix of fate, physics and dumb luck not intervened.

Just as the tarantula readjusted its position, swinging that bunched, painted back toward me, the sound of roaring hellfire quieted, to be replaced with the high whine of the spinning turret, now empty of the ammunition that made up its voice and all its might.

I nearly smiled, but then I saw the red lights do another of their hypnotic, demonic dances. There was a sharp, clipped metal sound, and a black coil fell down beneath the beast's belly like some cold discharge. Two clawed arms materialized at its back. They gripped a copper ribbon between them and began moving toward the base of the still-spinning turret.

With a half-strangled curse, I extricated myself from the wreckage of the railing, tried to leave the pain for later, and raced up the remainder of the stair, gleaming sword flashing like the pennant of a doomed hero from poems. I felt sick as I heard the metal ribbon—the next river of bullets—click into place, and lost my breath as I screamed in toward the beast's toothless maw.

I closed my eyes, let out a scream that likely sounded like the garbled mix of emotions—equal parts horror and rage—that it was, and brought the sword of Min's father in behind me like a humming prayer.

For a long second, I kept expecting the next river to tear me limb from limb and make me a mess of blood, rubber, resin and bone for some crawling metal janitor to find and secret away.

All was quiet but for the shaking sound of hydraulics and escaping gas.

I opened my eyes and nearly died from the sight alone. In the place of the red glowing eyes I'd already come to loathe, I was greeted by eight quivering black pearls set in a circle. The barrel of the turret shook and protested, and I only tore my eyes from the tip of the nightmarish weapon with effort, and saw that I'd plunged the sword into the guts of wire, cord and link of the turret's neck.

The beast seemed unable to think its way out of its current predicament. Its prey was present and in range—even laughably vulnerable—and yet, it wasn't dying.

I thought of pulling the sword out and attempting to duck below the restarted tube of death before it could renew its assault, and thought better of it. I tensed and heaved with a sharp pull to the left, jamming the cracked sword against another peg within the gears and breaking it off, lodging half of the blade in the mechanical creature's innards.

When I ducked under the tarantula's gun, it didn't try to follow me, just kept trying to get that turret to spin. I kept an eye on the shaft of folded steel caught in the neck and whispered softly to it to hold just a bit longer as I sucked in my stomach and slithered between the bent legs—any one of which could crush me in an instant—and the top of the rail.

I spared a glance around the rest of the gallery, ensuring that this one had killed all its fellows in its greed to be rid of me, and touched the dimmed gray arrow on the paneled wall behind the beast. The arrow lit white, and the bell tolled. The wall parted to reveal an elevator that was its own small room, and I entered, pressed the uppermost button on the panel to the right, and sighed as it closed over the pitiful image of the frustrated metal tarantula beyond, quivering, shaking and smoking with the broken blade of a katana stuck in its neck.

14

THE NEST

I expected any number of things to happen when I reached the top of the tower.

For starters, I expected to hear a delayed alarm—the one that should have sounded from the second my boot touched down in that cold cement courtyard just a few minutes before. Surely the crawlers were only the first line of defense, and no doubt the bigger one—we'll call him the dog—would have informed the higher-ups of its failure, whether they be of the human or mechanical variety.

I didn't see any obvious cameras. No black specks with tiny red dots leering at me from the corners of the elevator, but I knew they had to be there. Whoever roamed the many halls and slumbered in the many feathered chambers knew some fool had tried for the tower.

The white lights in the wood-paneled elevator—complete with its own potted plants and hung paintings—flickered, and I turned my halved sword over in my hand. I caught sight of my own reflection—cracked demon mask and all—in a polished section of steel above the control panel, and nearly laughed at the absurdity of it.

My shoulder throbbed where I'd rammed the rail. It was too early to know if it was broken or torn, but I'd never had great luck when it came to joints. My chin stung with the scabbed-over scrape the first crawler had left me, and I felt the same pulsing, throbbing sting from a dozen other places where my League suit hadn't fully protected me. My right ankle buzzed, caught between painful and numb on account of my too-fast roll to avoid the molten river of lead pouring down at me from the top of the stair.

I was a man playing at being a monster, and I'd entered a lair full of them.

I loosened the grip on the sword hilt and slid to the left side of the elevator as the box hissed to its final resting place at the top of the tower. I pressed my shoulder against the front panel, watching the doors quiver before opening. A thin beam of reddish-pink light spilled in from the room beyond, like bloody candy.

The door opened and I kept my eyes down, watching for shadows or signs of an ambush as the rose-colored sliver turned into a beam before filling the whole of the elevator floor. I paused there, counting the half-seconds before the door would start to close and listening for the now-familiar, haunting sound of whirring belts and spinning cogs, clicks and chirps.

There was nothing. No sound to signify an ambush. Only a light, lilting melody and an odd scratching sound that interrupted it on occasion. I thought it sounded like a cat scratching at a post, but it jogged a memory of an old music box Kenta had had in the attic of the dojo. It was built like a suitcase, and atop a small brass spoke, he'd place a black disc he called a record. A little tooth on the end of a flimsy arm sank into the grooved surface and belted out some of the worst-sounding drivel—all horns and jazz sounds—they'd tried to recapture of the prime America in the days of his youth, before the world had become what it was today.

I closed my eyes, breathed out a long, slow release, and stepped into the open doorway, which emitted a light beeping sound to kindly ask that I step forward or backward so that it might continue its empty, meaningless rounds. Up and down. Down and up.

My instinctual scan picked up nothing untoward, except for

the fact that there damn well should have been something unto-ward and, well, there wasn't.

I stepped forward onto a slate-tiled floor in a hall that was more narrow than I'd expected. I was standing in a miniature lobby of sorts, with a short entryway that narrowed to an alley between dark wood paneling. There were doorways on either side—likely luxury bathrooms, coat closets or odd billionaire sex chambers. At the end of the hall, the source of the pink glow revealed itself as a wide, carpeted bedroom with a bed larger than most apartments set squarely against a wall of black windows. I had to squint to make out the figure atop the many-pillowed surface, but she was unmistakably female, and unmis-takably attractive.

She was also naked.

Worst of all, she didn't look the least bit concerned, which either meant she had alerted the wrong authorities—more death machines or men dressed in black suits come from the Land of the Rising Sun—or I was already in the thick of an ambush. She was the queen spider and I a bold, willing fly.

I stepped forward anyway, and as I entered the dimly lit hall, I did my best to stay alert in the narrow confines. She moved, her blonde hair falling away from the breasts it had been cover-ing, and she quirked one eyebrow and the matching hip, letting a pink satin sheet fall away.

I dove past the first pair of darkened doorways and came up with my broken sword on one knee, facing back the way I'd come. Nothing. There was a single white circle illuminated above the elevator doors. The shaft wasn't moving. It was still waiting down in the lobby.

That eliminated one possibility, then.

When I turned to face the heiress once more, she'd moved a little to her right. Her face was still the red-lipped, cream-soft picture of calm and control, but I saw the way one hand gripped the covers.

Someone had put her up to this, then. Someone was waiting in the room with her—likely quite a few someones—and they were waiting until I joined them in the relative open of the oval room beyond, rather than entering my killing field one at a time.

"You're him, then."

She did a remarkable job of keeping her voice level, but I saw fresh sweat—sweat that had nothing to do with whatever late-night escapades she'd been up to under those silks just minutes before—pool into the hollow, alluring dip between her neck and chest.

"Don't get many visitors like me, Princess?" I asked, my voice echoing strangely behind the slashed and jagged mask.

"Demons?" She raised both eyebrows now. "Rivals? Scorned lovers?"

"Much as I'd love for that to be the case—"

"The Sword Punk."

I actually tilted my head in the way a dog might at an unexpected sound. Even beneath my mask, she saw the effect and the surprise.

"What did you think they'd taken to calling you?"

"I've seen the names," I said. "The Demon in Room—"

"Punk's the one that's sticking, if I get my way."

Now her voice took on an edge it hadn't held before. This wasn't the bearing of a girl playing at being a queen, then. Gabriella Burtahn might not wear a League suit or carry the jagged, broken end of a sword in high places, but she was a killer nonetheless. She'd stabbed, lied, cheated and stormed her way into the biggest media market in the Far East. Those three letters—SMC—weren't under the ownership of some shadowy board, they were hers.

Well, let her think I didn't like the name, that I didn't need the name. Let her take it with her, along with the message I'd leave her tonight, and let her plaster it with scorn on every imprint, corporate app and blue ticker she could.

Let them snigger at the name … while they could.

"So," she started, leaning back, arching her spine and sticking her chest out for good measure, "which is it, then? You run around in a mask, wearing a League suit—I like the red—"

"I can tell," I said, gesturing at our surroundings.

"And murdering lowlifes—"

"You mean you and Zoo weren't friends?"

"Never met him." She shrugged. "Didn't even know we were connected until I read it in one of the papers I own. I think it's one of the liberal papers." She laughed. It was a wicked sound. "Funny, that. Even the bleeding-heart writers who'd do anything to have my head on a pike and see the channels burn with the rest of the free world work for me. Most don't even know it."

I didn't answer, just kept watching the corners where the gray tiles met the pink carpet—or maybe it was white—alert for any signs of encroaching, impatient assassins. I'd never actually met an assassin before, and even though they'd existed in every empire, in every kingdom and palace since the far reaches of time, I'd always sort of considered them a fiction. Still, if anyone had them in her employ, I figured it might be someone as sickly rich as Gabriella.

"So, tell me noble Sword Punk..." She smiled, and then the smile turned into a threatening grimace, like a fox turned into a hawk. "What does Kuzu Tokoro have in common with one such as me? What tiny, shit-stained affronts could he have visited upon you that would cause you to aim so high, so soon on your quest for ... whatever it is you're on a quest for?" She raised a hand, fingers twirling up toward her chin with deliberate slowness, brushing a raised pink nipple along the way. "Or are you truly just mad?"

"Even the mad have ends," I said, voice husky and distracted. Well, distracted from Gabriella, and focused on everything but her.

"Many of them short ones," she snipped back. Now she was starting to remind me less of a beautiful, poisonous enchantress and more of a yipping, pampered lapdog. This one wore many faces.

I dived again, rolling on a dime and coming up in a low, wide stance just before the foot of the gargantuan bed, and calm, controlled Gabriella showed off her perky figure with a startled yelp as she crawled backward until that cream-colored skin shared its sweat with the back window.

The room was a bit smaller than I'd anticipated. It stretched a few strides to the left, where a pink couch took up the length of the windowed wall there. A flat screen hung above it, picking up more of that sick, red-pink glow from a series of cloth lanterns strung on wires in crisscrossing patterns throughout the room.

To the right, there was a series of leather chairs sat around a glass table with all manner of vials, pipes and ceramics atop it.

"Testing out the local imports, I see."

Gabriella didn't answer.

"Just because I'm not looking directly at you doesn't mean I can't see your hand inching toward that drawer. Move it back and use it to do something useful—like covering yourself—before you lose the hand."

I heard her swallow, a sticky sound, but she did as I said.

None of it made any sense. I was caught near frozen. I'd reached the top of the tower, and I had a naked princess quivering before me—though not in any way that should make a man proud or hungry—and yet, it all felt far too easy (allowing that I'd nearly been sliced to ribbons and then blasted to smithereens along the way).

"Surely the crawlers aren't the only things guarding the Princess of Seoul," I said. "Even if they had mommy watching over them from the gallery." As I said it, I noticed a door at the far end of the room. It was closed, but white light leaked out from the bottom. I couldn't tell if it was occupied or not, as little sense as it would make for someone to be taking a shit during all this.

"Surely not," Gabriella answered, her voice working to regain some measure of the control it had before. "Though, I must admit, given all the noise, I was sure one of my pets would have walked through that door bearing your head—mask and all."

She moved, and I rose and whirled toward her, flicking the broken sword from my right hand to my left and leveling it at her. She ignored me completely, clicking the black remote she held, and the screen flickered to life behind me. I didn't turn, but caught the reflection in the rear windows. It was a seemingly still image of the lobby, the shaft of white moonlight painting the final, grisly resting place of Gabriella's crawlers in stark detail.

"Didn't paint you as the sentimental type," I said, keeping my eyes on the bathroom door.

"How'd you like to paint me?"

There was a flushing sound, and the white light spilling out from behind the door was interrupted for a moment.

"You've got to be kidding me," I said, switching the sword back to my right hand. "Who the hell takes a shit in a situation like this?"

I saw Gabriella staring at me out of the corner of my eye, shoulders up, palms down, control suddenly regained.

"Someone who's not afraid of you, I'd guess," she said. The door eased open, and a lone figure framed the doorway. He was so splashed with a mix of white and red-pink light at first that I could barely make out his features, much less what he was fumbling around with in his hands.

At first, I thought it was his belt buckle. He wore jeans and no shirt. His body was lean, of similar build to me but slightly thinner, more gaunt. He was scarred all over, and one side of his chest appeared to be sunken in, as if he'd lost a mass of the muscle there. His hair was short, cut in a spiked Japanese style not unlike my own haphazard anime locks, but his features were undoubtedly local. He looked familiar. Even his black eyes.

"Mal Chin," I breathed.

His dark eyes widened some at that, and I swallowed. I didn't know why I cared whether or not they knew who I was, but now that I'd taken to wearing the mask, I suppose I'd grown into the character.

Mal Chin was one of the first League fighters. He'd competed in the opening season, making it all the way to the Semi Finals before he'd suffered a loss slightly less suspicious than the one I should have had against Janix. He'd disappeared shortly thereafter, but that was where the similarities between us ended.

Rumors had swirled that he'd got himself mixed up with the wrong crowd, that he was involved in low crime, but, knowing who owned the League, his presence in this very room shouldn't have come as a shock.

Most likely, Goro had caught wind of Mal Chin's extracurricular activities, and everyone who'd watched the inaugural season had caught sight of his skill. Goro would have many uses for a man like that aside from bringing in ratings, and a man like that would no doubt enjoy the anonymity the Hachinin provided.

As for said skill, some even say he'd have taken Korain out in the Finals that year, had they met. Not me. Not to League fighters who knew what they were watching. Still, Mal Chin was good. He even bordered on being very good. Of course, he wasn't as good as me. Assuming he didn't know who I was, it stood to reason that he'd like his chances against any old sword-wielding assassin. Assuming he did know, it didn't sit well with me just how stoic he was about the whole affair.

Now that my eyes had adjusted to the gaudy mix of light and color, I saw what Mal Chin held. He had already strapped on one glove—really more of a half-grip, like brass knuckles made of resin and Kevlar—and was adjusting the other, keeping his eyes on me all the while. Once he had both grips tightly fitted, resin bars set firmly over his knuckles, and he lowered them to his belt, which was an ugly, shining mess of obsidian, with finger-length arrowheads pointed down the whole way around. I heard a clicking sound as the grips latched onto the ends of two arrowheads, and Mal Chin yanked, pulling the arrowheads free. He lowered his hands—arrowhead gauntlets included—to his sides, and examined me in greater detail.

"I must say," I said, widening my stance ever so slightly, "it's disappointing to see you in such low company."

Gabriella let out a sardonic laugh.

"He's hardly the lowest I've entertained," she said. "And besides, he's quite talented, according to his lender. Private security doesn't come cheap these days. Some opt for sheer numbers. I opt for … talent. Mal here has already shown me some of his. Now, I reckon I'll see what else he's about."

"That's all well and good, but I wasn't talking to you."

Gabriella scoffed. She was showing more of her true, spoiled heiress self with each passing moment. Each moment that brought her closer to her presumed victory.

Mal Chin shrugged, his lifeless eyes taking on the sheen of a snake's.

"Got to find work where you can, these days," he said without emotion.

"Work steady, then?" I asked, moving my left foot forward, right foot back. He just stayed in his loose, shoulder-width stance, arms hanging limp by his sides, obsidian arrowhead knives already looking as if they'd been dipped in the colors of the night. Red and black.

"Steady enough. Looks like it's picking up."

I glanced sidelong at Gabriella, making sure she hadn't thought twice about reaching for that drawer. She looked rather bored by the whole exchange, more than likely perturbed that it had little to do with her. I was beginning to think she wasn't quite used to not being the center of attention.

"Gabriella, my dear," I said. "I'm afraid you're going to need more than this to get out of the mess your greed has landed you in. Mal here is a tough out for anyone, but I've seen better."

Those black eyes seemed to flash, though whether it was with anger or intrigue, it was difficult to tell.

"The League uses blunted blades," Mal Chin said, speaking up before Gabriella could. He lowered himself into a crouch, using a stance I hadn't seen before. He was too square for my liking, his knees bunched, abs straining. He raised his fists out to his sides, black arrowheads glittering like stalagmites below the lanterns. "It's a game, and not all who play at war know the true thing."

"That what you call it?" I nearly spat. "Running bloody errands for Goro and the Hachinin? Guarding an heiress whose empire is built on twisted truths at best and red lies at worst?"

Mal Chin didn't answer the challenge right away, but Gabriella did, guessing at all the wrong things.

"You're from Beijing One, aren't you? With our new sports and entertainment holdings, we've just beat out your Q3 projections for the first time, and in a country with a twentieth of the population." She laughed and shook her head, as if she'd figured out the secrets of the universe, right up until her next brilliant thought occurred. "Or is this a house call from Berlin? Burst Media? No. Don't tell me you've come all this way from North America. You've got some light in those demon's eyes of yours, and they don't look Viking to me."

"Let's say I'm from all of them, Gabriella," I said, bored, "and none of them. Let's say I'm the object of the people's vengeance, manifested as the karmic retribution for your past, and all those like you."

Gabriella looked from me to Mal Chin, totally at a loss.

"A noble quest, then," Mal Chin sneered, making it apparent that no mirth could find his voice unless you tortured it into him. "A hero of the people."

"What's the matter, Mal?" I asked, settling into my own stance. "Left your grand ambitions behind? Our gifts are just those. Gifts. And you've used them wrong, my friend. The toll comes due."

"Take off the mask," Mal Chin said, his voice now a low growl that was as close to emotion as he'd come.

"Make me."

His shoulders loosened slightly, his eyes taking on a new mode.

"What's got you excited?"

"The Sword Punk," he said, shaking his head slowly. He let out what I guessed to be a laugh, even if it sounded more like a toad's death rattle. "I wondered who it might be. Wondered if I might be the one lucky enough to meet him first. To kill him."

I frowned, wondering what collective he was referencing. Mal Chin caught it. He was a sharp one, and he was starting to get me inching away from fear and toward anger. A bad move. For me.

"You didn't seriously think they wouldn't have covered all ends, all partners, did you? You made a show when you took out Zoo. You wore a mask and a League suit you don't seem overly concerned with covering up, even if you have slapped form red plate over it. You can get replicas at any sports loft and specialty store. But I'd know that resin and rubber anywhere." He pointed with the tip of one of those serrated arrowheads. "That's the real thing. The genuine article. I wonder if the man beneath it is as well."

I clenched my fists a little tighter, feeling the sweat pouring down the nape of my neck, greasing the space between my back and my suit. The cuts on my leg and the piercings along my sides stung as the salt slid over the wet scabs the crawlers had left behind.

"The Hachinin take all affronts personally," Mal Chin said. "They protect all partners equally." He glanced at Gabriella, who had drawn the covers up protectively over her chest, feeling decidedly less in control the longer the two fighters spoke.

No. Not fighters. Killers. That was what I was now, whether I liked it or not. Looking into Mal Chin's lifeless eyes, that was what I knew him to be.

"Partners," I spat. "Slaves. How the hell did they know I'd come for her?"

Mal Chin laughed again. This one sounded more genuine.

"The media princess isn't half as important as you seem to think she is, but she made the list." I frowned again. "The Hachinin can afford more than just me for protection, friend." He bit out the last word. "They can afford to protect more than just Gabriella Burtahn. Still, I had a feeling I'd be the lucky one. I had a feeling you'd come to me, given your obvious desire to put on a show. To be known. Perhaps to be feared." He smiled, and the more genuine it seemed, the more sick it made me feel. "I can respect the last, at least."

"It isn't about fear," I said, hating the way my voice sounded. Hating that I actually felt the need to respond at all. Mal Chin was a murderer. A puppet. "It's about taking back what's ours."

"Ours?" Mal Chin said. "Take back what, I wonder? The Free City of Seoul? This is business, hero. It's the way the world has been since before those black boxes first turned on in the twentieth century. It's the world born after the sword and before the bomb. It's the world built with the gun, and the end of a businessman's—or woman's—pen. Ink is the new blood.

Contracts are the new slavery. Money is the new sin. Same as the old."

"Never had you figured for a poet."

"You never had me figured at all, friend," he said, emphasizing the last word again. "Otherwise, you never would have come here tonight. Or you'd have killed the princess and fled her lonely tower."

Gabriella swallowed. She glanced toward the nightstand once more, but wasn't about to move. She looked like a rabbit caught between a hawk and a snake, not thrilled with her chances no matter who came out of their disagreement alive.

"Don't suppose you'd let me make good on that escape now, friend?"

Mal Chin only smiled his dark, wicked smile. At least he got enjoyment out of something, after all. That showed me, judging people before I got a real chance to know them.

"Fret not, Princess," I said without looking at her. "I'm not here to kill you. Once I've cleaned up this mess, you might even thank me. Can't imagine you'd want the snake back in your bed after this."

"I've been wondering who the Sword Punk is," Mal Chin said as if Gabriella didn't exist. As if she were less than the pillows and sheets she nested among. "We've been taking guesses—"

"Who's 'we,' in this case, Mal? Not that it matters. No matter how many there are, it isn't going to stop what's coming for Goro."

"If what's coming is you," Mal Chin said, "it's going to stop right now. It's going to stop tonight. I only wish you'd accomplished more, ticked a few more boxes before I brought you down. You should have gone after a few more lowlifes. Tokoro was annoying, but there are plenty more like him. Should have started at the ports, cleaned up the suppliers, maybe even made a few friends before going after the propaganda arm of the Hachinin."

Mal Chin slid his eyes toward Gabriella again. He wore the ghost of a smile. I almost felt sorry for her, seeing the way she slid back, likely thinking that the only thing more sickening than seeing the way he looked at her was how recently he'd shared her bed.

"What do you say, Princess?" he asked her. "Who is the latest hero of Seoul? Who challenges the Hachinin—"

"And their servants," I bit. My tone must have made it clear I was through discussing things. Mal Chin didn't seem to mind.

"I think I've a guess," he said.

There was a pause as both of us worked through the myriad martial possibilities. This wasn't an arena. There was no canvas between us, no easy, regular geometry to navigate. Fighting indoors was like fighting in a minefield; even the corner of a cheap table could prove fatal. A crusted fork left carelessly on a grimy plate could take an eye and a life along with it. Still, the calculations were the same, even if they took a bit longer. And the fights were typically shorter.

For better or worse.

My knowledge of the first few seasons of the League was limited. I wasn't a fan of the sport. I was a fighter. I'd always shirked my more academic responsibilities. I preferred to learn on the job.

I did have an inkling, though. Something nagging at the back of my mind, warning me like the hot core of a smoldering fire. Mal Chin is fast, my mind told me.

As it turned out, I was right.

Mal Chin covered the distance between us faster than Sang Hee could have—maybe even faster than Joon. He came on with a killing speed, more wolf than hawk, and bearing fangs twice as long.

I leaned right, dodging one streaking arrowhead, but Mal's low fist—his left one—streaked in and punched me in the chest hard enough to send me reeling backward with a silent cough. I spun end over end and slammed into the back wall hard enough to shake the screen on its swivel above my head.

My breath rushed back in and my mind turned to more immediate concerns. There was a burning sensation, and I looked down to see that the prick had buried one of the arrowheads into my chest halfway. Given that there was at least an inch of League armor beneath the links in the red samurai plate, the wound was likely a shallow one. But I knew from Kenta's stories it didn't take much to kill a man where Mal had aimed.

A killer indeed.

I ripped the blade out with some effort—it stuck in the slick rubber—and tried to ignore the spurt of fresh blood that issued from my chest. Mal wasn't about to let me recover. He was on me quick, spearing forward with a thrusting knee that I only dodged by throwing myself to the left.

The strike broke the wood-framed couch behind my head, and before I could scramble enough to make for his blind side, Mal chambered his right leg and struck me full in the mask with an extended kick. The resin smashed my nose and a ceramic ridge split my lower lip. I tasted blood, but the force of the kick wasn't strong enough to send me into another tumble.

I came up and charged in, bringing my broken sword up with me. I anticipated Mal's forward stab as he squared to meet me and swung across my body rather than straight ahead. Mal was forced to watch the arrowhead streak away with a flash and clang as the shattered end of the blade took it from his grasp and sent it spinning across the room. My heart caught in my chest as Gabriella screamed, but a quick glance assured me the missile had missed her.

Mal Chin shot those gauntlets down toward his belt, looking to hook on a few more pointed arrowheads, just as I knew and hoped he would, and I used the opportunity to stab forward, aiming for the soft bit above his hip. He wasn't wearing any sort of armor. It made him faster than me—even more so than he already was—but it also meant that any blows I landed would be doubly costly for him.

He made his body into a blade, stepping back with his left foot and twisting so the sword missed him. He smiled as he caught my thrusting arm, but I simply used the momentum to bring the rest of me in behind it—hard and fast—and the smile turned to a grimace as my left shoulder slammed into his chin and crunched his teeth into his lips. He fell back with a spray, slamming the back of his head off the panel behind him. In the commotion my blade was embedded in the wall, and I left it there.

I went to work before Mal Chin could spring away, landing a hard volley of strikes to his ribs, working him like a heavy bag, up and down, climbing the ladder of his torso before I smashed an elbow into the bridge of his nose.

He started to slump, but I felt a fresh hot pain in my side and cursed, grabbing the slick hilt of the sword and prying it free from the wall with a dry, chalky suck as the plaster tumbled free.

I staggered back, clutching my side where another of Mal's arrowheads was firmly planted just under my ribs, this one deeper than the last. Blood loss was starting to catch up with me. The room was starting to spin ever so slightly, the bright colors warping it all and casting a gaudy haze on the proceedings.

Mal Chin wiped at his nose and chin, which were now an indistinguishable red mess, and straightened, prying his back from the wall. He tried to talk, but all that came out was a wet cough. Mal Chin had underestimated the damage I could do with League Armor and the damage he could take without it.

"I ..." he started and then stopped, and I saw that both grips were once more replete with obsidian sharps. "I do think I've seen a flurry like that before."

I frowned through my mask. Now that the fight was on in full, I felt like stripping it away, both for the added vision it would provide and the dripping need to let Mal know who it was that had beat him. That would beat him, rather. Still had to figure that bit out.

"Go ahead," Mal said as a syrupy bead of blood dribbled down his chin. "We're all friends here. Isn't that right, Gabriella?" I could hear her whimpering behind me, clutching the blood-sprayed and sweat-soaked covers to her immodesty. He turned his snake eyes back to me. "Isn't that right, Akio?"

My heart didn't stop like I thought it might. After all, how difficult would it be for a fellow League fighter to suss out who I was? I might not have landed any of my patented kicks, but the suit was the right color, and the mask didn't eliminate the hair.

There was also the small matter of motive, and how compelling mine might be after being killed—or almost killed—by Zoo just a week ago.

I nearly kept up the act. Nearly speared Mal Chin right there on the spot. Instead, I gave him a shrug and reached up with my sword hand, oily black-gloved fingers pressing into the red porcelain of the demon's mask.

"You sure you want to do that, Prince?" he teased. "Might undo the spell."

I couldn't know exactly what he meant by it, but I was beyond the point of caring much either way.

I whipped it to the side, and the mask—already compromised by our fight—shattered like an exclamation against the wall of windows. I raised my chin, and Mal gave me his appraisal.

"Akio Prince," he laughed and then smiled. "Back from the dead."

"Not so hard to do," I quipped. "Dying only sticks if you give it time to, in my experience."

Mal Chin detached himself from the back wall and took a step closer. He lowered his spiked fists, adopting the stance he had before he'd first attacked me.

"Let's see if it does this time, then."

I was ready for the blitz this time, no matter how fast. Mal Chin attacked between beats, which is to say, between breaths. I'd picked it up too late the last time. This time, I baited him. Breathing in made you slower. Breathing in made you vulnerable. I did breathe, but I altered my rhythm. I puffed out my chest while exhaling, and Mal flashed in, arrowhead gauntlets leading.

I had a kick ready this time. While Mal Chin and I had been exchanging mid-fight pleasantries, I'd slid my left foot back. It was a subtle movement, and one that wasn't easy to see in the close confines, but it allowed me to pivot and engage my right hip that much quicker. I had the side kick partway out. It wasn't enough to sink a full blow into Mal Chin's gut, and his widened eyes and toothy snarl showed that he knew it, but it did catch him on the hips, slowing him just enough and allowing me to push myself back.

I fell down toward the right side of the bed. Mal Chin was on me quick, but my left hand, questing backward, locked onto the handle of the drawer the heiress had been glancing toward earlier. I brought it out and smashed it over Mal Chin's face. It shattered with a violent crack that some bone in Mal's head echoed, bits of brown wood flying in all directions, with a center of dull gray metal soaring in the ether between the shards.

Mal Chin's eyes went blank for a split second, but he braced his fall on one fist, directly into my thigh, the arrowhead sinking in all the way to the hilt. I let out a sound that was part scream, part roar, and reached for the gun as it tumbled to the ground between us.

Mal saw it too, and even in his dazed state he was the quicker and the closer. He latched onto it with a hungry aggression, leaving his latest arrowhead behind in my thigh, and swung it toward my face.

His eyes widened again, only this time, it wasn't in excitement, or victory. It looked like surprise.

His fingers shook, and before he could drop it, I slapped the gun out of his hand, got my good leg under me and stood, pulling him up by the neck.

"Wh …" he started, but the red had filled his mouth, just as it was filling his lungs.

I tried to stand him up, but his legs were too weak. I let him drop. He looked at me, then at the stunned Gabriella, and finally, agonizingly, down at his own body. He didn't so much work at the hilt that was embedded into his sternum as brush the tassels along the end. It was like he couldn't quite figure out what the problem was, but knew it had something to do with the katana sticking out of his chest.

"You're fast, Mal," I said with a curt nod. "Fastest I've fought, I dare say. Though, they tell me Korain was quite the beast."

"Kch …" He made a sound that might have been an attempt to repeat the fighter's name.

"What is it?" I asked. I held no doubt that Mal Chin was an evil man, but I wasn't one to gloat over a fallen enemy. Well, not him, at least.

"Ctch … can't." He managed the word. "Can't w …"

"I can't win. That it, Mal? You saying I can't win?"

He didn't respond, which was answer enough. I sank down onto one knee, ignoring the throbbing pain that had started to course from the meat of my thigh down into the top of my foot.

"Surely you don't mean against you, Mal," I said. His eyes were mostly vacant, now. "Perhaps you mean Korain. I assume he's one of the glorified slaves you referenced earlier. Who was he set to guard on this night, I wonder? Surely you mean Goro, and the Hachinin. I can't win against men like that, can I?"

I wanted to scream that he was wrong, or else explain it to him, calmly, sickly even. Like he would have.

Instead, I fell silent, and watched him die, not realizing I hadn't told him he was wrong.

I stood up, feeling drunk and more than half dead. I'd know how to measure these things.

When I swung around, I half expected to see Gabriella brandishing the gun I'd knocked away. Instead, she merely looked at me with a cold, even defiant air.

"Akio Prince," she said, shaking her head. "The League fighter?"

"I'm flattered."

"I only heard of you very recently."

"And for reasons that are, as you can see," I bowed, wincing with the effort, "less than true."

"So it would seem."

I thought she might beg for her life. I'd just killed a man in her presence, and I'd implied that I was looking to kill quite a few more. But it seemed that Gabriella Burtahn had ascended to the top of a corporate throne through more than just her looks and the blood that had given them to her. She was a pragmatist, always thinking. She'd likely be doing it right up until a corporate assassin truly did come for her golden head.

"Am I on your list, Akio Prince?" she asked. She didn't seem particularly afraid of the answer.

"Not today, Princess," I said, taking a step forward. There was a faint sound like falling rain, and I looked down to see bright-red droplets streaming down from my limp gloved fingers, further staining Gabriella's formerly pristine sheets.

"You're really going after Goro and the Hachinin?" she asked.

"You reference them as if you're separate."

"We are," she said, quick enough that she meant it. "I am. I—"

"Don't," I said, holding up a hand. "Don't give me some sob story about getting in too deep with the local bosses, Gabriella. Better liars than you have tried. You take the money, you take the territory, you tell the lies—their lies—you're as bad as them."

"No, Akio Prince," she said, again demonstrating a backbone that could do more than strike suggestive poses. "Nobody is as bad as them. And nobody is as dangerous. You should have fled the country. Taken your life as the gift it was and—"

"Now," I said, leaning in. I didn't have time for this, and I was beginning to get the sense that there might have been more than obsidian coating the tips of Mal Chin's arrowheads. That got more of a reaction, sparked a bit of the former fear she'd done well to hide away. "Here's what your little puppets are going to say on the news tomorrow."

15

INFAMOUS

"You killed another one, didn't you?"

I didn't answer right away.

It was a mundane enough scene, if you ignored the broken katana on the coffee table. We were sitting in Min's living room, watching the night's broadcast. So far, they hadn't come to anything particularly noteworthy, which either meant Gabriella was going to get another visit from me very soon, or they were saving it for primetime.

Min was angry with me, but mostly, she was angry at being drawn into the whole thing. Here I was, bleeding through another stack of her bandages, waiting to see if SMC was about to do my unwilling bidding, like I was some rival crime boss looking to take down the Hachinin by their rules.

Still, Min's voice lacked its usual gusto. She was through worrying for me, but I thought her lack of bite had more to do with the fact that, on some level, she appreciated what I was doing. She watched the screen with equal parts trepidation and excitement, as if she hadn't quite believed my story.

"So," she said distractedly, "you said it was guarded by … spiders?"

A story I'd already told her three times …

"Crawlers," I said, tired. "And one … spider, yes. I guess that's the only way to describe it."

Min shook her head. "How the hell did they ship it in, get it through the port—"

"Min …" I said.

"Akio," she shot back, "I know you don't think we have a handle on anything at the department, but the port? That's federal ground, there. There's no way Goro controls it."

"He doesn't have to control the whole port, Min. He only has to control a finger of it, and clearly, he does."

She looked like she was going to argue, but maybe she had mercy on my tired soul. I'd nodded in and out of consciousness throughout the day, waiting for my wounds to scab over, wondering how many more fights I could survive with men and women at or above the caliber of Mal Chin. I kept thinking of Korain and his associates, wondering how many of them were out there, and what sort of targets they were guarding. Surely anyone being guarded by Goro was tainted by him and his foreign employers. Not a bad list to get ahold of, if I could.

"Spider tanks … crawlers …" she said with another shake of her head as she turned back toward the screen. "Sounds like the sorts of machines Kenta spoke about from the North African conflicts."

"I'm sure they're the same." I reached for the hilt of the broken katana. Min had cleaned it as best she could, but as I raised it, another chip of steel broke off and tumbled onto the floor. Min's eyebrow twitched. "I'm sorry about the blade, Min."

"Don't be," she said, and then, turning, "really." She smiled in a disarming way. "If I didn't want you to have it, you wouldn't. And judging by your night, it sounds like you'd have been dead if you hadn't taken it, even if it couldn't hold up against a … spider tank."

I gave it another spin. "Certainly got the job done."

"Doesn't look like it's up for another."

"No," I said. "I suppose not."

The gears started turning in my mind. I'd need weapons if I was going to continue the little game I'd started. I'd need better ones than what I currently had, and ones that wouldn't break at the first sign of decent trouble.

Min inhaled sharply and leaned forward, and I lost the thought. Despite my exhaustion, I found myself leaning forward as well.

The screen had changed; the platinum blonde and her salt-and-pepper desk mate were nowhere to be seen. In their place was a man I vaguely recognized. I'd likely seen him in any number of shops, bars and billboards across the city. He wore a blue suit with faint pinstripes that clashed with an all-blue background. He was sweating profusely, and had already tried to loosen a garish red tie on three separate occasions.

The blue ticker at the bottom of the screen showed his name emblazoned in bright capital letters.

BARRY FIN, INVESTIGATIVE REPORTER, SMC.

I frowned, wondering where they were going with this. I didn't realize Barry had yet to say a word until he looked off camera nervously, gave a sharp bark to clear his throat, and then launched into the evening's special report.

Lucky him. Clever Gabriella.

"Thank you, Micah and Kia," Barry said, *"the investigative team has put together what I dare say is … quite possibly the biggest … or, the most important report in this company's storied history. We've been at this for months, and, well …"*

Barry held up remarkably well after his lips loosened sufficiently. It took him a bit of doing to get the name Goro Hamada out, but once he did, he launched into a detailed breakdown of many of fair Goro's trespasses against the commonwealth of Seoul. This included but was not limited to money laundering through the League, bribery, extortion, corporate blackmail and espionage—the irony that I'd forced this situation through not dissimilar means was not lost on me—and even a few hints of fight fixing and conspiracy to commit murder. These last two were mentioned so closely together that any but the most dull-minded viewer would be hard-pressed not to make the Akio Prince connection.

"The old ass looks like he's watching his pension dry up right before his eyes," Min breathed.

"He's going to lose a lot more than his pension, if those lips keep moving in tune with Gabriella's strings," I said. Min didn't look my way, but I saw her frown as she turned the words over. "I suppose Gabriella wasn't going to make the address herself."

"Ah," Min said, a bit of her former ire returning. "So you've killed another man tonight, and an innocent one at that."

"Maybe not," I said. "Goro would have to be an even bigger fool than I think him to move against a reporter so blatantly. And besides, you're a cop, Min. If that isn't a witness worth protecting, I don't know what is."

"I'll have a team on it."

"Good."

Barry Fin finished his report, lips trembling, fingers twitching so badly he dropped his pen and blinked as it rolled inexorably toward the camera. He looked as if he was going to say more, and I leaned in, teeth bared like an overeager wolf.

"Come on, Barry," I whispered. "You can do it. Out with it."

Min switched between Barry and me, her curiosity piqued, along with a little bit of fear, if I knew her.

"All of this could be construed as business politics," Min said, throwing up a hand toward the screen. "There's nothing to connect it to your alter ego, nothing to build your rallying cry to a crescendo—"

"Have faith, Min."

She went to reply, but Barry opened his mouth and she closed hers.

"The Seoul Policing and Defense Force have attempted to fight against such injustices from foreign—and very close—shores using the limits of Korean law. Thus far, their attempts have proven … insufficient. Goro Hamada, also known as Goro of the Hachinin, is not welcome here. His money is not welcome here. His influence is not welcome here. He is not wanted, except for by one man."

I smiled broadly, my heart hammering away in my chest. Barry Fin might be the one talking, but anyone watching would start to get the idea soon enough, and I was guessing that Goro —fat, greasy, red-faced Goro—was getting the picture now.

"Some call him the Ghost of Seoul," Barry said. "Others, the

Red Demon. He's killed two men connected with the Hachinin, one of whom you know about. Neither was on his list, and neither lived to see it matter. The Sword PUNK has eight spaces on his list, and only one name in fresh ink, waiting to be struck through."

I started to turn my head toward Min, when Barry said something that caught me off guard.

"A dossier has been prepared by the SMC Investigative Unit and is already with the appropriate authorities," he said. "If I were you, Goro Hamada, I'd spend less time worrying over which pyrotechnics to unleash during tomorrow's League Finals and more time worrying about which of your army of lawyers will be preparing your defense."

"I …" Min started and then stopped. "What is Gabriella playing at here?"

"My thoughts exactly," I said, watching Barry intently. He was still sweating, but the quiver in his voice had quit. He had grown into the character Gabriella was having him play. Everyone knew SMC's investigative reports were bunk, more a glorified gossip column than anything, but surely even they wouldn't lie so blatantly.

"Min—"

"On it," she said, getting to her feet and scooping up her phone on the way to the kitchen. I heard her speaking a few seconds later, trying to confirm the veracity of Barry boy's claims while I sat in a somewhat stunned silence.

Barry's lengthy report ended, and the broadcast didn't bother going back to Micah and Kia at the desk. I heard Min reenter the room.

"Well?"

"Confirmed," she said, shaking her head as she made her way through the open door of her bedroom. "SMC dropped off a packet this morning. Boxes of packets, as a matter of fact," she called out. I heard her closet door open, metal handles rattling as she attempted to dress and undress at the same time.

"Clever thing," I said, shaking my head, albeit wearing a smile this time.

Min came back into view, fighting with an undershirt, black belt still dangling from frayed navy-blue loops.

"What's clever?"

"Princess Gabriella," I said as if it were obvious. I nodded at the screen, and Min finished pulling her shirt on and grimaced at a Japanese beer ad. "She's hedging her bets, and, much to my surprise, she's leaning away from Goro."

"I wouldn't call sending an incriminating dossier to the Seoul Police Force hedging, Akio. I'd say she's up and betrayed him. It wouldn't surprise me if Goro is on the first plane out tomorrow morning. We won't be able to get a warrant of that magnitude before then." She seemed disheartened by the prospect, but then let out a short, clipped laugh. "At least we'll get to see him whipped all the way back to his masters in Japan, tail tucked firmly—"

"He's not going anywhere," I said, my tone broaching no argument. "Gabriella's smart. Smarter than we're giving her credit for." Min watched me, arms crossed. "She didn't give you anything you didn't already have—"

"You don't know that, Akio."

I merely looked at her. She bit her lip.

"Gabriella may be embedded in Seoul, but she's got too many ties to Goro and the Hachinin," I held up the broken blade as a testament to that, "to turn on them completely."

"Maybe she's calling in favors from her homeland," Min reasoned. "She's a shrewd businesswoman, young as she may be. She knows when the tide is changing."

"Much as I'd like to believe it, I don't think I've done quite enough to turn the tide." I paused and tilted my chin. "Though, maybe the breeze is starting to shift a bit. You may be right, Min—"

"What?" She leaned forward, cupping a hand to her ear, as if she couldn't quite believe what she was hearing. "Can you repeat that, on the record?"

"Ha, ha," I droned. "Gabriella has friends in high places, and not just in the East. This is a shot across the bow. She's letting Goro know he's on his own, and she's letting him know that I—

someone who wants him dead—got to her, and on his watch. More so, she's letting the Hachinin know."

"It's a dangerous game to play," Min said. "Akio ..."

"What?" I stood. It took a little more effort than it should have.

"Goro won't run."

"I know."

"He won't run because he needs to see this through. See you through. He needs to put down this little fire before it fans into a blaze. His masters are watching, after all."

"Min," I said, holding my hands out to my sides, "I do believe you're finally seeing the point."

One of these days, she was going to launch herself across the room, and launch me into the next one with one of those lethal side kicks she'd perfected before Joon and I could even get the motion down. This time, she settled for one of her most withering stares.

"Yes, Akio," she purred falsely. "It's all going so well for you. You've managed to piss off the most powerful man in Seoul enough to get him to kill you, piss off his lackeys and partners enough to tell him he failed, and piss him off all over again so that he'll stop at nothing to see it done. For real this time. Gabriella isn't going to be fighting against Goro and the Hachinin. The Seoul Police Force—me and mine—aren't going to be fighting against the Hachinin."

She wasn't getting the reaction she wanted out of me. Her eyes began to shine as her voice rose.

"People like this fight in the shadows, Akio, not on backlit canvases with bright-lit blades that look more like toys than weapons of war. They're practically made of the stuff."

"Now," I said, "so am I."

"They know it's you, Akio!" Min shouted. She waved at the screen. The blue ticker was back, and Micah and Kia were as well, freshly powdered and with no sign that anything untoward had just occurred. The social media bubbles that popped up ad nauseam on the left column kept showing two words over and over, one of them in all caps.

Sword PUNK.

The words were often shot out into the ether as a declaration, complete with exclamation marks. That, or question marks, wondering who he was.

But there was another pair of words on the LED screen, white against the baby-blue background. White as a ghost, and just as solid.

Akio Prince.

I knew it would be the case; as soon as I'd cleared the compound walls beneath Gabriella's tower, I knew I'd be marked. That is, if I managed to get out of the penthouse alive. That was the point, after all. Not everyone was convinced, I'd later learn. The names were linked, but there was nothing to put me at the scene of either recent crime—Zoo's killing because I'd left no one credible to mark me, Gabriella's break-in because the whole incident hadn't happened, as far as she was concerned.

And yet, stood there, trying my best to ignore the silent screaming, the cacophonous, muted frenzy the social sphere had become on my account, I found myself short of breath, and felt again nearly as dizzy as Mal Chin's strikes had left me.

"They know it's you, Akio," Min repeated. She buttoned on her uniform as she went, yellow badge and tassels emblazoned like French pauldrons. "The public might not. You're more a ghost story to them, and a fun one. But those who matter—Goro and the rest—they know it's you—"

"They're meant to," I growled out.

"They know it's not some corporate assassin," Min continued unabated, "or some league of them. They know it's not the Russians, or the Americans. They know it's not some radical from the subcontinent. They know exactly what they're dealing with."

"And?"

"And?" Min returned, saying it as if the answer should be obvious. "And what, Akio? You think they're afraid of you? Why? Because you're possibly one of the best sport fighters in Season 6—whatever blasted season it is—of a League built off blood money and wagers? Why? Because you killed a billion-aire's errand boy, and then roughed up an heiress's penthouse?"

I was beyond the point of talking, and beyond the point of listening. Min wasn't wrong. I was a fool. Thing is, I thought I had Goro figured for a bigger one. You see, big things, powerful things, they've always got that fatal flaw, and it makes them vulnerable to deadly, foolish things.

"Goro is greed, Min. And the Hachinin is pride. If he hangs around these parts too long, waiting to smoke the fox out of its hole without bringing you lot down on him, he's going to find a tiger's got him flanked. Doesn't matter how many hounds he has at his beck and call then. Not when I step in."

I reached out with both hands, gripping her on the shoulders.

"Goro will remain in Seoul, Min," I said. "And the Hachinin will not lend him support, now that Gabriella's outed him, now that SMC and—by extension—the people hold him in open contempt. He'll stay, and he'll try to put the fires out. That's how I'll get him."

"The fires?" She started to look down, but I gave her a firm shake.

"Zoo and SMC are just the start, Min," I said. "Once I get going, once I get ahold of the names in that stack of files she sent—"

"You mean once I get ahold of them," Min said.

I shrugged. "Plenty of other names I know. Plenty of friends of Goro I know from around the League. Plenty of favors I can call in. Plenty of fires I can start. Before too long, the whole forest will come down, and then the fat, sluggish bear's got nowhere to hide."

Min looked at me with an odd mix of expression. It wasn't quite disbelief—after all, she knew what I'd already done, and, whether she liked to admit it or not, with her blessing—but it verged close enough to it.

"You're not going to be starting any fires with what you've got." She nodded at the League suit I'd discarded haphazardly on the side of the couch, and at the broken red plates that still clung to it, part of the shattered vest I'd put on over it. She kicked at the broken sword I'd left on the carpet.

"No," I said with a nod. "I'm not." I stepped away from her and reached for the phone she'd left on the divider between the living room and kitchen.

"Planning to start a fire right now?" she asked, watching me dial with suspicion.

"Not quite," I said, looking out the window. It was past dusk, and the moon wasn't yet out in full. "You said it yourself, Min. I need new blades. I need a new suit," I nodded at the torn one in its crumbled heap, "and I need a new place to stay."

She'd opened her mouth to argue against the first two points, but now only looked confused at the last.

"Like you said, Goro knows I'm alive. He might start asking around. Could be he'll skip right past asking and start knocking."

She made a shooing gesture with one hand, as if she could ward the truth away like a fly. "Nothing to connect us these days," she said, swallowing. She gripped her arms tightly, as if suppressing a shiver, and looked past me, staring down the dim kitchen hall and out the front door.

"There's never been much connecting me to anyone," I said. I said it softly and only just resisted the urge to brush an errant bang from her brow. I don't know if she saw. "Whatever there is," I said with a sigh, "I'd like to keep."

"You need to talk to him, Akio."

I almost groaned out of habit, but her words hit me like a dart. She was right. Again.

"I know."

"Before you start another fire."

"I know."

"But you're not calling him tonight."

"..."

She looked up at me, brown eyes earnest.

"No."

Min sighed and shouldered me out of the way on her way to the door, snatching up her keys as she went.

"What will you do—"

"Put out fires, Akio," Min said without turning. "Like I do every night." She hesitated by the door. "I assume you'll be gone when I'm back." I didn't answer right away. A moment later, I heard the door slam shut behind her.

I looked down at the backlit screen of her personal mobile and started tapping. "Let's see if I've got more than two friends left in the world."

16

FRIEND IN NEED

I didn't have a lot of time. At least, that's what I told myself as I stood on the sidewalk across the street from Ken's Place, staring at windows that were a good sight cleaner than Kenta had ever kept them.

There were figures moving on the other side of the pane. Figures that might've looked like wraiths to anyone else. Figures that looked like memories to me. There was a tall one with hair tied back in a tail. The class was mostly empty, with just a pair of youths toiling in the center of the dojo, taking turns throwing one another while Joon looked on. There was a small gray smudge against the window, likely one of their friends or siblings watching them, afraid to join in.

Joon had always been more patient than Kenta.

I was leaning forward, battling between the urge to go in and see him and the fear of doing just that. Surely he knew I was alive. Surely he could feel it.

If Joon had heard of the Sword Punk, chances were, he wouldn't be impressed by him.

Joon didn't like the thugs and lowlifes that hung around the dingier parts of town. He didn't like the Japanese gangsters or those who pulled their strings back on the mainland. Still, he'd always taken a more grassroots approach to stamping out their corruption. Maybe one of the three kids in the dojo that night would avoid the trappings of rain-soaked Seoul, the neon lights and drifting smoke from slime-choked alleys, and maybe it would be because of Joon.

I gritted my teeth as I thought of it, finding myself getting worked up all over again.

"See you around, pal," I said, nearly shouldering into a passerby as I turned from the spot. I pulled my hood tighter and adjusted the band in the oversized sweats Min had let me borrow unbeknownst to her—probably an heirloom of a more welcome houseguest than I'd been.

Initially, I'd been nervous at the prospect of making my way through the city while it was still daylight, given the news, given the buzz. Then again, I wasn't wearing glowing red armor or a demon mask, and I wasn't waving a sword around. As it turned out, Akio Prince wasn't a face people knew enough to catch beneath a gray hood as they passed him. I might as well have been the ghost some had taken to calling me.

I crossed the street and struck north, keeping my eyes down and marking my progress through the city by the reflections of the buildings in the puddles I glided over. I hesitated as a bright-red blur graced one of the deeper pools, and looked up.

A holographic billboard hung over the intersection in Seoul's major shopping district, the letters buzzing with that faint, maddening sound that only synthetic, evil things could generate.

League Finals. Tomorrow Night. Get your tick...

I smirked and kept on walking.

It didn't occur to me until an hour later, once I was coated in a thin sheen that mixed sweat and condensed fog, that the friend I was set to meet might have better things to do.

I tried to shake the thought as I came to a sheer wall that had once been the site of a dam that now stood as a gray monolith, or a tombstone to a river gone dry. There was a rusted iron stairway running up the side of it, and I took it achingly slow, my haphazard stitches pulling sharply with each step in what was becoming a familiar feeling.

At the top, I turned and looked back out over the city. Seoul was a land of steel and concrete giants with neon ghosts fighting through the mist. The shadows melded together, stretching away to the south, west and east. The manmade mountain that made up the southern border was only just visible as a suggestion, like a matte painting. When I turned around, I found myself on a mountain roadway heading north. There was a guardrail on the opposite side of the road, and beyond it I saw a hint of blue that caught my eye.

There was no traffic in the north but for the occasional bike. There were no condos here. The ground was too uneven and prone to slides, and the forests of Korea stretched to the north, reaching for hundreds of miles over dense valleys before shifting to barren and dry rock. The only folk who made their homes there were the very rich and the very poor, the former with hidden compounds with private gates and armed guards, and the latter with shacks and farms and grassy hillocks. One sounded far more ideal than the other to me, but then, I'd always been something of a loner.

When I was sure there was nobody around to grant me attention that was no doubt warranted, I crossed to the opposite side of the street and climbed over the silver guardrail. The rough, sodden ground sloped down and away, exposing a natural drainage system that snaked its way beneath the crumbling cliff and disappeared into a mix of green foliage.

The blue light I'd glimpsed revealed itself as a cycle, complete with golden accents. There was a long black bag hung on the side next to the seat, and a blue helmet hung on the handles. The bike had been ditched and leaned against the side of a trunk. Beyond it, a stream trickled through the unkempt brush.

I made my way to the water's edge, brushing the growth from my face and pulling my hood back. The afternoon was muggy and stale, sticky and uncomfortable.

"Even on the eve of battle, curiosity got the better of me."

The voice startled me and caused me to lose my footing. I slipped with a splash into the shallow, cold water. I looked to the left, where Sang Hee sat on a flat gray stone that broke the stream into twin currents. She was wearing a blue tank top— everything was blue with her—and black leather pants. Her hair was tied back in a tail. Her eyes appraised me with an intensity her relaxed bearing lacked.

"Akio Prince," she said, shaking her head so slightly you could miss the movement. "It's one thing to hear a ghost story. Another to see one."

I gave a mock bow and trudged through the stream. Sang Hee stood up on the rock. She met me at eye level, looking at me intensely. I opened my mouth to speak, but that stare had me caught at a loss for words.

"It …" I started. "It's good to see you, Sang Hee."

She actually smiled, a rarity from her, in my limited experience.

Sang Hee extended her hand and I took it, grasping her on the forearm and squeezing. We must have looked ridiculous, embracing in a sun-dappled grove like great heroes finally united. It felt good.

"I'm sorry to pull you away from your training—"

"No training in the midst of the League season," Sang Hee said. "It's all about rest from here. Rest and focus, both of which, yes, you are doing a fine job mucking up."

I nodded and gave a halfhearted shrug.

"I assume all of that trouble on the news is your doing?"

"Trouble? Not for anyone who hasn't had it coming a long time."

Her look shifted, then. She searched me and came up wanting.

"What happened, Akio?"

I swallowed. Min was the only friend I'd had contact with since Kuzu and the suits had tried to put me six feet under a river not too far from this one. Killing him had felt like progress, I couldn't deny that. Still, my heart beat faster as I remembered the lead ripping into my shoulder. The sound of the stream sloshing past us, carving its way around my ankles, reminded me of that black nighttime water I'd slipped under like a bad dream.

"Goro happened," I said. "And," I looked away from her, my eyes scanning the woods around us, "I suppose a bit of me happened as well."

Sang Hee made a great show of sighing. I didn't realize we still gripped one another until she yanked me up roughly onto the flat stone.

"You're not nearly the poet you think you are, Prince. Tell it to me straight. You're in bad with Goro, yes? Why? What did you do?"

"I won a fight, Sang Hee." I didn't intend for the venom to be directed at her, but where Goro Hamada was concerned, I had plenty to spare. Sang Hee's eyes widened, but she recovered quickly enough. She must have seen the flush spread across my face.

"He wanted you to take a dive," she reasoned. She stepped back and put her hands on her hips, shaking her head. She let out a sardonic laugh. "Of course. Your show with Janix."

"Not for the crowd," I acknowledged.

"I don't get it," she said, exasperated. "Why not let the chips fall where they may? You came off like a star in that one."

I shrugged.

"I started fighting in the League to pay off a debt. I've been what you might call … efficient thus far in my career. I don't play to the media, or make the blog rounds. I don't stir up bad blood with my opponents, and unlike you, my fighting style isn't known for being flashy. It's—"

"Direct." Sang Hee nodded. "To the point." She smirked. "You know, Akio, playing with your food can work wonders on the open sponsorship market."

"Figures," I said with a sigh. "The fight that puts me over is the one that gets me killed."

"Not from where I'm standing."

I felt strange in Sang Hee's presence. It was as if being here had me realizing that I was just the tiniest forgotten cog in all of it. Sure, I'd taken out one of Goro's best errand boys, and I'd even managed to get a bit of drama going between him and Gabriella Burtahn—drama I hoped had already reached the ears and tapping fingers of the bosses back in Japan—but what was I really playing at? I couldn't be seen in public. I couldn't go to the police, not after I'd literally killed the man who'd tried to kill me. I had nothing connecting any of it to Goro.

And then, it all spun back around, like a darkly comic wheel. The only thing left to do was the craziest thing, it seemed.

"You've got a look to you, Akio," Sang Hee said. Her voice was full of foreboding, and, unless I was sorely mistaken, perhaps a bit of desire. She seemed to come to her senses, stepped back again and would have gone over into the shallows had it not been for my reaching out to steady her.

We were standing very close, close enough to seem staged if it had been in a movie or play. I don't know if I leaned in or she did, but that kiss borrowed some of our remembrance from a week ago, and added a hell of a lot more to the mix than I realized had been there. Before we broke off, it became clear to me why Sang Hee would have come to meet me.

"So," she said, not so much breaking off from the contact as slipping out of it, "what now? What's your endgame?"

I told her. There, in a private forest on the borders of Seoul, I told her how I wasn't going to run. I told her I was going to stay, and that Kuzu Tokoro and Mal Chin were just the beginning. I told her my plans to make Goro sweat, and eventually to make him bleed, perhaps to kill him, if I got the chance.

I was nearly panting when I finished, and the stream seemed more silent after, as if the woodlands had taken in a long breath, uncertain of the killer in their midst.

If she looked at me differently, Sang Hee did a good job of hiding it.

She chewed it over for a time, standing with her arms crossed, more aloof than she had appeared before. She spit into the water. It was a vulgar move that somehow made me more attracted to her than I already was.

"I knew you took a fall," she said, returning to the earlier point. I frowned. Seeing it, she shrugged and threw her arms up. "What do you want me to say, Akio? I'm already doing my damnedest not to act like you just told me you were going to singlehandedly take down the Hachinin. I mean ... how? Just ... how are you even going to start—"

"One at a time," I replied evenly. Sang Hee bit back her reply. She might be flabbergasted, but the entire exchange had a markedly different feel from my arguments with Min.

"What's that stupid grin for?"

"You agree with me," I said simply.

She swallowed and raised her eyebrows. "Everyone in Seoul agrees with you. The Hachinin are a cancer. Their thugs have infected every street and corner, their product coursing through Korean veins like organic highways."

"No," I said. "No, no. Not that. I mean you agree with what I'm doing. You agree with how I'm doing it."

Sang Hee looked confused. She turned it over, and whatever conclusion she came to surprised her.

"You're going to get yourself killed, Akio. Is that what you want? To become a martyr?"

When I didn't answer right away, she took a step toward me. I'd yet to fight her under League rules, but I had my doubts over whether or not I'd prevail. Here, with no rules to protect me, I wasn't so sure I wanted to raise her hackles any more than I already had.

"You should have taken the fall, Akio."

I would have felt it more keenly if she had believed it.

"I didn't. And here I stand." I spread my arms out.

"For now."

"For now," I echoed.

Sang Hee looked toward the shore, scanning as a car whizzed past on the mountain road. The sun was getting low, and the fog was rolling back in. The water of the stream cast a mist that enveloped the rippled surface and rose up to kiss our fingertips.

"Killing Goro isn't going to solve this city's problems. You know that, right?" She didn't look at me as she spoke.

"It's a start," I said. "I may have been born to squalor, but it was a safe sort. The streets raised me and they did it well, all things considered." That drew another dubious appraisal, but I forged on. "But this city is poisoned, Sang Hee. You know it, I know it. Everyone knows it. And that fat prick's at the heart of it." I smiled. "I've already got him riled."

"More than riled." She seemed to try to say it with a hint of warning, but it came out more mischievous. Seeing my questioning look, she rolled her eyes. "He's released a press clipping this morning, responding to SMC's allegations."

"Did he, now?"

That was intriguing. I expected Goro to wall himself up in his offices, devote all attention to the League Finals tomorrow night, and put off addressing the media 'investigation' until it blew over, or until I was dead. He might be waiting a while on that last account, but Goro hadn't got to where he was without being a patient man. Gabriella was playing a game, and she thought she was using me as a puppet. Now, one of the great powers of the East was launching salvos across the bow of the Hachinin, even if not quite on their home soil. And I'd started it.

"He refuted all claims against his name."

"Yeah," I said distractedly, lost in my own thoughts.

"He's going to be at the Finals, according to my little birds."

Now it was my turn to raise my eyebrows. "And how many little birds do you have?"

"Enough."

Sang Hee was connected. I didn't know how and I didn't know the extent of it, but I did know that fighting was a hobby for her. She might not be an heiress at the level of Gabriella. For all I knew, she was self-made. I'd seen the sorts of purses she brought in from the League. Healthy. Much healthier than my own, despite my victories, but even with her lucrative sponsorship deals, she was known by many, and respected by more. It dawned on me then that she'd make a hell of an enemy, and that I should do everything in my meager power to keep her as a friend.

That probably shouldn't include asking more favors. But then, I was a ghost, after all. And what was a ghost to do but find people to haunt?

"I suppose a part of me expected him to hop on the first plane to Tokyo," I said.

"That would involve admitting defeat," Sang Hee said.

"Goro's weathered media storms and investigations before. They almost had him strung up four years ago on the port charges—"

"Not even close," I said, shaking my head. "They weren't close to a conviction. It was all a song and dance. They had nothing on him. Just some of his loose-lipped lackeys. Goro keeps a lot of friends, but he doesn't keep any of them particularly close. Not close enough to implicate him, in any event."

"Your girlfriend at the precinct tell you that?"

"Maybe."

"Hmm."

"No," I said, not willing to go down that particular road any farther. "Goro wouldn't run from me. He doesn't fear me enough yet."

"How do you know he fears you at all?"

"You don't try to kill someone you don't fear."

"That can be turned around, Akio."

"Fair enough." I smiled, flashing back to my recent League match against King Kwan. I wondered where the big fella had got to. "I guess it's a good thing that's my trick."

"Your trick?"

"It's nothing," I said, waving it away like so much smoke.

The silence stretched for the first time, and I didn't think this one was going to lead to a kiss. The realness of the situation was beginning to infect Sang Hee like a rot. She still stood with her arms crossed, but now they seemed to be holding in warmth and suppressing a shiver rather than displaying calm in the face of my madness.

"Maybe it is time we take the city back." She said it almost under her breath. Quiet enough to seem deadly serious.

"'We,' is it?" Not that I was complaining.

Sang Hee cleared her throat. "So, my ethereal Ghost of Seoul, my Sword Punk." She seemed to like the name, though not for the reasons others did. "Why did you really call me here, if it wasn't to profess your undying love?"

"How do you know it isn't?"

Her look might best be described as withering bored.

"What do you want?"

"I need a new suit," I said, a little sheepish. I'd stuck my hands into the pockets of my hoodie and turned them out like a teenager. "This isn't going to get me very far when I tangle with one of Korain's crew next time—"

"Korain?" Sang Hee looked nervous and surprised all at once.

"Mal Chin was one of his, apparently." I nodded. "Errand boys for the Hachinin."

"More than errand boys, Akio," she said, and now she didn't have to work to suppress the chill. "Korain's the best the League ever saw. How much money do you think it took to pull him away from it when he was on top?"

"Right," I said, only half ignoring the point. I spoke past the growing lump in my throat. "I also need new blades, and I've heard you know a guy."

"League blades?" she asked. "You want League blades to go along with a spiffy new League suit? Are you staging a coup, or a play? You may as well put up billboards that you're alive and—"

"He already knows, Sang Hee," I said. "Which is quite the point. And besides, how am I supposed to live up to the hype that's building on every forum across the land if I don't continue my rebellion with the same flair I started it with?"

"Rebellion ..." she tasted the word. It didn't go down right.

"You do know a guy, right?"

"Yes," she said. "I know a guy, but I'm guessing you're going to want a League suit that stops more than blunted blades and glowing batons, and I'm guessing you're going to want blades that can do what your little red flares never could. Namely, kill."

I didn't answer and Sang Hee began to turn it all over, tapping her foot and looking everywhere but at me. She must have examined every slick stone, floating leaf and errant bit of bark in the vicinity before she came back.

"That's it?" she asked.

"Wh ... what's it?"

"You were going to use me for the odd tumble before your epic and quite dramatic fall, and now you're going to use me to supply you with weapons to take down the most powerful man in Seoul, who would only be the eighth most powerful man in Japan."

"I—" I started but she wasn't finished.

"And all without inviting me into your little group?"

She seemed to be as genuinely hurt by the prospect as I was surprised and confused at it.

"Team?"

"Your rebellion, Akio," she said, twirling her fingers like she was ripping cobwebs. "Whatever it is. Clearly you haven't got this far alone. Someone's been hiding you, and I'd guess it's either that little minx you've got at the precinct or the cute one who teaches at Ken's old place downtown."

"It's not—" I started and stopped again.

The truth was, I hadn't done it alone. Sure, I'd made my grand, public stand against Goro, and I'd certainly been the one to kill Zoo. I had been the one to scale Gabriella Burtahn's tower.

But then, I hadn't pulled myself out of that river. I hadn't slain a mechanical demon in a broken lobby that may as well have been a throne room from a storybook without something borrowed, and I certainly hadn't stayed fed and warm on my own. My team was small, but I couldn't argue that it didn't exist.

"You're really not going to invite me to join your little group?" Sang Hee continued, misreading my pause.

I started to reach my hand out once more, but the sound of a cycle cruising by—slowly, by the sounds of it—had both of us perking up. There was a pop from the motor, and whoever it was sped off.

"Welcome to the team," I said, gripping her hand firmly. She took it reluctantly, not liking the idea of having to ask.

"But," I pulled her in a bit, leaned into her ear, "let's not pretend I provoked those pre- and post-match tumbles."

When I released her, she'd pursed her lips into a tight line to hide the smile. "And who're you calling cute?" I asked as she stepped down into the water, making her way back to the nearby shore. "Joon's hardly the dating type."

"And you are?"

"Well …" I didn't have much to say to that. Luckily, she let it go.

I spent a few minutes shaking loose pebbles from my shoes while Sang Hee made a call.

"Right. No. No. Yes. Exactly. Not like that. Well … it's private" were just a few of the clips I heard, and questions of who Sang Hee was and where she had found a man who'd not only make the best sponsored weapons the League had ever seen, but would also turn them lethal with little more than a phone call, flooded my mind.

She ended the call, slipped her phone back into her back pocket and bent over the seat of her cycle, rooting through one of the pockets in the long black pack that probably housed her brilliant staff.

I'd just finished retying my shoes when I felt it, like a threat on the breeze. Like ill intent drifting in my direction, fast as the crow flies.

I followed the drainage ditch back up to the guardrail along the side of the road. I didn't see anything untoward, but just before I returned my attention to the dirt clearing, I saw something black glinting in the fog-filtered sun. It was farther up the rise and obscured by a thicket of small trees and scrub. It was a cycle, likely the one that had taken its time in passing just minutes before. And it was riderless.

My pulse quickened as I scanned the surrounding trees. Sang Hee must have sensed that something was amiss. She paused in her rooting, frozen like a hare cornered by a snake. I saw the shadow detach itself from the tree line just a stride or two from her, and I knew I wouldn't reach him in time.

A different sort of black glinted in the filtered light beneath the trees as the masked hitman leveled his rifle, and even before I could shout a warning, Sang Hee exploded into motion.

She ripped her pack free and ducked behind her cycle. The gun flashed, but the barrel was longer than it should have been, and silent but for the horrifying ringing clacking sounds as bullets embedded themselves in the leather and plastic, and bounced off of the metal bits, of Sang Hee's cycle.

I knew I wouldn't make it in time, but I charged forward anyway, without the time to snatch up so much as a loose stone to hurl as a desperate distraction. The barrel of the gun swung up and scanned toward me, reminding me of the spider's turret at the base of Gabriella's tower. Only this had a man behind it. I don't know why it felt different, why it felt worse to be about to die that way, but it did.

I was less than two strides from him, and knew I was too far.

There was a flash that I at first mistook for the blinding light of the gun barrel, and I dove to the side, my shoulder slamming hard into the bank that rose up to meet the road above. I only realized the light had been blue when I was midway through a scramble that would have seen me shredded had the gunman had any sense of aim.

Had Sang Hee not skewered him on the spot.

I stood on shaking legs and stared at the scene before me, dumbstruck. Sang Hee had come around the front of her cycle, blue staff—more a pulsating blue spear, from the looks of it—in hand, and had thrown it with the might of a Greek god. It had taken the gunman off his feet, passed through his chest and planted itself tip-first in the hard-packed dirt a short distance away, taking him with it like a kebob.

He sighed a bloody sigh, arms drooping to his sides, chin lolling. The gun hit the ground with a thud, and the woods were quiet once more.

There was a pregnant pause that felt like a readjustment, and Sang Hee and I approached the impaled corpse with trepidation.

When we were close, Sang Hee reached out and ripped his nylon mask away with a savagery I found oddly disquieting. She was breathing heavily, but seemed remarkably calm, given the circumstances.

"Know him?"

"No," I said.

He was older than I would have guessed, with gray hair cut in a military style. His eyes had already glazed over, heavy lids half closed, and a trickle of dark blood ran from his chin like syrup. He looked European. Maybe even American.

"One of Goro's errand boys," she spat.

"An assassin," I said, "but military. Not a fighter."

I looked from him down to the blue shaft that was still pulsating. A foot length of it stuck out of his chest, while the rest had passed through him.

"The hell is this?"

Sang Hee shoved the assassin forward. He slid down the length of her glowing resin spear with a sickening squelch that wasn't as bad as the wet sucking sound as she yanked the weapon's tip free. The spear buzzed and crackled.

"That thing a taser, too?"

"When I want it to be," Sang Hee said. She pressed a button I couldn't see and the light faded from the shaft, along with the buzzing sound.

"It's like you said, Akio," she looked at me, caught between a smile and a grimace, "city's been getting bad. Can't be too careful."

We both looked down at the sorry soul who'd tried to cross us—that had tried to cross Sang Hee without knowing that she was some kind of lethal urban ninja.

"Guess that's a yes, then."

"What?" I asked, foggily.

"To joining the team."

"You don't have to kill someone to prove you're on—"

"A team of killers?" she interrupted.

I didn't have a good response to that.

"They came here. They saw me. They tried to kill me," she said, pointing at the corpse while looking at me. "That makes them my enemy just as much as yours."

"I ... I'm sorry."

"I know."

Sang Hee walked away, passing through the narrow, brush-choked trail toward the stream. I heard her splashing in the water, cleaning the gore from her spear while I stared numbly at the man she'd killed because of me.

Joon popped into my mind then, and I cursed myself for spending time outside of the dojo this morning. I didn't know if

I'd been followed, but I didn't see how they'd known where to find me. Maybe Sang Hee's cycle had simply been too conspicuously placed to escape notice. Or maybe they'd been tailing her ever since my reemergence, since we'd been connected even prior to being matched up in the League Finals.

I heard Sang Hee make her way back over, heard her zip up her pack and kick at the pipes of her cycle.

"Asshole missed the fuel tank."

"That's a good thing, right?"

"Sure."

She walked past me and leaned down, her hair spilling over and nearly brushing the top of his bloody face. She yanked something from his belt, and I heard a metallic jingle.

"Akio."

I blinked and looked at her. She held something out to me and I accepted the dead man's keys into my quivering palm. I didn't know what had come over me. I'd killed two men already this week. Bad men, I told myself. This one seemed no different, and I hadn't even been the one to do it.

Sang Hee frowned in consternation, reached out and squeezed me on the shoulder. "It's okay, Akio," she said. "We all make choices. Mine led me here, and they weren't all about you. I'll tell you about some of those choices when we have time. His led him ... well, there." She nodded at the dead man. "It isn't anyone's fault. Even if it is, it doesn't much matter."

I only realized after she forgave me that it wasn't guilt over what I'd caused her to do that had me feeling so off. It was the same thing that would have given me sleepless nights after Zoo and his thugs had filled my back and side with lead if I'd been conscious enough to turn it over. It was a feeling of powerlessness, and I knew it was one I could turn around, just like the fear. Could turn around and aim it.

"I hate guns," I said.

"What's that?" Sang Hee asked, distracted as she started up her cycle. "There we go. None the worse for wear."

She spun it around and came up on my right side. She held

something else out to me. I took what looked to be a spherical LED screen.

"Squeeze that and it'll bring up a map that'll guide you to the compound."

"The compound?"

"Farther north," she said. "It also works as a key." She nodded up at the road. "Take the dead man's bike. He won't be needing it."

My thoughts were starting to clear. Sang Hee revved the engine and went to start back up the trail, but I snatched her by the elbow.

"Don't do anything stupid tomorrow night," I said, my eyes boring into hers.

Her bottom lip was quivering, and not out of fear for me. She was in shock, or something like it. For some reason, it made me feel better.

"We'll talk after the Finals," she said. "We'll figure … all this out."

She sped off, spewing clods of dirt and dust over the dead man's face, and left me with the distinct impression that I'd just struck a match and sent it tumbling end over end into a hornets' nest.

17

DEFIANCE

I saw shadows all along the mountain road, and only some of them could be owed to the sinking sun as its rays died amongst the trees.

The sphere Sang Hee had given me was magnetized. I'd propped it up on the dead man's dash, and tried not to be startled every time it flashed out a new set of instructions. The road I traveled was illuminated in a faint-blue winding trail, with myself as the blinking dot. The forested hills on either side of me came up as 3D ghosts on the display. In the distance, a yellow dot that represented my destination had grown from a faint firefly to a glowing bulb.

And it was a good thing, since Mr. Assassin's bike was almost out of juice. Old-fashioned gasoline, this one.

The sky had cleared some since I'd left my streamside rendezvous, exposing the stars in the blue-black curtain above. It was almost enough to make me forget my plight, or those of the friends I'd pulled into the game with me.

There weren't many structures in the wooded hills around me. At least, none that I could see apart from the odd broken-down farmhouse. Of course, there was no farming in Seoul or its surrounding valleys. None that I knew of, anyway. Still, I thought of them like that, like the shells of homes that time forgot, uninhabited and overgrown, far from the sights, lights and sounds of the city and too wild to be tamed completely.

I saw gates. Some were wrought iron, but most were a mix of marble and plaster. They dotted the bends in the road. Ornate and imposing, they were an odd mix of new and old, as the security panels glowed a dull and bloody red in the night. Dirt roads stretched out behind them, disappearing up into the taller plateaus, where the rich and industrious kept their secret keeps.

I smiled to think that Sang Hee had one of her own, a castle to hide away from the worries and ways of the city in. As I thought of her, I thought of the moments we shared before she'd been forced to kill on my behalf. I thought of the kiss.

The road pulled sharply to the west, but the blinking sphere pulsed excitedly to get my attention, turning yellow and forming an arrow out of the electronic ether that pointed east. I peeled off and passed onto a dirt way. The trail was too narrow for a car to make it through, and the branches hung low, threatening to take an eye as I lost the stars overhead.

I came to what looked to be more a wall than a gate and brought the bike to a sputtering halt with a rattle, kicking the peg down. I tried to quiet the sphere, which buzzed excitedly, informing me that we had reached our intended destination.

I had to laugh as I took a step toward the wall, spying a faint-blue glow in the place of a red one. I approached the security panel and felt my heart sink as the sapphire-backed numbers leered up at me like mythic gatekeepers.

"Password would've helped," I muttered to myself.

I nearly turned around and slumped against the steel wall, when I noticed the little sphere blinking blue instead of yellow. I looked back at the panel set into the wall behind me, and saw it pulsing in time with the sphere.

"Fair enough," I said, walking back over to the bike. "Sorry I ever doubted you, little fella," I said, snatching the sphere up and walking it back to the wall.

It took some doing, but after a few moments spent trying to ignore the sphere's mounting annoyance, I found a button with a white key symbol carved into it and pressed. A compartment like an old-school disc drive slid out with an oiled hiss, and I placed the sphere into the basket like an egg.

A great grinding sound echoed in the hills, and I marveled as I examined the structure. The wall stretched away into the darkness on either side, and I wondered what sort of compound Sang Hee was hiding up in these hills, and how long she'd been hiding it.

After a hiss, a gap opened to the left of the panel, and the wall split on either side of the trail. The way beyond was brighter than I thought it would be, and I realized the night had only seemed deeper because of the trees. It took my eyes a few moments to adjust to the sudden, moonlit bright.

"Wow."

Didn't do it justice.

I spared a look back at the trail, ensuring that I hadn't been followed by another friend-in-waiting. My eyes scanned the darkness, looking for the glint of moonlight off an obsidian barrel.

Satisfied that I was alone, I stole into the courtyard as the gate rattled shut behind me with a clang.

I found myself in a yard that was surrounded on three sides by sections of wall that rose to twice my height, and on the fourth by a glass and concrete building that appeared to have two levels above ground and at least one below. There were towers set into three corners of the compound. It looked like a mix between a prison and a training yard, and I settled on the latter as the more likely pick as I padded over a large squared area raised above the surface of the dirt and grass in front of the building. It reminded me of the mats of Kenta's dojo, albeit harder. I certainly wouldn't have liked to take a fall on it.

"No apartment, then," I said aloud. Certainly no luxury abode. This compound had history. It wasn't the plaything of some aristocrat, but rather a place that had been built with a purpose in mind, and before Sang Hee had been around to see it done. Sure, aspects of it were modern, but the sloped concrete had gone out of style before we were born. It was something you saw in American military installations and Russian state offices, not prizefighters' hideouts.

Something bronze glinted in the half light, and I paused before a slab that was stuck like a flagstone on the other side of the platform. It was a star with a tiger's head in the center, white fangs glistening like stalactites. It took me a minute of pondering, but the image jogged something in me: a memory from long ago.

I remembered sitting in Min's house, stuffed like only they would stuff me when Joon and I would go over for supper once a week. Her father had pulled his old album out for what must have been the thousandth time for Min, judging by the way she'd rolled her eyes, but just the third or fourth for Joon and me.

He'd been a military man, he often told us, though Min's mother would turn away with a shake of her head and Min would roll her eyes so he could see.

"Why does Korea need a military?" I remember Joon asking.

Min's father had looked at him with a soft, almost wistful expression.

"There hasn't been a war here in ages," I'd added.

"Almost was one," he had said, his voice going from excited to grave. He adopted the same tone and the same expression when he told any of his stories, even more so when he told stories of the samurai he read about, and the great ninja clans from hundreds of years before, as if he'd been there.

Min's father had flipped through the book, showing us photos of him and his fellow recruits as they trained in yards a little less modern than this one but with a similar layout. They were dressed in gray and green. Gray from the South and green from the North, he told us.

It was all a bit of a foreign concept to the youths, that Korea had once been separate. Sure, we still referred to North and South, but only with a regional bias, not the enduring hatred and slow, powerful forgiveness that men and women like Min's parents—and plenty more beside them—no doubt felt at the dissolution of the line separating the two.

He'd hesitated over a page near the back, and I'd been so taken with it that he'd offered to rip it out and give it to me before his wife convinced him better of it.

I bent down in the yard and touched the emblazoned crest carved into the granite, and remembered the same seal embossed on that old velvet album. Tensions had been high with neighboring countries in the East for a long time, but they'd reached a boiling point on account of a unified Korea.

Tensions with Japan in particular had, and the mainland no longer had the best business relationship with its massive—and economically reeling—superpower to the south. China had checked out of the military game after overreaching in a series of brutally violent and ultimately futile conflicts with a temporary American-Russian alliance. As a result, the Land of the Rising Sun had its red eye fixed on its old stomping grounds once more. In the wake of American withdrawal from the Middle East, Japan got itself a military again, and one not ruled by the people, but by many of the precursors of the men who would go on to call themselves the Hachinin.

I stood and scanned the yard with renewed perspective. This had been one of the training facilities a unified Korea had sent its best and brightest to in the days of the country's youth, when it seemed our quiet corner of the world was set to join the West and the African continent in a contest to see whose bombs made the biggest craters and wrung the most tears from grieving mothers.

As it turned out, Japan took a few thousand reconnaissance flights, decided they didn't like what they saw, and called off their invasion, at least in the classic sense of the word. Of course, the economy of Seoul was largely based on entertainment, and the more enterprising members of the Japanese and defected American crime bosses living on the island found inroads that used violence as an invitation instead, with the League being the latest and greatest example of a way to funnel money out of the continent and back to Tokyo and Kyoto.

I stood in the yard as the moon fought its silent battle with the drifting clouds overhead, and imagined the men and women who had trained here. I saw them as wraiths, men and women of honor, not fighting for lights and crowds and adoration, but for unity and against tyranny.

"Sang Hee, I do think you have some secrets to share," I said into the cool night. It was beginning to feel less strange speaking to myself, the longer I was out here with nothing but the hills, trees and stars for company.

The picture was becoming clearer. No doubt Sang Hee had some connection to whoever had run this installation. Or maybe she'd simply snatched it up before some other rich asshole could, and rather than tear it down, had simply modified it to her liking, preserving its history, and its meaning.

I was beginning to like that girl, which made my heart flutter for all the wrong reasons as I thought of how she'd be stepping into the Soul Dome tomorrow night with Goro sitting in his box like a silent titan.

Don't do anything stupid, Sang Hee, I'd told her. And I didn't much like the look she'd returned.

I turned toward what I assumed was the front of the complex and eased the glass door open, admitting myself into a dim blue room with tiled floors and a tall, many-angled ceiling. Lights flickered on and cast a soft yellow warmth over the proceedings, and I made my way through the lobby toward a cement stairway at the back.

All in all, there looked like there may have been some modifications made to the place, but it didn't exactly have a residential coziness. I took the stairway down, growing more conscious of my increasing fatigue with each step, and sighed in relief as I discovered an underground lair that was much more in keeping with the Sang Hee I had known than the pseudo-military silo up above.

The lights here were softer still, and the ceiling low enough that I could brush my fingertips across it as I walked. The walls were poured concrete, and there was none of the glass in the basement to be found above. The room wasn't particularly wide, with plenty of openings on the right toward what I guessed to be dormitories, but the main hall stretched back almost too far for me to see. It was as if I'd wandered into a nuclear bunker, albeit one modified to the tastes of a twenty-nine-year-old millionaire.

To the left was a comfortable-looking seating area, replete with leather couches, lazy boys and a long black stem resting atop a stand against the slate-gray wall that looked to be a projection plate for one of those holographic viewscreens that had gone out of fashion almost as soon as they'd been released to the masses. Nifty technology didn't mean jack if nobody but the Sang Hees of the world could afford it.

I decided the rest of the complex could be explored tomorrow morning. For now, I plopped myself down on the longest, deepest couch I could find, and fell asleep before I had the chance to think too much on the man Sang Hee had killed or the coming trials.

Goro would get his. This week, this month or this decade, he'd get his. I only hoped nobody else took the chance from me in the meantime.

I woke in a state of panic that was exacerbated by having the distinct impression that an earthquake was about to bring several hundred tons of concrete crashing down over my head. I thrashed, nearly pulling a stitch that hadn't quite healed, and rolled to my left, falling unceremoniously onto the floor.

The whole building shook. Or, it had been shaking. I was almost sure of it.

I got to my feet and settled into a crouch as the dry crackle of speakers turning on after a long time dormant made the hair on the nape of my neck stand on end.

"Entrance, Main Gate, Section Zero," an electronic voice said.

I raced up the stairs, taking them two at a time. I rounded the bend and nearly fell face-first at the top of the main landing as my toe caught on the lip of a stair. I recovered my balance, but not my wits, and if it hadn't been Min standing in front of me, arms crossed in front of her chest and eyebrows raised in that expectant way of hers, I'd have been caught dead to rights.

"Catch you napping?" she asked.

I stared, dumbfounded and entirely at a loss, looking at her for a spell before I craned my neck to the side, trying to get an angle to see the front gate. It had been closed behind her.

"How …" I started, but Min tossed something to me. I caught it without knowing what it was, and shook my head, lamenting my own stupidity as the viewing sphere Sang Hee had given me settled into my palm, black and dormant.

"You left that in the door," she said.

"Okay," I said. "But that still doesn't explain how you found me here."

The sun was already nearing the end of its arc in the daytime sky, which meant I'd been sleeping a lot longer than I'd anticipated. It cast a burnt orange glow over everything, drenching the concrete pillars and casting yellow rays through the glass windows and skylights I hadn't noticed in the night.

As I drew to within striking distance—which could also be hugging distance, one never knew when dealing with Min—I noticed how tired she looked.

"I traced the call you made before you left my place last night," Min said. "Did some digging. Found an address under one of Sang Hee's holdings."

"Holdings …" I repeated, sounding dumber than I looked, which must have been mighty dumb already.

"Your *friend*," I wasn't sure if she emphasized the word for one of two reasons and didn't bother asking, "has a pretty extensive portfolio. But, most of it's locked up in real estate, and not the kind people typically pay top dollar for."

"It's good to see you, Min," I said, putting on a wan smile.

"But you're wondering why I'm here."

"Well … yeah, I am."

"I wanted to give you an update on the investigation."

"Okay …" I said. "Update away."

Min watched me as if measuring a reaction she hadn't got yet.

"Nothing's going to stick, Akio."

I pursed my lips, but the longer I thought about it, the less displeased I felt. Of course it wasn't going to stick.

"There's a lot of usable stuff in there," Min continued. She seemed worried over my lack of reaction. "But, we've been in contact with some of Seoul's best public prosecutors, and all of them side with the defenders."

"Side with them on what?"

"That Goro has a strong case against Gabriella Burtahn regarding blackmail, and that we're about to get into a legal pissing contest between billionaires that's going to result in millions in legal fees and probably no real consequences to either one apart from a few underlings' jobs being lost and a few corporate firms getting fat off their argumentative indulgence."

I nodded.

"I'm sorry, Akio."

"Sorry for what? This is fine, Min. It's great. Well, not great, but …"

She looked far from convinced.

"I told you this was the way things would go, Min," I said. "It's the way things always go for these people. Men like Goro only speak one language—"

"He speaks it through a lot of mouths, Akio. You can't fight them all."

I bit off my response. We'd been circling the same argument for years, even before recent developments had cast it in an entirely different light. Still, I was beginning to understand why Min looked so disappointed. Some part of her was still clinging to the hope that the law would be enough to see Goro laid low. That justice would prevail, and not on the end of a scorned fighter's blades.

"So …" Min said, walking around the lobby. She looked up, measuring the place as if it were hiding something. "Sang Hee a wannabe historian?"

"Hell if I know."

"Right," Min said without looking at me. "Because you two have never been close."

I swallowed and didn't respond, which was response enough. Min wasn't hung up on me like I had been on her once upon a time, but there was enough history there, and enough platonic love from childhood, to make things awkward, if not tense.

The stretching mood hid something else just beneath the surface. Min was hiding something, or taking her time in getting to it.

"You saw Joon," I said.

Min stopped a short distance from me. She didn't immediately turn around.

"I did."

When I didn't say anything, Min turned, her expression earnest.

"He thought you were dead, Akio, even if he hoped against it. He doesn't follow the gossip. Hadn't heard of your recent ... missions. Though," she paused and even looked to suppress a smile, "I'm not sure which made him madder."

"Wonderful ..."

"It's not just you involved in—"

"I know."

I didn't say it tersely. Just said it, like a dropped stone in a well.

"Have you had any unexpected house calls?" I asked, concerned. "Anyone following—"

"I'm fine," she said. "Either nobody's connected us, or Goro's too smart or too busy to move against a member of the SPDF so brazenly."

"Probably the former," I muttered.

Min nodded and shrugged, as if it didn't matter.

"Sang Hee killed a man yesterday," I blurted out. It sounded horrid and crass. Min raised her eyebrows and her chin. "My fault." I pressed a hand to my chest. "Again."

"She is involved, then," she said as much as asked. "Sang Hee. She's not just letting you squat. No, she doesn't seem the type to stay on the sidelines."

"Hopefully she does for one more night, at least."

Min nodded toward the glass door and wall behind me, at the

front of the lobby. The sun had already sunk, with just a bit of gold mixing with the lavender in the southwestern sky. Most of the yard was once more drenched in shadow.

"There a screen in this place, or just old charts? League Finals kick off soon. Let's watch your girl do work."

"Yeah," I said with a smirk. "If there's one thing that could salvage this shit month, it's watching Janix get pummeled again. He's already lost some pretty points. We'll see what's left of him when Sang Hee's through."

I tried not to let my nerves show. Nerves about what Sang Hee might do on Goro's stage tonight. Nerves about what he might do if he had connected her to the dead man by the stream and the Sword Punk that was starting to give him more trouble than he was willing to deal with quietly.

It took some doing, but eventually I discovered—quite by accident—that the best way to turn on a holographic display was to flail above and about it like an idiot until it sparked to life. It took several minutes before the floating image resolved itself into any semblance of clarity approaching a good old-fashioned LED display, and the sound echoed obtusely in the underground bunker.

"Place looks like it was designed to take a nuke," Min said as she came back from her cursory inspection of the dormitories.

She sat down on the couch next to me with a heavy plop and the tinging of glass. I looked over to see her set a six-pack of dusty brown bottles onto the knee-high table in front of us. She snatched one up and twisted the top off with expert precision, and took a drink. The first sip brought a grimace, the second nearly turned her green.

"The hell did you find that?"

"Beside one of the bunks," she said.

"The good ole boys leave it sitting?"

She turned the bottle over, searching for something.

"You really didn't look at the expiration date? Beer's good maybe a year tops."

She set the bottle down on the table with a heavy thud and waved a hand at our surroundings. "The hell is this place?"

"Unified Tactical Defense Installation, is my guess."

"Makes sense."

The commercials ended and the intro package started up on the screen, preceded by the red tower against a white background that was the symbol of Kyoto Sport. Highlights from the League's first few seasons played in a kaleidoscope of colorful graphics, all while trumpets and horns blared in an attempt to get across the majesty of the events of the past and the history of the one to follow. Sang Hee featured prominently, as did Janix, while champions from seasons past flitted across the screen on the heels of their most triumphant moments.

No matter how cynical I got, no matter how close to the sport and all its ugly truths and buried lies, I couldn't ignore the thrill that package called up in me, nor the sickening, raw anger that rose to supplant it when the screen faded to black, and one last highlight package rolled featuring none other than yours truly. It wouldn't have been all bad, if the next fade hadn't brought with it those gleaming, ghostly white words, like fangs in the darkness.

In memory of Akio Prince.

The screen hung there for longer than it should have, and when the words faded, the roar of the crowd was deafening. In one deft, utterly simplistic producorial move, Goro had not only thumbed his greasy fat nose at me, but won back a crowd who'd already forgotten his public shaming just forty-eight hours before and the implications of his role in Akio's—in my—unfortunate demise.

It was Finals night. Truth and justice be damned.

Min and I sat with arms crossed in ire as the announcer went through his routine. More highlight packages played, and two half-nude men with slightly more muscle than fat pounded a great canvas drum while spotlights made them hot enough to glisten.

"Get on with it," I said, chewing my lip.

Finally, mercifully, they did.

Janix was the first to enter the arena. He was preceded by an amber light show, and while he looked to be nursing a limp as he

came across the blue corner drawbridge, he looked largely
unharmed, though I noticed that the cameras kept a healthy
distance from his face. I couldn't help but smirk as I caught a
glimpse of a divot or two in that formerly impeccable jawline.

Janix bowed to either side of the arena crowd, as was customary, and then turned toward the Presidential box, dipping the
lowest for his master. He looked to have new armor on. It was
the color of ivory, and looked as if it had been fashioned from the
gathered and melted bones of mammoths. It had red painted
streaks on it that clashed with the orange trails of light that ran
in LED rivers through the seams. Two translucent handles jutted
up from behind his back, and when he turned to expose the X
sheath across his back, I noticed that they were longer than the
sticks he'd fought me with.

"Looks like he's learned a thing or two, after all," Min said.

"His weapons weren't long enough to deal with my unarmed
reach," I said. "I don't know what he thinks they'll do against
Sang Hee."

But then, that was why they played the game, after all. The
oldest adage in combat sports was also the truest: styles make
fights. Always had. Always would.

The crowd gave Janix some love, but there was a strange,
halting mood over his entrance, likely down to the fact that he'd
last been seen in the arena losing to me, and that I'd summarily
been killed by accident or otherwise, robbing them of what
should have been a Sang Hee versus Akio Prince League Finals
match. The match would have been made all the sweeter due to
the fact that the trades had recently made me at one of her city
condos.

Of course, Goro's team had managed to spin that one as well,
not-so-subtly drawing a link between tonight's match and Sang
Hee's desire to finish what her dead lover had started.

When the arena lights faded, the crowd let out a collective
gasp of anticipation. When the first blue lights streaked across
the horizontal displays, they roared. Sang Hee's bridge was
bathed in azure light, looking like magical ice. She let the crowd

steep in it for a space of time, the blue bridge hanging there above the black chasm. She let Janix soak in their cheers, and in the anticipation of her arrival.

When she finally crossed—trademarked blue armor polished to a metallic sheen—Sang Hee received the loudest ovation I'd ever witnessed in a League match. Even Min seemed impressed.

Sang Hee stepped onto the white canvas of the platform with grace and even reverence, and dipped a bow toward either side of the crowd. She took another step toward the center, toward Janix, and dipped one toward him. And then, in a sign of things to come, she pivoted toward the black glass box where shadowed figures watched with dispassionate interest, and stared. Simply stared, long and hard.

At first, the crowd seemed confused by Sang Hee's display. Was she going to bow to the Presidential box, as was customary? Was she going to address Goro, perhaps pine for her lost lover, Akio Prince?

As it turned out, Sang Hee's plan was, quite simply, to continue standing and staring with all the cold will she could muster. Soon enough, the silence of the crowd changed to an amused murmur, and soon, that turned. There were whispers and even a few shouts, some telling the fighters to get on with it, others asking aloud what Sang Hee was playing at.

I smiled, knowing exactly how that look came off to me, and thinking of how it must look to Goro himself.

The speakers crackled and the announcer coughed awkwardly into his microphone. He was sweating, unsure how to proceed, but Sang Hee was not going to bow, it seemed, and so, the only thing left to do was to proceed.

"Fighters! Finalists! Take your positions!"

Janix said something to Sang Hee as he drew his blades, flashing them to amber life. She drew her eyes away from Goro's box with effort.

"Fight!"

Janix exploded into motion, covering the distance between him and Sang Hee faster than I remembered him moving against me. Sang Hee either didn't have time to draw or decided against it, shifting her weight just enough to form her body into a blade. She dipped back and spun away, pulling the top end of her staff with one hand as she spun. The butt of the staff whacked Janix on the back of the head and caused him to stumble, and Sang Hee disengaged, unharmed and unperturbed as the crowd laughed maniacally.

"Careful now," I said through gritted teeth. Min was leaning forward, hands gripping her pants. She looked quickly at me before focusing back on the screen.

"She's fine, Akio," she said, pointing. "She's in control."

It seemed that she was.

Janix made for Sang Hee again, and Sang Hee dodged. Sometimes, she'd extend a palm, deflecting one of his reaching polymer batons. Most of the time, she simply flitted away like a leaf on the undulating surface of a river.

Janix looked more tired to me than frustrated. On more than one occasion, he followed up a lunging strike with some barked barb at Sang Hee. The Sang Hee I knew would have risen to any number of those challenges, but not this one. This one was cold and calculating, and deadly focused.

The thing was, she didn't seem particularly interested in doing anything about it.

Sang Hee reached for her staff when Janix managed to cross her up with a forehand jab into a backhand cross, and the crowd roared in excitement. Instead, she changed tack at the last moment, accepting the glancing blow off of her turning shoulder and lancing a kick into Janix's midsection that sent him sprawling.

"It's a wonder he made it to the Semis," Min said, her tone quickly going from enthralled and excited to bored.

"He's tired," I said. "He still hasn't recovered." Now that the fight was on in full—if you could really call it a fight—it was all too apparent. Janix labored with each lunge and pull. He winced with every pivot. Our fight had only been a week before, and Janix had likely earned himself some fractures and bone bruises that wouldn't be fully healed before the next season, never mind tonight's match.

In a way, as I watched him dart and spring, lunge and parry, I pitied handsome Janix. I knew how persuasive Goro could be, just as I knew how much money he was set to earn with a victory tonight.

As many had discovered before, both in the arena and in whatever venue they'd had the misfortune of coming up against her, Sang Hee was far less benevolent than her name would imply. Tonight, her ire wasn't directed at Janix. While that might spare him a good deal of pain in the physical realm, it wouldn't do much to help his standing among the public.

"She's playing with him," I said. Min nodded her agreement.

"Doesn't look like she's having a whole lot of fun doing it."

"No," I agreed. "No, it doesn't."

The crowd was growing restless. The vast majority of the arena was pro-Sang Hee, but even they could be stretched thin. Even they had their limits when their hero of choice played too long.

Janix lunged in again, this time disguising a sweep with that lead baton-flashing jab. Sang Hee stayed in the pocket as Janix ducked, planted his palms on the canvas and launched into a spin, sweeping his heel across the surface of the canvas. The back of his calf collided with Sang Hee's—or nearly did—but she saw it at the last moment, leaping and spinning over the kick and drawing her staff again as she came back down.

The crowd inhaled as Sang Hee landed off to Janix's blind side as he finished his sweep. It would take nearly a second for him to regain his feet, and his hands were low, batons nowhere close enough to stop the overhead chop from that blazing blue staff.

Only Sang Hee didn't bring the staff down. Instead, she merely twirled away, spinning the weapon along with her, and waited for Janix to regain his feet. If the fighter knew he'd just been spared—and by extension, humiliated in front of ten thousand arena fans—he showed no signs of it.

"That confirms it," Min said. "Akio, what is your girl doing?"

"I'm afraid I'm beginning to get a picture."

There. There it was, on the back of another Janix lunge. Sang Hee spun away, her feet a blur of defensive mastery, her knees bent just enough to allow her to move laterally or vertically. Sang Hee was making the whole thing look effortless, but those movements required expert precision and a lot more energy than it appeared. Her face might look serene to a casual observer, but to one who knew her, it bespoke deep concentration. Her temples were sweating, drips coalescing and making salted streaks that plastered her dark hair to her ears. Her eyes tracked Janix's every movement, but on the tail end of each exchange—or lack thereof—they tracked up toward the Presidential box, and held there just a moment too long.

Janix was good, but he wasn't as good as me, and he wasn't nearly as good as Sang Hee. Compromised as he was, the fight should have been over on the second or third exchange, and the confetti should have been falling from the rafters, illuminating Sang Hee's win and Goro's PR victory. Another record night for the League, and one built on the back of the tragedy of Akio Prince.

What a story.

Only, Sang Hee seemed to be the only actor not playing along. I only hoped she was nearly through playing, that her private point had been made to Goro—clear enough to be recognized, subtle enough not to be repaid.

"Come on, Sang Hee," I whispered, willing her body to move in a way that would cause Janix a little more than embarrassment. Willing that bright-blue staff to find a mark against suit and skin rather than amber baton.

Janix paused, his chest heaving so hard the scales of his League suit seemed to only barely be able to contain the movement. He winced with each breath, and I remembered a few of the shots I'd landed on his ribs.

Hunt the body and the head will follow.

Another of Kenta's mad, absolutely true axioms.

The crowd was growing more restless as Sang Hee—usually one to pace and stalk her prey—simply stood and stared, waiting for Janix to make the next move, and the next and the one after that, until it seemed he was near to the point of dropping from the exhaustion.

There was a crackle and a screech as the announcer tapped his microphone to life from the floating box above the center platform.

"Red Corner Fighter has been charged a warning for timidity!"

That brought with it a confused mix from the crowd, with some shouting their agreement while others shouted them down, defending their benevolent queen to the last. Surely Sang Hee was up to something, they thought. Surely there was something to clever Janix's style that the others—and they themselves —couldn't see.

Sang Hee gave an almost imperceptible shrug and began to stride forward with long, casual steps. She swung her glowing staff absently at her right side, and Janix shrank back at her approach. When she drew nearer, he brandished his batons, crossing them before him in anticipation of a sudden leaping attack, perhaps an overhead chop.

Instead, Sang Hee stopped almost an arm's reach from her opponent, looked him up and down and promptly dropped her staff. Now the crowd seemed to be on the verge of panic, with Sang Hee's fans going so far as to cry out in anguish, as if they couldn't believe what they were seeing.

Min and I leaned forward as far as the couch cushions would allow us, waiting for Janix's strike to fall. Sang Hee collapsed, falling to her knees as if she'd been shot, though Janix hadn't so much as flinched.

Sang Hee knelt there, shoulders slumped, head down and black hair falling in a sorry cascade around one shoulder. Janix looked from his fallen foe to the encircling crowd. He stepped back and then forward, raised a baton and then lowered it. He looked wild, like a deer trapped in a rocky gorge and surrounded by wolves.

Finally, he looked to the Presidential box, and even on the

screen, we could see shadows rushing to and fro behind the opaque surface, like eels in a black pool.

"Red Corner Fighter," the announcer intoned. "Do you … do you forfeit the match? Are you injured?"

Sang Hee raised her head, craning around Janix to squint up at the spotlight that bathed the announcer's form in gaudy radiance.

"I do," she said. "And I am not."

Now there wasn't so much a gasp as an outright denial, as if the crowd truly could not believe what they were seeing. Some threw debris. A bottle made it as far as the canvas of the arena before skipping harmlessly off of the giving surface and careening into the darkness and the netting below.

"Repeat, Red Corner Fighter," the annoyed, confused announcer said. "You are injured?"

"Negative," Sang Hee said, light and lilting as a songbird. "I am unharmed. Have you not been watching?"

"I … I have been."

"Have you not all been watching?" Sang Hee threw her hands out to her sides, palms up. "Surely you have seen it."

The crowd fell silent.

"I am defeated," Sang Hee said. She looked up at Janix and gave a smirk before bowing her head once more. "I have taken the measure of my opponent, and I have come up wanting. I cannot defeat him. Surely, my fans will forgive me. I'll come back stronger next time."

A roar of anger and denial spread, only now it was difficult to know whom it was aimed at. Some made Sang Hee the object of their rage, while others cursed Janix's name. Still more screamed with almost directionless hate, but I smiled as the plan became clearer. Smiled even as I recognized the danger Sang Hee was now putting herself in.

Those jeers, those screams of rage that could only come on the backs of consumers whose money had been spent and whose bloodlust had yet to be sated, had only one direction. Suddenly, it looked as if Goro's no-lose situation wasn't quite as ironclad as he or I had believed. Suddenly it looked very much like there was a way for him and his League to lose the night, and Sang Hee had discovered it without landing so much as a resin-backed strike.

"Red Corner Fighter," the announcer said in a tone that mixed annoyance with confusion, "please confirm: you forfeit the League Finals to Janix. You will not continue …"

He let a question hang at the end of the supposed statement, giving Sang Hee every chance to give up the charade.

She actually raised a hand to her chin and stroked it. She frowned in concentration, like continuing to fight—even winning—hadn't occurred to her as a possibility.

She made a great show of sighing, and her shoulders drooped further still, her form nearly folding in on itself with its despondence.

"I am defeated."

The crowd had begun to chant Sang Hee's name, but now they seemed truly and summarily defeated. A few still cursed her and others hurled their drinks and insults at the black maw that was the President's box. Most of them had fallen silent, and the first lines had begun to trickle out of the arena like mourners abandoning a funeral, the better to beat the traffic. The better to find some bar to drink away their sorrows and curse demons that would have lost a face by the time they hit the third bottle. Ill will that would grow into disdain, and disdain that might someday soon change into that emotion that all promoters—that all businesses—feared more than anything else.

Indifference.

Sang Hee's victory was at hand. All she had to do was keep kneeling there. Janix wouldn't strike her. He'd thought about it, his face playing over such a range of emotions that he was the picture of chaos. Ultimately, he had settled on a more genuine, frustrated version of the despondence Sang Hee was only playing at.

Only, she didn't keep kneeling there. She didn't wait until the arena emptied and the sportscasters could begin spinning their sponsored yarns about what had gone wrong and about what sort of an effect Akio Prince's death must have had on the former champion to keep her from competing up to her fullest ability. Goro's spin doctors were already hard at work on that narrative, no doubt.

Sang Hee got to her feet, and the droning murmur in the crowd quieted some. The announcer's microphone let out a soft whine, but he didn't speak, waiting for Sang Hee to shed some light on the situation, to bail him out. Many of those who had gone halfway toward the exits had now paused on the slick and sticky stairs, while others who had already passed into the halls filtered back in, drawn in by a halting curiosity.

This better be good, their looks said.

Sang Hee walked toward the lip of the platform, the one just beneath the President's box. She smiled, cameras tracking her likable, charismatic features. She raised her hands and crossed one foot over the other like a court jester.

"This is what we do now, is it not?" she asked. Spectators looked from one to another before focusing back on Sang Hee. "This is what the League has become, and through it, what Seoul has become. Performance. Drama. Lies."

The words were like hurled stones, each one burying itself in the thick plate glass of Goro's suite.

"If it seems to the audience that my performance was not up to par, I must apologize. Though I may have his skill with resin and light, I must say, I'm not half the actor Akio Prince was." Another murmur. "Or," she stroked her chin again and began to pace along the edge. "No. I suppose Akio didn't give the performance he was meant to, did he Goro?"

I had a sudden image of Goro slamming some red button in his booth that would see the whole platform disappear from sight, casting both Sang Hee and poor Janix into the abyss.

"Forgive me, audience," Sang Hee said. "You did not know. Akio Prince was meant to fall, isn't that right, Goro? Akio was meant to fall, as I have fallen. He was meant to lose."

Sang Hee turned, her eyes sweeping past Janix and convincing him to stay in place. She found each and every sweeping camera, forcing them to focus on her every word.

"This is what we do here, in the Free City of Seoul," Sang

Hee said, finishing her spin until she was once again facing the President's box. "We make stories. But not all are as willing as I. Not all are as complacent nor as cowardly. Alas, not all can be as brave and foolish as Akio Prince."

Now there was a cheer, though it seemed to be a halfhearted one, tinged with need. The crowd had taken Sang Hee's meaning, but threading my name into it all had brought back the stink of SMC's investigation of Goro. She had just accused him of fixing fights—a more egregious affront than murder from the perspective of the audience—but she had also done so while hinting that my refusal to go along with the charade had resulted in my untimely demise.

"She just told them you're alive, Akio," Min said. "She just told them the Sword Punk is Akio Prince."

I supposed I should have been worrying—knew I would be in time—but for now, I couldn't help but smile as I pictured Goro's cigar-smoke-obscured face in that luxury box.

"Now, audience," Sang Hee said. The floor was still hers, with the announcer uncertain how to proceed and the broadcast unwilling to wink out until those black lenses had soaked up every last frame of Sang Hee's address. "How shall I do it? Shall I cast myself into the abyss, or should Janix strike me down? Which would add more … drama to the proceedings? Which would cash more bets?"

The crowd began to shout with ten thousand voices. Some told her to go for it, while the vast majority began to say something else, something that coalesced and formed into a chant. Something that had Sang Hee smiling.

"Goro! Goro! Goro!" they shouted, calling for his blood.

When the chanting had grown loud enough, the spotlight winked out, bathing Sang Hee in the dim lights from the rafters and the ethereal blue fairy glow of her staff. She looked like a glowing hero from yore, like a magical princess standing before her people, and before the black maw of some fell beast that was too frightened to move against her.

The phone lights turned on to chase away the enveloping

dark like ten thousand candles. The flashes were cheers all their own, casting a glittering brilliance over the dim arena.

Then, a row of lights turned on. They were set into the black steel above the Presidential box, and they shone down on Sang Hee, washing out the glow of her staff and forcing her to shield her eyes as she squinted up.

The crowd jeered and screamed, salivating at the prospect of seeing Goro, and in a light altogether unbecoming. Normally, he made two appearances per season, at the beginning and at the end, to crown a champion. How strange, then, to see him now.

"I've got a bad feeling about this," Min said, her former good humor sucked out with the titan's threatened arrival.

She was rarely wrong about such things.

The glass looked to warp, and then the whole box seemed to shudder. The glass window that was more a wall began to slide down with a silent hiss, exposing soft red lighting that made the interior look like a bloody mouth. I half expected a room full of suits—investors and gamblers and the occasional guard—to appear, but I should have known Goro more than that. He was about nothing if not appearances, and it wouldn't do to appear cowed in front of Sang Hee.

I had to admit, bathed as he was in the combined light of his bloody box and the burned orange tip of his rich cigar, he looked less fat than immense. He stood at the very edge of the box, with nothing to stop him from plunging into the chasm below him, and only a forward step away from Sang Hee. He took a long pull on his cigar, and the burnt orange light inched up closer to those fat lips as he blew out a billowing plume of smoke that obscured the spotlights on the top of the box for a long minute.

He waited there a long time. Long enough to make it all a bit uncomfortable, and long enough for the crowd to quiet their complaints. It was like a show, and judging by the way Sang Hee began to fidget, it wasn't one that Goro was entirely willing to cede control of.

"What happened to him, Goro?" Sang Hee asked. Now she looked like the caged tiger she usually emulated in the arena.

She paced back and forth, her eyes fixed on Goro, right hand gripping her blue staff fiercely. "What happened to Akio Prince?"

The crowd was utterly transfixed, and it was all I could do to keep my eyes from drying out as I fixated on the surreal scene before me. Here was my lover and rival, pacing before one of the Hachinin, inquiring as to my death.

"How are you going to weasel your way out of this one, Goro?" I asked, too caught up in it all, too intoxicated by the welcome threat of possibility to think of an answer Min had already arrived at.

"Akio Prince," Goro said, his voice deep and baritone, with none of the slick grease you might expect, "was a champion."

The crowd shouted him down, told him to answer Sang Hee.

"Akio Prince is gone, Sang Hee," he said. "But he is not forgotten."

The crowd seemed less sure how to react to that, but they kept their anger burning hot enough to let him hear it.

"Now, we look to the future of the League without him. We look to the future, as we always have."

Sang Hee didn't know where he was going with this. She didn't respond, only paced and growled up at him, teeth bared.

"Audience, surely you can see what's happened here, and do not let it be said that Goro or the League has turned a blind eye to it. Do not let it be said that we have shirked responsibility, or avoided blame."

"Out with it, Goro," I growled, both fearful and fascinated by how he'd managed to wriggle out of it, to spin it without a stack of market research and obituaries in his hand—his usual means for solving PR nightmares.

"It is clear that the League as it stands has grown too stale for someone with the talent and skill of Sang Hee," Goro said. "Just as it had grown too stale for the late, great Akio Prince, who never put a premium on performance but who stopped at nothing to win. More so, Prince was a man who stopped at nothing to challenge himself." He dipped his chin to Sang Hee. "Perhaps if he had met you in the Finals—and you him—the two of you might have had the challenge you so desired. As it stands,

Akio chose to forego his League blades, and you have chosen to forego the event entirely. This, I cannot blame you for. But …"

The crowd had stopped their shouting and chanting. Now, they hung on Goro's every word. Even Sang Hee did.

"Now, you can cast yourself into that abyss, take your amber licks on the end of Janix's batons … or, you can put your money where your mouth is, and accept a challenge worthy of one of your skill level, and worthy of the memory of Akio Prince."

Sang Hee swallowed, knowing Goro had her just where he wanted.

"What challenge?" she asked.

"Oh, Sang Hee," I said, putting my head in my hands.

"At least he can't outright kill her now that the feud is so public. Public challenge. Needs to be collected in front of these same people, and many more watching like we're watching. He can't move against her in any real, material way until this whole episode has faded from the public consciousness. Even then, people would draw lines between you and her. More so, between Goro and the two of you."

"You said yourself that any lines your investigation might draw are less than meaningless—"

"Legal lines, Akio," Min said, like a parent explaining something to a child. "For men like Goro, those are always the easiest lines to cross. I'm talking about the court of public opinion. It's a lot for politicians. It's everything for men like Goro."

I shook my head, but knew Min was right. At least Sang Hee would be safe a little while longer. Now, it only remained to be seen what sort of challenge Goro had in mind.

"Sang Hee," Goro intoned. "What say we put your skill to the test in the most primal and potent way? What say we avoid the pageantry, the glitz and glamor? What say we abandon Seoul rules, and bring Kyoto out, just for one night?"

"Oh," Min said.

"Yeah," I agreed. "Shit."

On paper, there wasn't a lot separating Kyoto rules from Seoul rules as the League dictated, nor from Shanghai rules, nor from Moscow rules. Each division of the League had its own playbook, all of which included a mortality clause. Regulators were less concerned with death in sporting events now than they had been in the early aughts. The modern world was all about freedom, and freedom of choice.

In a sporting sense, I suppose that meant freedom from life as well. At least, freedom to die.

Still, while opponents and organizers couldn't be held responsible for death or serious injury in a set of League rules that allowed strikes with resin blades and heavy batons—even Janix's sticks packed more than enough punch to do some serious long-term damage—the spirit of the rules tended to emphasize the martial spirit, including mercy.

Not so in Kyoto. In Kyoto, they adopted the samurai way, which is to say, fighters were disgraced for losing with their consciousness intact, and fighters passed into legend for fighting far beyond their physical and mental limits, collapsing into sad, bloody heaps of exhaustion, and later being pronounced dead at regional hospitals via press release.

The only true difference between Kyoto rules and Seoul rules lay in what was forfeit when one signed on that red dotted line. Namely, the right to forfeit.

"You want me to fight Kyoto rules," Sang Hee said, "against him?" She jutted her staff back toward Janix, who couldn't help but take a shrinking step backward. That drew a laugh from the audience and a groan from Min.

"She's playing right into his hand."

"Not Janix," Goro said. "Brave and capable though he is, it's clear that Janix's recent appearance left him in a state unbefitting a finalist. No, Janix is the League champion. He won under Seoul rules. He won the season, fair and square."

The crowd groaned and Janix hung his head in shame, though he was no doubt running the calculations in his mind. His estate was about to get much healthier.

"No, we'll find a new foe for you, Sang Hee. One from across the sea. What say you? Audience? What do you say to the first-ever cross-League championship match?"

"Cross-League championship?" Min asked. "Who's the Kyoto champ this year?"

"A local boy, I think. Yusuke something. He's good, but ..."

"But what?"

"Not good enough to beat Sang Hee. Seoul may be 'softer' than the other Leagues," I said, "but nobody would argue that we're not the best of the best."

"I wouldn't be so sure of that," Min said.

"Goro's playing at something," I said. "There's more to this than meets the eye. If he wants Sang Hee to fall in the arena for some kind of pride play, he should bring Korain back out of retirement. Take him off of his latest assassination mission."

"What? Korain's an assassin?"

"Pretty sure," I said with a shrug. Min was staring at me as if I'd finally snapped. "What? You've got no problem believing that Mal Chin went dark. Where do you think Korain's been since dominating the League? He's completely off-map."

She focused back on the screen. "I suppose Goro feels it's a win–win for him. No matter who wins and no matter who dies, the whole thing is going to run the news cycle for the next week. Sang Hee's entire address—from implications surrounding poor old Akio Prince to fight fixing in the League—is going to look like some sort of brilliant promotional rug pull from Goro's office. They'll be lauding him a marketing genius on the same channel that's currently investigating him for fraud and corporate espionage. And the Sword Punk remains a myth. A conspiracy. Here I was giving modern audiences more credit than the folks who used to eat up that retro American wrestling crap, where fighters railed against promoters and very, totally for-real crimes were committed between rival factions who then chose to settle their differences with steel chairs and microphones."

"That's only if she says yes," I said.

"Akio, my boy," Min said, reaching for one of her skunked bottles before she remembered herself and set it back down with a heavy sigh, "you really need to get better at this."

"Better at what?" I asked distractedly, watching Sang Hee intensely as she measured Goro for all he was worth.

"Us," Min said, waving a hand around.

"Well?" Goro asked. He extended his cigar out over the abyss and tapped the top. Red motes of ash flitted down like fireflies, lending the whole thing an ominous, choreographed air that the audience was eating up. "What say you, Sang Hee?"

"I say …" Sang Hee started. She swallowed, her eyes darting from side to side, measuring the audience's reaction. Taking in their anticipation. Goro had her. "I say, give me your best shot."

With that, Sang Hee gave her blue staff a twirl and set it back onto its catches on the back of her League suit, the light flashing once more before winking out. She turned on her heels and walked right past a Janix who wouldn't meet her eyes, before taking her blue bridge across the abyss and into the halls beyond.

Cameras extended out of the shadows, hovering around her, measuring every angle, mapping every contour of her face. The crowd was silent up until the moments following Sang Hee's withdrawal, and then they exploded into a cacophonous, celebratory malaise that carried them out into the streets and bars and message boards beyond.

The city was buzzing. Sang Hee was trapped in a potential deathmatch that would no doubt be skewed against her. Goro had won the night.

The League broadcast faded to that red tower over a white background, which hung in a buzzing silence before switching over to the post-event broadcast. The broadcasters were already sweating with anticipation as they delved excitedly into the fallout from Sang Hee's brave address, and wondered aloud how the League had changed to suit expanding consumer interests right before our very eyes.

What a historic, brave, legendary event.

I stood and waved at the holographic screen in an attempt to shut it up. It called up a menu instead and I kicked the glass table halfway across the room before storming out.

Min caught up to me in the lobby upstairs, snatching me by the arm as I made for the front door and the gate beyond it.

"Wait, Akio! Wait!"

I stopped and spun on her, breathing heavily. For an instant, Min looked worried that I might lash out at her. I took a steadying breath.

"I'm sorry," I said. "Min, if she comes back here, tell her to wait for me. We need to talk, figure out our next move. She's in, now. She's in deep, just like everyone else I ... everyone else around me."

"Okay," she said. "Okay, Akio. But, where are you—"

"I need to take a ride."

18

LIKE OLD TIMES

I only realized I was crying when I slowed the cycle around a bend in the road, allowing the tears streaming down the crags of my face to settle before the wind rushed back in to take them.

The dead man's bike was faster than any city bike I'd taken. That's what good old-fashioned gas would get you.

It wasn't that I was sad, or mourning, though I did worry over the domino effect Sang Hee's stunt was about to have. It wasn't purely anger, either. I'd had plenty of that over the last two weeks, and I knew I'd have plenty of it to spare even if I realized my dream of plunging a glowing red blade up to the haft in Goro's slimy chest.

I didn't know what the tears were for, at the end of it. I didn't know who they were for, though I suspected it came down to the same as the rest of it. The same selfish end of all my intentions.

The tears were for me, just as the vengeance was for me. Just as the blood—every last drop I could get my hands on—was for me. To pretend otherwise was to disrespect those who followed me, who tried to protect me, who held me up as a symbol even if they wouldn't admit it except into the far cold reaches of the neon nights.

It was all for me. It was all for Akio Prince, hero of the downtrodden.

It was dark in the hills at night, and it took another twenty

minutes before the bright jewel that was Seoul was laid out like
a beacon before me. Alluring and dangerous. I hit a patch of
gravel near the place where Sang Hee had killed a man not long
before. The front wheel skidded and nearly spun out, and I tailed
the bike into a ditch, somehow keeping upright all the way to my
skidding halt.

I released the breath I felt like I'd been holding for the last
ten miles. The air seemed heavier down here, so far below Sang
Hee's complex, as if the weight of all my decisions had collapsed
on me at once.

I closed my eyes and took a steadying breath, ignoring the
soft yellow glow of a car that passed me by.

I thought of everything. Sang Hee's fight, Min's investigation.
I thought of the night on the bridge, when two of Zoo's bullets
had found my flesh, if not my heart. I thought of the burnt end
of Goro's cigar, and the pink rug in Gabriella's nest, and how it
had got all sticky and fat off of Mal Chin's blood. More blood I'd
spilled.

Lastly, I thought of the crowd from tonight's match. I
thought of how happy I'd been when they'd been calling for
Goro's head, and then how quickly it had turned when he'd
simply given them what they wanted. Surely some of them—
most of them, even—smelled something fishy. Surely there were
those in the arena and watching at home that knew it wasn't a
work—that Sang Hee had been earnest in her defiance.

But then, we were living in a cynical world, and deep down, I
knew that men like Goro hadn't made it that way, they had
simply taken advantage of what was already there.

Tonight, Goro had won. He'd convinced the city that Sang
Hee was doing his bidding, albeit in a roundabout way. As a
result, Min was already saying that there were some who
believed the entire investigation was nothing more than a
publicity stunt designed to deepen the supposed rift between
Goro and the League's top star. It was a callback to American
wrestling organizations, before combat sports had adopted cages
and made the violence on the ends of their rivalries real, even if
the storylines supporting them were often far from genuine.

In the end, people followed rivalries in sports more than the good guys and gals because they wanted it to feel real more than to be real. Most of them probably thought the changed rule set was nothing but window dressing. I knew better. Goro would play to their collective fantasies. He'd use Sang Hee's bravery to prop up the whole storyline, and then, if he could, he'd make sure she never saw fit to trouble him again, and the crowd would be drunk off of the shock that such a glorious, obvious work ended with something as tangible as death.

What theater.

I took off again, screaming toward the city with renewed focus, even if I didn't quite know where I was going yet. A part of me considered driving right up to Goro's offices, or any number of his private abodes, barging through the front door and demanding an audience. Maybe his head had grown large enough on the back of the night's seeming victory that he'd admit me, if only to watch me grovel for my friend and lover at his feet before killing me.

No. Goro was smarter than that. He was cunning, and things like him didn't live so long on the backs of such violent acts and orders by allowing anything even smelling of danger into their presence.

Goro had to die. Sang Hee's address and his ensuing response only confirmed it. The way the crowd had lapped it all up like kittens at an ocean of milk made it all the more clear that the city was sick, and that Goro was the tumor.

There were others to deal with, both above him and below him. But Goro was the one pressing on my windpipe, threatening to strangle me. He was the one I'd cut out first, and his present course had only solidified my own.

Before I knew it, I was leaning my bike against a half-full rack on the side of a well-lit street. I looked up, blinking and half expecting to be standing in front of the Soul Dome.

I turned around, realizing with a mix of dread and inevitability where I'd gone in my rage and confusion.

The glass was polished to a squeaky sheen, and the trophies were already gleaming with the reflected light of the street lamps. The mats beyond were wet, but only half of them had been gone over. There was a drenched mop leaning against the redwood timber.

A bell rang as the door to my left opened, and I swallowed before swiveling to meet Joon's eyes.

"Going to stand there all night, or coming in?"

Joon, bedecked in his faded blue gi that could have been the same one he'd been wearing for the last twenty years, ducked back inside but threw the door open wider, forcing me to catch it before it closed. I dipped inside and pulled my shoes off on instinct, shoving them into a cubby to the left of the door.

Joon bowed and stepped back onto the mats, snatching up his mop on the way, and set to cleaning once more. I stood on the laminate square that marked the entryway, and scanned the dojo I'd spent more time in as a youth than everywhere else combined.

Joon had given me the silent treatment before. It seemed that was how most of my friends and those who'd grown close enough to call me family decided to deal with me in times of crisis. But Joon had always had a particularly infuriating knack for it. He wouldn't rise before I would, but for now, I let him mop and delighted in the familiar smell of sweat and bleach, leather and pine that made the place up. There was even a slight hint of sweet mold blowing in from a rickety vent at the far end of the room. We'd had it checked back when I was teaching here and had been assured it wasn't deadly.

"At least grab a broom."

Less patient than usual. Which meant he was royally pissed.

I bowed onto the mats and walked along the red borders on the left side of the room. I took the short stair up into a narrow hallway where Joon's room—doubling as an office—rested. I stole a glance inside as I passed it, shaking my head as I spied the old cot and mussed covers littering the place, along with a small black desk and a computer that looked like it still had its software and hardware packaged separately.

I squeezed the brass knob to the door at the back of the hall and shouldered my way in. It was dark and musty inside, but everything was still in its proper place. I navigated by feel, snatching the handle of a mop and dragging it and its dingy old bucket-on-wheels back into the hall.

By the time I managed to negotiate the rolling heap of plastic, metal and bleached sludge down onto the mats, Joon had already finished. I sighed and shoved the cart against the wall, letting the handle rest just beneath a cracked picture of Kenta and his squad from the olden days.

Joon quickly moved from mopping to the windows, snatching up a rag that looked like it would make everything dirtier. He set to polishing trophies he'd already gone over before I arrived— likely more than once—and I moved into the center of the dojo floor, leaning against the timber support pole and watching him work.

"Bet you're wondering what brings me here," I said, my throat cracking oddly due to the silence.

"Judging by the look on your face when I opened that door, you're wondering the same thing," Joon said, short and clipped. Damn it if he didn't know me.

"Things have been …"

"Yeah," Joon said. "Aren't they always, Akio."

That got the blood going a bit, but I choked back my initial response. Joon had a right to be angry. Sure, I'd been shot three times, knocked into a frothing river and nearly been assassinated—by everything from former League members to spider tanks to one guy on a bike—but I'd been alive, and I hadn't told him.

"Have you figured it out?" Joon asked.

I blinked and watched him. He raised an eyebrow, finally deigning to look my way for longer than a split second.

"Figured what out?"

"What you're doing here. Surely it isn't to tell me you're alive. Min did on your account. Seems she's doing a lot of things on your account. Seems a lot of people are."

"You watched the Finals, I take it?"

"Caught the highlights."

"I see. Well, contrary to popular belief, I've never been as convincing as I've thought. I can't make people do anything, Joon. Min—"

"Cares about you, Akio. And so, apparently, does Sang Hee. Listen, I know why you didn't come to me first, and don't give me any bullshit about protecting me, thank you very much. But I'll do you a favor and tell you that you don't have to worry on my account, not about protecting me and certainly not about including me in whatever it is you've got going on. You want to know if I approve. I don't. I don't know what kind of war you're waging, but I know it's got a lot more to do with vengeance than whatever you've concocted as your reasoning in that thick— growing thicker—skull of yours."

He sighed, seeming to have to work to calm himself.

"You don't have to ask my permission to do anything, Akio. I'm not your father."

"I know that," I said, knowing it made me sound just like the child Joon was telling me I wasn't.

"Then why are you here?"

"Not to ask your blessing to do something that should have been done a long time ago. That's for damn sure."

Joon almost smiled. Just like that, he had the rise out of me I swore he wouldn't get.

"You're really in deep, aren't you?"

"I'm not here for your help, Joon," I said, not caring now that my voice was rising. I straightened from the pillar and took a step toward him. He just watched, arms crossed. At least he wasn't pretending to clean anything anymore. "I'm not here to ask your permission. And I'm certainly not here to apologize for not coming sooner. I … you and the kids … I couldn't—"

"Apology accepted."

I closed my eyes and clenched my fists. When it came to situations like this, there were two ways to go: I could either shout Joon down or laugh and defuse the murderous intent that he could build in me faster than anyone.

"I'm here to warn you, Joon," I said.

"Warn me of …?"

"Goro, the Hachinin, Seoul," I said. "All of it. I'm marked. They know I'm alive—"

"And why is that?" Joon's look changed, and now we were coming to what was really eating him up. "Min told me she offered you a way out—"

"A one-way ticket west, Joon!" I shouted. "She offered me a chance to run, tail tucked between my legs. She offered me nothing. Less than nothing."

"She offered you your life."

"I have it," I said, jabbing my thumb into my chest. "I have it."

"How much longer will that be the case, now that you've got Goro and the Hachinin on your trail?"

"So far, so good."

"Yeah," Joon said, looking like he wanted to spit. "I saw. The war's going so well, Akio. You've killed a small-time errand boy, exposed a corrupt cop without actually exposing him, since he's dead, inserted yourself into a feud between two of the most powerful business interests in the city, and somehow even managed to drag Sang Hee—"

"I haven't done any dragging," I said, and my tone must have showed Joon he was treading dangerous ground. He paused for the moment, and I relaxed a bit. "Good to see you still keep abreast on some of the goings on in the city you call yours."

"The kids talk," Joon said. "They tell me what I need to know, and plenty that I don't need to know."

"You talk like you want what's best for them, Joon," I sneered. "Was Kuzu Tokoro operating a den not two blocks from here in the best interest of the precious children?"

"Don't," Joon said, raising a finger. Now he was growing into the father act he claimed he didn't intend. He swallowed and sucked on his lower lip, chewing in frustration as he searched out my expression. "You really think you're doing something, don't you?" He leaned back, planting his hands on his hips and adopting a posture of such profound condescension it was a wonder he didn't topple over. "You really think—"

"It doesn't matter what I think," I said, not caring how it

sounded. "It matters what I do, Joon. It matters that I do. That's what Kenta—"

"Don't."

"Don't what? You know it's true."

"I know he'd agree," Joon said, tilting his chin. "That's a far cry from a ringing endorsement of the truth, in my experience."

"He taught you—"

"Everything I know, and plenty more besides," Joon said. "It took me years to pick up on the latter, but I can trace virtually every poor decision I've ever made back to that man's influence."

"Shame," I said. This wasn't how I'd wanted tonight to go. I didn't know how I'd wanted it to go, but not like this. "You should be—"

"I am," Joon said. "Now that that's out of the way. Now that we're both terribly sorry, I'll ask you again, Akio Prince, the Ghost of Seoul, the Sword Punk … why are you here? And don't say it's for me. You might have the others fooled—Min should know better—but I've known you long enough to see what happens when you've got an idea in your head. It becomes you. It consumes you and everything around you. Not me, Akio. Not this time."

He had me there. He gave voice to all the silent, whining doubts that had been creeping in at the corners, and that not even my blind, momentous anger could chase away entirely.

"Guess you've got it all figured out," I said, making a show of looking around at the dojo.

"Guess we both do," Joon answered. He didn't sound victorious, only tired. Tired and regretful. Still, calm as Joon liked to act, I knew this had been his version of an outburst. Calm, measured but full of venom, just like the old days.

"Well, then," I said. "Guess I've made my point." I began walking to the side of the room. Joon had gone back to polishing his trophies—most of them were mine and Min's, as Joon had never been as interested in competing. Come to think of it, he'd never been as interested in anything.

"Yes," Joon said distractedly. "Your warning is well heeded, Akio. I'll keep the children safe, and we'll watch as you burn the city down around you. Only take care around those flames, Akio. They catch."

I closed my eyes again as I reached the opposite wall. I reached out, my hand closing around the rough wood of the bo staff I'd first learned on as a boy. I pulled it free from its hooks and turned, sending it end over end toward Joon. He caught it in his right hand, not so much as threatening to drop the rag in his left, though the trophy he'd held clattered to the floor with a hollow sound of cheap marble and painted plastic.

I smiled at him and reached back with my left hand without turning. I found another length of wood, pulled it down and strode toward Joon.

He dropped the rag and followed me into the center of the dojo, where the blue mats went from rough to smooth as polished glass, not worn down due to the sliding passage of hundreds of pairs of feet, but rather due to the passage of two pairs thousands of times.

The sparring square had no firm boundaries marked by lines or tape on the floor, but we two knew where it started and where it ended. We stood on opposite sides, a few feet from the red pillar where Kenta would lean with his stopwatch—another heirloom of his Africa campaigns—and enact some semblance of structure over our wars.

Joon and I eyed each other on opposite sides of the square. If we extended our staffs from the hip, they would just meet in the middle.

"Sure you don't want to change into a gi?" Joon asked.

"I'll give you that small advantage." I shrugged, though my riding pants were more geared toward avoiding skinned knees on the pavement rather than engaging in pirouettes and lunging kicks. "You've been out of practice."

"All I do is practice," Joon said.

I almost laughed at him, but then he filled the space between us and brought his staff lancing in behind him. Our conversation —our true conversation—started on that first dodge, as I sucked in and spun away from the nose of the staff and brought my own back around, screaming for the back of Joon's head.

Wood met wood and the first crack filled the echoing silence of the dojo. It was soon followed by the smell of ozone as the staffs made small pops of smoke at their meeting points, like fresh lightning in the rain. We came together and drifted apart, moving like ghosts in the growing mist our collisions made. Our faces were painted with concentration, tight and even grimacing at first, and then looser, relaxed and soon bordering on serene.

Joon slapped the top of my hand hard enough to send shards of pain lancing up into my shoulder, and I rewarded his aggression with a streaking elbow that made a packing sound as it collided with his ear. We spun away with a grunt and a hiss and then closed in again, our feet twisting, turning, pivoting and hopping to tell the story of our clash that our staffs only punctuated with those violent cracks.

I got too close to Joon on our fifth exchange, and he switched his staff to his opposite hand, swung it around my back and snatched it on either end, pulling in. I gritted my teeth and struggled against the strain as the wood of the staff ground into the soft bits between my vertebrae. Joon had the harder head, so I resisted the urge to headbutt him. Instead, I snuck the blade of my foot inside his stance and raked down his calf, slamming my heel into the top of his foot.

"One of mine," Joon said with a wincing smile as he streaked away once more. He ducked into a side stance and took the wind from me with a kick as I lunged in too soon. "And one of yours."

Instead of allowing Joon to extend his hip and send me sprawling onto the floor, I dropped my staff and snatched his kicking leg behind the knee, falling down as I used my top hand as a lever. In fighting, it was easy to get lost in the details, in the minutiae of manipulating the human body to achieve one's competitive ends.

One thing had been and would always be true regarding the most effective martial arts techniques. They simply moved your body in ways it was not designed to go. Joon was too good for me to move his body in opposite directions, just as I was too good for him to do the same to me. The next best thing, then, was to freeze movement for long enough to cause a delay between the fighter's mind and his body. When I hooked Joon's leg and straightened it before he could plant it, I caused one of those momentary freezes. Joon had already sent the requisite signals down to that kicking leg, first telling it to extend out farther to sink his kick in deeper into my midsection, and then, when that failed, to retract it.

I stopped the former and the latter, and the result was us tumbling to the mats with my mind working on the basis of what I wanted to do, and Joon's working overtime just to reevaluate.

Again, if we can paint the whole picture of fighting with just a few strokes, here's another gem for you: if you're busy worrying about what your opponent is doing to you, you're not making him think about what you're going to do. In short, think too much, and you're losing.

"Caught you think—" I started to say as Joon's back slammed into the mats.

I felt the sickening sensation as Joon's left foot rocketed up between my legs.

"Caught you talking!"

Joon's foot met some of the soft stuff, but I did manage to turn my takedown into a haphazard roll that took some of the sting out of the strike. The ensuring scramble saw both of us landing short punches that wouldn't do much aside from purple and bruise as we spat and jockeyed for position. Joon tried to stand and then dived for his fallen staff, and I hooked the front of his ankles with my feet and assisted him in another quick fall.

I followed Joon down and was rewarded with an elbow to the bridge of the nose. That one had me rolling to the side, my hands swiping the floor in search of one of our fallen weapons. Alas, I came up empty-handed and seeing stars.

When I managed to blink away the tears long enough to focus on the scene in front of me, I saw Joon standing there with both staffs in hand. He smirked and tossed one to the side, where it rolled toward the shelf below the front window, and leveled the other in front of him.

"Come on, then," I said, shaking my head to clear the last of the cobwebs.

Joon's smile disappeared. He brought the staff up and spun it around the top of his head, moving his feet in a quick rotation that was just a hair too long. He was trying to build power in the strike—more power than was necessary for a spar—and as a result, the spin came on a delay.

I didn't.

I speared forward, driving the balls of my feet into the mat as hard as I could as I shot toward Joon like a cannonball. I raised my arms in a cage block that likely saved my nose from finishing its shattering. As it turned out, the staff wasn't nearly as sturdy as my forearms, which Kenta, Joon, Min and every partner and opponent—friend and foe—had helped to mold into weapons. They doubled as shields.

I saw Joon's eyes widen as his weapon turned to splinters on my bare skin, and then I heard the breath leave his chest as I continued the momentum and slammed into him, bowling him over. I rolled again as soon as I hit the mats and came up in a bounce, ready to charge again.

Only Joon wasn't up yet. I paused for a moment, and then a stab of panic hit me as I wondered if I'd done some real damage to him. Joon sat up wincing, one hand wrapped around his chest like a seatbelt while the other posted up on the mats.

"Joon," I said, straightening. There were splinters littering the floor, and wet spots I was only now recognizing as the blood that was leaking out of my nose. "I'm sorry."

I expected him to cough out some curse, to tell me to hit the road and not to come back, or even to simply jab a finger toward the polished glass door. Instead, he made a sound that I at first mistook for wheezing, and that soon resolved into a madman's laughter.

I smiled nervously at first, and then, when Joon looked up at me through his sweat-soaked black bangs, and I saw the truth of the sound, I joined him.

"Jesus, Akio," he coughed. "Must have learned that one in your cage-fighting days. I never took to it."

"There's a time and place for finesse—" I started.

"Just not a china shop," Joon finished and I laughed all the harder.

"Not one of Kenta's best."

"No," Joon agreed. He extended his hand and I hooked it in mine, pulling him up.

"You good?" I asked.

"Something cracked," he said, looking around at the floor. "Something more than that old thing, I mean."

"Rub some dirt on it," I teased. "Besides, I guess you win if we're playing by the old rules." Joon looked up from the floor to me, frowning. "First blood," I said, indicating my nose.

"Of course I won," Joon said, deadly serious until the goofy, awkward smile I'd known since he'd first trusted me enough to show it broke his face. "Doesn't matter what rule set. Now," he nodded toward the floor, "since I won fair and square, and since, obviously, I can't really move much right now, what say you get to work cleaning all this up?"

I wiped some of the blood from under my nose and went to pat Joon on the back with the opposite hand as I passed him. Instead, I gave him a healthy pat on the stomach, delighting in the wheezing sob he made before he stumbled back over to sit on the trophy shelf beneath the front window.

It took a lot longer to clean the mats this time, but I wasn't in a rush. Joon and I spoke of old times spent in the dojo on nights like this, and he tossed in little asides on how to clean the mats better—the same asides Kenta had drilled into the two of us and that I'd heard a thousand times over the years—but I let him. It was a good feeling, sharing something like this. Reconciling like Joon and I had might hurt more than a night of heavy drinking, but it killed fewer brain cells and reminded us why we were friends in the first place.

"So you and Min had it out like this too?"

"In her father's old dojo." I nodded, wiping the sweat from my brow as I finished and set the mop handle back to rest against Kenta's pillar.

"The spar turn into anything else?" Joon asked with a mischievous smirk. "You know, like old times?"

I shot him a look. "Those days are long gone, Joon," I said. It didn't feel as awkward to talk about these days, even if that particular episode had left more scars on the three of us than anything in the years before or since.

Joon shrugged. "Maybe you should try pissing us off less often there, bud. You wouldn't have to have so many ... 'conversations.'"

"That's fighters for you," I said.

"I'm no fighter, Akio," Joon said. "Neither is Min. Not anymore."

Now I turned a different look on him as I leaned against the pillar and crossed my arms, facing him with a heavy sigh. "What?"

He threw his arms up and then coughed with the effort. I winced in sympathy as I waited for the fit to subside. "You've always been the fighter, Akio."

"Not because you couldn't be," I said. "You could have won any of the tournaments I did. You could have entered the League—"

"Didn't want to," Joon said, waving the thought away like so much smoke. "Bunch of lights and sounds and half-nude men banging drums."

"Exactly my point, Joon. You never wanted to. Lacking the will is a far cry from lacking the ability."

"Never said I lacked the ability, Akio," Joon said. His voice changed, got more serious, almost somber. He didn't meet my eyes for a few moments as he thought how best to say it. "Anyway," he said with a shake of the head, "will counts for a lot, is all I'm saying. Min has it. You're right on that account, but she's taken her own way, aimed it at the badge and all that. We never had the stuff you had."

"The issues, you mean." I smiled. Joon shrugged and gave a smile of his own.

"We are all imperfect machines."

"Trained perfectly," I finished. "He did get pretty philosophical at the end, there."

"I think he was reading Russian lit," Joon said. "Not sure he understood it much."

"He took what he wanted from it."

"That he did."

The next silence stretched a bit longer, and I closed my eyes and breathed in deeply, allowing the bleach and the slight metallic hint of metal and blood to fill my nostrils. Familiar and comforting smells, which told you a lot about us. Told you a lot about people, and what they could count as comfortable, depending on the circumstances.

"You sure you know what you're doing, Akio?" Joon asked. He was looking down at the mats, watching them dry in their own time. Now he looked up at me. "You shouldn't be here, out and about like this."

"Goro knows I'm alive," I said.

"But the people don't, Akio," he said. "They're not quite as sharp as you might think. Sure, some have drawn parallels between the Sword Punk's mission and Akio Prince's untimely demise, but it's all looking like a work now, including the reports of the sword-wielding madman hunting down Goro's thugs. According to the mainstream, the League Finals were a final farewell to your memory, now inextricable from the League, forever immortalized in their archives."

"Such a tribute," I said.

"You really mean to go through with it, then," Joon said. He could always tell more judging by what I didn't say than what I did.

"I've killed two men and half a third."

"Half?"

"Sang Hee did most of it, but he wouldn't have been there if it hadn't been for me." Joon watched me. "Yes, I'm going to go through with it, Joon, though you haven't exactly asked what 'it' is."

"You're going to kill Goro of the Hachinin, and you think—"

"It doesn't matter what I think," I said, my tone showing I

had no desire to revisit the argument. Joon was more wont to drop an argument he couldn't win than Min. He let this one go.

"Right," Joon said. "It matters what you do, and all that."

I nodded.

"So, then," he said, straightening a bit, easing some elasticity back into his ribs before they seized up on him completely, "what is it you're going to do, and how will I know?"

"I'm sure it'll make the news." I smiled.

"You running the SMC now, too?" he asked. "Min said something—"

"Long story," I said. "Involves killer robots and many-bladed assassins."

"Ah," Joon said, "and here I thought my week was more exciting than usual. Three new signups, Akio. Three. And one of them might actually stick around."

I smiled. He spoke like he was tired, like he'd rather be doing anything else but running an old dojo in the center of a sprawling neon metropolis. We both knew better, both knew I had no pity for him, even if he had plenty to spare for me.

I opened my mouth to speak, but something felt wrong. In moments like these, it was the little cues that added up to form a patchwork of wrongness that started the body moving before the conscious mind could formulate it all into any semblance of sense. The way a pair of shadows passed by the glass twice, heading in either direction before pausing on the third time they passed. The way a pair of headlights on the opposite side of the street illuminated the sidewalk in front of an idle and empty car for longer than any errand would explain.

"Down!"

Joon had started to turn his head toward the window. Heeding my warning, he stood and started forward in a dive.

The window shattered in a hail of glass and lead, and I ducked around the side of the red pillar, hearing the bullets whiz by me, feeling them thud into the back of the pine frame and ting against the copper piping on the inside. I scrambled around the opposite side and brought my knees up to my chest, my eyes working furiously to scan the room, searching for something to fight back with, searching for some route by which I could turn and sprint back toward the shattered window in time to intercede.

The machine guns screamed their fury into the night, a signal from Goro and the Hachinin to the city that they were here, and that they would do what they wanted, take what they wanted, like wolves on the borders of a peaceful flock whose protectors had grown fat and lazy.

The bullets thumped into the mats on either side of me, tore chunks of rubber and padding up from the floor Joon and I had cleaned twice already. Before the trail of death reached me, I heard the telltale clink and annoying chatter that sounded like confused machinery.

The twin shadows which were illuminated against the back of the dojo wall reached into their trench coat pockets, and a third shadow joined them, rising from a glass-strewn pile on the floor.

"Joon! No!"

I rolled over, narrowly avoiding slitting my wrist on a shard of glass that had embedded itself in the post, and shot toward the broken gap where the front window had been. I cleared the shelf and all the fallen trophies as Joon did, each of us hitting a different leather-clad man full on, our knees extended.

I landed atop mine with a heavy crunch and shot my fist down, breaking the black shades and the sockets behind them. I looked to my left, and saw Joon dropping a bloody shard of glass from a shaking fist. At first, I thought it was his blood that had stained the piece, and then I looked down at the ruined neck— the female neck—of the second shooter.

"Joon ..." I started.

"Go," he said. I thought everything had come undone, that Joon would hate me now and forever. And then he looked at me, and I knew he hadn't meant it that way. "Go, Akio!" he shouted, the role of big brother falling on him like an expectant shroud. "I'll take care of things here."

"But—"

"Min gave me a contact at the department," he said, eyes

scanning the opposite side of the street. It was deserted this time of night, but I could hear people screaming and saw them running east, toward the more lit areas. Joon nodded across the street to where the idling car—nobody left to man it—shined its ghostly lights on the black cycle I'd taken off of their associate two days before.

"Go, Akio," Joon said, calmer now. He stood, and I grimaced at the amount of red on him, from the stuff that was his on his sliced feet to the stuff that most certainly wasn't that dripped from his clenched fists.

I stood, ignoring the sting from the cuts I'd suffered as best I could. I saw blue lights lighting the bottoms of the clouds. I kicked at the form at my feet and heard a groan. "This one's still good."

"Akio," Joon said, snatching me by the crook of the elbow before I could start across the street. I can't say I'd ever seen him look that way before. "Could have been kids here."

"I know," I said. "I'm sorry, Joon. It's my—"

"Just make them pay. Show him who you are, Akio." He gripped tighter before releasing me. "Show them who we are."

I nodded hurriedly and sprinted across the road. I didn't have time to fetch my shoes. Once I'd spun the cycle back toward the west, and rounded the first of many bends heading back up into the northern forested hills of Seoul, I found myself smiling.

Who smiled on a night like this but a demon?

My pocket buzzed, and I didn't realize I still had Sang Hee's sphere on me until I pulled it out. It flashed blue letters across the surface.

"What can't you do?" I asked it.

My place. Now. – Sang Hee

"Yes ma'am," I said, leaving the crying city behind, but not for long.

19

THE GAME

Hot off of the nausea-inducing thrill of the fear and adrenaline the latest attempt on my life—and those of my friends—had called up, my ride into the forested hills of the north was fraught with tension.

Not for me, although I couldn't help but wonder which of the shadows between the trees might reach out to snatch me into its waiting maw, which of the rockslides atop the cliff-like bends might shake loose as I trundled past. No, I worried for them. All of them. My little clutch of friendly souls in a city full of them.

Finding the security gate to Sang Hee's compound left open did nothing to dispel my fears, causing me to ditch my bike and effect something of a controlled crash as I struck the training platform with my bare feet and tumbled across the expanse toward the compound.

Lights were on inside, but they were dim, emanating from a chamber off to the left of the main entrance, and although I saw two figures sitting comfortably, two silhouettes very likely having a chat over a cup of tea or a rancid beer from the bunkers below, the darker corners of my mind mistook their stillness for death.

I threw the glass door open and spilled inside the many-angled concrete labyrinth, my gasps echoing in the silence. I nearly went down, feeling fresh stinging on the bottoms of my feet as small, edged pebbles of glass reintroduced themselves after the scene at the dojo.

Finding Sang Hee and Min unharmed and relatively stoic was a relief. The way the two of them put aside whatever conversation they had been engaged in to give me the biggest double dose of side eye I'd ever got was most decidedly not.

The two of them sat in old-looking cloth chairs on opposite sides of a knee-height table. There was a large black duffel bag on top of it, which looked to be military make. It had the red logo of an anvil sewed into the stitching.

"Akio," Min said with a curt nod, as if she were a mother waiting to read my report card. She looked tired, as she had for the last two weeks, but otherwise none the worse for wear.

"Prince," Sang Hee said, looking me up and down in a way that was most certainly not to be taken as suggestive. She looked wide awake, even wired, though she was trying hard to project an image of calm. Her black hair was tied back in a tail, but her bangs were plastered to her brow with sweat that likely still hadn't been wiped clean from her row—if you could call it that— with Janix in the arena.

"Ladies," I managed to wheeze out before bending down with a huff and gripping my sweat-soaked knees. There was a trickle of blood filling one of the gray, grouted seams between the stone tiles in the floor. "Good to see you both looking well."

"Better than you," Sang Hee said.

"Isn't that always the case?" Min added. That drew a tight, grudging smirk from Sang Hee, and acted as further confirmation that the two hadn't quite become fast friends in whatever time they'd been sitting here.

"Fair enough," I said. There was another chair beneath the back row of windows that peered out onto the black steel wall that encircled the compound. I stepped gingerly around Sang Hee and grabbed it by the arm, pulling it over and settling into it on the opposite side of the table.

"Min," I said, unable to bear the silence anymore and hoping my tone showed it, "Joon—"

"I know," she clipped. "Here I was thinking my calls from the precinct were over for the day—what with Sang Hee's Akio-like stunt—and then I get a panicked one from one of my guys, telling me Ken's Place had been shot up. One dead, four very close to it by the time officers arrived on the scene."

"The shooters," I said, then my breath caught. "Wait. Did you say four?"

"Four," Min said flatly. "First crew had backup. Joon's fine, in case you were wondering."

"He said he would be."

She looked from me to Sang Hee.

"Where is he, Min?"

"Seoul Regional," she said, her tone softening some. "Probably where you should be, given—"

"I'm fine. Just need to clean out these cuts."

Min nodded, and I saw that outer shell crack just a bit to reveal the concern beneath it.

"He's okay," she said. "Shaken, obviously, and I don't think because of what happened to him. What almost happened to him."

I didn't know what to say.

"He's with two of my best," Min said. "Two of my own, Akio. Hand-picked. He's safe."

I watched her for a while and then nodded, looking down at my feet. The sting resurfaced, and I snatched one of the water-filled mugs off of the table and poured it over both of them, wiping the water gently over the callused soles and prodding to dislodge any lingering twinkles of glass.

"Thank God for Kenta's mats," I said absently, then to Sang Hee's questioning look I said, "calluses."

"Ah," she nodded. "I always trained in boots."

"Were you born with a League suit on and a resin staff in hand or something?" I asked. She shrugged.

I turned back to Min.

"Joon killed a man because of me," I said, and the way I said it seemed to garner the first true look of sympathy from both women. "Seems everyone around me is becoming a killer these days."

"Killing days," Sang Hee said with a shrug. "Don't assume you're the catalyst. Killing happens. Sometimes it just happens in a direction we're not used to."

It was an odd way to put it, and once again, it made me question everything I had known—thought I had known—about Sang Hee up until very recent days.

"So," I said, eager to change the subject lest the guilt rising in my gut threatened to consume me once again, "how long have you two been … talking?"

Sang Hee smiled and Min matched her, the two sharing some sort of telepathic bond. That was the only way I could rationalize it, in any case.

"Afraid we might've found common ground, Akio?" Min asked in a sadistically playful manner.

"On what might we do that?" Sang Hee added.

I shrugged, pretending not to be as terrified at the prospect as I so clearly was. "Wouldn't be the worst thing, given the circumstances."

They each made a noise that, again, could only have been the result of some sort of silent ESP bond developed in the last two hours. It was a mix of amusement and open derision.

I made a weird waving motion with one hand, trying to undo whatever shared spell the two were weaving.

"You shouldn't have challenged Goro like that, Sang Hee," I said.

"There's your common ground," she said, nodding toward Min. "Officer Min here said the same thing."

"He's up to something—"

"Isn't that exactly why we're going after him?" Sang Hee asked, amused. "Because he's up to something. Up to many somethings."

Sang Hee's tone shifted sharply, her eyes flashing as if they held a light all their own.

"Spare me the theatrics, Prince," she said. "Goro put himself in my sights the moment he sent one of his goons after me."

"He was sent after—"

"He made the connection, Akio!" she shouted, planting her

black leather boots on the tiles and leaning forward, her hands blanching as she dug her fingers into the armrests. "I was always going to be on the list. He knew we were," she glanced sidelong at Min, "involved."

Sang Hee suggested it was the assassin's attempt on her life that had got Goro in her sights, but I couldn't shake the feeling that she'd already had the League President marked. After all, her Finals match with Janix wasn't the first time she had leveled a cold stare on that black glass box in the Soul Dome.

Min rolled her eyes. "Point is, we know he's up to something, Akio. But so are we. We'd better be, if we want to live out the month."

I put my forehead in the palms of my hands. "I should've listened to you sooner."

"Yeah," Min said.

"Yup," Sang Hee added, almost at the same time.

"Which part?" Min asked.

"I should've fled the country, gone into witness—"

"He would've found you," Sang Hee interrupted, earning a wicked glare from Min, though she bit back her waiting reply. "He always does."

Now both Min and I looked to her with questions forming on our tongues. She waved them away.

"You're not the first to challenge Goro, and I'm not the last. If we play this right, anyway." She reached over the left side of her chair and rifled around in a plastic bag. I heard the ting of bottles and she brought out three clutched in fingers I only just noticed were trembling. She snapped the top off of each using the edge of the wood table and the heel of her palm, chipping the table's surface, and handed them out.

We each took a long drag and sighed it out in unison. Sang Hee laughed first and Min and I joined her. We expelled the stress and tension of the day and night like opened kettles. When I looked up, Min and Sang Hee were staring hard at one another. Min inclined her head toward me.

"Tell him," she said.

I looked from her to Sang Hee. "Tell me what? I don't think I can bear any more good news."

Sang Hee took another pull. "It's nothing much," she said. "Just the rules for the Finals. Well, the second Finals, seeing how the last went."

Now it was my turn to raise my eyebrows. "Kyoto rules, no? I know. We watched it together, Min."

"Kyoto with a twist," Min said, nodding for Sang Hee to fill in the gaps.

"I really don't see what the big deal is," Sang Hee said, addressing Min in an attempt to avoid eye contact with me. "Kyoto rules means Kyoto rules. No mercy, unless it's wanted."

"Not many deaths in the Kyoto League," I said, the mystery and the dread sprouting like a seed in my mind. "Even with their rules. Not easy to kill someone as well trained as the fighters that make it up. Most are incapacitated. Even if they don't ask for mercy, they're usually granted it. We know whoever Goro puts you in there with isn't going to give it."

"Bet you they'll ask," Sang Hee said, but Min cleared her throat to keep her on course, bring her back around to the point.

"Sang Hee," I said, drawing it out.

"Fine," she sighed. "I signed the papers in Goro's office—"

"You went in there?" I asked, nearly standing up in my disbelief. I could see it, smell it. The tinted President's box with its looming suits and swirling smog of cigar smoke. Cheap cigars, too. Dry and musty. Goro could afford better, but it seemed a point of pride for him to smoke the shit when he had visitors.

"He wasn't going to kill me," Sang Hee said with an easy roll of her eyes. She had more of a talent for it than Min, which was saying something. "Yes, I went in there to sign. Kyoto rules. The works. It wasn't until I sent the packet to my agent before I left for the compound that the fine print came clear."

"Fine print," I said.

"Just a slight change of the equipment variety," Min said, watching Sang Hee, who swallowed, though she was trying hard to appear unconcerned.

"Blades instead of blunts," she said. "Sharps. You know, like they use in South America."

The South American League was unaffiliated with that which dominated the East, that which was run by the Hachinin. It was a cheap knockoff that paid less than a quarter the rate of ours, and less than a fifth what the Kyoto League coughed up. They called it the Blood League, and the name was well earned. Same rules, largely, albeit fought in dustier arenas and on redder mats. Same rules but for the equipment. Sharps instead of flats. Blades instead of blunts.

The LigaSA had been founded in the midst of the American Wars, when the twin continents had fractured their relationship beyond repair, at least in this century. It had been founded and informed by the conflict. They believed in the sanctity of violence, not martial arts. They peeled the facade off of prize-fighting and reduced it to its roots. For fighters like me, it was like looking in a black mirror.

"Akio?" Min said. Judging by her tone, it wasn't the first time. Sang Hee watched me with her arms crossed, as if prepared to defend herself.

"Can't be," I said, then shook my head to clear the fog. "Even here, even with Goro's blessing and the League's coffers and Sang Hee's signature, it can't be legal. Can it?"

"It's not illegal enough to stop outright," Min said. "I looked into it. Precinct is looking into it now, but they just got another package dropped off last night, one from Tokyo—anonymous, of course—and outlining all of Princess Burtahn's many sins. The shit's started piling up, and they're caught in the midst of crossing streams of billionaire piss—"

"Really?" Sang Hee cut in, echoing my grimace.

"Sorry," Min said, looking tired. She set her drained bottle down with a hollow thud and leaned back.

"Point is, the League's been lobbying for years, and they've stepped it up in the last few months, since before the start of last season. Rules are getting more lax. At least, liability is. Welcome to the free market, for everyone but the free citizens of Seoul." She stretched her arms out in a faux messianic gesture. "Where you're free to die under the benevolent gaze of your corporate masters, and free not to seek recompense."

"How many has she had?" I asked Sang Hee, only half joking. She shrugged.

"Media's in a frenzy," Min said, ignoring my jibe. "Most are calling it a publicity stunt, and only some seem aware of the equipment change. Even most of the detectives think it's a work —a way to make the League seem more real, distract from recent controversies. Even disappearances, on both sides."

I nodded along with her, putting the threads together. "And for those who matter, the masters in Japan, it's a clever way for Goro to address and double down on Sang Hee's challenge. It's a funny thing about the League being classified as entertainment instead of sport."

I thought about warning Sang Hee again, about telling her to back out while she still could, but when I met her eyes, I saw the same steel that made me up, that made Min up and even Joon, though he'd managed to temper his better than the three of us. We were blades, ourselves, all fighting, swinging in the dark for years and looking for somewhere meaningful to aim it. Min had come the closest, but the system had stifled her just as it had stifled so many good men and women before her.

"It's a setup," I said. Before Sang Hee could raise a complaint. "I know you know. I know." She settled back down, glancing at Min before giving me her attention. "It's a setup, but I'm not sure Goro's entirely thought this one through."

"What do you mean?" Min said, and all three of us leaned closer.

"Goro means to make an example of Sang Hee to his masters, and very likely to me. He knows—thinks—I won't show. He knows he'll be eliminating my most public ally. Gabriella's hand has been played, but that conflict, though I kicked it off, has nothing to do with me. This has everything to do with me. It has everything to do with the people. The League is a monument to the Hachinin. It's a monument to Goro, and he means to sacrifice its brightest star to it."

"He's going to need to find someone better than Janix if

that's what he means to do," Sang Hee said matter-of-factly. The nonchalant statement made an image of Mal Chin flash behind my eyes, and others from seasons past. Those who hadn't entered again. Those who were rumored to be working in the shadows, earning their purses for more silent and less honorable deeds.

"But," I continued, "what if I did show? What if I—"

"He could be trying to bait you out as much as kill Sang Hee," Min said, concern evident. "Either way, he wins."

"But only if we lose," I said. "Think about it. The people already made the connection between Sang Hee and Akio Prince. The smarter ones—the more connected, I should say—have drawn the line between Akio Prince and Kuzu Tokoro, Gabriella Burtahn, Goro of the Hachinin and the pest that's cropped up in the League champion's seeming absence. A pest who seems bent on causing the Hachinin of Seoul undue stress."

"I follow you," Sang Hee said, nodding.

Min looked either unconvinced or reluctant to be convinced. I concentrated on her.

"Think of how many eyes are going to be on that stage tomorrow night," I said. "If people do think it's a work, my appearance will fit in with that narrative nice and snug. For those who see through the seeming charade, they'll know I'm still here, that Sang Hee is with me, and that someone's fighting back against Goro. They might not know exactly why, or how, but they know resistance when they see it, even if it's in the guise of a story for the masses to soak up."

"The red pills," Min said, almost distracted.

"What?"

"That's what they call themselves on the web," she said. "Those who see through the games and the politics, who see the SMC for what it is. They connect dots and tie strings, trying to get a look under the hood at what's really going on. Lot of them are better at it than the professionals. They're not bound by warrants, nor limited by closed-loop thinking or five detectives in a room, bouncing ideas back and forth until the edges are rounded and smoothed out and they are no longer able to effect change. Not all of their conclusions are sound, but enough of them are. They're the ones championing the Sword Punk name. They're the ones who'll be watching closely, to see the game beneath the game."

She looked up from the table and the empty bottle, and back at me. "You're right, Akio. He won't be able to move against you. Not in the open. Not then."

I smiled. I wasn't going to enter the arena in the open. I wasn't going to walk across the red corner bridge alongside Sang Hee. I was going to have a conversation with Goro Hamada, whether or not the public learned of it.

Sang Hee stood. She reached down and started on the zipper of the big black bag. I helped her throw open the flap, and marveled at the collection of resin, rubber, Kevlar and steel inside.

"That was quick," I said, lifting out a red mask that was meant to cover the nose and mouth. It had a sharp-angled top and bottom, like a double-hooked eagle's beak.

"You wanted to be a symbol, Prince," Sang Hee said. "Be it."

I leaned back, turning the mask over in my hands and looking beyond it into the shadows of the bag. I saw red blades whose edges caught enough of the dim lights above to clue me in as to their intent. No blunts here.

"We'll play into Goro's little story," I said. "We'll play our parts to a tee. He thinks he wins either way. Sang Hee dies on a public stage, or the Sword Punk comes back and dies along with her. He can spin it as the most elaborate work ever pulled. Only it won't be that simple."

"Why is that?" Min asked.

"Because while Sang Hee performs in Goro's little show, I'm going to kill him. I am."

20

FAIR FIGHT

There was a lot of artifice in the new world. Everything was plastic and resin. Alloys. Nothing was pure. Nothing was just steel or iron or flesh. Everything had been combined to try to make something better.

It was an ugly world. A synthetic world, especially in the New East. But then, that was my Western half talking. The half I'd never really known.

I suppose every generation felt the same way about the next. The good bits of change took hindsight to see. The bad bits stuck out immediately.

But as I stood on the edge of a rain-slicked rooftop staring out over the neon-lit streets of Seoul, I saw the beauty of the place. Where Tokyo was said to be all reds and poisoned greens, Seoul was blue. Azure and white. Not unlike Sang Hee.

The Soul Dome was less than a stone's throw across the alleyway. The massive, billboard-sized screen that showed League matches to those too poor to attend the fights in the arena or too smart to throw their money away was buzzing, the vivid light and colors of the display fizzing and even smoking in places as the rain tried to wash it along with all the rest of the city.

The League had never fared as well in Seoul as it had in

Kyoto, in Shanghai. Even, if it were to be believed, in Australia. Still, this night had an energy to it. I could see it in the cars idling along both sides of the wide, black street, and in the way the crowds gathered on the sidewalks spilled out from under the amber and red-lit eaves for a better look.

Cigarette smoke drifted up, slithering under my new mask and making me wrinkle my nose. I tensed, clenching my gloved fists to test the give in my new suit for the hundredth time that hour as the highlight packages started up. I'd be a dead giveaway as the red veins of my suit lit up in response to my muscles, but this was a bright city, and all attention was focused on the Dome. On Sang Hee, whom I'd potentially sent to die on my behalf.

I stretched for the tenth time in a dozen minutes, checking the give of the suit Sang Hee had had fashioned for me in record time, and by unknown sources. The suit was black, like my old one, and had thick veins of light that responded to both heart rate and movement. But this one was made of a resin-Kevlar hybrid material. Organic rubber, Sang Hee called it. It allowed my skin to breathe and my muscles to flex outward, while hardening as they tensed. On offense, it should allow me to move like a dancer. On defense, it would form a dense, protective shell. In essence, it was the best sort of soft that money could buy, but meant more, I think, for corporate assassins and rooftop ninjas than League fighters. Sang Hee's wasn't made of the same material. She probably could have gotten away with it, but her honor forbid her from gaining an unfair advantage over a League opponent, Kyoto rules or otherwise.

The new suit was more flexible than the old, and, if Sang Hee was to be believed, significantly more resistant to blades, although it wouldn't spare my ribs from blunt force trauma. Better to survive the former and accept the latter, in my very recent experience. I wasn't likely to come out of many more encounters like the one against Mal Chin and Gabriella's spider bots as unscathed as I had. Still, I had kept some of Min's father's armor, strapping the brilliant red pauldrons to my shoulders, greaves to my forearms and insteps to my shins.

I felt at once more and less nervous than I did before a typical League match. Tonight, I wouldn't be going up against resin and buzzing neon, nor League kicks and elbows. I'd be facing down steel and cobalt.

I tried to distract myself from the coming violence, focusing on the highlight packages. The Season 6 summary played through quickly, the package showing a liberal amount of footage of my fight with Janix, before flashing a few tantalizing bits of imagery of me leaving Sang Hee's condo, and continuing on with her masterful performance against the same man.

The camera focused on the glare Sang Hee had turned on Goro's black-tinted President's box. And thus, as the lights went down and the white and blue flashes started, the stage was set.

With little more than some PR spin and production value, Goro and the League had managed to gild the very real—though imagined—death of Akio Prince on the meta narrative of a League storyline. Some thought it was in bad taste. They still watched. Others ate it up, wondering if the Sword Punk had been little more than a media figure invented for the sole purpose of drumming up interest in this very event.

They'd wait to pass judgment on Goro and the League until after the show. The city had been promised blood in the form of Kyoto rules. Sang Hee had promised them victory over Goro, and by extension, the Hachinin, even if many assumed it would be of the Pyrrhic variety.

In short, every side had a rooted interest in the night's proceedings.

Originally, we had considered having me enter the arena alongside Sang Hee. To take the red corner bridge with her and stand in the middle of that cream-colored canvas, giving Goro my own unsettling stare. The crowd would have eaten it up. Those naïve enough to believe I'd come back seeking vengeance —it didn't matter that it was the truth—along with those who believed the whole storyline to be little more than the work of the League's increasingly active writers' room.

Surely Goro had wanted me in the arena, Sang Hee said. Surely he knew I wouldn't go, Min had argued.

I knew the truth of it. Goro knew that I would be unable to pass up the opportunity at vengeance, just as he knew I wasn't dumb enough to walk right into the arena with Sang Hee, no matter how many eyes were watching. Goro knew that, while the millions of eyes were focused on Sang Hee's trial, the true fight would take place in the luminescent halls of the Soul Dome.

I hadn't wondered for long if he was there or not. Of course he was there. Goro knew the only way to catch the tiger was to leave out fresh meat, and he was a tantalizing piece. No doubt he had surrounded himself with a considerable retinue.

Waiting was always the hardest part. Sang Hee said she had friends on the inside. Friends that would do their best to get me as clear a path to Goro as possible. She seemed to have friends all over, including those with talents particularly geared toward fashioning League resin into lethal paramilitary-grade equipment. Not that I was complaining.

The trick would be to get to him before his full plans regarding Sang Hee—whatever they were—could go into effect. And if there was one thought that kept me salivating, it was the thought of what I'd do once I got to him.

The pounding of the ceremonial drums went on for longer than was normal. The reedy, shrill announcer prattled on, spitting and gyrating longer than was normal. And when the screen faded to shimmering black once more, the darkness settled longer than was normal.

The screen remained gray-black, with the fuzzy unreality of static. The crowd was little more than hushed wraiths. Ghosts of unrest. The Soul Dome loomed behind the rectangular screen like a monolith. A structure built of sin, and bathed in violence. To me, in that moment, it resembled an eggshell, one whose innards I was eager to be at. My mask felt like a bloody hawk's beak, my sheathed blades talons.

I crouched, settling down onto one knee and eyeing the fire escapes, the vents with their white condensation issuing into the musty wet of the night.

When the screen flickered back to life, a bright-blue bridge materialized out of the darkness, and a tall, thin figure strode into the void, marching toward the screen like an apparition. When her boot touched the white canvas, she drew her bo staff and lit it, bathing herself in storm light.

Sang Hee received such an ovation I could see the sweat of her pre-fight workout shivering on her brow under the vibration of the crowd.

The camera switched perspective, Sang Hee and her blazing blue staff now peering in the direction of the opposite tunnel. A red bridge materialized there, and in the place of one shadow, two emerged from the darkness. I frowned, my suit expanding slightly in response to my racing heart.

The shadows cut in opposite directions as soon as they touched the bridge. Their suits lit with deep violet veins that carved armored plates from their profiles. They were relatively small. Smaller than me and shorter than Sang Hee. One was male and the other female. Their features were Eastern. Possibly Japanese. They could have been twins. The female had her hair pulled up in a bun, while the male had his cut short except for the front, where black bangs hung down over his eyes. Dark eyes.

I didn't recognize either of them, and judging by the hushed, pregnant pause of the audience, they didn't either.

Assassins brought in from across the sea, most likely.

The male crossed his arms over his chest. In the place of a glowing weapon, purple razor fins emerged from seams in his forearms, with half-foot spikes jutting out from behind his elbows like folded sickle wings. The blades pulsated. The female crossed her arms in front of her chest, clenched her fists and then shot them down to her sides. Ten-inch amethyst claws jutted out of holes above her knuckles, two on each hand. These, too pulsated.

Sang Hee frowned, partially because the lights had come back up, and partially because she was wondering what Goro was playing at. She glanced in the direction of the President's box. No looming shadow this time.

"Ladies and gentlemen!" the announcer screamed into his

spit-infused microphone. "Welcome the twins from Kyoto. Names redacted. Titles, Spark and Glow."

I nearly choked on the absurdity of it. They weren't even trying to hide the hit. All the more entertaining for the audience. All the more dramatic.

Sang Hee could have forfeited right then and there. Called bullshit on Goro's last-minute rules change. Instead, she brought her blue staff down in front of her face and spread her feet out into her martial stance as the twins stood motionless, purple razor blades glowing along with matching luminescent contact lenses.

"Ah, but don't start yet, champions!" the announcer said as Sang Hee tensed, settling her weight onto her back heel. "Goro would be remiss if he did not afford Sang Hee the opportunity to bring forth an ally."

Sang Hee frowned and swallowed. I did too.

Another pregnant pause, and then the murmuring of the crowd morphed, changing from whispering to excited tremors. A chant started and then died. And then another picked up its memory, and the words echoed in the Soul Dome. Soon enough, those watching in the alleys and under the glowing, smoke-choked eaves below me joined in, and Goro's imagined victory was at hand.

"Sword … Punk … Sword … Punk … Sword PUNK!"

They chanted. They yelled. They screamed, throaty and raw, knowing now that the Sword Punk was little more than a story. A masterful, brilliant story invented by Goro Hamada on the backs of a few well-timed deaths in the media. And if some guessed it had been real, that the Sword Punk had been real, that Akio Prince had risen from the dead, or that he had really died at all, it was all the better for Goro's story.

As I crouched there, I resolved that the display—the taunt—would be Goro's last. For Akio Prince had died that night. The Sword Punk was real, and tonight, he'd go a long way toward earning the various titles he'd been given too early. Names written in the blood of corrupt underlings.

"Do you have no ally to call, then?" the announcer taunted. "No hero-in-waiting? No ghost? No demon? No savior?"

Sang Hee glanced up toward the announcer's table. She seemed to consider hurling her weapon—I now knew from experience it was one hidden switch away from turning from bo staff to spear and impaling the screeching parrot where he squawked.

"No matter. Goro is nothing if not generous."

Goro had never made himself a major part of the promotion. He was always on the edges. But there was no President Blue tonight. Tonight, Goro had decided that the best way to dispel controversy was to lean into it so fully that the whole thing came off seeming as bright-lit and produced as the rest of the city.

If there had been any doubt remaining over whether people watched the League for the sporting, martial arts aesthetic or for the stories it produced, they were dispelled then. Akio Prince was alive, the collective unconscious seemed to say. He'd been paid off, paid to retire. Smart of Goro. Shrewd. A clever way to turn your most dominant, and yet your least popular, champion into an asset. Surely he'd been given a nice severance. Surely he was set up in one of those glass and steel compounds in the mountains to the north.

I gritted my teeth, and licked the blood from the lip I'd been chewing. Blood, with its metal smell and copper taste, had a way of bringing the real out of the artifice, lest I too get caught in the spell.

Before the battle could be joined, the blue bridge Sang Hee had traversed from the tunnel to the center platform flickered, and the lights went down once more. My heart beat a little faster as I wondered whether or not Goro might just kill her then and there, then catch a waiting helicopter back to his brothers and sisters, his masters in Tokyo.

The bridge went dark, its LED lights dimmed. When it flared back to life, it did so with a warm yellow glow. The crowd cheered and my frown turned from anger to confusion. Sang Hee kept most of her attention focused on the pacing twins on the other side of the platform, but she stepped off to the side, angling herself away from the golden bridge.

The doorway to the tunnel opened, now with bright-white light framing it and painting the newest arrival in splendor. When the lights dimmed a bit, Dae made his walk, his golden armor standing out against his pale skin and short, dark hair with white streaks. His twin hand axes glinted on his back, and his armor—thicker than most in the League—reflected the flashing lights of the mobile devices in the crowd.

Dae bowed as he crossed the threshold from his flickering sunlit bridge to the martial canvas. When he raised his head, he nodded to Sang Hee, then to the crowd, many of whom went weak in the knees at the sight of his glowing blue contact lenses, which matched Sang Hee's armor.

"*Introducing,*" the announcer screamed, seizing on the excited confusion in the crowd, "Dae! Dae will be fighting alongside Sang Hee in the first-ever team League Finals!"

Sang Hee's look would have been humorous if she wasn't in mortal peril. She eyed Dae like he was something she'd just dragged in on the bottom of her shoe. That look showed plainly that she would much rather have faced down the poison-colored twins from Kyoto alone than do it in his company.

I didn't know much about Dae. He seemed a fine enough fellow. He was good. Not good enough to beat Sang Hee, as evidenced by her besting him in the Quarters, but good nonetheless. Still, I couldn't help but think he was wrapped in Goro's plan in more ways than one, and I couldn't imagine that any of the potential scenarios Goro had made peace with included Sang Hee emerging from the Finals victorious after denouncing him so publicly. His ego wouldn't allow it, even if he had managed to convince a good portion of the crowd that he'd been pulling the strings all along.

"What are you playing at, Goro?" I asked. The rain had picked up. The screen went fuzzy and then came back with some clarity. The streets had gone relatively quiet as every available eye in the street-side bars or looking through the intermittent wipers in idling, humming cars was fixed on the arena.

When the screen became clear once more, the bridges had

withdrawn, leaving the four fighters on the center platform. The lights dimmed enough to afford an extra bit of glow to the League weapons: the twins with their deep purple, pulsating blades; Sang Hee with her ice-lightning blue staff; and Dae with the double-sided golden axes he ignited as soon as they were drawn.

I saw Sang Hee's lips moving and Dae twitching an eyebrow in her direction. Her eyes were fixed on the twins, but she was addressing him.

I leaned forward, realizing with a flutter that if I leaned any more, I'd go right down into the alley with a crash. With how rapt the city seemed to be on the Finals, it was doubtful anyone would have noticed.

"As a final note," the announcer said, his voice affecting a grave, mock-serious tone, "tonight's contest will be fought under Kyoto rules, in honor of our guests. No quarter need be given, even if it's asked for. No mercy is expected."

The twins bowed toward the President's box, and a worried hush fell over the audience. Not worried in the genuine sense. More worried in the way an audience worries over a character in peril in a film, or dying in a virtual game. That's all this was to them, after all. They'd warm to the sudden shift in intent quickly enough.

As soon as the diminutive twins straightened out of their bows, they tore across the canvas trailing amethyst streaks. They were fast. Fast enough to look enhanced from a distance. Cybernetics weren't allowed in the League—they weren't even allowed in Korea—but there didn't seem to be many regulations in Kyoto. Perhaps we were playing by all of their rules tonight.

The twins crossed paths in the center of the canvas, one darting and the other spinning toward their respective foes. At the top of the screen, the male ducked low then leapt high—high as an acrobat—spinning in the air and coming down with an exaggerated overhead slice with the glowing spine on his forearm. Sang Hee raised her spear to block, and purple and blue sparks lit the gloom and littered the canvas. As the Kyoto fight-

er's feet hit the canvas, the female blazed across the bottom of
the screen, her claws stabbing toward Dae's chiseled features.
He turned them aside with a hard stroke of one axe and followed
it up with the back hand.

I was so caught up in the initial exchange that I hadn't
noticed another light shining in my eyes. Now it blinked on and
off, and I tore my eyes away from the screen with effort. A hatch
had opened up on the roof of the Dome, off to the right, in the
shadows of the towering screen. It flickered again, on and off. I
tensed, the red light in my suit grooves responding eagerly, and a
figure ducked out of sight, taking the light with them but leaving
the hatch open.

I stood and backed up ten paces, and breathed in deeply,
feeling the sinuous suit respond in kind, feeling the stiff, rigid
blades across my back. Feeling the hatred grow as I imagined
Goro stuffing his fat face with something greasy as he watched
Sang Hee fight for his entertainment, and winning back the
crowd the ghost of Akio Prince had thought was his just a few
days before.

Time to do something. Something more than nothing.

It wasn't so far. Even still, I backed up another few paces,
then started forward. I pushed in hard, the resin-rubber grooves
of my boots giving me purchase on the slick rooftop as I sprinted
toward the alley.

Three strides, then four, and on the fifth, I took the ledge and
put all of my strength into the leap, soaring over the gap. I saw
the falling rain droplets framed against all the colors of Seoul.
The amber and yellow from the bars and dens in the streets
below. The white halogen of headlights lancing shards up into
my lids, the purple of the twins' blades on the massive screen,
along with the gold of Dae and that steady, buzzing azure blue of
Sang Hee. The moment seemed to take an eternity, and if anyone
saw me make the leap, they might have thought me a red apparition. A demon in the city night, come to take my revenge.

And that's exactly what I was.

My landing wasn't graceful. It was animalistic. I slammed

into the tangle of steel and rain-slicked cement and scrambled, leaving the bright of the screen behind and crawling up the sloped roof of the Soul Dome until I came to the open service hatch.

I peered over the edge, and saw nothing but a cement landing below. I dropped in, landing in a crouch, my hands straying up toward the black resin hilts in my suit. I breathed out, checking down the stairwell to my right. Nothing. Up to my left, nothing, but my mystery ally on the inside had left their flashlight hanging from the chrome handle of a gray painted door.

Up, then.

I left my blades sheathed, for now, and tore up the stairs. The door opened easily, admitting me into another brightly lit hall that seemed to go on forever. I didn't know the Soul Dome well, since I only entered and left when I had a fight scheduled, but I guessed that I was above the locker rooms, and certainly above the arena. It was quiet, but the long fluorescent lights above me flickered at odd intervals. They seemed to be punctuating something, and I guessed it was the roaring bass of the crowd.

The thought of the arena brought with it a renewed sense of urgency. I walked with purpose, passing service closets and closed steel doors, back offices where any number of legal and illegal practices might take place. My focus was ahead. Forward.

When that hall ended, I turned right, following the only path laid out before me. The lights here were more a smoldering blue, like lantern light, the sort that drew moths. I passed under these with an even more steady gait and stopped at a juncture where another hall split off to the right. I paused and closed my eyes, feeling the condensation on the inside of my mask. There it was. A distant rumble, but grown closer than the last. I opened my eyes and waited for the tremors to rise again. When they did, I saw that the lights in the hall up ahead responded more vigorously than those to my right, almost as if they were panicked.

Gray painted steel doors were replaced with glass ones with steel mesh between the panes. The first few were unoccupied, but the farther I got, the more inhabited the Soul Dome was. I passed a room full of what looked to be clerks—mostly women, typing away at screens and likely counting the night's concessions or bets. Most of them paid me no mind. It wasn't particularly strange to see a fighter in a League suit at the Dome, even one wearing a mask.

I should have met resistance by now. If Goro knew I was coming, and I was guessing he did, I should have met resistance, if not been killed ten times over. The next hall was a little darker than the others. I paused as I walked past another large office, this one with a wall of screens. There was a group of technicians fussing over the automated camera controls, and a pair of managers with headsets on barking out orders. I squinted, trying to get a view of the action. I couldn't make out much detail. There was a lot of flashing light. Sparks, which meant the action was getting quite furious.

Desperate curiosity got the better of me, and I shouldered my way through the door. The techs kept their attention on their screens, but one of the managers swung his head back toward the door, ready to bark out orders. He didn't look frightened by my appearance, more confused. Even irritated.

"What's the work?" I asked.

"The … what?" the manager/director replied. "Wait. Who are you, and what are—"

I drew one of my blades, the quick movement lighting the veins of my suit, and brought it down in a flashing blur. The ruby-steel alloy split an expensive-looking monitor to my right, carving through it like butter and showering the control center with sparks.

The screens flickered but didn't die, and the techs and another director ducked comically while the one that had initially addressed me shrank back, his eyes wild.

"Goro didn't tell you to expect me?"

"N … n …"

"Expect who?" the other director, this one a blonde woman with bright-green eyes, asked.

"P … punk," a diminutive man with greasy brown hair said, clutching the back of his chair with sweaty palms.

"That's right," I said. I had my teeth bared like a wolf, but they couldn't see it behind my mask. I think my eyes did the trick. "So then," I pointed up at the wall of screens with my pulsating red sword, "what's the work, here?"

Now that I was closer, I could see the action in greater detail. Sang Hee was bleeding from a slash on her cheek. The Kyoto twins were using sharps. An inch higher and she'd have lost an eye. Dae was bleeding as well, albeit from his knuckles. He and Sang Hee fought separately, while the twins switched between the two of them, occasionally giving one a respite and joining forces to launch a particularly nasty purple salvo at the other.

They seemed to be concentrating the bulk of their attention on Sang Hee, and Dae … there was something about the way Dae was moving. Not his body. His body was in the fight. His feet worked expertly. His arms swung those golden glowing axes. But, his eyes kept tracing back to Sang Hee. He was tracking her around the ring, even when one or both of the twins was on him, harassing him like jackals.

I narrowed my eyes, focusing with my martial mind, which was ever-present, floating just beneath the surface. It was how I saw the world. Everything was a violent equation.

The twins were good. The male threw straights despite his elbow blades pointing to hooks as the more efficient option. The female threw hooks and swipes, fighting more like a rabid cat than a streaking assassin. When they pirouetted, crossing over each other's glowing amethyst paths, their attack patterns changed. The female launched herself at Dae, claws going straight this time. It was all he could do to frame his axes up, directing the purple glowing claws over his sweat-soaked brow. He had to bend backward to duck, and the claws raked him on the way by.

"Convincing," I said, frowning.

Dae spun away from the exchange, whipping his trailing axe out to cover his retreat. The Kyoto girl ducked and rolled, then came up stabbing again. The two had been in the foreground, but now the camera focused on the exchange behind them, where the Kyoto male leapt as often as he darted. Sang Hee was able to keep him at bay with her lashing staff. The blue resin flashed like lightning each time it met the purple fin blades. The Kyoto male extended a cross, missing wide.

"Bait," I breathed.

Sang Hee recognized it. She had been prepared to counter, framing her staff out in front of her and stepping into an overhead strike. But I saw her eyes widen as she traced the path of the punch, the lavender glow lighting the whites of her eyes. She pulled her staff back and hopped backward just as her opponent pulled his arm back, the hook of his fin blade scraping against the retreating staff. If she'd have left it in place, he would have torn it from her grasp and left her unarmed.

Sang Hee twirled away, her whipping staff keeping more distance between herself and her attacker than Dae was able to keep between himself and his as she skirted the edge of the platform and sidestepped back into the middle. Dae was driven back, and soon the two were back to back, weapons of gold and blue flaring out at their flashing, speedy adversaries.

As the camera panned and as the each fighter rotated on their central axes, I watched their eyes. The twins were intent on their kill. No faking that. They were in it to win. Sang Hee switched between them, and occasionally glanced backward, often as she could spare, suspicious of Dae's axes every time a swing brought one of the blades too close to the nape of her neck. Her suit was thinner than mine and much less armored than Dae's. Sang Hee favored movement, and the twins were wise to it. They were trying to corral her. Their attacks seemed more vicious when aimed at Dae, and more probing when aimed at Sang Hee. I suspected that would change as soon as they had her where they wanted her. A staff was an excellent weapon for maintaining spacing. Not as much when harried from multiple fronts.

As for Dae, he was being forced to defend himself. I was convinced the twins were at him, fighting to kill. But his eyes … there! They switched toward the President's box, that obsidian, reflective and opaque den of corruption and opulence. Once. Twice. Every time he and Sang Hee completed a rotation, his eyes grew increasingly desperate.

It was as if he was waiting for some signal.

"There." I leveled the tip of my ruby-red sword toward the monitor focusing on Dae's expression.

One of the directors had inched toward the doorway, but he knew he'd get no farther without the risk of being cut in half. The woman remained still, and the technicians had resumed their work, though I could see them sweating as they wondered when the armed and masked ninja in their midst would start hacking away at more than controls.

"What's his play?" I asked.

"Whose—"

"Dae's!" I shouted. "And Goro's."

The blonde woman and the man directly in front of me exchanged glances. Nervous on one face and confused on the other.

I sussed out which was which quickly enough and stepped quickly forward, smashing my left fist into the soft mix of tissue and cartilage on the man's face. He crumpled into a heap and rocked amidst the sparking wires and glittering glass. I stepped over him and around the first row of unmanned controls. The blonde woman stepped backward, haltingly.

"What's the play?" I asked again. Calm. Even. Deadly.

Her light eyes twitched and watered. Sparks danced from the broken controls beside me, and yellow, blue and purple flashes lit the wall of screens as the tempo in the arena took on a desperate air.

I growled and swung my blade toward the soft, exposed skin of her throat, guiding the tip up just under her chin, just as I had with Kuzu Tokoro. She tilted her chin up, keeping her quivering eyes on me.

"I suggest you find your voice," I said as she swallowed.

"I don't know … the particul—"

I pressed the tip of the razor-sharp blade up so it just touched the soft flesh of her chin. The techs had stopped. They leaned over their chairs in various states of fear and unease, wondering if I was about to rip out their boss's throat, and, likely, whether they would make it to the door before I could do the same to them. The other director had quieted his whimpering and had devolved into a controlled moaning as he fussed over the remnants of his nose.

"As you can see, my blades won't mind the blood. Quite goes with the whole outfit, really." She looked me up and down again, noting the armor, the glowing red veins of my suit, and the length of glowing ruby steel parked under her chin. "Is Dae fighting to win?" I asked.

She nodded too quickly and winced as the sword nipped. That worked for me.

"And what else is he—"

"He's to betray Sang Hee," she said too hurriedly for it to be a lie. "Soon as he finds an opening. He's supposed to swing too wild, score a hit that lets the twins do the rest."

I nodded. It was simple. And yet, as I watched the way Dae fought … more importantly, as I watched the way the Kyoto twins went at him, I wondered if they had got the memo that he was on their side. Most likely, Goro had given separate orders to each outfit. The twins were to fight to kill. If Dae died in the chaos, that suited Goro so long as Sang Hee followed suit. Less people who knew, and that sort of thing.

Dae must have been at least half as bright as his name. He'd caught on to that bit, at least. Still, he seemed desperate for a signal. Those eyes kept finding the black glass of Goro's box as often as they could.

I tried to focus back on the director but something on the broadcast caught my eye. Amidst the glowing white canvas and Dae's golden axes, Sang Hee's rod of lightning and the Kyoto twins' shards of charged violet, there was a deeper glow. A small, ruddy blossom of light coming from behind the black glass of the President's box.

It was too small on the broadcast to make out details, but I could see the hint of that great, bulky form—an immense and intimidating figure in silhouette who was more flab than muscle in person, more jowl than jaw. Goro, watching the fools in the audience more than the dancing fighters on their lonely canvas. Watching Dae.

My heart caught in my throat as Dae and Sang Hee executed another unplanned and yet coordinated spin as the twins increased their tempo. Dae's face—the picture of focus—changed as the President's box and Goro's burning cigar blossom came into view. He set his feet as the female twin slid in front of him, halted the backswing of his right-hand blade and started it forward. The twin's eyes widened, her own martial mind working over the calculations as Sang Hee came in on her right. She darted backward as Dae's axe swept across his body.

Sang Hee was unaware that Dae had stopped his spin as she continued her rotation. Her staff was streaking to her left as her body went right. Dae's axe was now speeding in from the opposite direction, a strike in the guise of an attack on the Kyoto twin that would soon bite into the soft section of Sang Hee's side.

There was nothing I could do to stop it, and I had an impression of red. I saw Sang Hee kneeling on the canvas, staff pulsating as if with her own life energy as she examined bloody hands. I saw myself tearing through the control room, filling it with red to match, and continuing on to do the devil's work on anyone else I might deem responsible.

The vision passed in a blur, but Dae's strike never landed. At the last moment, he tucked the right-hand axe in, swinging it across his body at an angle. He guided the glowing golden weapon down past his left hip, between him and Sang Hee, switched his feet and used the momentum to bring his left-hand axe up and around his body ... and straight ahead.

The Kyoto twin's eyes had no more whites to expose. She had shifted back just enough to avoid Dae's Judas strike and then to close back in with her claws before he could think to defend himself from the double cross. But his overhead had a spin and a step on it, and she was out of position.

The golden axe came down like a righteous sunbeam, landing on the twin's resin armor between the links of her collar. Even on the broadcast, the crunch was audible, and the twin's face screwed up in pain as she rolled out of the exchange, avoiding Dae's follow-up.

The twin came up with her right arm curled, claws glowing,

while the left hung limp, claws and suit veins dimming on that side as the suit responded to the slackened muscles. She tried to step backward and stumbled, glancing down toward her compromised limb as if compelling it to obey her.

The blow had been brutal, and the twin had rolled too late. Her collarbone had shattered like a bird's wing. If she was lucky, the bones hadn't punctured anything vital. If she wanted to ensure survival, she'd concede. As her brother spun and slashed his razor wings out at Sang Hee enough to get her to give an inch, he retreated toward his sister, watching her out of the corner of his eye as he kept Sang Hee and Dae in front of him.

"There's hope for you yet, Dae," I whispered.

The audio from the stream was being fed into headsets adorning the control panel at the front of the room, beneath the wall of screens. I couldn't hear much more than static, but as the contest experienced its first organic pause, the very walls shook with the outpouring of energy from Seoul's citizens, within the arena and without.

The azure and golden fighters from Korea stood firm. Sang Hee looked at Dae, her expression searching. Had she noticed the strange sequence? Had she sensed the change of heart? The killing intent before the sudden shift?

Dae looked straight ahead. His brow was sweaty and bloody, and he blinked away the mix, keeping his axes out in front of him as wards. Sang Hee quit her examination of him and measured the twins.

The brother looked back at his sister with concern, but when I saw his sister's eyes slide toward the President's box, I knew there was no quit in her. She was Kyoto, through and through. That, and Goro had likely made himself all too clear. The terms? Victory. Or death.

Sang Hee came to the same conclusion. She lowered her staff as I finally, slowly lowered my own blade from beneath the chin of the director. Sang Hee activated the hidden catch on the shaft of her weapon and the tip extended, the staff transforming into a sparking spear that made the twins' faces go ashen. Sang Hee's lips moved, and while I couldn't read them clearly, the intent was all too obvious.

The Princess of Seoul offered mercy.

She was better than me, in that respect.

21

ALL STOPS

"Where's security?" I asked the director, feeling steady now that Sang Hee and Dae seemed to have the upper hand. "Or does Goro really value his staff so little?"

The director swallowed. She still kept her chin frozen with a tilt even though I had lowered my blade. I smirked.

"He's holed up in his cave, yes?"

A nod so imperceptible I might have imagined it.

"How many does he have?" I asked. "Guns or blunts?"

Nothing. She was either a stone-faced badass or, more likely, in shock.

I shrugged. "Doesn't matter, I suppose. As you were." I nodded back at the techs. "Fight could use some better angles. Things are heating up."

The techs bent back to their work, fussing over the camera controls and donning their headsets as blue, gold and purple flashes overtook the screen once more. The director kept her eyes on me until I turned around and strode from the room. I took extra care to step on and not over the groaning male director, drawing a pitiful squeak.

It wasn't really his fault, all things considered. Still, guilt by association, and all that.

The lights flickered as I stole back out into the hall, likely a residual effect of me carving up the control panel. I quickened my pace, knowing I had to be getting close to the locker rooms and, by extension, the narrow lane of a hall that would take me to the door I most wanted to get behind. Sang Hee and Dae appeared to have the fight under control, which only meant Goro would get more desperate if he really did intend for the League's most popular fighter to die today, as he'd intended of me not so long ago.

I came to a familiar junction. Ahead, the hall spilled down a steep staircase that led to a more dimly lit walk. At the bottom, the red corner locker room was cut into the bowels of the Soul Dome, along with the mini fridge I had rigged. I wondered if any of my green German bottles were shivering in there, frosted over and crystalizing. The sounds from the arena were more pronounced here. More bass than anything, though I could hear snatches of that reedy announcer's voice as he attempted to guide the narrative he had not been expecting to call.

Zoo had taken me up these stairs after the Round of 16, and had brought me to Goro's office. I don't know if I had expected a reward, a promotion or a restructured contract. Maybe even a sponsorship opportunity, since Kenta's debt was almost paid and I was the highest-level fighter in the League not to have accepted one. Either way, I had prepared myself either for a heated argument preceded by empty platitudes or to respond coolly and stoically to Goro's pleading as bean-counters peered at me nervously or condescendingly over their inch-thick glasses.

Instead, it was Goro who had been stoic. Calm. Clear. And firmly in control. There were no platitudes. No conditions. Nobody offered me a seat. Instead, Goro had announced himself with that red blossom of cigar light, revealing his greasy bulk only in impressions as he sat on a leather throne. He didn't even speak. He had people for that. A diminutive man—wasn't it always the way?—had explained that I was to lose my Semi-Final match to Janix, that I would be paid for the fall, and paid handsomely, and that no questions would be asked and no answers given aside from that.

I could be quick and snappy in the ring, and doubly so with my words when it came to shouting down Joon or Min, and

especially Kenta, back when we'd had the good fortune of arguments. With Goro, I had only stood and stared. He hadn't even
had the decency to surround himself with more than a few unar-
mored mercenaries, of which Zoo was captain.

Well, I'd make my argument tonight. I'd get the last word,
even if Goro had had the first one.

I sheathed my right-hand blade, reforming the X across my
back, and flexed my core and my fists. The red veins of my suit
responded.

I didn't take the corner so much as blur it, sprinting around
the intersection and into the adjoining hall that would take me
to Goro's office.

I had the barest impression of shadows at the end of the hall,
all clustered together, when the lights—all of the lights
—went out.

I slid to a halt, not even halfway toward the wooden door
with no placard, and cursed myself for freezing. A blossom of
light cast a red glow over the proceedings. I was reminded of
Goro's cigar, only this light was coming from me, as my suit
drank in the tension of my muscles and put it back out, casting
the hall in the color of blood.

For a heart-stopping instant, I expected to hear the telltale
click of a trigger. The cold cobalt sound that may as well be a
death sentence. Min's father's armor was probably more ornamental than effective, and it wasn't made to stop spider tanks or
auto rifles, in any case. I doubted the resin suit Sang Hee had
gifted me was up to the task either, and I was hardly going to
deflect any bullets with the ruby blades on my back, fast as I
might be.

But as my eyes adjusted to the red gloom, I saw that the
clutch of shadows at the back of the room weren't kneeling in
firing positions, but rather inching their way toward me, arms
locked and a mix of batons and black marine knives clutched in
their own black leather gloves. They had helmets on, and even in
the dim, hellish light, I could see the faint green glow beneath
their visors. As if seeing me better than I could see them would
do them any good.

There appeared to be a dozen of them. Paramilitary, no doubt, and it wouldn't have surprised me to find out they were from Tokyo. More likely, a mix of international ne'er-do-wells Goro kept on the payroll for emergencies just like this.

They looked like the creeping shadows of demons, which I took to mean I was in good company.

"Lucky for me," I said, stopping a couple in front, "Goro's smart enough to know he can't bring guns to a League fight, especially not with the police force sniffing around lately." They started to edge forward again. "Unlucky for you, I plan on defending myself to the best … of my considerable ability."

I unsheathed my swords and squeezed the hilts, allowing their brighter ruby glow to light up my quarry in the only color I planned to share with them tonight.

The group paused again. A few glass helmets tilted toward one another in what I imagined was consternation. A tall, beefy fellow in the center of the pack pushed through, barking something at the others.

Russian. That was a surprise. Another answered him from the side. Not Russian.

"Just in case I wasn't clear enough with that last bit of foreboding," I said. "I will fight to kill. I'm sure Goro's paying you enough for it not to matter, but … fellas … the best way for me to put this is, you're just not the final boss here, and I do plan to play him."

Guns would have done the trick of giving me enough fear to work with. As it stood, being in an enclosed arena with limited horizontal movement and utilizing close-range weapons had me feeling more excited than terrified.

Maybe Commander Red Star would give me a fit, though. He certainly seemed up to the task, and there were a lot of sharps in the mix, I reminded myself as I sank into my stance, sliding my right foot back as I raised my twin dragon's fangs.

"Come on, then."

They did.

The commander was a big fellow, but he wasn't particularly quick. He barked something at the others and then rushed forward. It was a feint. I slashed a backhand at his midsection, scraping a line in the cloth and drawing a spark from the armor underneath. He had a meaty baton with obsidian spikes on the head, like a caveman's club, and I had the inappropriate and poorly timed epiphany that brutes just hadn't evolved all that much in the last several millennia.

On instinct, I brought my right heel up to my left and lanced a side kick into his hips. Red Star's spiked club still came down, but when it struck, it did so glancing. A backhand–forehand with my blades—more hilt on the first and punch on the follow-through—had him stumbling off to my left, and the two that came for me next did so much more quickly, and much more directly. Straight-line, and with knives.

I felt the jolt of fear in my heart that immediately injected a shot of adrenaline into the situation. I ducked right, feeling one knife glance off of the red plate armor strapped to my left shoulder while I swept my left hand across to slap-block the other knife, and likely snap a finger in the process. As I spun through the pair, I felt a burning slash on the back of my thigh and noticed Red Star up to his old tricks. He'd dropped the club in favor of a blade and managed a backward stab that had found its way in. Shallow, but a nice reminder.

No playing.

When I spun, I raised the right sword high and slashed with the left. The relative lack of resistance the sword met, combined with the commando's scream on that side, told me their armor didn't stretch all the way around the torso, and that was one down who wouldn't be getting up without some assistance.

My right-hand blade carved a crescent up and then forward, chopping down in a very un-sword-like maneuver. But hey, it had worked for Dae just a short while before, and I wasn't fighting Kyoto League fighters. It bought me spacing as the thicker pack of soldiers slammed backs into chests in their flight from the glowing red sickle, and in fighting, spacing bought you time.

There are a lot of details in every sort of fighting, and, if you haven't figured it out by now, I was pretty good at the details. But as Kenta had drilled into Joon and me on more occasions than I'd ever wish upon any unfortunate orphaned soul, finesse was for the ring. Even efficiency, the staple of Joon's game, wasn't what kept men alive in the trenches. Sometimes, in the case of a classic last-stand-type scenario, it came down to guts. Who had more, and who kept more in their bodies in the midst of the chaos.

I was reminded of those talks. Of those lectures, as I spun through that darkened hall, red sabers flashing, heels shifting, toes pirouetting like a dancer's. Sometimes, when there were just too many opponents, too many blunts and blades, too much blood on the other side, you had to bring will into the mix.

I'd landed more hits than I'd received. I'd carved an electrical wire from the panels in the ceiling that added a sparking strobe effect to the formerly hellish styling of the battle, but I'd received quite a few hits in return, most of them on the ends of blades.

My resin and ornamental plate spared me from anything too deep, and I'd like to think my defensive prowess did as much or more in that regard. Even my mask sent a slashing combat knife off the mark that would have given me a wide smile.

Things started getting a little rough when I added an unnecessary spin on the back of another slash across the back of one of the commandos. The one nearest Goro's mahogany door didn't jump backward like the rest had. He ducked, and then he came forward, charging like a bull. He hit me square in the hips and bowled me over, landing us in a tangle.

I kept ahold of my blades, but the bleeding, enraged pack of hired men with batons and carbon fiber closed in like a wave, kicking, striking and sometimes stabbing at the glowing League suit that squirmed, bucked, kicked and slashed desperately on the floor. The rubber of my hilts squeaked like mice as my back slid over blood whose origins I didn't want to puzzle over. I took an Achilles from one and the front of a knee from another as I dislodged the bull and flipped myself over.

Things slowed down as Red Star closed in. His club landed against the side of my head, and I was only spared a particularly gruesome death due to the fact that the blow was slowed on its path by an errant limb. Still, the vision in my left eye went black, and the vision in my right eye went red.

I tried to make the best of it, and framed out with my left blade, bringing my right across in a slash. I flipped the right, pointing it downward and punching Red Star in the square jaw visible beneath his visor. His teeth went bloody, but he was very much alive, and growing angrier. The lead wolf, with a pack at his call and at my haunches.

I heard Kenta in my head. I saw him in the sparking, flashing shadows, his white mustaches and beard making him look like an old lion as he judged the manner of my death. As he judged my mercy and spit a gob of saliva and disgust to join the rest of the wet in the hazy, violent chaos.

Too soft, Kenta would have said. *When wolves are at the door, show them a tiger, not a hare.*

He was right, of course. I was outnumbered at least ten to one, and I could hack away at heels and armored, weighted cloth all night. These men had a job to do, and I had less blood than them. I was holding fangs, and thus far, I'd only been using them as claws.

I suppose it was guilt. Why did these men have to die on the path I'd set out for myself?

But then, we all make choices. Mine had led me here, fighting a pack of wolves in the bowels of the Soul Dome in front of Goro Hamada's door of judgment. In front of the gates of hell, for all the difference it made.

I had made my choices, and these men had made theirs.

I lanced a kick to the right, catching one commando on his glass helmet, which shattered and planted shards into his eyes. He screamed, and the tiger woke up. Red claws turned into fangs. The difference would have been subtle to an outside observer. I still punched and kicked, but the strikes had no pull to them. They were meant to stun. One to the chest and another to the throat that might have killed even if a three-foot length of glowing red steel hadn't plunged in behind it. I tore the sword across, taking the throat of the unfortunate commando with it.

A momentary respite in the bloody chaos as I looked down,

shaking, over my kill. Black visor. Black helm. Black blood that only turned red because everything in that hall was. I looked forward, and saw Goro's door. I turned around, feeling burning more than pain with the myriad slashes and stabs I'd received, and looked out over the pack.

The wolves were stunned. Stunned and scared. But Red Star stood in their midst. He'd dropped his club, and had his hands balled into fists. The alpha was angry, so the wolves mimicked him.

We met in the middle, and I launched myself forward, plunging my sword into a belly and punching out with the other. A knife sank into my bicep and I pulled back, kicking Red Star in the chest with all the force I could muster. He stumbled backward and I went to work on the pack as it closed ranks.

I didn't see individuals in the press, and I was spared a look at the eyes as most of the visors left the souls covered. I still struck with closed fists and booted heels and plated knees more than the razor-sharp glowing blades, but those found homes too, and before I knew it, most of the pack was either still or squirming. Two scrambled and ran, slipping due to a mix of injury and blood on the tiles, half supporting and half pushing off of each other in their desperation to be away from me. They fled into the bright of the adjoining hall.

But one stood firm.

Red Star slammed into me. A clean cross dislodged my mask and caused it to bite into the skin of my cheek. I responded with a cross of my own that broke the strap under his chin and sent his helmet clattering off of the wall, and we spun in a bloody tangle. No growling, no shouting and no swearing. No words anyone would understand. Just breath, haggard and strained, hot and angry. Desperate and hateful. Red Star had the sort of face you'd have guessed. Blond hair cut short in a military style, and enough scars to let me know he'd done a lot more of real fighting than I had. A man after Kenta's own heart, and, if the eyes could tell you anything, a killer.

He reared back and brought his head down toward my nose. I tucked and squeezed my eyes shut, accepting the butt on the crown of my head. It hurt like hell, and sounded like the snap of a baton off a rail, but he went just a bit slack on the back end of it, absorbing the worst of the blow.

I pushed, surprising him with my strength, but I was lower and I had him up on his heels. He clenched his hands behind my head, grasping the nape of my neck in order to keep me too close to stab. My arms had got crossed in front of me. I'd have to drop the blades to free them. Instead, I spun him around and pushed, gritting my bloody teeth, running him backward.

Joon was always a better grappler than me, but I knew all about leverage. Red Star might have had some sambo chops in his repertoire, but it wasn't going to do him any good with the angle I had him at. He tried to bring a knee up as I pushed him backward, sliding through the blood of his fellows as I guided him inexorably toward Goro's door. With a quick exhale and heave, I turned my left shoulder down and used the extra half inch to turn the push into a short ram.

His back collided with the door, rattling the frame and bringing bits of dried paint and plaster down on our heads. Now the growling started. He kept ahold of the back of my neck, and I got two inches of space this time. The second ram caused a crack in the door and drew a cough from his chest. For the third ram I had three inches, and made two cracks. The fourth broke his grip and sent a brass hinge spinning in the sparking electrical light.

I had turned myself into a ram of the animal variety and Red Star into one of the battering variety. The fifth ram cracked his sternum, and the ensuing cough was wet. I hopped backward, uncrossed my arms and dove back in.

I plunged both red blades in this time, one just beneath the ribs and the other straight through. His body was feeble resistance, and even the door behind parted around the high-grade steel alloy. I stepped backward, leaving the Russian pinned quite unceremoniously to the door, two glowing red swords sticking out of his torso which were fading toward the color of all the blood in the mix without my hands gripped around the hilts.

Red Star's eyes were milky. He saw me as a shadow, and I gave him a demon's nod before I sighed out the anger of our brief, bloody embrace. I tensed, flexed every fiber in my body, red suit veins flashing like a dragon's glare, and whipped around, launching the hardest side kick I'd ever thrown into his chest between the hilts.

The door shattered and the Russian died on impact, admitting me a rather dramatic entrance into Goro's den.

The lighting was dim, but it was brighter than the hall, despite the flashes from the hanging electrical wires. I had expected a red blossom of light from the end of a dipped cigar, Goro staring at me over a second retinue of commandos.

He was there, but he wasn't sitting. He was standing behind that great leather throne in the center of the long room that was the President's box. He was even bigger than I remembered, and his eyes were even darker. Dark enough for me to see my own reflection in them.

The Red Demon of Seoul. The Ghost of Akio Prince. The Sword Punk, framed in a flashing hallway filled with dead and dying, and painted in my colors.

I was so taken with the sight of Goro and his sweat-streaked face, his fat sausage hands gripping the back of that leather chair nervously, and the wrinkled kerchief in his pocket, that I hadn't taken stock of my surroundings.

There was another in the room with us. He sat on Goro's throne. He was unassuming. He had long silver hair and a black, form-fitting shirt that covered his upper body completely, along with leather pants. I thought he was wearing sunglasses, but when I blinked some clarity into my watering eyes, I recognized them as thin lenses under his lids. Spectral lenses. He had thin brown gloves on with small metal beads stitched into them.

This was a Tokyo man. An enforcer. A soldier of the Hachinin, and here to look after one of their own.

If he wasn't chemically enhanced, he might be cybernetically. It was still a new science, and faulty as all hell. But unpredictable.

I don't know if it was the work of the supposedly intelligent binding fibers of my suit or that chemical rage that had yet to recede from my fight in the hallway, but I was feeling more alive than I should have been given the number of knives I'd just met.

"Your brothers and sisters think so lowly of you, they only sent the one," I said, examining the stranger. "A dog to guard a dog."

Suit or not, I couldn't afford to let this drag out. Whether it was blood loss, Goro's reinforcements or the police force Min couldn't keep out of the Soul Dome all night, the night was getting old.

I could only just see the platform in the arena from where I stood at the back of Goro's office. There were flashes of gold, blue and midnight purple as Sang Hee and Dae continued to fend off the attacks of the Kyoto twins. Given what I had seen on the monitors in the control room, it looked like the fight should be winding down. That was Kyoto for you. Whole other league over there. I only hoped the twins would surrender before forcing Sang Hee and Dae to kill them. I could see the glow of blue screens as the fans in attendance took to the socials in force, likely to see if the rest of the city—if the rest of the world —was seeing the intensity of the fight they had the fortune or misfortune of witnessing firsthand.

The sounds of the arena were muffled behind the thick tinted glass that covered the entire right-facing window. It seemed Goro liked to see, but not hear.

A brief wave of dizziness came over me. I tried to stop myself from swaying and flexed my core. I felt a trickle of wet under my suit and knew some of my wounds were deeper than I had thought. The veins of my suit responded to the tension, reigniting their red glow like blown coals. The Tokyo assassin's soulless black lenses shifted, the microscopic synthetic gears within the organic silicon solution not missing anything. He seemed the picture of ease, unlike Goro.

"Goro Hamada of the Hachinin," I said, extending my left-hand sword out into the room, pointing directly at him. I gripped the handle and let the ruby-red glow brighten for emphasis. "I, Akio Prince, sentence you to die. I only wish the glass in your throne room were more clear, so they might see you beg before the end."

There were no escape routes that I could see behind Goro. Just a lavish blackwood bar replete with aged whiskey, wine and cigars, each of which could likely be sold to support a family of five for a year.

Goro tried to remain as calm as the man he'd hired or been sent by the Hachinin, but that greasy neck and those shivering jowls couldn't hide a nervous swallow.

The assassin took my threat as an invitation. He had seemed only mildly interested in my presence before. More curious than tense. He stood up. He was tall, and though I couldn't see any truth in his eyes behind the shifting black lenses, he looked vaguely Scandinavian to me. He was thin, but his body seemed lithe and solid, like condensed iron.

He stepped forward, his black leather shoes silent on the thin carpet. I moved to the right, starting to circle. I caught a glimpse of Sang Hee's shimmering blue spear as I did, and blinked the image away. If I got close to Goro, I'd risk an exposed flank to kill him. The assassin knew this, and apparently his charge was clear. He stopped circling, paused for a brief moment and then came on, straight and true, those dark gloves with their silver beads flashing.

I had expected him to brandish a weapon on the way in, but his confidence confirmed that the gloves were what I had to be wary of. I dove to the right, tucked and rolled as the silver-haired assassin launched a right cross toward the place where my head had been. He was fast, but not impossibly fast. Not enhanced in any obvious ways besides the eyes.

Still, I knew making a try for Goro would be impossible given the intent with which the assassin had thrown that strike. Besides, bait could be used both ways. As I came up onto my right leg, pain lancing through my muscles as the blood pooled in tiny crevices within my suit, I leaned toward Goro. The assassin bit, darting toward me.

I reversed my lean, and switched my eyes from the fright-ened-looking Goro back toward the streaking assassin. I jabbed my left sword forward, and the assassin spun, his feet moving expertly as he slapped the blade aside with the flat of his palm and came in. I meant to have the other blade waiting to carve a crescent to the right, expecting him to try to get an angle on me, but it seemed the man was a straight-line fighter. His right foot planted on the carpet well inside of my reach and he pumped a right jab that I leaned back to avoid. A left cross had me spinning to my right, back toward the glass. I swept my jutting blade toward the back of his head and continued my spin, bringing the right one around in a flash.

Either would have taken his silver-haired head from his shoulders with ease, but he ducked, followed my path with his shifting black eyes and shouldered into my side.

I hit the glass without much force, but it was enough to jar the grips on my blades. The assassin came on, lancing a fast, straight combination toward my head. I dodged two punches, and the third slammed into the glass. There was a flash and a jolt as I felt like a mule had kicked me in the back. I jerked forward as the assassin sidestepped. I managed to get my left hilt up just in time to partially deflect the next gauntlet-charged blow, but the ensuing shock sent me tumbling.

When I came up from my latest roll—one I hadn't planned to execute—I looked up to see the assassin standing with his back to the glass wall. Blue and white sparks played out along the edges, matching the chattering of my teeth.

"So, that's your trick," I said.

The assassin didn't wait for an invitation to resume our fast acquaintance, and I didn't either. We met in the middle of the room, a double slash of my blades forcing him to spin again, right into a roundhouse kick. He blocked that one with both forearms, but the force of the blow surprised him, causing him to stumble. I followed it up with a knee, and he blocked that one with his hands framed down in an X.

A shock blasted into my leg, the resin suit doing some work to distribute the charge. It gave me the boost I needed, and I stepped quickly forward, planting myself firmly inside the guard of the assassin, which he didn't expect given my use of sharps. I launched another double slash, but this one after reversing the grip on my swords. I led with my elbows, with my swords forming razor fins on the outside of my forearms, glittering bloody tips forming spikes that curved out from the edges of my elbows, mimicking the male Kyoto fighter.

The first elbow missed, but the second bit deeply into the assassin's shoulders, and now it was his turn to fall backward into a roll.

When he came up, he did so wearing a different expression. He wasn't afraid. This one looked like a sociopath, through and through. But now he had been forced to concentrate, if nothing else.

I almost smiled, knowing I'd given him plenty to consider in the last exchange, but then I noticed the empty room behind him, and the black sliver between two panels in the wall. No sign of Goro.

I gritted my teeth.

"I do hope you're not planning to run like your charge," I said. "I need somewhere to put all this ..."

"Rage," the assassin said with a nod. He nodded again toward the body of the Russian commando lying on the splintered door and the sparking, bloody hallway I'd left behind. I didn't turn around. "Looks like you've got plenty to spare." He secured his black and silver gloves, and gave a curt nod, along with the barest whisper of a smirk.

When he came on again, he did so with urgency, exposing his covered fear. I wasn't afraid as I met him in the center of the room. I was angry, and for once, I let that run.

We'd see where it took me.

22

RAGE

For a rather thin fellow, the vaguely Swedish Tokyo assassin packed a hell of a punch.

Then again, he was wearing electrified gauntlets that added an extra little mule kick of 50,000 volts into each strike. It wouldn't be enough to kill even if it landed on exposed flesh. The fact that I was wearing a half inch of carbon resin—or whatever the hell Sang Hee's mysterious benefactors had provided for her—did a lot to mute the effect. Still, I couldn't pretend it was entirely pleasant.

If there was one advantage to being tased every time he of the silver-spun locks landed a punch, it was the fact that it was getting really, really annoying, and while I was never one to fight angry, I found that the emotion was working a hell of a lot better than fear would. I probably owed that to the amount of blood I'd left with my soviet comrades in the hallway that had finally ceased its sparking behind me, but Goro's entirely predictable retreat had done nothing to slow the boil to a simmer.

The assassin closed the distance repeatedly, doing a remarkably disciplined job of staying inside the reach of my flashing ruby blades. Every time I swung, he moved forward instead of backward, crowding the strikes and making every blow I landed a glancing one. Changing to backhand grips and razor fins had allowed me to land a few cuts, but after he had adjusted to that,

I found that I was landing less and less and he was landing more. It didn't take a genius to surmise that those shifting black lenses had something to do with the way he was able to adapt and seemingly anticipate my next move.

I might be stubborn in virtually every aspect of my life—Min and Joon could attest to that easily enough—but I'd never been one to let pride into the ring. And while the rules may have changed, and the consequences with them, fighting a silver-haired assassin with Thor-powered fists and robotic eyes was just like slapping a new coat of paint on an old house.

This was a fight, just like any other fight, and if anyone was going to find a way out of it, it was me.

Thus, it came as quite an unpleasant surprise to Mr. Tokyo Stockholm when I released my grips on my swords and let them fall, dimming, to the carpet as I met his next volley of close-range strikes with a series of rattling, bruising blocks. Each block stung. Each one, whether on the insides of his flashing wrists or the tops of his knuckles, caused those little chrome beads to bite, but I'd already thrown him off.

We spun, only instead of doing so independently, the assassin and I waltzed around Goro's dark den of corruption with our fists a red and silver-blue blur. Our feet stepped with purpose, in and out, trying to get the most advantageous footing. The assassin attacked, attacked, attacked, and I attacked his attacks, concentrating every chop, hook and upturned elbow into his oncoming fists.

When I saw his tight, thin lips open ever so slightly to expose a bit of yellow-tinged bone, I exhaled, deepening my concentration.

Kenta had always detested the term blocking. To him, there was no such thing as defense in a fight. Only offense in disguise. Why block an ongoing blow when you could meet it with one of your own? You see, fighters threw strikes expecting resistance, but only in the form of soft tissue or yielding muscle and flesh. They didn't throw with the intent to clash with hard-boned shins or elbows, or even the crown of the head, which I used to duck-block a high cross that veered off the mark.

That one had the assassin wincing, and he backpedaled, skittering toward the tinted glass.

"That's it?" I asked, striding forward confidently. "That's the only trick?"

The assassin came on again, and now he did so displaying a bit of the emotion he had kept so well hidden before now. A lead jab came out slow, and I slammed it away with a left hook. The follow-up cross was disguised well, but his ensuing hook was aimed too low. It met a resin-reinforced elbow I tucked in to protect my liver.

He was growing increasingly desperate, and while he upped the tempo of his strikes, turning three- and four-punch combinations into five and six, each had less pepper on it than the last, and while I wasn't wearing fancy Tokyo spectral lenses, I was hopped up on all sorts of adrenaline and natural painkillers as my body kept the anger flowing in an effort to fight off the inevitable shock such violence and trauma produced in the less martial among us. Among the prey.

My eyes saw as much as his now, and as he retracted his fists after the latest assault, I saw that several of the shiny silver beads on his gauntlets had either been cracked or dislodged entirely. We stepped among them, our shoes crunching them like pearls.

The Tokyo assassin was good, but he had exposed a few faults with his game. He had a blistering close-range attack, and the tools to back it up. His footwork was expert, but it was all too one-dimensional. He was devastating up close because he had to be. Because he had nothing else. He concentrated on probing the body with blistering and lightning-infused punches. But when that strategy was turned on him, when my blocks hurt as much as his blows and my suit proved up to the task of absorbing his offense, he had nothing to fall back on.

How many skilled combatants had he faced and broken down? How many had focused on defending themselves, hoping he would tire out or expose some opening a well-timed counter could exploit?

There were no holes in his game. There were no lapses in

judgment. No careless mistakes or open windows to crawl through. If openings weren't presented, however, they could be made.

He came on again. He was determined. I'd give him that. Then again, he had seen a hallway full of dead mercenaries just a few minutes earlier. Every creature had survival instincts. Every creature had a quiet desperation that you could make loud with enough motivation.

My blows were red blurs as the veins of my suit were washed in red light. I lifted my arms in a cage block, elbows pointed straight ahead, and crashed into him, breaking his next combo before it could start and smashing him into the glass wall. One of his arms ricocheted off of the glass and I launched a cross into it, shattering the hand. I darted backward and then sailed forward with a hopping side kick. It had a lot on it, and pinned as he was to the back wall, his spine had nowhere to go. I heard another crack, and this one was going to be tough for him to walk off.

He tried to say something as he started to slump, but all that came out was a rattling sigh.

"What's that?" I asked, remembering to rechamber my kick and planting my foot. I lowered my lead fist but kept the back one cocked in case he was playing possum.

He kept himself from falling completely, and then pushed his back against the glass and willed himself into a standing position. His gauntlets trailed tiny fins and worms of white light that skittered between the chrome beads that hadn't been smashed in our exchanges. He looked like he tried to straighten, but I'd likely taken out his central supports like breaking down a building from its foundation pillars. He wasn't going anywhere.

"Nothing personal, right?" I said, relaxing as I approached him. I shot my left hand forward and grabbed him around the throat, then slammed his head against the glass. The stuff was thick. It hadn't so much as cracked during our fight.

The assassin gritted his bloody teeth and gargled something. Now that I felt him, he had more strength left than I'd anticipated. The wounds wouldn't be mortal. That made him dangerous to keep alive, but it also meant I might be able to pry some information out of him. I searched his eyes. They were tough to find behind the lenses sliding over and under one another amidst the glass and silicon of his optical system, but I did find them. They were a glacial blue the filters had turned gray.

"Still some man in you, then," I said. "More than a lot of your compatriots in the employ of the Hachinin, I'm guessing. What sort of attachments do they have? What sort of upgrades?"

I loosened my grip slightly. Enough to keep him from feeling the need to strike out. Enough to make him reconsider a last-ditch attempt. Maybe the Sword Punk would let him live, if he proved useful.

"W ... what do ... you want to—"

"Quite a bit, actually," I said, releasing him. He started to slide against the glass, but I steadied him. My eyes had already roved over the rest of his form-fitting shirt and pants. No hidden compartments or pockets that I could see. The only weapons he had brought into this fight were himself and those sparkly gloves. "Nifty things," I said, nodding at them. The energy had dissipated, with just the barest flicker of light winking around the base of some of the cracked eggshell beads. They must have worked on kinetic energy, charged by his movements, similar to the way my suit was.

I craned my neck and looked over the assassin's left shoulder. The fight was still on in the arena, with the canvas close enough to leap to from this height. The female twin still knelt on the far side of the platform, clutching her shattered arm to her side, keeping it locked, while her brother spun with those glowing elbow blades in the middle of the canvas.

Sang Hee and Dae had him penned in, with Dae biting at him with his golden axes while Sang Hee probed with her spear. If anyone in the audience noticed any sort of commotion in the President's box, they made no move to show it.

"Those two are from Kyoto, yes?" I asked without looking at the assassin.

He sighed and I pressed my palm into his chest, pushing just enough to cause him great discomfort, given the likely state of his insides.

"Yes."

"Anything special about them? Anything enhanced?"

He winced. At least, I think it was a wince, though it was possible that it had been a smirk.

"Not ... enhanced," he said, not wanting to experience another friendly, persistent push in the solar plexus.

"Hmm," I said, nodding. "Didn't think so. They're good, but ... not any faster or stronger than the next elite martial artist."

The assassin nodded along with me.

"Though, I wonder at Goro's play." The assassin's shifting lenses traced their shaking way back up to my eyes. I could see my reflection in the glass circlets from this angle. My red mask had been cracked. It was slightly askew, and my black bangs stuck up at chaotic angles. My eyes were steady. I had to admit, I looked quite in control of the situation.

"P ... play?"

I sighed and the assassin panicked.

"You kn ... know his play," he said, trying to recover before I decided to retrieve one of my discarded blades. "K ... kill you. K ... kill them." He flicked a head toss backward, bouncing it off the glass and spotting it with a bit of blood.

"Yes," I said. "I gathered that much. But, no offense to you, it's just, I was expecting a little more from Goro of the Hachinin."

His lenses wobbled toward the open door and then back to my face. It was a fair point. The Tokyo-Swede hadn't been the only one guarding Goro. I had been forced to fight my way through half of Siberia to get into the room.

Still ...

"That's it?" I repeated. I had been feeling disrespected, but it had started to turn slowly, inexorably to a feeling of dread as the adrenaline slowed and the first waves of pain from my myriad wounds fought their way through the tightness of the suit. Surely there was more to the plan.

"G ... Goro is not ... Hachi—"

"I know Goro is Hachinin," I said, cutting him off. I continued to watch the fight in the arena during our conference. I didn't feel a particular urge to go after Goro in the moment. If Sang Hee hadn't provided a bit more info from her various mystery contacts, I would have thought he was already on his way to Tokyo to join those very men and women in their own shadowy, smoke-filled rooms. But that wasn't where Goro was headed. I had to hope she was right.

Dae executed an impressive upward strike with his lead axe. The blow caught the Kyoto male's blade and forced his hand up, exposing his midsection. Sang Hee came in behind Dae and planted a leaping side kick of her own firmly into the fighter's midsection, sending him in an uncontrolled roll until he came up with a cracked blade and a bloody mouth next to his prone sister.

"Fight's over," I said. The crowd seemed to know it, too. They leaned forward, gripping their sticky plastic armrests and smudging their interactive screens in their greasy excitement. Now, it only remained to be seen if the Kyoto twins knew it.

Judging by the look of worry in the male's eyes, it looked like he did. Judging by the look of defiance in his injured sister's eyes, however, her hanging black bangs unable to conceal it even from this distance, I was doubtful they'd be retracting those amethyst sharps back into their League suits.

A choking sound emanated from the assassin's throat. I only realized it was laughter—hoarse, cracking laughter—when I looked back at him and saw him smiling. Blood leaked from the corner of his pale mouth, looking like running lipstick.

"What's funny?" I asked. "Where's the rest of Goro's plan?"

"Goro …" He choked and devolved into a fit of coughing. I glanced back in the arena and saw that the male twin had reengaged. Dae was holding him off while Sang Hee kept a wary distance, twirling her glowing blue spear. She looked up toward the glass and something seemed to hold her attention. Her eyes widened. I looked down at my suit and saw the red veins pulsing in time with my heartbeat.

I seized the assassin by the shoulders, lifted him and

slammed him back into the glass, blinking away the mist of blood that issued from his mouth and coated my eyelids.

"Out with it," I said. "What's Goro's plan? This can't be it. A few commandos and whatever the fuck you are ... a couple of Kyoto League fighters—good as they might be—to defeat Sang Hee and Dae? A gamble, and not a great one."

Bullish as I may have been about the whole endeavor of taking Goro out tonight, there had been a doomed knowing in the back of my mind. It was the same doom that infected Min's worried glances as the three of us had planned it. Sang Hee and I were fighters who could play at thinking. Min was a thinker who happened to be able to fight. She had managed to keep the police force from interfering, for now, and she was doing all she could to prevent him from boarding one of those planes Sang Hee assured us he wouldn't, but she didn't expect us to get out of Goro's den of corruption with our lives.

Truth be told, I didn't either. My only hope was to do as much damage as possible, to spare Sang Hee a grisly fate for her defiance if I could manage it, and to die doing something ... if not good, then at least worthwhile.

Now, as I stood holding the broken shell of a Tokyo assassin, standing in seeming victory, I knew I had lost. I knew there was something I wasn't seeing.

"G ... Goro ... not Hachin—"

"I already told you!" I said, spittle flying as I slammed him again. He squeaked like a mouse or a wounded bird that time, but he kept on smiling. Kept on laughing his croaking laughter.

"Hachi ... Hachinin are ... even less forgiving than you, Prince Akio."

"Spare me the threats, Stockholm," I said. "I knew what I was getting into when I killed Kuzu Tokoro."

I knew what I had been getting into with Goro, at least. I hadn't spared a whole lot of thought to what I was getting into when the rest of the Hachinin came after me. I was never great at multi-tasking. I was a man of focus, I told myself, without allowing that creeping certainty to come to the forefront of my mind. The certainty that I wouldn't make it that far.

"Not ... you," he said. "Not yet. No." His eyes widened, exposing bloodshot spider veins on the outside of the lenses that were entrenched with microscopic anchors. "The Hachinin do not suffer failure."

"Unlucky for you, friend."

"Yes," he said with a single nod, his eyes looking distant. "Unlucky me. Unlucky Goro."

"Ah."

Now it made sense. Goro's feeble defenses, as much damage as they had managed to inflict on me, weren't enough to stop a single man with enough anger aimed in his direction. Not a hallway full of mercenaries and not a Tokyo assassin, tricky though he was. It was a defense unbecoming of one of the Hachinin.

"Goro's been cut off from them," I reasoned.

The assassin nodded, head lolling a bit as he either fought with or embraced the loss of consciousness. I gave him a shake and he gritted his teeth against the fresh pain from his core.

"And you?"

"Not ... not one of Goro's," he said.

"Right. So, then. The Hachinin dangled Goro out like bait? They wanted me to win?"

A feeble shrug. "Not sure they cared much how the slob died. Just that he did, either on the end of your red blades ... or—"

"On the end of your black stare," I said. "You weren't sent for protection. You were sent as insurance."

Another smile. The assassin tapped the side of his head. His temple. Then he did so again, his fingers pinching in at the corner of his eye. "Insurance ... and research."

"Research?"

"You fought well, Prince Akio. Better than I imagined, certainly. They've been watching."

I swallowed. Of course I expected the Hachinin to be watching the night's festivities, if only to see how Goro planned to deal with this small, annoying inner-League insurrection. I didn't quite expect them to be looking out for me specifically, and certainly not to be watching me through the creepy, bug-eyed lenses of an assassin.

"Do I need to get an application ready?" I asked, looking into those disconcerting lenses now, and ignoring the human eyes beneath them. I was talking to the Hachinin, or whoever was looking at me through the feed. "I assume a spot is opening up on the assassin roster."

I worked to affect a calm demeanor. In this small situation, it appeared I had control, but it was a veneer thinner than the synthetic covering on the assassin's eyes. The Hachinin might not have wanted me to live, but they certainly wanted Goro to die. Once I was through with the situation at the Soul Dome, I fully intended to track Goro down and kill him. If I won tonight, the Hachinin did as well.

I suppose it should have provided me some measure of comfort that Goro had been left for dead. That it would be up to me and me alone how he met his end. It didn't. Instead, it all gave me the feeling of being a small gear in an infinitely complex clock, one whose time I couldn't get far enough away from to read.

The Hachinin had seen it all. They'd seen me refuse Goro's command when I fought Janix square. When I won square. They had seen my death and likely heard of my resurrection before Goro had, and they had most certainly noted my assault on Princess Gabriella's tower. They had let it all happen. Watched it play out, either for sheer entertainment, or because they wanted to see what they could gain from it.

Korea might be a corrupt shadow of what it had once been, but it was still free, in a manner of speaking. Far freer than the mainland to the south, and certainly than the islands to the southeast. Goro had been assigned a difficult task in spreading the influence of the Hachinin throughout Seoul. Perhaps the Hachinin felt it was time for another to take over, and I'd just paved the way for whoever it was.

Still, there was a more immediate feeling that served the purpose of supplanting the fear easily enough. I was still angry.

The Hachinin might feel like they were all-knowing and all-seeing, but things that skulked in the shadows were not things to be feared. They were things that feared.

In that moment, I decided two things: one, that Goro Hamada would still die by my hand. Two, that each and every one of the Hachinin would follow in his red wake. The Sword Punk might be a term of trollish endearment among the scattered pockets of attuned internet dwellers leading up to now, and a fun distraction for those still watching blue tickers slide across the bottoms of corporate-controlled screens, but the name was soon to get a lot less funny for a select few.

But then, that was all to come, and in my long, slow moments of revelation and deliberation, I had quite forgotten the situation at hand. And, as it turned out, that situation was far from settled.

The assassin had straightened some. His bearing was still crooked, but now it was rigid, as if every muscle and cord in his body had been stretched taut. His black lenses flashed and turned bright white, making me wince. I released him and stepped back quickly. I hadn't noticed it before, but now I saw a blinking green light tucked in the very corner of the assassin's eye, in the white and pink between the bright lenses and the fleshy underside of the socket.

He hadn't just been tapping the side of his head for effect. He'd tripped something. Some failsafe.

The assassin lurched toward me like a zombie, only he closed the distance faster than I was anticipating. In my shock and with my adrenaline having cooled some with the fight having ground to a halt, I made the wrong decision and bent to scoop up my discarded blades. The assassin didn't throw a cute combination at me, or even seize the opportunity to try to catch my ducking head with a knee or a scythe kick. He leapt on me like a beast.

We went down in a rolling tangle, and I knew I was no longer fighting a conscious man when he began spitting and biting at my glowing red forearms. He felt stronger than he had before. I didn't think it was a result of something chemical or technological. It felt more like the strength of madness. He was rabid.

Raving mad, and intent on smashing my face in just as readily as tearing my throat out. Whatever it took.

As shocking as the sudden turn was, and although the assassin seemed to be ignoring the significant injuries he had incurred, he was in no position to beat me. I framed him away from my body with a knee against his chest, managed to plant a boot flat against it as we struggled on the carpet, and then launched him backward.

Once again, he smashed against the glass wall, and this time a crack split the pane all the way to the far corner of the room. Muffled sounds from the arena spilled in through the tiny opening in the airtight barrier, tumbling discordantly into the box. As I shot to my feet, I was forced to cover my eyes when a blinding white flash lit the room. The assassin's gloves had been badly damaged in the fight, exposing wiring and chrome shards where there had been nodes. He ignored the currents of electricity that animated his body like a carnival creature and his hair like a swimming wraith, and came on again.

I tensed, adopting a side-facing stance. The next kick I planted would kill him.

Before the zombie assassin could get more than a swaying step away from the glass, a bright-blue flare went up, causing me to flinch. I exhaled and planted the chambered kick in his chest. The crack the sound made as it struck his chest was echoed by a second one as he struck the glass again.

The assassin would have slumped over and started dying on the floor of Goro's office, but the blue flare rising up out of the arena hadn't been a flare at all. Sang Hee's azure spear completed its journey in quick fashion, bursting through the cracked glass with ease and continuing right through the assassin's body. The glowing tip tore through his wiry frame and flickered as it stopped, sticking a foot out of his chest. The assassin looked down, the spectral lenses that covered his eyes flickering along with the razor resin weapon that had dealt the killing blow. The cracks from the puncture in the glass wall splintered and joined, creating a mosaic, and then it all crumbled.

The assassin, spear still shining in his torso, fell backward and followed the shards of Goro's barrier into the arena, down below the combat platform and into the glittering netting in the depths.

A wash of hot, sticky air enveloped the exposed President's box where I stood. The soundproof glass was gone, but the effect was surreal, as the sudden turn of events had settled a hush over the audience that even the announcer's shrill voice paused long enough to consider.

I swallowed and walked to the edge of the box, my boot kicking away a clinging shard of tinted black glass. Sang Hee stood poised on the edge of the platform facing me and the box, her throwing arm still extended, fingers still splayed. Her eyes were wide. Seeing me standing on the edge, she blinked and let her arm fall to her side. Dae stood behind her. He was looking my way, but his body and golden axes were still facing the right side of the platform, where the Kyoto twins cowered, the male standing over his sister protectively. They looked in my direction with the same stunned expression that thousands in the arena and potentially millions on the live feed—if it had been allowed to continue—likely wore in the moment.

If they knew they had just witnessed a very real murder at the hands of their beloved Sang Hee, they made no consensus move to show it.

The chatter started. At first, it was like a breeze of whispers whose words I couldn't parse. But as it got louder, and more varied, I heard snatches.

"Him," was the word that stuck out. They might have called me the Sword Punk, or the Ghost of Seoul. Many no doubt recognized my colors, even if the getup had undergone some recent changes. They recognized Akio Prince, but they didn't call me by name.

It was impossible to say how I knew in that moment, but the fact that they called me "Him" in whispers and emitted shocked, slack-jawed exhalations meant quite a bit. They knew this wasn't a work. It wasn't a storyline. Seeing the state of me, seeing the desperate look Sang Hee had adopted fade to one of relief as she saw that I was alive, they knew I was real, and they knew the crazed conspiracy theorists who followed the events surrounding Akio Prince's untimely death a little too closely had been right.

Just like that, it all snapped into place. And just like that, I started talking.

"Goro Hamada is dead," I said, not planning the words. Even in the midst of the bright lights and the thousands of sets of eyes on me in the moment, I saw Sang Hee's frown. From her angle, she couldn't see anything of note in the President's box. "And," I added with a swallow, "Goro of the Hachinin is soon to follow."

That provoked a cheer from a few pockets in the crowd, but more looked at one another, confused. I saw the spindly hair of the announcer up in his aluminum nest. He gripped the microphone loosely, unsure how to proceed.

I cleared my throat, ducked back into the President's box awkwardly and snatched up my red blades. When I reappeared, I gripped them tightly, encouraging their ruby-red glow.

Sang Hee had me pausing once more. She jerked her head to the right, probably trying to indicate that I should be running into the night, either chasing the escaped Goro or evading capture by his goons or the police, rather than making some unplanned treatise to the city.

I settled for a middle ground, raising one sword and pointing it forward, out into the ether of the arena where I'd fought for these same people so many times before, and where I was supposed to fall.

"You know me," I said. "You know the name Akio Prince. You know who I was. And some among you know who I am now."

They were all looking at me, and, I realized with an uncomfortable palpitation and a renewed stinging of the various wounds under my suit, they were waiting for me to continue.

"The Yakuza are not dead," I said. "Corruption is not dead." The sound the crowd made was a strange mix of cheers and jeers. I felt emboldened. "The Free City of Seoul is not free."

I thought I might have gone too far with that one. There was a pause in the crowd, a brief inhalation, but then a cheer went up. A raucous, focused one. Some stood, spearing their fists into the air.

"We've all known it," I said. "The Hachinin still reign. They've got their hands in everything. Our industries. Our companies. Our media. Our entertainment." I traced a path with the tip of a blade, scanning along the balconies and drawing every eye along the trail. "The police do what they can. Some speak out. Some rebel. All are silenced. And all the while, we suffer. Our children succumb to vice. Our elders to despair. Our strong to bitterness. They want us divided. They want us weak. But we are not weak."

"Seoul! Seoul! Soul! SOUL!"

"The Japanese are as much prisoners as the rest of the East," I said. "More so. The East is safe, they tell us. That may be true. We know about the wars in the West. Germany. The Reformed Bloc. Madrid. The Americas. But I ask you now, do you people feel free? Do you feel empowered as you accumulate debt and toil away for companies wearing the flaking, dried skin of dead snakes? There is no Korea but for its people. There is no humanity but for humans. A shadow has taken the world. A shadow with many heads, in many lands. But, for now, I'm only intent on a precious few."

"HA!" they cried. "CHI!" they screamed. "NIN!"

They repeated it, screaming for the heads of the shadows in Japan. Screaming for the heads of devils. They knew it. They had always known it. Their lands were not their own. Their houses were not their own. Their careers were distractions. Their victories were brief respites from defeat.

In the moment, I felt like a conductor. In the moment, I felt dangerously powerful.

"Akio Prince is dead," I said, quieting them again. "Dead and gone." Sang Hee, who had been smiling during my speech, looked saddened at the prospect. "But I live on in his memory. And I plan to make it a long one. Bright for the many," I squeezed the left sword hilt, pouring as much light into the blade as it would give off, "dark for the few." I relaxed the grip on the right blade. The sword dimmed, darkening until it resembled frozen blood.

"And you." I nodded toward the Kyoto twins. "Would you be a tool of the Hachinin? Fighting in foreign lands on dark orders? The best in the world ply their trade here. Rare talents. Talents who would have been soldiers in empires past. Guardians. Heroes. Even punks, to some."

The audience laughed and cheered. They started up a new cheer.

"KYOTO!"

It was likely that some—if not many—still thought the whole thing was a work. Some brilliant meta commentary staged by Goro and the League to juice ratings. That everything, from the supposed attempt on Akio Prince's life to Sang Hee's defiance to the speech the Sword Punk gave now, was little more than opium disguised as hope. But there was truth in the words. Too much truth, they knew. Too much that couldn't be said, except for in those few-and-far-between places in the net where anonymity was still prized, defended and increasingly quarantined.

The crowd before me was so plentiful, so multitudinous that it might as well be anonymous.

"Goro of the Hachinin is as good as dead," I said, again addressing the twins. "But Goro Hamada will confess. You are free. Lay down your weapons, turn evidence against your masters. You are in Seoul, not Tokyo. You are free."

The male straightened. One of his forearm blades had been cracked. He looked at me, then scanned the crowd, seemingly willing to take me up on the offer.

Startled shouts and screams started as the entryways to the lobbies filled with flashing lights and clutched badges. The police began to fill the stairways. Some in the crowd shouted at them and even threw sodas and popcorn. Others held them back and called for calm.

Min had been kind enough to allow me to finish my address, then, which gave me the impression that the feeds hadn't been cut. At least, not in Seoul. I suppose I had Gabriella Burtahn to thank for that. I looked to my right. The hallway where I'd met Goro's commandos had gone dark. No flashing lights and shouted warnings. Not yet.

All that remained to be seen was how the Kyoto twins would choose to surrender. It hadn't quite occurred to me that they would not.

These two were from the island, where hope wasn't even packaged and sold to the masses anymore. Where the Hachinin reigned supreme, and where many snakes waited to take the place of the old serpents. Where dragons laid in wait.

It started with the female. She struggled to her feet. It seemed she had had enough of my pontificating, and judging solely by her bearing and the look in her eyes, visible even from my vantage point just above and beside the platform, she wasn't in an overly merciful mood. That was rich, considering it was us offering the mercy.

Her left arm didn't hang limp, but she seemed to be having trouble uncurling it, clutching it in toward her stomach as if it were in a sling. The purple claws on that fist had dimmed, looking like syrup, while the blades on her right gauntlet continued to pulse. The male fighter reached his hand out to steady her, but a cutting look stopped him.

She looked up at me with a glare, then scanned the crowd, watching the police attempt their forced evacuation. I hadn't seen Min, or heard her calling to me. The police hadn't shouted any orders at anyone but the crowd, but I knew they wouldn't suffer me to lord over the arena for much longer. It only remained to be seen if they would try to bring me in.

None of it concerned the fighter from Kyoto. If there had been any chance remaining that she might see reason, that hope quit as soon as she leveled her gaze on Dae once more. Her dark eyes reflected the golden-amber hue of his axes. He frowned at her, but remained firm.

In a quick movement, she shot her right hand down toward a compartment at her waist and pulled something out. It looked like a black pill, only as long as a middle finger and almost as thick as a cigar. My heart redoubled its pounding when I thought it might be some kind of explosive device, but she activated a switch and the pill opened, the two sections coming apart to reveal something smaller inside.

She was quite dexterous operating with one hand, and freed what looked to be a glass vial containing brackish liquid. It was impossible to tell the color from where I stood, but it was dark, and its oil-slick sheen reflected the purple of her claws.

I didn't notice there was a syringe on the end of the vial until the fighter jabbed it into her neck, much to the shock of her partner. He looked like he wanted to slap it out of her hand, and then he looked horrified as she injected the liquid.

She dropped the empty vial and fell to the floor, her convulsions starting as soon as her knees touched the canvas. Sang Hee took a step toward the twins, but Dae held an axe out to block her as the male twin stepped in front of his pain-racked sibling.

I was so taken with the sight of the convulsing fighter from across the sea that I didn't recognize the echoing pops of gunfire until one of the bullets struck a hanging shard of glass above my head. The broken piece flashed in front of my face, showing me my masked, bloody reflection as it descended into the depths of the Soul Dome.

The crowd screamed for an entirely different and more immediate reason, now. The high drama of the night was replaced by that of the low variety as they scrambled and surged toward the very exits Min's police had been trying to push them toward moments earlier. Goro's insurance policy was working for us in that respect, at least. Even the reedy-voiced announcer and the half-fat, half-muscle bozos manning the branded ceremonial drum in the rafters had fled.

I ducked on the ledge, my eyes searching out the source of the attack. Dae had stepped back to shield Sang Hee. His armor was thicker than hers, more plate than resin. There was a pack of officers tumbling like a mass of ants over a section of seats. I saw a man in a dark suit in the press, teeth gritted as he attempted to free himself. Similar struggles were taking place by the entry-ways. It was difficult to tell if it was all officers identifying potential shooters or if members of the crowd had taken the initiative in their stead.

More pops and trails of shrill gunfire echoed, and more screams. My stomach threatened the back of my throat with hot, acidic bile at the thought of people dying because of me, Goro and his ilk notwithstanding. However, it was over in relatively short order. The gunshots ceased, and the screams became less frequent as the stands emptied out of all but the officers and their new prisoners.

When I looked back into the ring, the Kyoto girl was writhing, screaming in pain. She clutched her bent elbow with her good one, and pulled at it. There was a pop followed by another scream. She moved like a rabid cat, not fully in control of her body. Like she was having a seizure. The suit bunched. She was small, but no longer diminutive. Her muscles seemed to slide over each other, coiling and bunching.

I knew what it was, then. It was a rumor in the fight game. A substance so prized that it only ended up in the hands of those with the darkest—and highest—means. It was rumored to be bestowed upon any who ascended to the top of the Kyoto League. I didn't think these two fit the bill. They were good, but they weren't good enough to get far in that League. No. This was desperation. This was Goro's one last trick. The one he'd kept up the sleeve of his second set of assassins, and not the one guarding him.

"The Kyoto Serum," I whispered.

It was a simple term for a substance whose supposedly occult origins remained wholly intact as it wended its way through the military industrial complexes of the West until it was perfected in the East.

Steroids had never really gone out of fashion. I'd never been partial to them, but I didn't really care if my opponents were. You might get a little faster and a bit stronger, but I told myself there was always a trade-off. Kenta used to say that you couldn't put any steroids in your chin. That it was liquid weakness, indicative of everything a fighter couldn't do rather than what he could.

I was willing to chalk this vial of Kyoto poison up to more of the same. Until she stopped shaking.

Now, she knelt. Her bun had come undone, and hair hung down over her eyes. Her chin was tucked into her chest. She breathed deep and exhaled slowly. Her brother, still standing in front of her, had been unable to concentrate on the potential threat Dae and the weaponless Sang Hee posed to them due to her episode. He edged toward her like a snake charmer, or someone cornering a leopard.

"You in the ring! Stop!" An officer shouted from the stands. Lights flashed in the red corner hallway, but the officers were having trouble figuring out how to get the bridge extended toward the combat platform. "Freeze! Sharps down! The contest is over!"

There were other shouts that seemed to be echoing from behind me. I glanced toward the darkened hallway once more. There was no way I'd be going that way. Min might be able to keep them off of me to some degree, but not if I walked headfirst into a squad of Seoul's finest with blood-drenched swords.

Speed kills.

It wasn't a new axiom in the fight game, but it was one I'd taken to early on. You might be stronger than your opponent. You might be tougher. You might be flat-out better in all the other ways that count. But if you couldn't catch the bastard, you can bet they could catch you.

Every martial artist learned the truth of that statement the first time they came up against someone faster than them. Every once in a while, the best were reminded of it. That said, speed wasn't going to win you the fight alone. You needed power to back it up. Or, in the case of our Kyoto friend, a few six-inch-long blades.

It all happened so fast, it seemed to be in slow motion.

The girl was up and on him in a flash more literal than usual, her blades leaving amethyst trails like neon taillights. Dae looked guarded, but he'd let his guard down. Truth be told, I'm not sure I would have been able to stop her on that initial burst. To his credit, Dae was trained enough to react on impulse. He slashed from his right shoulder down across to his left hip, pulling his left boot back as the Kyoto demon ducked low enough that her sickle bangs brushed the canvas. She turned inside of his strike and angled behind him as he spun, following the motion like she was his lavender shadow.

The Kyoto girl followed Dae's spin, shouldered him roughly in the back as he turned and caused him to stumble. The hitch threw his backhand off, and the left axe whipped harmlessly over her head as he came back around. The Kyoto fighter had frozen in front of him, and as Dae's left arm swung wild while his right swept in from down low, she ended their acquaintance.

With her right hand, she slashed upward with an uppercut that tore a golden plate from Dae's sternum. The left gauntlet —on the end of a formerly ruined arm—followed it, plunging into the thin rubber suit the slash had exposed. The stab came on the end of a wicked blow, the force of it causing Dae to wheeze on impact as the Kyoto girl lifted him up off of the canvas.

Dae let go of his axes and grabbed the girl's wiry arm with both of his golden-gloved hands. His boots kicked wildly, thrashing like a panicking child held over the edge of a cliff.

Sang Hee must have been caught in the same disbelieving trance I was. Now she yelled and charged in, diving toward one of Dae's discarded axes and coming up in a roll. The brother seemed at a total loss. He reacted too slowly to stop Sang Hee's attack on his sister.

From a distance, I could see that the girl, while holding the dying, struggling Dae two feet off of the canvas, had swung her eyes toward Sang Hee without moving her head. Her right arm was tucked at her side, and ready to turn. Sang Hee planted her left knee and swung with the right hand, Dae's axe flashing on the end of her blue reach.

"Back!" I screamed.

I saw Sang Hee go rigid as she tried to comply, but her strike was already in motion. The Kyoto girl spun, ripping her left gauntlet and claws out of Dae's chest as she brought her right around, slashing toward Sang Hee's neck.

Dae fell to the canvas and curled into a bloody heap, his hands clutched over the leaking wound in his chest.

Sang Hee must have been able to reverse some of the momentum, as she was able to lean just out of reach. The blazing purple claws swiped, the left backhand slicing a black bang from Sang Hee's brow while the right caught the golden axe just under the head, tearing it from her grasp. Rather than rolling backward, the ever-game Sang Hee pushed off of the canvas, looking to dive at the other fighter now that both strikes had missed her.

The Kyoto girl was too fast, enhanced as she was. Sang Hee had barely managed to rock forward onto the balls of her feet when a boot smashed into her chest, snapping her head forward violently. Sang Hee slammed into the canvas, the back of her head landing with a slap. She managed to turn the fall into a roll.

The officers shouted, and I could see some of them aiming guns into the arena. If they shot, there was no telling whom they'd hit. I knew some were likely aiming my way, even though they had just saved me from the snakes Goro had placed in the crowd.

"Hold your fire!" I thought it was Min's voice echoing from somewhere in the stands, but I didn't have time to search her out.

Sang Hee got back to her feet. Her spear had fallen into the netting below, and Dae's axes were out of reach. I realized with mounting dread that the Kyoto girl hadn't missed her completely on that initial exchange, as blood trickled down Sang Hee's right forearm, forming a stream that pattered onto the canvas. Dae's axe had deflected much of the blow, but a claw had found a way into her blue resin.

The Kyoto male had recovered some of his initial shock. He looked willing to jump into the melee, but the officers had their weapons trained on him, and he wasn't close to Sang Hee. He hesitated.

His sister wasted no more time. She followed up her savage gutting of Dae and her swift attack on Sang Hee with a blistering assault. She darted at Sang Hee, coming in straight on, now that

Sang Hee held no spear to ward her off. Lesser fighters would have been gutted on the initial exchange, but Sang Hee spun away from the edge of the platform, lancing a hook punch at the back of the assassin's head.

The blow missed, and the Kyoto girl folded Sang Hee over with an elbow to the sternum. Sang Hee stepped in and framed her arms out, catching the twisting assassin's next blow at the elbow. The assassin continued the blow regardless, her right gauntlet folding Sang Hee's block in and stabbing partially into the meat of her upper arm. The impact of the blow sent Sang Hee rolling again.

The Kyoto girl was too strong and too fast. I regripped my swords and crouched, ignoring the sting of the gashes under my suit. The moment I leapt onto that platform, my little rebellion was finished. Even if we managed to defeat the Kyoto fighters, the police would have no choice but to take me in.

A last-second thought occurred to me before I leapt. I looked to my left and saw the crack in the paneling behind the dark wood bar. I didn't have time to turn it over.

"Sang Hee! Jump!" I said. I tossed my right sword back into the President's box and leaned out over the chasm as far as I could, extending my hand.

Sang Hee was too caught up dodging the Kyoto girl's increasingly desperate, violent attacks to look my way. Each swipe of those shining purple claws got closer to scoring a lethal blow. Sang Hee ducked under the latest and dove forward. She came up out of her roll sprinting. Her blue armor was covered with a sheen of red, but her legs were unharmed. She was strong, and she'd need all of it to close the gap.

She raced to the edge of the platform, planted on the ledge with her right foot and leapt, her eyes meeting mine as she soared through the air.

Talk about slow motion. There might as well have been a lightning strike behind Sang Hee to highlight her as her arms churned over, legs extended, riding the dead currents of stagnant arena air as the red corner bridge extended toward the combat platform.

I lunged forward, snatching Sang Hee by the wrist as she started to fall below the lip of the President's box. As soon as I closed my grip, I yanked and rolled backward, heaving with all the strength I could muster. Sang Hee yelped as she smashed through broken glass on the ledge on the way up. She hit the carpet and rolled to the back wall, and then came up onto her knees.

I almost sighed out a bit of relief, but the nightmare continued when I saw a black-suited figure with glowing shards of amethyst for claws pass over my head. The Kyoto girl made the jump with ease, landing in the middle of Goro's office in a crouch.

I was flat on my back, and met Sang Hee's eyes before the assassin whirled on me, her eyes a blank mask of rage. I tried to scramble up, but she was on me, one knee slamming into my chest and forcing the air from my lungs as I slid back, my shoulders hanging over the edge of the chasm. The fall might not be fatal, depending on the angle, but I had no idea if this crazed beast would follow me right down into the netting of the Soul Dome.

The claws came flashing in, and I framed my remaining sword out in front of me. I caught the first gauntlet, the strength of the blow shocking me, but the second one went right in, sinking into the thick resin on the right side of my chest and burying the blades several inches deep.

I growled as I kept the sword framed out with my left hand and grabbed onto her stabbing wrist with my right, trying to resist the inevitable push as she attempted to bury the claws the rest of the way in. We bared our teeth at one another, though she couldn't see mine beneath the mask covering my mouth, and while I was in a worse way, hers seemed to be more pained, as if she were burning up from the inside out.

I saw a red glow behind the assassin, illuminating the ceiling. The Kyoto girl wasn't all animal rage, after all. She must have seen the glow reflected in my eyes. She rolled off of me, yanking her claws out of my chest with a disgusting sucking sound and slashing backward toward Sang Hee as she did.

Lucky for me, Sang Hee had the good sense not to stab straight down. She followed the assassin's roll and slashed at her, then followed the fighter's momentum, attempting to spear her on the spot.

I groaned and got to my feet a little slower than I would have liked, and diverted the Kyoto girl's charge toward Sang Hee with a slash of my own. She spun away from the red sword and made herself small, ducking backward at an impossible angle to make Sang Hee miss.

She came up with her back against the wall, while Sang Hee and I stood framed in front of the opening to the arena, each of us holding a glowing red sword.

"Ready?" I asked.

"Was going to ask you the same thing."

"Quickly, now," I said.

The Kyoto girl snarled, as eager to be done with the thing as we were.

The fight was ugly and desperate. In the glass and blood-stained office, none of Goro's possessions survived the blur of red swords and the fury of purple claws. Shelves broke apart as we hurled one another into them. The bar broke at the pillars. A glass table shattered, encrusting Sang Hee's suit with diamonds. The walls had as many scars as recessed alcoves with broken vases, trophies and statues praising the symbols of the zodiac.

We fought like beasts more than warriors. Midway through the short, desperate encounter, there probably wasn't enough blood left between us to fill one of us to the brim. And on we fought.

The Kyoto girl was fast and strong, but she'd left her martial mind behind her. Her moves left her open, and she hadn't adjusted well to fighting two enemies. Her brother was unable to support her now, having taken damage in the fight with Sang Hee and Dae, and now he had the police to deal with. She fought with the certainty that not to fight was to die. I couldn't say if that was true or not. Even if I managed to kill Goro tonight, or the next night, it might not spare this one a grisly fate. It might not spare any of us.

But mercy was as likely to get you killed as saved in times like these, so I set all thoughts of it aside, as did Sang Hee.

The Kyoto girl slowed as myriad cuts leaked onto the carpet. She lurched when Sang Hee punctured the back of her calf, Sang Hee wielding the sword like it was her usual spear or staff. The Kyoto girl spun and fell when I crashed inside of her range and cracked the flat of my blade against her temple.

When she came on again, Sang Hee and I sensed that the time was at hand. Still, she had more in the tank than I had thought, her assault forcing both of us back in a blur of purple. She screamed and raged at us, driving us toward the edge of the box.

Before I could think to do anything else, Sang Hee slapped one gauntlet aside with her sword and shouldered into the Kyoto fighter's chest.

"No!"

The Kyoto girl smiled and plunged her free gauntlet into Sang Hee's side, and the two spun in a deadly embrace. Before the assassin could free her claws, Sang Hee spun her toward me, her eyes meeting mine.

I saw the opening and drove in, plunging my sword into the Kyoto fighter's side as hard as I could as Sang Hee stumbled out of the exchange. It parted the resin of the Kyoto girl's suit easily, the glowing tip fighting through the blood to emit a demon's light as it emerged from her other side. She shuddered and started to stumble, and I pulled the blade out as she grabbed onto my shoulder to steady herself. I stepped back, bringing my sword with me, and her grip slipped. She fell back, her eyes glazing and confused, and before she could follow the Tokyo assassin's path, I steadied her from going over, and she fell to her knees on the inside of the ledge with a long sigh, her shoulders bowing in.

Her brother let out a primal, heart-wrenching scream, his eyes pinning me on the spot as I stood with a glowing, dripping sword on the ledge. He was already in cuffs, a squad of officers pulling him bodily toward the bridge. Another group was clustered around Dae's lifeless form, and I felt only grim certainty.

The Kyoto girl died quietly, and I turned back into the room and saw Sang Hee leaning against the only piece of furniture that hadn't been reduced to splinters. Goro's leather throne was gashed and ruined, but Sang Hee sank into it clutching her side. She looked more pale than usual, but her eyes held plenty of life. She smiled at me, and nodded toward the sword she'd left in the middle of the room.

"Going to be needing that, Prince," she said.

"Sang Hee ..."

"I'm ... okay," she said. "Really, Akio. I'll be fine." She heard something and looked toward the hallway. Flashlights speared their white circles into the room. "You've ... got to get going. Get Goro. Finish this."

I heard a crackle and pop from the arena and turned back toward the stands. Min stood in the center of the platform wearing the deep blue-black uniform with white lettering of Seoul's finest, looking up at me. They had taken Dae and the Kyoto fighter away. She stood alone, while officers checked every seat in the stands, every compartment. Every door. Every cubby.

Still staring at me, she reached up and pressed the box on her own shoulder. I saw her lips moving, but couldn't hear the sound.

"Stand down!" the officer in the hall said. "Down. Stand down."

"Get lost, Akio," Sang Hee said. "I could use a med kit, and I'd bet one of those goons is holding one."

I pulled my eyes from Min, limped toward the middle of the room and retrieved the other sword. I leaned over and kissed Sang Hee on the forehead.

"Thank you," I said.

"Don't let the snake talk too much," she said.

"You still think he'll go there?"

"Nowhere else he can go. Hachinin will be after him. Seoul will be after him. No ... no place to hide. He'll be drunk, I'd guess. If not dead already."

"Hopefully not."

"Go," Sang Hee said. She sounded weak, and I felt a pang in

my heart for the part I'd played in it. I winced and limped toward the back panel.

"Thank you," I said before pulling the panel aside and slipping into the dark.

"Don't thank me until we've won," Sang Hee said as I closed the door behind me.

I didn't think she was referring to Goro alone.

23

LOOSE END

I'd thought about stripping out of my modified League suit and armor after reaching the destination in the wee hours of the morning, but then, sometimes the skin wasn't quite ready to come off.

If my wounds had been life-threatening, I guessed that I would have taken a nasty and permanent spill on the slick, mist-covered valley roads during my flight from Seoul.

As it turned out, the commandos had managed only shallow, superficial punctures during our hellish hallway encounter. The Kyoto demon had managed to get a little closer to the point, but my organs had been spared.

There was something to the suit Sang Hee had given me. If the wounds festered, they'd kill me. My head was already starting to pound, but the pressure of the fibers seemed to react to the gashes and cuts in the resin, the cells in the suit constricting around the wound enough to quiet them. I had it in mind to ask her exactly where she had gotten it from, and what sort of technology it was using. Certainly nothing that would have been legal in the League.

But that could wait.

I found myself at the top of a gravel road. I'd followed the directions of the spherical tracking device Sang Hee had left wrapped on the handle of the black cycle that had been waiting for me in the alley behind the Soul Dome. Apparently Goro had made other transportation arrangements.

I leaned the bike down onto its side and stood, adjusting my mask and wincing at the pain in my jaw. The mask was not made of the same resin polymer as the rest of my suit. It recalled the painted steel and iron of Min's father's armor. I'd still kept the samurai insteps attached, as well as the greaves, though they had seen better days. The mask was the only piece that hadn't cracked, and that had come with Sang Hee's paramilitary getup.

I breathed in long and deep, filling my lungs with the fresh, water-touched air. It had been a miracle that I'd got out of the city without the police catching me. I had Min to thank for that, no doubt. But the greater surprise that should not have been a surprise was the fact that Goro had had no more traps lying in wait for me in the alley, or on the neon-lit streets of Seoul—or anywhere along the rest of the ensuing three-hour drive.

Goro had been abandoned by the Hachinin. He was alone. And soon, I'd be alone with him. There was nowhere to go. With no allies and likely limited access to his Tokyo funds, he had apparently chosen to settle down in the countryside, rotting away on some yacht or another. Or maybe he had already saved me the pleasurable trouble and taken his life in the traditional way. If he had, I might manage a nod of respect at the demise of Goro Hamada, but I knew men, and I knew cowards. Goro was one. And cowards never fell on their own swords.

The road continued down into a long, narrow valley. A mountainous and heavily forested peninsula bent to the right, extending far out and encircling the jagged bay. It looked like the sea might lie beyond it, but I guessed I wasn't quite that far east. It could have been Jecheon, but I hadn't paid much attention to the signs. My attention was focused. Singular.

Dozens of boats bobbed on moorings in the bay, and wooden buildings leaned beside dark brown docks. The boats weren't particularly noteworthy. Certainly not the ritzy sort you saw floating among the many marinas on the edges of the Yellow Sea. Not the glass and fiberglass monstrosities that were docked below the mansions on the edges of the Han River.

There were only a few people moving about—fishermen and the like. There weren't all that many residential homes along the water, and most of the mountain roads snaked their way up into the green and blue of the land, lost to the ghosts of nature.

It seemed like a strange place for Goro of the Hachinin to make his escape, but then Sang Hee had been convinced that, should Goro make the rational and expected choice to flee when I encountered him, he'd end up here. I'd have to drill into her sources later on. Clearly, Sang Hee of Seoul had secrets covering her secrets. She seemed to operate more like a high-powered spy than a professional athlete and heiress.

Then again, sometimes people with means just adopted unique hobbies.

I left my swords sheathed in the X scabbard across my back, snatched the blue tracker sphere from the bike handle, and started down the hill. I didn't expect there to be a big police presence in the area, and I didn't expect the fishermen to care much about what a man in a League suit might be doing down at the docks, but I moved as quietly as I could anyway, ducking into the bushes when I heard a truck approaching from the rear. It was still pre-dawn, and the sun had yet to fight its way up above the hills, though bits of the bay had started to glitter.

I snuck down to a small blue-gravel ramp, walking into the water until I was knee deep and running my glove along an old, moss-covered cement sea wall. It didn't take much guesswork to locate the right boat. Most of them were fishing vessels, open to the air and with traps, crates and boxes on top. Some had small cranes and others industrial rods anchored into the sides.

No. That wasn't Goro's style, even if shivering in a pile of damp blankets in the hold of a schooner would have increased his chances of survival. His boat was set apart from the others, swaying under a rocky overhang to my left. Close to the shore, but sheltered from prying eyes. The boat wasn't a gargantuan ode to status. It was a modest yacht, if there was such a thing. It had yellowing white rails and black glass around the second deck.

Goro might be smart—it was unlikely he'd have gotten as far

as he did without a little bit of brains to go along with the cash. But, there was more than one way to succeed in the business world. If Goro truly had an intellect to be feared, he wouldn't have stayed in his glass throne room during the Finals.

Men like Goro, no matter where they came from, no matter the lessons they'd learned along the way, always forgot many more. It was ego that ruled a man like that. Ego made him stay, so he could take pleasure in watching me as I watched Sang Hee being hacked apart by glowing sharps in the arena that had made her name. Dae had betrayed him, and that had been inconvenient, but his soviet squadron and his Swedish-Tokyo ghost had not been enough to stop the spirit of vengeance that hunted him.

The water was cold. I didn't mind. In fact, it quieted the renewed sting of my wounds as I slipped into it and began a swim that I knew would be longer than it looked. My suit and swords weren't as heavy as I thought they'd be, and the water wasn't as foul. For as many boats as there were in the bay, there wasn't a lot of oil in the water, and I saw fish darting under the surface, though the water was dark and opaque.

My suit glowed with the effort as I parted the water with slow, wide breaststrokes, trying not to disturb the surface too much. The red looked like blood under the surface. It wasn't the best thing for stealth. If there were any great ancient beasts lying in wait at the bottom of the bay, they'd be unable to pass up the chance to make a try for me.

Despite the feeling of almost Zen-like calm that had come over me during the dizzying drive from the north, my heart started pounding so loud I could almost hear it disturbing the water like a drum beat when I left the smaller boats and the longer docks behind and entered the shadows beneath the cliffs.

Goro's salvation loomed in front of me. I kept expecting a sniper to poke his head over the rusted chrome rails up top and end my rebellion then and there. There was nothing. Nothing to stop my midnight ride. Nothing to stop my swim. Nothing to stop my climb as I gripped the top of the rail and lifted myself up and over. I landed on the deck in a crouch, my suit pulsing as the water drenched the fiberglass. The back deck was bare, with yellowing mildew having taken root. There was a tinted glass door and windows on either side, and I could see a living room on the other side of it with old-style shag carpeting and teak counters. There were bottles and cans strewn about. Deeper within, I could see the light of a galley kitchen at the bottom of a slight staircase, and I saw myself reflected in a bedroom mirror at the back.

There was a stairwell to the left, curving up and out of sight, onto the second deck. Rather than entering the boat, I jumped up and gripped the overhanging ledge of the above deck from the outside to pull myself up.

At least, I started to, when the pop-bang of gunfire I had expected sounded off. I felt the wind of the bullet kiss my cheek as it ripped the atmosphere on its escape, and I released my hold and fell back down. As soon as my boots touched the lower deck, I pushed off and charged forward, ramming into the glass and bursting into the room. Another gunshot sounded, and then a third.

Reckless shooting.

I tore up the teak stairway to the left and freed my blades on the turn with a red flash, and then came to a stop.

I found myself in a slightly brighter room with windows on all sides. This was the pilot's room, complete with an old-fashioned wooden steering wheel and a white captain's chair. There was another hold to the left, and likely another bedroom. To the right, the sliding glass doors were open to the deck I'd tried to climb up to, and the mildewed curtains flapped in the early morning breeze.

Goro sat at a small circular table in the middle of the room. It had a faux wooden stem and a chrome base drilled into the white fiberglass floor. There was an empty chair on the side closest to me. On the other, Goro sat with his black pistol held loosely in his right hand, the barrel winking in my direction. In his left hand, what I at first mistook for a glass of whiskey now looked like an enclosed glass cylinder. It was thin, about the width of your middle finger, and there was a dark, oily liquid inside. It looked green, then red, and swished around with the viscosity of blood.

An image of a diminutive, vicious Kyoto girl with blazing purple claws flashed in my mind's eye.

Goro had always been big, but now he looked fat and gaunt at the same time. His eyes were tired. He was wearing the same suit he'd had on the night before, what now felt like an age ago. He smelled like stale cigar smoke and booze. He'd removed his tie, and his shoes and socks.

Goro looked like shit. Furthermore, he looked pathetic. A small part of me, secreted away in the same corner alley I'd slept in night after night before Kenta had taken me in, pitied him. It was the part of me that looked for the good in everyone. The part of me that looked for the victim in Goro Hamada.

Perhaps he hadn't been responsible for every horrible deed he'd witnessed. Maybe he'd been coerced, or forced at various times on his way up the ladder. Maybe he'd once slept in a rain-soaked alley like me. But I could usually tell that about someone, and I didn't think Goro fit the bill. No. Goro might not have been the architect of his climb up the ladder in Japan, but he'd climbed it, putting one hand in front of the other, rung after corrupt, bloody rung, not paying much mind to those he stepped over on the way up.

"You look drunk, Goro," I said. I could have leapt on him and ended it ten times over, but something about the whole situation just seemed so horribly, disappointingly mundane. He really was just a rich asshole sitting on a boat in the mountains of Korea. A broken, rich asshole.

Goro only stared at me. His eyes were still sharp, even if the rest of him wasn't.

"You're no innocent," I said. It was a strange thing to say, and came out sounding like a defense. A twinkle lit Goro's dark eyes.

"No," he said. His voice was deep and commanding. I'll give him that. "No, I suppose I'm not. But then, you don't get to the position I got to clean. You don't get to be sitting here," he tapped the nose of the gun on the table, "or standing over there, without being a killer."

That was true enough.

"Nowhere left to run, then? This is it?" I made a show of looking around. "I have to admit, I'm disappointed. The great Goro Hamada. Goro of the Hachinin. Run out of friends in so short a time. And all it took was a little tree-shaking."

"Don't act so surprised at your victory, Prince," Goro said. "It's unbecoming. Besides, you're smarter than that."

I sighed. "Yeah."

I don't know what came over me, but something did. I walked over and pulled the white padded chair out, and sat down in front of Goro of the Hachinin. I laid one sword across my lap and let the tip of the other twist in the sandblasted fiber-glass decking. Goro watched me, curious.

"We both know I'll kill you before you get a shot off," I said, answering the unspoken question. "You'd probably miss anyway, given how unreliable the things are."

Goro smiled. It seemed genuine. Still, he kept the gun in his hand, the barrel resting at an angle that would probably see the bullet skipping off of my shoulder armor. By the time he adjusted his grip well enough to get a squeeze off, I'd have buried three feet of red steel in his chest.

"I was expecting ... more," I said.

"Me too, Akio," Goro said. "Me too."

"They really did leave you out to dry, didn't they?"

Goro was silent.

"Why?"

"The Hachinin—"

"Heartless bastards," I said. "Part of the game. All the rest of it. I get it. But, I mean, I don't understand why they gave you up so soon into ... into—"

"Your righteous crusade?" Goro asked, smiling. He shrugged. "Let's just say my brothers and sisters across the Sea of Japan accept opportunities when they come up. Seoul is a difficult tiger to tame. Impossible, some say. I went at the city through the entertainment sector, and established an alliance with Gabriella Burtahn, she of the preternaturally perky tits." I was too tired to blush. "Others of my ilk would take more direct means."

"You weren't exactly subtle," I said. "Everyone knows the League is corrupt, and everyone knows the media is."

"And yet, they watch anyway, letting it rule their choices and influence their passions. Letting it fill foreign coffers with their earnings. But, the city's remained remarkably clean in spite of our best efforts and in spite of what you might think. Moving product isn't easy in Seoul."

"Drugs," I said.

"For now," Goro said.

That did get my blood rushing all over again. I knew what men like this considered product. I knew the stories from other lands, where children went missing. It didn't take a past like mine to take less than kindly to that sort of thing, but it didn't help.

Goro seemed to recognize how close he'd come to being killed then and there.

"I've never been partial—"

"How direct is direct?" I asked, cutting him off.

"Come again?"

"What sort of direct action do the rest of the Hachinin plan to take with the mainland?"

"War. False flags. Annex. The usual fare, Prince Akio. The things those who seek power use to get it."

How ironic, that the one who was set to die seemed to be the one more bored by the exchange.

"Power is the the final aim, then," I said, spitting onto the decking. The saliva was pink. Goro caught that, too.

"You're not looking so good, Prince Akio," he said. "Suit's keeping all the blood in, I take it." He looked me up and down. "Nifty thing. Not made for the League, I don't think."

"World's full of war," I said with a shrug. "Wars need weapons."

Goro looked at the gun he held, almost as an afterthought.

"It's never been the weapons winning wars, Akio, but the wielders."

I just looked at him while he considered the gun. Then I nodded at the vial he seemed to have forgotten. "What's the story with this shit? Saved a little extra for yourself, or was that supposed to be for Brother Kyoto?"

"Good fighters, them," Goro said. "And yes. He didn't accept. He thought his sister didn't either, but she was sharper than him, in more ways than one. She knew the arrangement, and the consequences for failure. This ... 'shit,' as you call it, can help you out of one jam, but it might land you in some others. I thought about taking it, seeing how I might fare against you. I did some boxing in my day. In the underground. In Tokyo. I couldn't bear the thought of the pain, though. I've never been partial to it."

I didn't know if he was talking about the pain inherent in a potential fight with me, or something caused by the liquid itself. I remembered how the Kyoto girl had thrashed and writhed. I didn't think the Kyoto Serum was lethal. Then again, most fighters didn't think it was real.

"You're in quite the jam now, Goro," I said, stating the obvious.

"You're less of a jam than you think, Akio," Goro said. "And that's accepting that I'm not going to make it off of this boat alive. To think, I'll be killed by my own fucking sponsors." He laughed. A mirthless sound.

I frowned.

"The fall you didn't take," Goro said by way of explanation. "Sponsors, but you're smart enough to have figured that much out. Unsponsored fighters aren't a good look for the League, Akio. Not a good look in any business, now. I'd have let you off the old man's debt."

"Doesn't seem like much to die for," I said, ignoring the subtle barb.

"No," Goro agreed. He looked up. There was a gap between this deck and the pilot's nest up top. You could see the cliffs, and what looked to be a collection of old, traditional-style homes. "Would you believe I grew up in these hills?"

He didn't seem to be talking to me, anymore. He was a ghost, and for the first time in a while, I felt like I wasn't.

The gun moved fast. Much faster than I could have anticipated. I kicked off of the decking hard and threw myself over the back of the chair as the bang resounded. I rolled on impact and stayed low, with my chin almost brushing the ground, blades out to either side like wings.

Goro's big legs and bare feet hadn't moved from their place, and I noticed with dumb, blinking eventuality that both of his arms hung slack by his sides, the tips of his fingers brushing the popcorn fiberglass decking. The gun rested on the deck under his right hand, and the glass vial, unbroken, beneath the left. The blood started dripping from his pant leg a few seconds later. His suit was so dark, it had obscured the liquid before then.

I stood and stared at Goro Hamada, who was now quite dead. I hadn't managed to slash his throat or stake him in the heart like the corporate vampire that he was. He'd simply planted his most recent bullet in the soft matter between his ears.

I'll admit it. Goro was a lot faster than he looked. Maybe it had been that final moment of clarity that had brought it out of him, or maybe I was feeling the effects of my marathon of a night—of a month, in many ways—more keenly than I had thought. Either way, it left me feeling more than a little unsettled that Goro could just as easily have planted the bullet somewhere else.

I sheathed my swords, walked around the table and collected the glass vial, depositing it in a compartment on my belt. I grunted against the pain as I bent. I'd been sitting too long, and now I really did have to get myself seen to.

I hadn't expected to walk down the stairs and calmly slip into the water after seeing to Goro's death. I kept expecting to catch a rapid blinking light out of the corner of my eye. One last trick from Goro of the Hachinin, who were now one less than eight.

Nobody came to check on the origins of the gunshots. I saw some people in the distance as I swam back to shore. They walked along the mountain paths, between old cottages like the one Goro had been raised in. The village was just starting to come to life as I walked up a gray gravel beach littered with weeds. A pair of fishermen watched me stomp up toward the road, their expressions mildly intrigued at the red and black glowing ninja samurai assassin in their midst. Maybe I'd become a story they'd tell here. Maybe I'd come back in a generation and see a statue of me.

Man, I was getting as foggy as the road would be.

The drive back north felt agonizingly long. The roads were mostly empty until I approached the outskirts of Seoul. But this was the modern world, and few people seemed to pay me much mind as I weaved in and out of the morning traffic. The sun brought out all the pain and fatigue the night had masked.

I didn't think about Goro on the drive up into the mountains north of the city. I didn't think of the Hachinin, and how they'd be coming after me soon enough. I thought about Kenta, and Joon. I thought about Min and Sang Hee. I thought about the Kyoto fighter I'd killed, and hated that I was starting to get used to the feeling.

I don't know if Seoul seemed like a cleaner place after what I'd done, taking out one dark hand of corruption in a sea of grasping, reaching shadows. But I can't say the place was worse off without him.

I must have passed out somewhere along the way. I was lucky I didn't go over a rail. When I woke up, I blinked away the sun and held up a hand as I groaned through the pain. Two figures leaned over me, looking like angels, one with shoulder-length hair and the other a long ponytail.

"I must be dead."

They frowned and looked at each other. Matching eyerolls followed a few seconds later.

"Just because I dragged you up here doesn't mean you're going to survive," Sang Hee said.

"Don't put it past either of us to rescue you just so we can be the ones to kill you," Min added.

I went to sit up. Sang Hee touched a hand to my chest to slow me. It was a tender motion, and one that Min caught. As I eased myself up into a seated position, I noticed that Sang Hee's arm was bandaged with white cloth up around her shoulder and around her elbow, forearm and hand. I was similarly bedecked, with a thick swaddle around my torso, and I was also wrapped in bands from shoulder to hip and across my chest. I was wearing black gi pants, and I could feel wrapping underneath them. The pain came on a few moments later, the blood rushing in all different directions and filling up the healing tissues where I'd been wounded the previous night ... or was it the previous week?

Min handed me a perspiring glass of water. I drank deeply, feeling the cold envelop my stomach and spread to my chest. I set it down on a glass table I dimly recognized, and then did a cursory inspection of my surroundings.

I was in the weirdly geometric cement megastructure that acted as Sang Hee's secret base-slash-repurposed training facility. I wondered how she had the thing classified for tax purposes. A luxury condo, probably. The rich were eccentric. Nothing that would set off any alarms.

The sun filtered in from the myriad windows and chutes between the massive blocks and beams of poured concrete. Despite the cold architecture, the place was well lit and warm, with a pleasant minimalist design I'd begun to appreciate. Sang Hee was minimalist herself, with nothing but a few tables, chairs and the holographic screen I'd been watching the last time I was here.

Speaking of which, where Min was wearing navy-blue cargo pants, brown boots and a white tank top, Sang Hee was wearing little more than the bandages that wrapped her wounded arm and happened to cover her chest. Her lower half left little to the imagination, with skintight blue shorts and plenty of leg. She had bruises all over her, from the tops of her feet to the hollow of each hip, and had a thick patch stapled to her side where the Kyoto girl had found a home for her claws.

Sang Hee was never one to be self-conscious, but she seemed to shrink a bit under my wandering stare. I swallowed and looked at Min, who had quirked one eyebrow up.

"So," I said. "What's the story? What did I miss this time?"

"Oh," Min said with another eye roll, "just the fallout of your dramatic insurrection. But don't worry, us little folk are always around to clean up your messes."

"Hey," I said. "This wasn't my plan alone. We all decided to move against the Hachinin—"

"We all decided to move against Goro," Min amended, her tone going hard. Sang Hee tensed, looking like she was about to come to my defense. Min sighed and relaxed her shoulders. "But, yeah. You're right, Akio. This time wasn't entirely your fault."

"Fault …" I said. "What's the damage?"

"To you, or the city?" Sang Hee asked.

"My body is starting to remind my brain about the damage I've suffered," I said with a wince. "Tell me," I said with a wave of my hand.

I'd been out for a full day and the following night. I'd wiped out just a short ride from the long, vertical drive through the forest to Sang Hee's front gate. Sang Hee had found me on her way back from the city. With Joon's help, she'd brought me inside, and when Min arrived, Min had undone the patchwork Sang Hee and Joon had managed and wrapped us both up properly.

"Where is Joon now?" I asked, confused.

"Here," Min said as Sang Hee nodded toward the glass door and transparent wall over by the entryway. "Keeping himself busy in the yard."

"Continue," I said.

Apparently the networks had covered the entire event with something approaching objectivity. This was due in part to the recent changes Gabriella Burtahn had made on the SMC board, but Min assured me that legal letters from the department and various Seoul governmental offices had convinced the heiress to be even more accommodating to the truth than she might have been otherwise.

The media, with Gabriella's prompting, debunked early rumors that the whole thing had been a work and acknowledged that it appeared Goro had been embroiled in a complicated plot against Akio Prince and other League fighters. Akio was not dead, and had come back to settle the score, while Goro had used his connections from Japan to stage a lethal contest in order to take out Sang Hee.

The story played perfectly into the public drama surrounding my not-so-secret escapades with Sang Hee that had immediately preceded my disappearance. As for Goro's connections, it was the first time anyone could remember him being linked to the Hachinin in public view. Everyone knew it, but Hachinin wasn't a name you threw around on the airwaves. It was akin to a declaration of war Gabriella's media empire had made toward the island, a fact that she reminded Min of in no uncertain terms. She expected protection, and not just of the spider tank variety. Even after she had the commitment, she had decided to flee to Germany to avoid the fallout of the Hachinin's vengeance, now that their Seoul puppet and media master had not only fallen, but smeared them in the process, and in public view.

It would be difficult for whomever the Hachinin had had on deck to swoop in and claim the spoils of Goro's entertainment empire. Goro had been a meticulous record-keeper, Min said. The bag of flesh had been smarter than he had looked, and Min and Seoul investigators had begun to unravel many of the inroads the Hachinin had made into Korea using Goro's domestic slush funds. Their product lines would be halted, and sting operations were already being prepped for the various ports along the borders of the Sea of Japan.

As for Akio Prince, he wasn't being talked about so much as the Sword Punk was. So much as the Red Demon of Seoul. Goro's death had only just hit the airwaves today. The police were said to be looking for Seoul's unelected vigilante, but they weren't looking hard, and they hadn't commented on what they might do once they found him.

"Great," I said. "Now, when does the army get ready to board the ships and head over to Tokyo?"

Min only stared at me.

"Organized crime is one thing, Akio," she said. "Tokyo isn't our business."

"Well, they've certainly made Seoul their business, and the mainland of China, and everywhere else."

"As the Germans used to say," Sang Hee cut in, "the first

country the you-know-whos invaded was their own. The same is true of the Hachinin."

"True," I said. "True." I went to stand, growling and grunting like an old man as I did. "Well, at least we know they can die." I ignored the look of concern that passed between the women as I quickly attempted, and then quickly abandoned, a series of stretches.

A thought occurred to me that had me feeling a new wave of panic. I started patting my pocketless pants, searching for something.

"Vial was in your suit," Sang Hee said.

"Where is it now?" I asked.

"Safe," she said. "What is it, and where'd you get it?"

"From Goro," I said. "Same shit the Kyoto demon had—"

"Her name was Aneko," Sang Hee said. "She was as much a victim in this as anyone else."

"Sure," I said. "And her brother?"

"Daichi," Min said. "We've got him down at the precinct."

"Not the most imaginative parents," I said absently. "The names, I mean."

"Yeah," Min said. "Well, he's been fairly useless from an information standpoint. Goro's records have told us more about the Hachinin than the twins ever could."

"He's as good as dead as soon as you let him out, you know," I said.

"He seems comfortable enough in custody," Min said. "Don't see that changing anytime soon."

I tried not to focus on the guilt I knew I shouldn't have felt at killing his sister. That was the way of the world. Kill or be killed, and I tried not to be the one who tried the killing first. I supposed the Hachinin could be something of an exception to the rule, once I got around to them. But, Goro was one of them, and he'd tried to have me killed. That was all the justification I needed. Besides, what was I going to do to fill the time now? I was wanted, for questioning and probably a whole lot more if the wrong people in Seoul and beyond got ahold of my case, no matter what Min had to say about it.

"Going to go talk to Joon," I said.

"Good idea," they said in unison. They looked at each other then away quickly. Min leaned back and crossed her arms while Sang Hee leaned forward and popped on the holographic screen on the other side of the room.

"You two have been spending too much time together, I think," I said with a smile. It wasn't taken all that well. "Sang Hee," her eyes swung up toward me, but she kept her head pointed straight. "You going to tell me where all this shit came from?" I gestured at the complex. "My suit. Those swords. Your spear."

"Spear's gone," she said.

"I'm sure you'll have another in short order."

She was quiet. Min watched her out of the corner of her eye, clearly as curious as I was about Sang Hee, an enigmatic, spear-wielding heiress with no public family and no public military record who seemed to be a lot more than she appeared.

"Yeah," she said with a short nod. "We'll talk."

"Good."

I turned and walked to the door. The sun was nice through the thick panes of glass, but when I stepped out into the court-yard, it felt like a blessing. I walked out into the grass, and then toward the center of the walled complex, my eyes mostly closed as I took in what the heavens could give me.

"It looked like a damn movie."

I opened my eyes and saw Joon standing in his customary blue gi. He was standing on a black grappling mat that was still covered with a thin film of gray cement dust. There were dark-black streaks along the surface from his katas that looked like calligraphy. He was sweating in the sun, his black bangs sticking to his brow.

"A good one?" I asked.

"Precinct doesn't have the best monitors," he said with a shrug.

I walked over and was happy to see Joon extend his hand first. I took it and squeezed, looking him in the eyes.

"Everything good? With the school, I mean."

"Closed down for now," he said. "Repairs. But, tax breaks be damned, it looks like me and the kids are getting an anonymous grant to help out. It's paying for their temporary housing and a hell of a lot more." He nodded toward the gray complex behind me.

I smiled.

"Who the hell is she?" he asked.

"Sang Hee? I can't say I know for sure, but, for now, I'd like to think she's proven that she's a friend."

Joon nodded. He wasn't one to pry unless he was in a mood.

"And who are you now?" he asked.

The question caught me off guard.

"Depends who's asking," I said, but Joon wasn't joking.

"Sword Punk." I shrugged. "Demon. Ghost. Prince. Does it matter?"

Joon only watched me in that infuriating way of his. I felt my blood begin to boil, and then saw the ghost of a smile on his lips. I started laughing, and Joon mirrored me. It felt good, as much as it hurt in the moment.

"You know the people of Korea weren't the only ones watching," Joon said while I took my time gripping my knees after the unintended bout of laughter.

"Yeah, well," I said, wiping the tears from my eyes, "the point wasn't really to make friends."

"Because you've got so many," Joon said.

"Too many, if you ask me."

Another silence that stretched. We both looked up at the flag flying over the compound yard.

"Goro's death has been bothering me," Joon said.

"That makes one of us."

"I can't decide if he was a coward or not," Joon said, undeterred.

I shrugged. "Not sure it matters."

"He wasn't afraid of you."

"I wouldn't quite go that far."

"He was afraid of them, though. Too afraid to stay alive."

"He wasn't getting off that boat alive," I said, firm.

Joon didn't seem to know if he believed that.

"I'm guessing the idea of retirement, witness protection and all that doesn't really appeal to you right now."

"You guessed right," I said.

"You're going to go after them, aren't you?"

I chewed my lip, not having the energy for an argument.

"You've never been one to play defense," he said after a bit.

"No," I said.

"Come on, then." Joon stepped back and made room for me at the imaginary doorway onto the mat.

I smirked until Joon gave me a whack on the shoulder, jolting me.

I stepped onto the mats, bowing as I did, lest I earn another whack. Joon took a few steps back, and gestured for me to do the same. The mats were small, and relatively thin. Barely a quarter the size of a boxing ring.

"Welcome to my dojo," Joon said. "Today's lesson: defense."

I went to sigh, but Joon shot toward me like he'd been fired out of a cannon. I twisted out of the way and slapped his spearing fist as I turned it aside. Joon came on again, and I blocked three quick strikes before absorbing a kick in the hip that folded me. I gritted my teeth and came up in a growl, only to see Joon standing with his fists cocked and his lead leg chambered, wearing the old competitive smile he kept hidden so often these days.

The pain of my wounds faded away as we sparred in the hot afternoon sun, and by the time the day turned from golden yellow to burning orange, Sang Hee and Min had pulled up steel chairs and were chatting over sweating green bottles as Joon and I hashed things out in the way we always had.

It felt good to remember the good. It felt good to ignore all the bad that was still to come.

AFTERWORD

Dear Reader,

You finished the book!

Sword PUNK is unlike anything I've ever written before, representing a major departure from my epic fantasy and superhero LitRPG fare. But I have to say, it's the most fun I've had writing in these last ten years, and if you guys want to join Akio Prince, Sang Hee, Joon and Min on their continuing adventures in the near-future far-east, I hope you'll consider leaving a review for this book on Amazon and/or Goodreads to let others know it's a journey worth taking.

Until next time,
Steven

Keep in touch with Monolith Books

Monolith Books publishes a wide range of speculative fiction, but especially fantasy. We hope that you will enjoy our novels as much as we do!

If you'd like to stay up to date on our releases, discounts, sales, author news and giveaways, sign up to our mailing list at the link below:

https://portal-books.com/monolith

You can also find us on on Facebook at our Page or Group:
https://www.facebook.com/MonolithBooks/
https://www.facebook.com/groups/monolithbooks

Thanks for reading and we hope to see you again for another adventure soon!

The Monolith Books Team

About the Author

Steven is a fighter turned writer who resides in the Boston area. He wishes all disputes were still settled with a friendly game of hand-to-hand combat, is a fan of awesome things, and tries to write books he'd want to read. He hopes you like them.

You can follow his writing career at his official web site www.StevenKelliher.com

Or Email him at author@stevenkelliher.com

Also By Steven Kelliher

Mastermind: Titan Online #1 - A Superhero LitRPG Series

In Titan Online, the greatest superhero rules with an iron fist. Seeking revenge, Karna re-rolls as a villain and plans to take him down.

A must read for fans of the TV show The Boys!

Find it on Amazon in ebook, on Kindle Unlimited and on Audible.

ALSO FROM MONOLITH BOOKS

Ascendant - A Dragon Rider Fantasy

In the mood for a brand new dragon rider epic? We got you covered with *Ascendant* by Michael R. Miller!

The start of a new dragon rider epic combining the best of Eragon with the hard magic of Brandon Sanderson and Will Wight.

Holt Cook was never meant to be a dragon rider. He has always served the Order Hall of the Crag dutifully, keeping their kitchen pots clean.

Until he discovers a dark secret: dragons do not tolerate weakness among their kin, killing the young they deem flawed. Moved by pity, Holt defies the Order, rescues a doomed egg and vows to protect the blind dragon within.

But the Scourge is rising. Undead hordes roam the land, spreading the blight and leaving destruction in their wake. The dragon riders are being slaughtered and betrayal lurks in the shadows.

Holt has one chance to survive. He must cultivate the mysterious power of his dragon's magical core. A unique energy which may tip the balance in the battles to come, and prove to the world that a servant is worthy after all.

You can find Ascendant on Amazon in ebook, on Kindle Unlimited, in paperback and on Audible narrated by Peter Kenny.

Ever Winter - A Post-Apocalyptic Survival Thriller

In the aftermath of a devastating apocalypse, Earth has become a desolate ice-world, in the grip of perpetual winter.

Henry and his family have managed to survive on the tundra of what was once a vast ocean, far from the savage remnants of humanity.

When the family is discovered, their peaceful existence is shattered and their lives are changed forever. Henry's siblings are kidnapped, leaving him alone in the ruins of their home.

Broken, altered and tormented by all that has befallen him, Henry must bring vengeance to those that assume him dead. By any means necessary.

You can find Ever Winter on Amazon in ebook, on Kindle Unlimited, in paperback

Copyright © Steven Kelliher, 2020

Published by Monolith Books, 2020

The right of Steven Kelliher to be identified as the Author of the Work has been asserted by him in accordance with the Copyright, Designs and Patents Act 1988.

All rights reserved.

No part of this publication may be reproduced, stored in a retrieval system, or transmitted in any form or by any means, electronic, mechanical, photocopying, recording, or otherwise, without the prior permission of both the copyright owner and the above publisher of this book.

All characters and events in this book are fictitious, and any resemblance to actual persons, living or dead, is purely coincidental.

www.portal-books.com